Praise for

WEDDING ISSUES

"You'll giggle all the way through *Wedding Issues*, then immediately text your girlfriends that they have *got* to read this delightful debut. This is the book you want to take on vacation, to bring to book club, to turn off the television to read. In short—a smash!"

—LAUREN EDMONDSON,
author of *Wedding of the Season*

"*Bride Wars* meets high-society haughtiness in this laugh-out-loud, feel-good story of how far we are willing to go for love and friendship. Elle Evans's voice sings—it's sharp, witty, and full of flare. I am a fan!"

—NEELY TUBATI ALEXANDER,
author of *Love Buzz*

"A rollicking ride through the highs and lows—or the I dos and I don'ts—of the wedding and media industries. Elle Evans reveals truths about friendship, ambition, and the heady intoxication of a crush. RSVP to this delicious debut."

—AVERY CARPENTER FORREY,
author of *Social Engagement*

"Brimming with humor and heart; you'll laugh your way to the very last page of this marvelously entertaining novel."

—LIZ FENTON and LISA STEINKE,
coauthors of *Forever Hold Your Peace*

WEDDING ISSUES

WEDDING ISSUES

a novel

ELLE EVANS

Zibby Books
New York

Library of Congress Control Number: 2023946587
Paperback ISBN: 978-1-958506-74-5
Hardcover ISBN: 978-1-958506-75-2
eBook ISBN: 978-1-958506-76-9

www.zibbymedia.com

Printed in the United States of America
10 9 8 7 6 5 4 3 2 1

To my parents, Kellianne and Christopher, who have supported and embraced my writing my entire life

To Steph, this book's fairy godmother, who provided endless insights and love

And to my husband, Alan, who enjoys reading my books even more than plastic surgery textbooks

1

September

It was my third breakup of the month. Seventh of the year. I should be a pro at this by now. I *was* a pro. And yet . . . the words still weren't right.

"Aren't you *done?*" Aditya twitched nervously. "You've had my phone for ten minutes!"

"Shh! I'm trying to concentrate." I drummed my nails on the neon-green table and stared at the screen, willing the right words to appear. Aditya had asked for help crafting an it's-over-for-good message to a clingy fling. They'd been on and off for months, but she ghosted him whenever he was ready to commit. It was time for Aditya to put his metaphorical foot down. Which happened to be my specialty.

Leighton reached over and snatched the phone out of my hand. "*Hey, good to hear from you! I'm down to catch up, but I want to be honest—I'm looking for a relationship.* What's wrong with that, Liv?"

I bit my lip and replayed the words in my head. Hearing them out loud was crucial. That was my father's first golden rule of negotiation: it didn't matter what you *meant*, it mattered what they *heard*. I shook my head and reclaimed the phone. "The last part's wrong. Gives her an opening."

Leighton tilted her head, her honey-blond curls falling across her shoulder. "An opening?" she asked. In the twenty years I'd known her, she'd never once had a bad hair day. Witchcraft.

"She could say she's looking for a casual relationship. Which—"

"A casual relationship?" Aditya interjected, sounding hopeful. "But that could be—"

"—exactly what he'd fall for!" I finished. Leighton laughed. "Aditya, this girl's your own personal boomerang."

He frowned. "Boomerang?"

"Every time you throw her away, she ricochets right back."

Leighton grinned. "Okay, love that. Don't be mad if I steal that line for an Instagram caption."

I hadn't intended to become the Relationship Grim Reaper. I'd sort of . . . stumbled into it. I had a knack for conversation. Not just fluffy cocktail chatter—*tough* conversations, the ones that scared everyone else. Asking for a raise. Persuading an enemy. Breaking up with an SO.

On our second day of classes at Vanderbilt Law, I'd coached Aditya through a polite thanks-but-no-thanks response to a post-first-date text. A classmate overheard and asked for help with a tenacious ex-girlfriend. And then word spread. In my first year of law school, I'd broken up with nine people, asked out six, negotiated three raises, and convinced a dog-walker to switch from an hourly rate to a per diem.

"Hey, good to hear from you! I want to be up-front—I'm looking for something serious, and I'm just not feeling that with you. Wish you all the best. There." I slid Aditya's phone back across the table, savoring the satisfaction of a deftly worded text. "My work here is done." I might not have my own love life under control, but at least I could help Aditya with his.

Aditya pressed send and spread his arms dramatically. "Done! Free at last." He stood and ran a hand through his shiny black hair. "That's my cue to leave, before I get tipsy and start texting her again."

"Sure you don't want to stay for another drink?" I asked.

Aditya grimaced. "I wish. I'm way behind on prep for these malpractice interviews. Switching industries sucks. Catch you later."

I glanced around the trendy Mexican restaurant, known as Insta-bait for its electric-green furniture and shockingly pink margaritas. The content-friendly décor was exactly why Leighton had chosen it. To my law school friends' amusement, Leighton was an online influencer. She'd always had a knack for fashion and photography, a winning combination for someone growing up in the social media era. Her brand, Peach Sugar, was a blend of old-school Southern lady and feminist modernity (per her bio). She'd started a Tumblr in middle school, joined YouTube in high school, and was thriving on Instagram by college.

Since graduation five years ago, she'd been dividing her time between growing her brand and working part-time retail. As her closest childhood friend, I'd seen it all. I'd witnessed the time and energy she'd poured into Peach Sugar, and how hard she'd fought for every one of her seventy-eight thousand Instagram followers. Some scoffed at Leighton's "fluffy" career, but they hadn't seen her grueling content schedule or her three-inch-thick design sketchbook. It was hard work. I'd happily choose another Torts midterm over masterminding one of Leighton's photo shoots.

Once Leighton had documented our photogenic drinks for her fans, I fixed her with a stern gaze. "I know what you're doing."

She fluttered her long, thick eyelashes. Extensions, but good ones. Half of Leighton's time was spent maintaining her immaculate appearance; I didn't envy her that. "I don't know what you're talking about."

"You're buttering me up. Which you don't need to do!"

Leighton slumped against the table, abandoning all pretense. "Are you *sure*? Liv, this is such a huge thing you're doing for me. I still can't believe it's real."

"It's real! And it's gonna happen."

"Do you want to practice again what you're—"

I grabbed her hand, wincing as her three-carat diamond monstrosity cut into my palm. "Stop. If it were *you* pitching Emma DeVant tonight, then yes, you'd have reason to be nervous." Despite her online success, Leighton was terribly shy in person. "But come on. You're insulting me."

"I know, I know." Leighton toyed with a lock of glossy hair. Her whole family looked like they'd stepped out of a beach volleyball ad: tall, lithe, and golden blond. Me, I looked as if I'd stepped out of an ad for vitamin D deficiency. "But what if—"

"Did I or did I not talk you out of that speeding ticket?"

"Yes, but—"

"And convinced that first boutique owner to sponsor your brand?"

"Yes, but—"

"But what?" I raised my margarita and toasted myself. "Why doubt me now?"

"Because this is *so* important," Leighton said, green eyes widening in angst. "Landing that *Southern Charm* cover would be career kryptonite."

"Isn't kryptonite bad?"

"Is it?" She waved a hand. "Ads can only take Peach Sugar so far. The next level is a clothing collaboration. I've had some brands reach out. If I got the *Southern Charm* cover, I could land a deal."

While *Vogue* and *Cosmopolitan* dominated Manhattan newsstands, in-the-know Southerners read *Southern Charm*, the women's-magazine-turned-cultural-phenomenon favored by those who preferred Atlanta to Boston and Nashville to New York. Each year the magazine highlighted a high-profile spring wedding, with one lucky bride winning the coveted June cover, typically a country music star, football wife, or old-money family. Leighton's following was *just* large enough to make her a reasonable choice. And the timeline worked: Leighton and Matt would be married next May, right ahead of the June issue. The newsstand and social media coverage were exactly what Leighton needed to level up Peach Sugar.

"Lest you forget, I proved my magic by *getting* this meeting."

"That was lucky! You ran into her pumping gas."

I wagged a finger at her, mentally wishing last week's Emma DeVant encounter had occurred in a slightly more glamorous locale. After all, optimizing the environment was key to a successful persuasion. But Olivia Fitzgerald would not be held back by little things like catcalling hooligans or eau de gasoline.

The location hadn't been ideal, and neither was the timing; I'd returned to Nashville from my Manhattan internship only hours before. A layer of airport grime still clung to my clothes, and my head reeled from boy troubles of my own. But when I'd spotted Emma DeVant across a Mobil gas station, I'd recognized her at once. A successful alumna of my Nashville prep school, Emma had given our commencement speech. I'd kept tabs on her via LinkedIn, and knew she was a senior editor at *Southern Charm*.

So I'd seized the moment. I'd barreled over, complimented her pumps, mentioned our shared alma mater, and struck up a conversation about a recent *SC* article. Ten minutes later, I insisted on setting a meeting to pitch my up-and-coming bestie for the cover. We'd arranged to meet for drinks a week later. Like my dad, a tough-as-nails Big-Law-litigator-turned-high-profile-mediator, always told me, "You make your own luck."

Tonight, I'd win Emma over, clench the June cover for Leighton, and cement my title as Best Maid of Honor *ever*. Anyone could plan a killer bachelorette party or stuff a hundred envelopes. But *I* got my friend a magazine cover.

And Leighton wasn't just any friend. She was practically my sister, only without the sibling rivalry and coordinated Christmas-card outfits. We'd grown up together in a leafy Nashville suburb and stayed close even after we both left Tennessee for college. When we'd returned postgrad—me for a paralegal job and then law school, her for the state capital's cultural cachet—it felt only natural that we'd spend our twenties together in Nashville. It'd been an amazing five years. Except, the end of this phase was rapidly approaching. In the spring, Leighton would marry and move in with Matt, starting her grown-up married life. And I'd graduate and move to New York to start my grown-up adult job.

I'd do anything to make this last year spectacular. Our Nashville friendship deserved a highlight-reel-worthy final year. That was enough motivation to chase Emma DeVant across a dozen gas station parking lots. And then . . . there was also the line I'd crossed two weeks ago. A major lapse in girl code required an equally major good deed in return. I needed a card up my sleeve to make sure I could smooth things over.

But then something clicked. "Wait." I put my margarita down. "Did you say brands had reached out to you? Leighton, that's huge!"

Leighton chewed her bottom lip. "I know."

"What brands? When? What's the offer?" I couldn't understand why she was so quiet. Leighton had been trying to land a clothing collaboration for years. "Why didn't you tell me?" Mentally I kicked myself for not asking Leighton earlier. I'd gotten back into town only last week, after a ten-week stint in Manhattan as a summer associate for Holmes & Reese, my dream Big Law firm. I'd now returned for my last year at Vanderbilt Law. My last year living in the same city as my best friend, who had an ironclad rule against living where it snowed. I squashed that thought; it was too depressing.

She blinked a few times, like she was working up the courage to spit something out. "This DTC fashion brand based in Houston, Kenne's—"

"DTC?"

"Direct-to-consumer. They reached out earlier in the

summer for a sponcon, and I brought up the idea of a collaboration." She hesitated. "They weren't interested then . . . but yesterday I told them I might be on the *SC* cover. And now they want to set up a Zoom meeting."

I would've laughed if she didn't look so genuinely tormented. "*That's* what you're worried about? That you jinxed it by telling someone?"

Leighton flushed. "It's too good to be true!" She took a long sip of her drink. "Tell me again about what Emma's like. *New Yorker*–style."

Patricia and Charles Sawyer, Leighton's parents, were longtime *New Yorker* readers and always kept a stack on the kitchen table. Back in high school, the *New Yorker*'s flair for pretentious interviewee descriptions had become a running joke among me, Leighton, and her brother, Will.

"The unruffled editor wears her success like an understated designer bag—you find yourself impressed, without consciously understanding why." My cheeks reddened, but Leighton didn't notice. I'd had my answer ready because I'd imagined telling Will about the run-in. Since Will was currently off the grid on a dive trip in Thailand, I'd been stocking up on clever things to tell him.

Leighton laughed. "And in English?"

"Confident. Speedy but not rushed. Vaguely unapproachable," I added. "You'll know it when you see it. She oozes *Southern Charm*."

"Are you describing yourself, or . . . ?"

And that's when I smelled it, a second before the talons closed over my shoulder: the sickly sweetness of Givenchy's Very Irresistible perfume. The petrified expression on

Leighton's face confirmed my dread: the Evil Empress had arrived.

"*Southern Charm?*" floated the soft, feminine drawl. "What's this, Olivia?"

I shook a mental fist at the happy hour gods—was this not sacred time?—before spinning around. "Hello, Aunt Lotte."

My aunt Charlotte pursed her plump lips, expertly lined in a blush pink that she never left the house without. Today she was clad in a peach sheath dress and nude stilettos, her signature look. I'd never seen her in flats, let alone sneakers. A boxy designer purse swung on her elbow like a shield, the sharp corner hovering dangerously close to my left eye.

"Hello, darling." Charlotte's Southern drawl sounded reserved and proper, like everything else she did. What was she doing in Nashville? Atlanta was her domain. Leighton and I had nicknamed her the Evil Empress, since Georgia's the Empire State of the South. "What's this about a magazine?" Her eyes bored into Leighton, who's always been the weaker-willed of us.

Exposure to Charlotte Harlow was an unfortunate side effect of spending your childhood with me, like Leighton had. Although Charlotte lived in Atlanta, she'd made frequent trips to Nashville to visit my mom and drag her to benefit dinners, galas, and glamorous rich-people "charity" work. Their secondary purpose was allowing Charlotte to critique everything about my life, and, by extension, Leighton's.

"Olivia's pitching me as *Southern Charm*'s next June cover star!" Leighton chirped, the news bubbling out in a combination of pride and fear.

"June?" Charlotte arched a dark eyebrow. "Isn't that the wedding issue?"

Leighton held up her left hand and wiggled her fingers.

"Congrats, darling." Charlotte's smile didn't reach her eyes, although that could've been the Botox. "What a . . . bold ring."

Leighton twitched, elation draining out of her faster than air from a punctured balloon. I coughed to draw the Empress's attention back to myself. I've always felt bad that Leighton had to put up with my ridiculous aunt and her comments. One Halloween, Charlotte had told eleven-year-old Leighton that her handmade Snow White costume was "derivative" and "uninspired." In retaliation, I'd taught myself to use a bottle opener and stuffed gummy worms into all of Charlotte's best wines.

Charlotte refocused on me. "I was unaware that *Southern Charm* found cover stars through public submissions. Although I'm not surprised my niece is involved. She talks her way into everything!" She tittered unconvincingly.

Charlotte's always thought that I meddle too much. Takes one to know one, I suppose.

"It's not *public*," I said, nailing the balance of disdain and disinterest, like I barely cared to correct her misunderstanding. "A drinks meeting with a senior editor. No big deal."

Charlotte lifted an eyebrow. "And you chose *here?*"

Leighton snorted. "Of *course* not." I widened my eyes at her in a stop-talking-now way. "They're meeting at MM Baxter in an hour."

Dammit. I smiled sweetly at my aunt, aiming for composure as my mind churned through possibilities. Would Charlotte call ahead and cancel my reservation? Book out the whole patio for herself? Phone in a phony bomb threat? Phone in a *real* bomb threat?

You're being crazy, I scolded myself. Charlotte and I were family enemies (famemies?), the type of relative whose visits you endured with patronizing bless-your-hearts galore. Mostly I despised her because she'd brought out the worst side of my mother: the status-obsessed "philanthropist" who'd attended countless gala dinners while her own daughter reheated frozen pizzas and taught herself precalculus. It was a sleep-deprived surgeon who'd T-bone my mom on the interstate, killing her instantly three months into my freshman year of college. But I couldn't help blaming Charlotte for taking my mom away from me years earlier.

"Have a lovely time." Charlotte's brown eyes rested on me with a curious intensity. "I'd say good luck, but Olivia could talk Chevrolet out of making trucks! Enjoy your evening, girls."

"Bye, Aunt Lotte," I called after her, taking pleasure in the irritation creasing her forehead as she stalked away. She hated when I called her that.

Leighton leaned forward. "What's she doing in Nashville?"

"No idea. I thought she wasn't in town until next week— I'm supposed to have lunch with her."

"Ew, why?"

"It was her idea. She's been in Nashville a lot lately. I think she's getting involved in some 'charity' work here." I made air quotes around "charity." "Maybe she feels some familial obligation when she's in town?"

"As long as she doesn't move here." Leighton shuddered. "I don't want anything keeping you from visiting me next year!"

"Nothing could," I promised, holding my margarita high to toast her. "I'd battle a thousand Empresses if it meant—"

My wrist jolted sideways, and my lap was immediately drenched. I was so stunned, it took me a second to piece together the facts: Charlotte's bag had swung in a whistling arc as she whirled, toppling my drink.

"Oh, I am *so* sorry," Charlotte cooed, her voice dripping with insincerity as my blouse dripped with spilled margarita. "So clumsy of me!"

Leighton gaped wordlessly. The image should've been funny: jalapeño margarita splashed across my white blouse, my messy bun turned to pure mess. Except I had an hour to get across town and impress a magazine editor at a swanky cocktail bar. I couldn't show up looking like this.

"I only wanted to confirm we're on for lunch on Tuesday?" she purred.

I had to hand it to her: the woman was cold as ice. She'd dumped a drink on me like we were filming a reality TV special, but her poise might fool you into thinking it was an accident.

If you didn't know Charlotte.

"Yup, I'll see you then." I pasted a smile on my face. "But if you don't mind, I've got to head home to change before—"

"Of course, your big meeting! But I insist on making it up to you." Charlotte snapped her fingers. A nearby waiter produced a fresh margarita (had she kept him on standby?), which she handed to me with a firm politeness.

I accepted the drink, even though I wanted to toss it in her face. But you can't fight Charlotte; I've made that mistake before. She's well versed in the Art of Indirect War, the science of slippery attacks and verbal daggers that could pass for butter knives in the right lighting. And I had a big reason to keep the peace with her, at least for one more year. "Thanks."

"No trouble," she trilled, and then disappeared again, this time for good.

Leighton glanced at her watch. "Liv, you'll be cutting it close—"

"Call me an Uber." I took two hearty swigs of margarita, never one to let a good drink go unfinished. "I'll schedule another for pickup in twenty minutes. I have a backup outfit sitting on my bed. I can be in and out of my apartment in six minutes flat."

"I hope so—"

I leapt to my feet and swept my stuff into my bag. "Leighton, relax. I've got this. By tomorrow morning, we'll be celebrating your June cover."

Flashing one last reassuring smile, I hurried toward the restaurant entrance before she could notice that I was convincing myself, too.

I should've spent the Uber ride to MM Baxter rehearsing my pitch. But I was too worked up over my run-in with the Empress. I'd spent much of my childhood waging war against Charlotte, aided and abetted by Charlotte's daughter, my cousin Kali. When I was little, no one had faulted me for being open about my dislike. One Christmas, Grandpa even congratulated me for replacing all of Charlotte's presents with coal.

But once I was in high school, Mom's tolerance for my "hijinks" evaporated practically overnight. I was now expected to *admire* my glamorous aunt, like Mom did. To *aspire* to accomplish as much philanthropic work as Charlotte. To *emulate* Charlotte's composure and refined elegance.

I did none of those things. But after several groundings and a missed homecoming dance, I'd revised my war strategy to better align with my aunt's. Some would say there's no difference between a thrown margarita and a spilled one. But others—like me and Charlotte—know there's all the difference in the world.

And since Charlotte had driven Mom away from me, I'd chosen to emulate my father instead. It didn't take a therapist to unpack my reasons for following Dad into law: Mom had become a stranger. If I wanted parental approval, I needed to look elsewhere. And the easiest way to get my father's attention was achievement. There was a well-trod pathway to Big Law, the term for the elite, cutthroat law firms where the real money was made, and where my father had launched his mediation career. All I had to do was follow it. At eleven, I'd first pinned up the steps on my vision board, my own yellow brick road leading to the Emerald City of giant checks and ruby-soled shoes. And, if I were really lucky, more than one phone call a month from Dad, the wizard himself. The steps:

A. High grades and SAT scores (extracurriculars a bonus)
B. Acceptance to an impressive college
C. Continued high grades and killer LSAT score

D. Name-brand law school

E. Summer associate program at a Big Law firm

After working my ass off during my first year at Vanderbilt Law, I'd landed a coveted summer internship at Holmes & Reese, one of Manhattan's most powerful firms. High-performing interns ("summer associates") were typically asked to return the summer after 2L, the final "tryout" before a full-time employment offer was extended in the early 3L year. Some firms sent offer letters during the summer before 3L started, but H&R was notorious for keeping you waiting. According to office rumors, a senior partner had once caught his wife screwing a summer associate on the associate's last day, right after his new employment contract had been signed. Since then, they took their sweet time with contracts.

So last January, when I'd agreed to return for a second summer with Holmes & Reese, I'd known a formal job offer wouldn't materialize until the fall. I'd adjusted my expectations and looked forward to celebrating come September.

But two months later, my well-laid plans were ripped to shreds. In a cruel twist of fate, Charlotte's new husband, Hank, transferred to Holmes & Reese at the senior partner level. Meaning that Hank now wielded power over my soon-to-be-incoming job offer. And if Hank could influence my future in Big Law . . .

Charlotte, for the first time in my life, had real leverage over me.

Six minutes later, I was still pulling myself together as my Uber turned into the drive of the swanky hotel. *Focus, Olivia,*

I chanted. Leighton was depending on me. And *I* needed my plan to work. If I could snag this opportunity for Leighton, she'd be ecstatic. The *Southern Charm* cover could solve my boy problems and my friendship problems in one fell swoop. *If* I pulled this off.

The hotel interior was a sea of glossy marble and tasteful gold accents. I headed to the elevator bay and hit *R* for rooftop. My reflection stared back at me from the elevator's mirrored doors. I looked like garbage.

Internal alarm bells rang in my ears. How was this possible? I'd changed into a fresh outfit fifteen minutes ago. But I looked . . . wilted. Like a Southern belle after six straight hours of Kentucky Derby sunshine. My face was unpleasantly flushed, my chest was tinged a weird green, and my roots looked downright greasy. A bead of sweat dripped down my neck and ran down my lower back. I might not hold a candle to Leighton, but I wasn't a gremlin. Not normally. What was going on?

The elevator doors slid open, and I dashed inside, frantically digging through my purse. As the elevator soared thirty floors, I fluffed out my hair, dabbed up the sweat, and popped a breath mint to counteract the sickening dismay in my stomach.

"You *can* do this, and you *will* do this," I muttered to myself. It was something Dad always said, a way of toughening me up before a big exam or internship interview.

The elevator dinged, and the doors opened to an airy, modern-looking space, all glass walls and exposed metal beams. Small trees were planted in tiny squares of soil, creating a pleasing juxtaposition against the concrete floor.

Ahead, the walls curved outward to reveal a glistening balcony, crowned by a giant bonsai tree. In the distance, the Nashville skyline glittered.

The place was gorgeous and hummed with Friday-night energy. Every table was crowded with young professionals with money to burn on nineteen-dollar cocktails. I'd never been to MM Baxter, but I'd researched the place all weekend. I was relieved to have chosen well. Emma's auburn hair was nowhere to be seen, as expected. I'd timed my Uber to ensure I was seated when she arrived.

"Can I help you?"

I turned to face the bored-looking host. "I have a seven-thirty reservation. Olivia Fitzgerald."

He glanced down at his iPad and scrolled through a list of names. My stomach twisted unpleasantly; had Charlotte canceled my reservation?

Finally, he looked up. "We already seated the other member of your party. She's right over there, near the balcony—"

"Really?" I followed his gaze across the restaurant. "But she's not supposed to be here for—"

And then I saw the platinum-blond head of hair: Charlotte. My stomach churned again.

"Un-freakin'-believable," I muttered.

"Are you okay?" He frowned. "You look like—like you've seen a ghost."

"More like the devil."

Leaving him staring confusedly after me, I strode across the restaurant and threw myself down at Charlotte's table in a show of indignation. My butt, slamming into a trendy steel chair, did not appreciate the flashy entrance, but my flair for the dramatic sure did.

"Aunt Lotte," I said through gritted teeth. "What're you doing here?"

Composure intact, my aunt reached forward and took a sip of her white wine. "Don't make a scene, Olivia. I'm here to meet with Ms. DeVant."

"This is *my* meeting!"

She inclined her head. "Yes, and I'm so grateful for the introduction." Her eyes caught mine. "Family connections can be oh-so-useful."

A not-so-veiled threat to my Holmes & Reese dreams. My cheeks flushed. "Why," I said with forced calm, "do you even want a meeting with Emma? *Southern Charm's* audience is young professionals."

Having slightly emphasized the *young*, I fake-laughed to twist in the dagger. Her eyes narrowed. My cheeks were flush with victory—or was that nausea? My stomach rolled.

"Not me," she said primly. "Kali."

This time my laugh was genuine. "Kali? Come on, Aunt Lotte, you'll need a better cover story than that."

Charlotte's daughter, Kali, my only cousin on my mom's side, was—there was no other word for it—*cool*. Looking back, her being three years older probably meant I'd have idolized her no matter what. But she earned every ounce of that adoration. In middle school, she'd played truant from every fancy-schmancy boarding school Charlotte shipped her off to, until my aunt had finally given up and enrolled her back in the public school system.

As children, we'd united at family gatherings to rebel against our mothers and their hoity-toity expectations. Kali'd been the first to identify the chinks in Charlotte's Chanel armor. When I was nine, she'd shown me where Charlotte kept the "real" trash cans, instead of the fancy, stain-free ones she put out for company. We'd spent one glorious summer swapping trash cans at every opportunity. As Charlotte's fury intensified, we clung to our declarations of innocence, and the rest of the family sided with us. After all, who could get mad at two preteens for throwing their tissues in the wrong container?

I felt a stab of nostalgia at the memory. For us, growing up had meant growing apart. While I bonded with my dad over my journey to Big Law, Kali didn't have that option: her father, my uncle Mark, died from colon cancer when she was thirteen and I was ten. Kali had always been close with her dad, and she took the loss hard. After struggling through high school, she took a gap year before college to backpack around Europe and Asia. Then she'd gotten her degree and landed a job in advertising for Patagonia.

Charlotte smiled without warmth. "It's Kali who'll get the cover story."

"What're you talking about?"

"Didn't you hear the happy news?"

Charlotte slid her phone toward me: Kali and her long-term girlfriend, Greta, beaming on top of some mountain, both wiggling rings on their left hands.

"Kali's engaged?" I was caught off guard; how had I not known? Were we so distant that I didn't even merit an *FYI, we're engaged* text? My surprise made me slow in putting it all together, until I realized what Charlotte had said. A cover story . . .

"You're here to pitch Kali's wedding for *Southern Charm.*"

My aunt sat back, triumphant. "As convincing as you think you are, Olivia, I assure you that mine is the more compelling story. Kali and Greta are an environmental power couple. I hear saving the Earth is *very* hot among your generation."

"An unfortunate choice of words," I muttered.

"And, as I'm sure you discovered in your research, *Southern Charm* is struggling to remain relevant. Kali and Greta would revolutionize the wedding issue. The first same-sex cover stars!"

A sour taste rose in the back of my throat. Her angle was good. Even worse, I agreed with Charlotte: *Southern Charm* was long overdue for a progressive overhaul. In the last decade, it had successfully expanded from a print magazine to an online media company, like most of journalism. But it'd been slower to widen its narrow definition of aspirational womanhood, which tended to feature thin white women marrying rich cowboy types. Diversity was not a strong point of *SC*, and I loved the idea of that finally starting to change.

But . . . that change didn't have to start with the next wedding issue. *SC* could choose a queer woman for any of its upcoming covers! Or feature a badass lesbian wedding the following June, after Leighton had already risen to fame. Besides, my cousin would never want a splashy magazine wedding. Not the Kali I knew.

I didn't have a rebuttal, so I focused on yet another unknown. Charlotte was speaking like someone who'd done *her* research, but Leighton had spilled the beans only an hour ago. "How'd you have time to prepare?" I said blankly.

"Isn't there a saying about this?" Charlotte took a dainty

sip of her wine and regarded me with a curious glint in her eyes. "Youth underestimates age, or something of that nature? You forget, darling niece, that I have a bachelor's from Harvard and an MBA from Wharton. I am a capable woman with many connections. I simply called a friend who works in the magazine industry and asked for her advice." She leaned forward and the glint hardened. "Some of us do not rely on nepotism alone."

I hated to admit it, but she'd rattled me. A bead of sweat rolled down my temple, and my stomach was in outright revolt. I forced myself to stay calm. I needed this. Leighton needed this. Kali swooping in to steal the spotlight made no sense at all. Unless Charlotte had arranged for a personality transplant, my cousin wouldn't be caught dead on a magazine cover unless it was *Rock Climbers Today*.

"Leighton has a following," I said weakly. My mind seemed foggy; how had I forgotten the talking points I'd rehearsed all week? "She can bring additional readers and clicks to *Southern Charm*. She's a perfect fit for their brand—"

"She already *is* their brand," Charlotte countered. "A repackaged Carrie Underwood, without the singing. There's nothing exciting about that, Olivia. Novelty sells. Even in the South."

My head throbbed. The corners of the room swam in and out of focus. "That's not true, and Kali's not some novelty to trot out—"

"Are you all right? You look dreadful—"

A sudden wave of nausea crashed over me. I pushed my chair away and lurched to my feet. If I could get to the bathroom before Emma arrived, maybe I could still—

"Olivia Fitzgerald?" said a bright voice behind me. "So good to see you again—"

And with that, I turned and emptied my stomach all over Emma DeVant's magenta Jimmy Choos.

2

The next morning, I woke with the bitter taste of failure in my mouth. Along with the lingering taste of vomit. How had everything gone so wrong last night?

My mind replayed the chaos for the hundredth time: The horrified look on Emma's face. Charlotte graciously swooping in with stain remover. My stomach threatening to return for round two. Me, forcing out a strangled, "I'm so sorry!" before rushing out in disgrace.

Gingerly, I sat up. My stomach accepted this without further revolt. How had I gotten so sick, so fast? It made no sense. Food poisoning? The only food I'd eaten yesterday was an acai bowl and a coffee-shop muffin; neither seemed a likely culprit. A vicious twenty-four-hour bug with an unlucky onset? Embarrassment aside, I felt fine this morning, and I'd never heard of a six-hour bug. Maybe Charlotte had cursed me at the cantina.

Charlotte. Who'd almost certainly nabbed the cover for Kali, after my awful showing last night. How was I going to tell Leighton I'd failed?

And, almost more important, how was I going to tell Leighton about *everything*? How could I come clean without some glorious news to offset the hurt? I pictured calling her up: "Do you want the bad news or the other bad news? The news about losing that big career boost, or the news about me sleeping with your brother? You know, the one thing you asked me never to do?"

Even I couldn't pull off that conversation.

A knock distracted me. After wrapping a blanket around my grey tank and boxer shorts, I padded through my small living room and opened the door to reveal Aditya, his face bright with expectation. "How'd it go?" he asked without preamble. "Did you kill it?"

Aditya and I had met on the first day of law school, bonding over mutual love of the shade (orientation was outside in the scalding Tennessee sun) and cynical mistrust of the law-is-the-purest-profession propaganda our professors were peddling. When we realized we lived in the same apartment building, we both committed to the friendship for selfish reasons. (Aditya had been searching for free dog walks for his pup, Circe, and I studied best when I could monologue trial arguments to a captive audience.) Hence, everybody won. One of my proudest successes was that Leighton and Aditya got on well. I'd been nervous that my tenderhearted bestie wouldn't mesh well with my blunt, sarcastic classmate, but they'd given each other the benefit of the doubt.

"Got killed, more like," I mumbled. "Come in, I've got cold brew in the fridge."

Once I'd poured us both coffee, we settled on my plush grey sectional.

"You look awful," Aditya observed, nodding thanks as I handed him a cup. "What the hell happened?"

I locked eyes with my reflection in the mirror across from the couch. A bedraggled raccoon in ratty PJs stared back, last night's mascara smudged down her cheeks. Even my normally bright blue eyes looked dull and defeated.

"Not what I expected," I said truthfully. I filled him in on the whole disastrous mess. "No idea what happened. I was so sick, so fast."

"You seemed fine when I left." Aditya tugged at the sleeves of his black sweatshirt. "It makes no sense. Unless Charlotte really did curse you? Or poison you?"

"You've been watching too much true crime."

"Nah, just reviewing overdose cases." Aditya had originally gunned for corporate law like me, but a crappy summer associate experience had prompted his recent pivot into medical malpractice. "How bruised is your ego?"

"Beyond repair."

He snorted. "Impossible. Your ego is indestructible. I've never met someone more impressed with themself." He ducked the pillow I threw at him. "You still gonna tell Leighton?"

Although Leighton was my closest friend in the world, two years of law school had tightly bonded me and Aditya. Last week, we'd celebrated my return from New York with a few too many beer flights, and I'd come clean about the whole

Manhattan mess. Aditya had been skeptical about my use-*Southern Charm*-cover-to-make-it-better plan from the start.

I rubbed my temples in preparation for the incoming lecture. Aditya was a good friend, if sometimes a little blunt. Right now I wanted to vent to a friend who'd enable my schemes, not question them.

"I'll . . . figure something out."

He hesitated, his awkwardness warning me that he was about to drop some serious insight. "Look, Liv . . . I know you're good with words. But even you can't manage every situation to work out the way you want."

"That's not what I'm doing," I protested, heat rising in my cheeks. I grabbed a pillow and hugged it to my chest. "And this isn't over yet. I'm gonna fix things."

"Liv, how are you possibly going to—"

Inspiration struck faster than a bolt of lightning. "First thing Monday morning. I'll handle it."

"There's no way Emma'll give you another meeting! Not after you puked on her—"

"I agree." I locked eyes with my reflection again. Dishevelment aside, there was a new fire behind her eyes, the kindling of a real idea. "Which is why I'll take the meeting to her."

I stood on the corner of a bustling street outside the *Southern Charm* office and took a deep, steadying breath. Traffic streamed by me while irritated pedestrians swerved to avoid collisions. If I closed my eyes, I could easily pretend I was the heroine of a glamorous Manhattan rom-com, poised to make a grand gesture like a Penn Station flash mob or an Empire State Building proposal.

As much as I loved my hometown, downtown Nashville was not *quite* as grand as Manhattan. The few buildings that passed for skyscrapers would've been runts in NYC, and there weren't nearly as many pedestrians. Or bagel places. I'd loved my time in Manhattan the past two summers, living my Big Law dreams and soaking in the wisdom of the best litigators in the city. I'd worked hard, of course, but I knew what I was signing up for by choosing the eighty-plus-hour work-weeks of a top firm.

Or at least I thought I did. Like all Big Law firms, Holmes & Reese pampered its summer interns, working us hard but not break-your-spirit hard, funding endless open-bar socials, and dispensing hefty paychecks. After graduation, the coddling would disappear and the hours would lengthen. This fact—that my actual Big Law experience would be much tougher than my summer positions—had seemed worth it when I'd taken that first internship two years ago. But now that I'd finished my second cushy summer stint, Real Life was looming nearer and nearer. The grind would be intense.

That's temporary, I reminded myself. My first few years out of law school would be grueling, but eventually I'd make partner and scale back. I'd have minions to do my grunt work and the freedom for higher-level case strategies, the part of law I loved best.

Shoving these new anxieties aside, I took another steadying breath. Today's stakes were higher than the Holmes & Reese office skyscraper. To be extra-safe, I'd gone to the grocery store on Saturday, double-checked every expiration date, and hadn't eaten a single meal outside my apartment over the weekend. Whatever bizarre affliction I'd come down with on Friday, I would *not* be derailed again.

And Will gets back into the country tomorrow, my subconscious reminded me. Immediately I shoved that knowledge into a dark mental crevice and rolled a metaphorical boulder on top. I couldn't afford any distractions today. I had no idea where Will and I stood, but if I wanted any hope of a future with him, I needed to stay in his sister's good graces.

"You can do this, and you will do this," I announced loudly.

A passing man gave me an extra-wide berth and a suspicious look. I felt a stab of longing for New York, where whispering mantras on city streets was encouraged rather than ridiculed. One day, I'd be living there for real. As long as I didn't piss off Charlotte.

I strode into the building and beelined to the reception desk, walking confidently like a job applicant who needed to impress.

"Hello," I said to the receptionist. "I'm here for a job interview at *Southern Charm.*"

"Name and ID, please."

"Landon Smith." I handed over my old fake ID, last used sophomore year of college to buy wine spritzers from the corner store, trying not to wince at the eight-year-old photo that claimed I was now thirty-four.

The receptionist clacked away on her keyboard. "Hmm. I don't see you listed for today."

I let a trace of exasperation creep into my voice. "I had to move up my interview—family emergency. A last-minute change."

The receptionist nodded, her eyes still on the screen. "When was your original interview date? If I can verify that—"

"Second week in October, first thing in the morning," I said, intentionally avoiding specifics. "They might've canceled that to open space for more applicants. I'm so sorry to rush you, but I'm running late. Can we finish this whole process later?"

"I'm not sure—"

"I can leave my license here for collateral." Still talking, I edged sideways toward the security gate. "You can call up to confirm, but I'm late and I really, really need this job. Can you just . . ." I gestured toward the barrier with an impatient air. "I promise, I'll sort this out after!"

For an infinitesimal moment, the receptionist teetered on the precipice between allowing me passage or making a scene. My mind raced through my Plan B options: A sob story about said family emergency? Did I still have tissues in my purse?

The waist-high security gate slid open. I waved cheerily and strode into the elevator bay before the receptionist could change her mind. My fake ID was a small price to pay for sneaking my way into the *Southern Charm* office. It was crazy how much you could get away with if you acted confident. Dad had taught me that, too.

Two women in business attire followed me into the elevator, both dressed too stuffily to be working at *SC*. Then another woman entered, this one rocking a fuchsia leather skirt and a black satin top. Eyeing her skirt, I said a silent prayer of mourning for all the killer outfits I'd never be allowed to wear in my corporate Big Law career.

On the eleventh floor, the elevator opened into a startlingly bright foyer. The floor was made of illuminated white-and-peach tiles, and the walls were covered with neon mock-ups of past *Southern Charm* issues. Funky farmhouse furniture was scattered around the room, adding a rustic Southern touch. Over the reception desk straight ahead hung a glowing sign: *Howdy, y'all!*

Pink Skirt slipped out. I followed her across the glowing floor. Given their Southern schtick, I'd half expected the place to resemble an old barn, not a flashy advertising office. But, as I reminded myself, *Southern Charm* was a giant brand, and a subsidiary of an even larger media conglomerate, Marshall Sheldon. No matter how much they emphasized their old-timey roots.

Walking with purpose, I followed Pink Skirt past another receptionist, who was distracted by arguing with someone on the phone. We headed down a hallway patterned with vibrant wildflowers, and I slowed to let the woman drift ahead of me.

The hallway opened into a large communal workspace filled with long glass desks. Two dozen stylishly dressed employees perched on fluffy stools, tapping away on sleek Mac laptops. A large print of Dolly Parton hung on the far wall, under another neon sign: *In Dolly we trust.*

Along the left ran several external offices with names on the door. Continuing down the hall, I found it: *Emma DeVant, Senior Editor.*

Taking a deep breath, I strode inside the corner office.

It hit me immediately that Emma DeVant was not a native Southerner. Unlike the rest of the offices, everything about her space screamed theme. Her desk and the back of her bookcase were patterned with a baby-blue gingham.

Random knickknacks dotted the shelves: a leather cowboy hat, a ceramic pair of cowboy boots, and mason jars filled with plastic flowers. The effect suggested she'd googled "Southern things" and filled her entire office with the first page of search results. Emma may have attended my local high school, but I'd bet my left kidney that she'd spent her childhood somewhere else.

And when my eyes traveled to Emma herself, sitting behind another gleaming MacBook, I felt an immediate kinship. In her sleek black sheath dress, topknot, and scarlet-soled pumps, she looked like a New Yorker. The confident, assertive sort of person that I identified with. And she had amazing eyebrows.

Channeling that New York energy, I plunged ahead. "Hi, Emma! It's great to see you again."

She looked up, startled, as I strode forward and held out my hand. "Olivia! I wasn't expecting you this—"

"Let me start by apologizing for Friday," I said, talking right over her. Nailing the first two minutes of this conversation was crucial; I needed her to hear me out. "I'm so sorry about that; it's never happened before. Here's a list of local dry cleaners that specialize in shoe cleaning, and here's a check to cover the cost."

I placed a manila folder on her desk and settled into the plush armchair as her eyes widened, impressed. If you do something small for someone, they'll feel obligated to do something for you in return. Like listen to your pitch.

"That's very kind," Emma said slowly, her forehead furrowed in confusion. "But you didn't have to do that—and you definitely didn't need to come all the way here!"

An opening. I seized it. "Well, I owe you more than a clean

pair of shoes—I owe you a pitch!" I took a second, thicker folder out of my purse and placed it flat on my lap.

Emma's face clouded over. "Olivia, I'm sorry to tell you, but I stayed to chat with your aunt on Friday. She made a compelling argument for your cousin's wedding. And I have to say, I'm liking the idea."

I took the offensive. "Let me guess: She told you it'd modernize *Southern Charm* to finally feature a same-sex wedding? That Kali and Greta would appeal to a more diverse set of advertisers and potential readers?"

"Yes, actually." Emma leaned back, clearly reevaluating me.

I opened the folder and handed it to her. "Those are valid points. But they pale in comparison to what Leighton brings to the table." "Pale in comparison" was a stretch, I knew. Queer representation would be game-changing for *SC*. But as I'd learned from my father, the way to win pitches was downplaying the opposition's angle and overselling your own. And it wasn't as if I'd be taking anything away from my cousin; it was Charlotte who wanted this, not Kali.

"Which is?"

"For starters, she's a perfect demographic match for your audience. Mid-twenties, native Southerner, politically safe, and genetically gifted, aka gorgeous. And if you look at the sales data for your last ten wedding issues, your three best-selling issues stayed true to that formula. Last year"—I flipped open the sales sheet—"y'all deviated from that formula with the Alabama gymnast, remember? The one with the double tattoo sleeves? Great artwork, in my opinion, but not *Southern Charm*."

"The formula is stale," Emma countered. "Predictable. Overdone."

"You're right, and you're wrong." I pulled another sheet to the top. "The formula works, yes, but it's also predictable. Sometimes boring. That's why you sell Leighton's wedding as the launchpad for her upcoming clothing line. Her bridesmaids will be wearing never-before-seen dresses from her very own line."

This wasn't, strictly speaking, something Leighton and I had ever discussed. True, Leighton had been designing and sewing dresses for years, but she'd mentioned bridesmaid dresses only once in passing. I was inventing a new project on the fly, but Emma was nodding thoughtfully, so I ran with it. "Choosing Leighton means flipping that whole antiquated script about a wedding being the most important day of a girl's life! For Leighton, it *will* be—but because she's launching her clothing empire, not because of an exchange of vows." I pushed another sheet of paper to the top. "Here's Instagram's breakdown of Leighton's followers—you'll see she ranks in the ninety-third percentile for follower interaction, and eighty-seventh percentile for click-through conversion rate. She's got a great story and a built-in audience. What more could you want?"

Emma's brown eyes darted across the data for a few moments. I waited, triumphant. I could sense sweet victory in the air—

"You've made a solid case," Emma said at last. "And if I'd heard this on Friday, I'd probably have signed Leighton. But I'm not sure it's different enough. We're under a lot of pressure to bump up our subscriber numbers." She gestured around the office. "It's why I agreed to this ridiculous décor. Trying to immerse myself in the Southern way of life."

Neglecting my true feelings on her décor, I focused on what she wasn't saying. "You think Kali has a better angle."

"Definitely more different."

"You're not worried it's *too* different?"

Emma stared at me for a moment, then shrugged in a what-the-hell sort of way. "Frankly, I am. But I don't have another slam-dunk bride. I could go with another NASCAR fiancée—"

"—but your last NASCAR couple cover was—"

"—our worst-selling wedding issue in five years, yes." Emma didn't appear to be bothered by my interjections; if anything, she seemed to appreciate the work I'd put into this meeting. Even if she wasn't buying what I was selling.

I paused and chewed on my bottom lip. She and I were on the same page about some parts of this decision—

"Honestly, Olivia, if I could do two wedding issues, I totally would," Emma went on. "They're our blockbuster issue every year. Even outsells September. And highest engagement on socials."

"What if you did have two issues? Kali in May and Leighton in—"

"No dice. Headquarters doesn't want us cannibalizing sales from *Bridal Today*. Since they're also in the Marshall Sheldon portfolio." She sighed. "We've carved out a once-a-year niche covering a 'Southern' wedding, but if I so much as *look* at another white dress, the *BT* editor in chief will have my head."

"That's a shame." I tried to quell my rising panic. I was running out of runway, fast.

"Right?" Luckily, we seemed to have touched a nerve; Emma was in full-on vent mode. "And to tie my promotion to the magazine's annual performance is completely ridiculous. I already subsidize every winter issue! We bring in so much new advertising in June alone."

I nodded. "You're totally right." Then my head shot up. "But—what if there was a way to stretch out the revenue from the wedding issue? Like, over six or seven months?"

"You mean renegotiate our advertising contracts?"

"No, I mean rethink your whole wedding coverage." I leaned forward, brimming with excitement. This was it; this was the solution. "Planning a wedding takes at least a year, right? There's so much more than the day of. Most couples have multiple pre-wedding events: engagement parties, bridal showers, bachelorette parties!"

Emma's eyes lit up. "We could cover pre-wedding events in preceding issues," she said slowly. "Drum up interest in the eventual wedding—"

"And encourage readers' investment in the happy couple!" I tapped a photo of Leighton and her fiancé, Matt. "By the time they see Leighton on the cover, they'll have been following her journey for almost a year."

Emma jumped to her feet and paced behind her desk in tight, excited circles. "As long as we keep the covers non-bridal, it's totally within our scope—" She turned and wagged a perfectly manicured nail at me. "You're good, Olivia. Really good. But it doesn't change my decision. Kali and Greta are exactly what this magazine needs. And they'll have plenty of wedding prep for us to cover."

My elation screeched to a halt. Frantically, I cast my mind backward over everything Emma had let slip.

"You said yourself that Kali wasn't a slam dunk," I said, pitching my voice to sound measured and reasonable. I was going for the logical argument; I had to sound like it. "Leighton was a compelling choice."

"Yes, but I've made up my—"

"And if it's a tough choice for you, it might be a tough choice for others, too, right?"

Emma eyed me suspiciously. "What're you getting at?"

"*Southern Charm* readers love the wedding issue. Giving them months of pre-wedding content will boost sales and eyeballs all year. But what if we took that to the next level?" I placed both hands flat on her desk, power-pose-style, and waited a beat before delivering the punch line. "Cover the planning for both weddings until the spring, keeping readers guessing about the June cover star!"

Emma stopped dead, mid-pace. "So we'd still cover the pre-wedding events . . ." She paused. I remained frozen, afraid to move lest it distract her from agreeing with me. "Which would let readers learn more about each couple. We could keep a record on the website, do live Instagram feeds each month—" She whirled and faced me. "Yes! I think this is it!"

Victory pumped through me like adrenaline. I'd done it! Well, sort of; I still had to make sure Leighton was chosen in the end. But I was sure I could make that happen. "Awesome! I'll let Leighton know."

"Great. Tell her my assistant will reach out with the paperwork this week. You're her maid of honor, right? Email over a schedule of her wedding events ASAP. Rough dates are fine for now." Emma scribbled a note to herself on a Post-it. "And I'll touch base with Charlotte about Kali's events."

"Will do," I promised.

Emma was furiously scrawling notes. "What did you say you do for work, again?"

"I'm in my last year of law school. Headed to corporate law afterward."

Emma chuckled, head still bent over her desk. "Well, your talents are wasted writing corporate merger agreements, that's for sure." I edged backward, not wanting to interfere with her creative process.

When I reached the door, she finally looked up. "Olivia?" Her gaze landed on me and sharpened. A businesslike edge crept into her voice. "It's a good idea, and I'm glad you brought it to me. But I won't be playing favorites. I'll make my choice based on how the events go."

I grinned back. "I understand. Let the best wedding win."

I'm sorry, *what?*"

"It'll be a competition, with Emma choosing the winner in April—"

I cut off mid-explanation, distracted because my feet were now drenched. I looked down to see the remnants of Leighton's iced coffee dripping all over my legs, with her dropped cup smashed into the pavement between us.

"A *competition?*" Leighton repeated, her left fist still clenching empty air. "Olivia! You said you'd get me the cover!"

A power-walking mom sped by us, throwing an annoyed look over her shoulder at the ruckus. I'd intentionally chosen to have this conversation in Centennial Park, a lush Nashville landmark that (a) provided Leighton with gorgeous Instagram content, and (b) was public enough that she couldn't push me into the lake.

"It's a formality, honestly!" I hurried to a nearby coffee

stand and collected a few napkins. "You're the perfect fit for *Southern Charm*'s demographics. And you have me! You'll totally win."

Leighton accepted a napkin and dabbed at her shins reluctantly. "Isn't it weird? With Kali being your cousin?"

"Not at all," I promised. "We barely talk."

"And Charlotte agreed to this?"

"I'll handle Charlotte," I assured her. "Leighton, you're my best friend. I told you I'd get this cover for you. Honestly, it's even better this way—you'll be featured in three extra articles about your pre-wedding events! That's more exposure for you and Peach Sugar."

"I guess . . ."

"And you can design your own bridesmaid dresses," I added, realizing that I'd left out how I'd promised Emma a career-launching dress debut at Leighton's wedding.

I peered over anxiously, trying to deduce if this would tip my stressed bride-to-be over the edge. But to my surprise, Leighton perked up. "The made-for-tailoring ones?"

"Um, yes?"

"Good thing I've been working on designs," she murmured, half to herself. Then she refocused on me, her dark green eyes deepening with something like pride. "Thanks for pitching that, Liv. Honestly, I'm surprised you remembered. I only mentioned it the one time."

Casting my mind backward, I finally dragged up the memory. The June night before I'd left for Manhattan, Leighton and I had shared a pitcher of margaritas and discussed our goals for the summer. She'd mentioned some new bridesmaid dress idea, but I'd been distracted, laser-focused on my own imminent adventure in Manhattan. I had no idea what made-for-tailoring meant, but now wasn't the time to ask.

Leighton had already slumped down on a nearby park bench, her eyes wide and anxious. "But it won't matter, if my wedding's not featured—"

"Are you honestly worried about winning? I'll be by your side every step of the way. Emma told me all about what *SC* readers like and don't like, and Kali doesn't know periwinkle from lavender."

"It's not that." Leighton sighed. "Hold on. I need another coffee for this. Be right back. Save that bench for us, okay?"

I commandeered the one open bench overlooking the Parthenon, the life-sized replica of the ancient Greek temple that dominated Centennial Park's landscape. It was one of Leighton's favorite backdrops for photo shoots. Early on, before Leighton had taught herself about DSLR cameras, Will had sometimes been drafted as our photographer. Over time, Leighton's skills with a self-timer had surpassed her older brother's half-interested attempts, much to ten-year-old me's chagrin. Even before I was old enough for crushes, I'd liked having him around.

Will, who was returning from his two-week Thailand trip sometime today.

Stop it, Olivia, I ordered myself. Leighton was almost back, laden with an extra-large coffee and a worried expression. I had to stop obsessing. One problem at a time.

Settling on the bench next to me, Leighton sipped her coffee morosely. "My brother's back," she announced.

"Oh?" I fixed an innocent expression on my face. Had I been mumbling his name, lovestruck, under my breath? Or had she read my mind? "Back from . . . ?"

"Somewhere in Asia. He just landed, five hours late," she said, gesturing toward her phone. "Classic. Every flight he's on gets delayed. He's got the worst luck."

"Hmm," I said, surreptitiously sliding my phone out of my bag. Nothing. "His new job's in North Carolina, right?"

"Yeah." Leighton looked surprised. "How'd you know about that? Did I mention it?"

"I think so. Or I saw on Insta." I shrugged casually. "Anyway. You were saying . . . ?"

"Right." Leighton tucked the phone away. "I hadn't realized how much I was counting on the *Southern Charm* thing until . . . until it wasn't a sure thing." She wound her arms tightly around her chest. "It's why Kenne's wanted me. And it was the only thing that made my mom back off."

Leighton's relationship with her mother was only slightly less tumultuous than mine with Charlotte. Her parents were old-fashioned (or, as they'd gently correct, *traditional*) and had never been enthusiastic about Leighton's social media. Her dad was a hard-ass surgeon at a downtown hospital, but his iron will paled in comparison to his wife's. Patricia Sawyer believed in stable careers, marriage at a young age, and regular church attendance. She'd never quite forgiven Leighton for turning down a corporate job in lieu of pursuing online influencing. Although Leighton earned enough to cover non-rent living expenses, she still lived in the rental property her parents owned in East Nashville, an ongoing source of strife between them. (She'd also committed the nearly unforgivable sin of waiting until the ancient age of twenty-seven to become engaged.)

As high-schoolers, we'd shared many late-night vent sessions about our overbearing mothers. Interpreting our fathers' hands-off parenting approach as respect for our autonomy, we viewed Patricia as a controlling tyrant. Around Patricia, I'd always made a point of emphasizing outside validation of Leighton's talents, from the local photography contests she'd won to the gorgeous costumes she sewed for school musicals. Leighton, for her part, offered me companionship and support when my parents dropped the ball. When our debate team made it to the national finals my senior year, my mom's Swan ball preparations and my dad's upcoming trial prevented either from traveling to Chicago to attend. But Leighton was there.

Normally Leighton and Patricia's relationship simmered in a constant state of low stress, but this sounded acute. Like the pot had boiled over. "Back off? Did something happen?"

Leighton rubbed her forehead distractedly. "This whole last year, they've been all over me to get a real job, to stop 'pretending' like I'm an online celebrity. They don't understand how hard I've been hustling, or how social media has always been a launchpad to a clothing collaboration. My mom thinks that all I want is to take pretty pictures."

This was unfair. Leighton worked hard to cultivate and grow her audience. Without a trust fund for luxurious vacations or shopping sprees, churning out endless new content required creativity and grit. And as talented as Leighton was at Instagram curation, her clothing sketches were even more impressive. I knew; I'd seen them. Or at least I'd seen the last round, back in the spring. I should probably ask to see the new ones soon.

But Leighton's parents struggled to understand the lack of specificity in their daughter's aspirations. She didn't have her heart set on any one avenue—clothing collaborations, creative directing, pure design work—and was open to whatever fashion-related opportunity came her way. Unstructured goals were hard for Patricia to take seriously. Sometimes I thought it took a lot more courage to choose something nebulous like Leighton had. Me, I'd chosen the predictable, linear route. Not easy, but no surprises. Three years of law school, followed by seven to nine grueling years as a Big Law associate, and then either partnership or a lateral move to another firm. I knew everything about the next decade of my life: my city, my employer, even my tax bracket. The structure was both reassuring and restrictive. But Leighton could go anywhere. Do anything.

"Anyway, we got in a big fight back in the spring, right after I got engaged. She told me that I was getting married and needed to act like a grown-up. I told her I wasn't done with Peach Sugar and that this next year could be big. She flipped out. Told me they'd be kicking me out of the apartment as soon as I walked down the aisle."

"You're moving in with Matt after the wedding anyway, right?" Without ever saying it outright, Leighton's parents had communicated their total opposition to cohabitation before marriage. Leighton had chosen not to die on that particular hill.

"It's not that. Things got really ugly that night. It was like I finally saw how little they think of what I do. Which is so frustrating, because I'm working my *ass* off!" Leighton mimed strangling someone in midair, and I nodded supportively, as behooved a dedicated maid of honor.

"And you told her about the *SC* cover?" I guessed.

"Yeah. Last week." Leighton wrapped her knees up under

her arms and stared at the ground, the picture of beautiful young angst. "My mom's face lit up. Finally, a sign that my career is actually *real*. So I'd really been counting on this. Not to mention the Houston Kenne's collaboration. Thank God I hadn't told my mom about that yet."

I felt a twinge of guilt. I knew the cover was huge for Leighton career-wise, but I hadn't realized how much it meant to her personally. Leighton was a happy-go-lucky person; most grievances rolled right off her. The ones that stuck, she tended to bury deep inside. If I didn't specifically ask her about her problems, she'd keep everything bottled up. (I was the opposite; Aditya had once accused me of collecting grudges the way some people collected stamps, and I didn't hesitate to vent about them.)

"You're *going* to win that cover," I told her, putting the full force of my persuasive abilities behind the sentiment. "Trust me. And you're gonna land that collaboration and show your mom how legit your career is. And how beautiful your bridesmaid designs are!"

She smiled weakly and leaned against me. "You're lucky I already had some ideas. So, how are you going to break the news to Charlotte?"

I swallowed hard. I had lunch plans with Charlotte in two hours, and I was dreading every moment of it.

"It's not like you stole the cover from Kali," I reasoned. "You were the default going into Friday's meeting, right? I'll say that Emma never stopped considering you, and she reached out to me about the competition since I know both you and Kali. It'll be like an act of God."

"M-hmm."

"Don't look at me like that!"

"Like what?"

"All doubtful."

Leighton blinked a few times and shaded her face from the sunlight. "The cover's a big deal, but I don't want you to lose your job over it."

Sometimes I felt like I didn't deserve Leighton's friendship. She was too selfless, too *good*. It was one of the (many) reasons it frustrated me when people wrote her off as a ditzy, image-obsessed influencer. Leighton was the most loyal friend I'd ever had. Even now, leading up to her own wedding and on the cusp of a huge career move, she was still thinking of my future.

And you're the opposite, said a nasty voice in the back of my mind. *You knew sleeping with Will would hurt her, and you did it anyway. You're only doing this out of guilt.*

"Don't worry." I squeezed her hand. "I'll keep my job, and you'll win the cover. We can have both."

Leighton grinned at me. "Have our wedding cake and eat it, too?"

"Exactly."

Despite my assurances to Leighton, I felt a gnawing sense of unease as I hurried into Stream & Field, the high-end restaurant overlooking the golf course at my father's country club. Although Atlanta-based Charlotte wasn't a member, Dad had secured the reservation at Charlotte's special request. I'd been dreading this little get-together. Normally it was easy to avoid her company. Outside of holidays, we'd rarely seen each other since my mom passed. She'd probably arranged this lunch to lord Hank's influence over me, but now there'd be a new topic of conversation: the *Southern Charm* competition.

Charlotte was already seated at a white-clothed table on the balcony. She was gazing over the driving range, where brightly attired men and women swung their clubs enthusiastically. Idly, I wondered how much it'd take to bribe a caddy to "accidentally" spin and fire a ball up toward Charlotte.

"Hello, Aunt Lotte," I said stiffly, as a way of announcing my presence.

My aunt turned. "Olivia. So glad you could make it." I felt a sudden chill despite the warm September sunshine.

She knew. She had to.

I'd emailed Emma yesterday afternoon, requesting she not disclose to Charlotte that the competition had been my idea. My standing as Leighton's maid of honor and Kali's cousin offered me pretext for not wanting to get caught in the middle.

"Well, their kale salad can't be missed." I tucked my napkin onto my lap and smiled at her—but not too brazenly. Gloating would confirm her suspicions.

We exchanged meaningless pleasantries. Finally, when the waitress had refilled our sparkling waters and departed with our lunch orders, Charlotte abandoned all pretense.

"I heard from Emma yesterday with some very surprising news."

"Oh?" I fixed an expression of polite interest on my face.

Charlotte's dark eyes drilled into me like lasers. "She wants to add a little excitement to the June issue. A competition between two brides. Magazine coverage of pre-wedding events, with Emma determining the eventual cover star in the spring."

"Oh yes," I said mildly. "Leighton told me about that. She's very excited to be back in the running."

A muscle jumped in Charlotte's jaw. "And you know what I thought, Olivia? What a *creative* idea. And how *convenient* that my niece's best friend is the one my daughter is competing against."

"Well, Leighton was already in consideration—"

"Don't insult my intelligence." Charlotte leaned across the table and dropped her voice. "This has your fingerprints all over it. A bold move, considering how Hank was just asked to give his opinion on the job offers made to H&R's summer candidates."

My throat went dry. "I let you take that meeting on Friday," I managed. "You had a fair shot." "Let" was a generous interpretation of the situation. Even if Charlotte hadn't crashed the meeting, I'd been in no fit state to convince anyone of anything.

Charlotte laughed. "Hasn't anyone told you, Olivia? The whole point of nepotism is to get more than your fair shot."

I changed tracks. "Why do you even want this? Because Kali sure as hell doesn't."

Something more than surprise flitted across her face—she hadn't expected to defend her motivations. She paused before replying. "Raising your public profile is enormously helpful in philanthropic work. I have hopes that Kali will follow in my footsteps. This could be her launchpad to high-profile, high-income donors."

Part of me had thought that Charlotte simply wanted to destroy my happiness, but I should've suspected her true social aspirations. From the way Mom had always told it, my aunt ruled Atlanta's charity scene with an iron fist. She'd twice been in talks to appear as a "friend of" *The Real Housewives of Atlanta*. I knew this because it'd been a family disaster each time Charlotte had been passed over; Mom had even forbidden me from watching reality TV in solidarity. Right. Like I'd ever let Charlotte's TV dreams derail my *Bachelor* fandom.

Even though the *Housewives* hadn't panned out, Charlotte had still managed to climb the ladder of society fame. She sat on the boards of half of Atlanta's most powerful nonprofits and was slowly increasing her social media presence. Ironic, given how she'd always looked down on Leighton's online profiles.

My aunt coughed delicately. "And . . . I regret that . . . in the past, I was not as supportive of my daughter's relationship choices."

Charlotte showing a sliver of humanity threw me off. There had been some drama when Kali had first announced she was bisexual. From what I'd heard through the familial grapevine, Charlotte had assumed Kali's girlfriends were "a phase." This manifested as passive-aggressive comments referring to Kali's partners as "friends" and repeated attempts to set up Kali with young men, even when she was in a relationship.

"I think it's great that you want to support Kali and Greta," I said, choosing my words carefully. "Honestly."

"Thank you." Charlotte inclined her head slightly. "I can

admit that I was wrong to question Kali's previous partners. I'd like to publicly celebrate her marriage to Greta."

My aunt seemed genuine; maybe this *was* her way of supporting her daughter. Even if it wasn't Kali's style. It always freaked me out when Charlotte's façade cracked. It was easier to reduce her to status-obsessed villainy, which was how I usually described her to Leighton or Aditya. And that's how I'd understood her as a kid. The summer before I left for college, Charlotte and Mom had wanted me to spend the summer in Atlanta for one of Charlotte's pet Young Leader philanthropy programs. I'd refused, outraged at the prospect of leaving my friends two months early. Mom had even officially enrolled me, prompting a blowout fight the night before graduation. I'd won, although at a heavy cost. Mom had been frosty toward me all summer, so I'd spent most of it at the Sawyers' lake house. Then I'd left for Duke, and three months later my mom passed away.

I still blamed Charlotte for driving that final wedge between us. Looking back, adult me could appreciate the huge network boost of Young Leader. (It was an elite program, and Charlotte had pulled some major strings to get me in.) It made both my head and my heart ache to dwell on memories like that. So instead I focused on the more uncomplicated part of Charlotte: the selfish, power-hungry striver.

"Doesn't Kali get a say in this? I'm not sure she's into *Southern Charm*."

Her eyes tightened. The brief tenderness vanished. "My daughter might not see the value of high-level philanthropy *yet*, but Kali's passionate about environmental advocacy. Her heart is in the right place. With time, I'm confident she'll see that following in my footsteps is the best way to accomplish her charitable goals." She recrossed her legs, flashing her $300-but-apparently-very-charitable shoes at me.

Twenty feet away, a gaggle of pastel-clad businessmen roared in laughter at their fellow's pathetic tee-off, distracting us both. I wrenched my gaze back to Charlotte.

"Well, I wish you and Kali the best of luck. I'm sure it'll be a lovely wedding."

"Of course it will." Charlotte's smile widened in a way that sent the hair on the back of my neck spiking straight up. "You'll make sure of it."

"Excuse me?"

"You may have talked Emma into this competition, but there's hope for you yet." Charlotte paused as the waitress reappeared with two kale salads. She set our plates down at lightning speed and fled, sensing the electrical charge radiating from our table. "Of course, I'll do anything to protect my daughter. As will my husband. And I know you want that job."

I stabbed at my salad, angry at how off-kilter she'd kept me during this whole conversation. She'd unseated me by admitting regret in her past treatment of Kali, but now she was right back in Evil Empress territory. She was building up to something; I could sense it. *Spit it out!*

Charlotte dabbed at her mouth and set her fork down. She laced her fingers under her chin and delivered the kill shot, serenely triumphant:

"You'll be Kali's maid of honor, and you'll make sure her wedding wins."

"What?" I yelped, so loudly that several nearby diners cast

us alarmed looks. A grandmother type fixed me with a withering hairy eyeball; at a place like this, causing a commotion was an imprisonable offense. "Are you insane?"

"She's your cousin; it makes perfect sense."

"Nothing about that makes sense." I ticked the reasons off on my fingers like I was performing a dramatic closing argument for a skeptical jury. Not that I'd ever argued in front of a jury (yet), but I'd practiced plenty of times in front of Aditya and old episodes of *The Good Wife*. "One: Kali and I aren't close anymore. We're not even bridesmaid-level friends, much less maid of honor! Two: I'm already Leighton's maid of honor, and she's getting married a week after Kali! Even if I wanted to—which I don't—and even if Kali wanted me to do this—which she doesn't—there's no way I'd have time to help plan *two* giant weddings."

Charlotte started to answer, but I steamrolled right over her. "And, three: Kali and Leighton are competing! I can't help both at once!"

"You won't be," Charlotte said swiftly. "You'll be helping Kali."

"But I'm Leighton's maid of—"

"Be Leighton's flower girl, for all I care." Charlotte straightened her already ballerina-like posture, towering over me even while sitting with her legs crossed primly at the ankles. "But you'll be Kali's maid of honor, and you will make sure she wins."

"I went through all this trouble to"—I paused, realizing I was about to tip my hand, but then plunged ahead; she knew anyway—"make sure Leighton had a chance at the cover! Why would I throw that away now?"

Charlotte reached into her purse and pulled out a black folder. "Your uncle asked me to pass this along."

Heart thumping in my ears, I reached forward and took the folder in both hands. If this held what I thought it did—

"Go ahead," Charlotte said, watching me in satisfaction. "Open it."

I opened the folder. Inside was a single sheet of paper with the Holmes & Reese header. A letter, addressed to Ms. Olivia Fitzgerald. I scanned the first line: *Congratulations! We are pleased to extend you an offer of full-time employment, contingent upon graduation from Vanderbilt University Law School in good standing . . .*

"This can work out for everyone," Charlotte said silkily, her drawl barely more than a whisper. "Be Kali's maid of honor. Plan flawless events and help her win. Even your little friend benefits—she'll have several pre-wedding events covered, and that's something, isn't it? And after they both go skipping off to their honeymoons, you'll head back to Manhattan for your dream job."

I stared at the offer letter, the words blurring as I tried to process. A jumble of thoughts ran through my head. I wanted this for Leighton so badly. And I'd put so much effort into getting her a chance at this magazine cover. But this was my chance at Big Law. Leighton's following would still increase with coverage of her pre-wedding events. Maybe that would be enough to greenlight her Houston collaboration . . .

This is Leighton, I reminded myself. *Your best friend in the world!* The one who'd—mere hours ago!—put my own best interests before her own. The one who'd refused to join any kickball teams in fourth grade until I was picked, too. The one who'd spent hours helping me prep before every mock trial debate in high school. The one who'd dropped out of sorority rush to FaceTime me every night for months after my mom died, even when all I could do was sob. And I'd betrayed her. Jeopardized our friendship for a shot at a guy who hadn't even texted me back.

And Kali . . .

The doubts pooling within me hardened to a steely certainty. I arranged my thoughts like I was arguing for a judge. My own inner judge.

Your Honor, there are three parties at stake in this issue: myself, Leighton, and Kali. (The Empress is a demon; only human interests are considered in this courtroom.)

There was no way Kali cared about a magazine cover. So Leighton winning the cover would be a satisfactory outcome for all involved.

The important thing was to honor my oral contract with Charlotte—that is, convince her that I was helping Kali. And I would—just not as much as I'd help Leighton. It all depended on the whims of one magazine editor. Emma and I were on the same wavelength. I could make it look like a close competition.

And Kali . . . I couldn't believe that my badass, wild-child cousin cared one iota about a *Southern Charm* wedding. She struck me as the type to drop in at City Hall on a Tuesday to get married for tax benefits, or to elope somewhere ridiculously cool, like during a scuba-diving excursion off the Great Barrier Reef. Charlotte might think she was acting in Kali's best interest, but I doubted my cousin's wedding goals involved a high-profile magazine feature. Maybe I could convince Kali to elope and drop out of the competition! If Leighton won by default, I'd be blameless.

I traced the glossy letterhead of Holmes & Reese. I'd have to make sure my official employment contract was signed well before Kali announced her decision to drop out. Or before Leighton won the competition. Even though I had an offer letter in my hands, entry-level positions at Big Law firms were insanely competitive. Last year, a summer associate attended the holiday Christmas party three months after her offer letter, had too much to drink, and fell off the chartered yacht into the East River. Her offer was quietly rescinded before the new year. A senior partner like Hank could make my offer vanish with one email.

But the closer I was to my actual start date, the harder it'd be to throw any wrenches into my future. Most high-achieving graduates would be locked into jobs by mid-spring, and Big Law wasn't designed for efficient mid-year recruiting. I had a stellar track record from my two summers at Holmes & Reese. I'd pretend to help Kali all winter, and then in the spring I'd really gear up my efforts to talk her out of this whole thing.

And by the time Charlotte saw Leighton on the cover of *Southern Charm*, I'd be fully onboard and the newest junior lawyer at Holmes & Reese.

"Olivia?" Charlotte's faux-concern broke into my inner monologue. "Are you all right? You look whiter than a wintertime Yankee."

Pull yourself together, I scolded. I couldn't go all quiet and contemplative in front of Charlotte; she'd know I was plotting. And I needed to sell this. I scrunched my eyebrows together and bit my lip in a show of indecision. "You practically plan events for a living. How would me being Kali's maid of honor change anything?"

"You understand the *Southern Charm* audience." Charlotte raised her shoulders slightly, the closest I'd ever seen her come to a shrug. "And the maid of honor plans the pre-wedding events—the things that'll win Kali the cover. I will, of course, handle the actual wedding."

This hadn't occurred to me, but it was a good point. If events like the bridal shower and bachelorette would drive Emma's decision . . . those events were even more important than the wedding, at least for *SC*. A tiny part of my brain clutched its skepticism. If Charlotte was this intent on the competition, she could take over planning *every* event, traditions be damned. Was she concerned that bachelorette planning was out of her opera-gala wheelhouse? Then again, she could hire a young party planner instead of bullying me. But I was probably overthinking this. Charlotte had that effect on me. My plan was complicated enough; I didn't need to be thinking myself in circles, too.

"Okay. I'll be Kali's maid of honor."

"Good. You focus on Kali. I will handle Leighton."

"Handle?" I repeated, the back of my neck prickling. "No. Leighton has nothing to do with you."

"So you'll help Kali win, then."

"Aunt Lotte, at the end of the day it's still up to Emma—"

"You're a smart girl, Olivia." Charlotte reached forward and tugged the Holmes & Reese folder away from me. "You'll find a way to make it happen. Isn't that what you always do?"

Make it happen. Make it work. This was what I did, right?

I persuaded people to see things like I did. Some would say this was an impossible situation. That if I agreed to this, everything would inevitably blow up in my face.

But I was Olivia Fitzgerald. And where others saw an impossibility, I saw opportunity.

I held out my hand and met my aunt's icy gaze. "We have a deal."

And right as we shook hands, a golf ball landed in my drink.

I looked up to see a white-clad guy jogging toward us, an unrepentant grin on his face. A very handsome face. And a very familiar one. My stomach did three loop-de-loops and settled two zip codes over from its normal location.

"Will!"

Leighton's brother, Will, arrived at our table to mop up the last drops of water dripping onto our legs. I was getting a lot of drinks spilled on me lately.

"Hey, Liv! Thought that was you." Will slid a sweat towel off his neck and draped it over the already soaked napkins. "Sorry about that. Tyler dared me to try a spin shot and, well, let's just say I lost that bet."

Charlotte dabbed her silk blouse as if she were fingerprinting a crime scene, iciness stealing across her face. But when she looked up, her expression morphed into reluctant appreciation. Even women twenty years his senior couldn't resist the striking attractiveness of Will Sawyer. All six feet three inches of him were tanned and glowing with a light sweat from the still-oppressive summer heat.

The new dampness under my armpits had nothing to do with the blazing Tennessee sun. My mind was wiped clear of anything remotely intelligent. Will had that effect on me. He was my longest-running crush, the literal boy next door who bore a blinding resemblance to the sun god Apollo. My face flushed at the memory of the last time I'd seen him. The night a striking chemistry had crackled between us, so new and unexpected that I'd half convinced myself I'd dreamed it all. The night I'd slept with my best friend's brother. And the last time I'd spoken to him.

Two weeks ago, I'd been a few days out from finishing my summer term at Holmes & Reese. Will had flown to Manhattan to visit a friend and we'd met up for a drink. It was supposed to be casual: he was killing time during his buddy's work dinner; I was venturing outside of my Midtown bubble. We'd arranged to meet for happy hour, but I'd gotten stuck in the office with a last-minute briefing. I'd texted him apologetically, sad to cancel a drink with my longest-running crush. But Will's buddy had a work crisis, so Will remained fortuitously free. We met up around ten p.m. I'd walked into the dimly lit bar in my sheath dress and Rothy's flats, wishing I'd worn something a little more day-to-night. I felt stuffy and overdressed for the casual neighborhood pub.

But then I'd seen him, sitting in a booth against the dark-paneled wall, and as soon as our eyes met a mutual spark ignited. Maybe it was the new environment, or the late hour, or the promise of a summer night, but all I could think about was how long it'd take him to kiss me.

(An hour and forty minutes, it turned out.)

My memory of that evening was tinged with the crispness

of a cool August night, the thrill of the illicit, and the sheer joy of a longtime crush *finally* being reciprocated. Will in Manhattan was both familiar and exotic, reassuring yet exciting. Each time we left a bar and paused outside on the sidewalk, our eyes met for an exhilarating millisecond. Neither of us wanted to be the first to suggest either of our places— that felt like an irreversible step. But neither of us wanted the night to end. So we stayed out until nearly five a.m., hopping from neighborhood bar to after-hours speakeasy to hole-in-the-wall jazz club.

With anyone else, the electric chemistry would've tugged us into bed together after a single drink, maybe two. But with Will, the strength of our shared history tempered that pull. Somehow, every innocent question birthed a newer and more intense discussion. Halfway through our first drink, he'd asked if my dad was proud of my Big Law achievements so far. Twenty minutes later, I was telling him—something I'd never told anyone, not even Leighton—how sometimes I resented my mom for dying, for leaving me no choice but Big Law if I wanted a shred of parental attention. For taking something that I'd already been interested in and removing the choice. Most of the time it didn't bother me. But occasionally it did, and that had been one of those nights.

Two bars and two equally intense conversations later, we'd stumbled out of the jazz club and onto the wide, empty sidewalk.

Will laced his fingers through mine and pulled me in to his chest. "What the hell happened tonight? Did we lose our minds?"

"Something like that." I giggled, and rose on my tiptoes to

kiss him. Another group of drunken revelers stumbled out of the bar behind us and whooped loudly at our PDA.

Will kissed the side of my neck. "I don't want this night to end."

This was it: the decision. The inflection point that would change everything.

"It doesn't have to," I whispered. And that was all it'd taken for us to end up together in Will's hotel room, tangled in fresh white sheets and lost in the thrill of each other. In the exhilaration of ignored consequences and forgotten promises.

Afterward, we rested among the fluffy down pillows, exhausted, yet neither of us ready for sleep. On some level, we were both aware that tonight had been an anomaly, that life would never be as simple and uncomplicated as deciding which drink to order next. I nuzzled against Will's chest, trying to memorize the scent of his woody cologne.

But before I could puncture our happy little bubble and mention his sister, Will kissed my forehead and sat up. "I hate to do this, but I've got to jump in the shower. I've got an early flight to catch."

"Oh. Right." I sat up against the padded headboard and watched him as he moved about the room, collecting remnants of his clothes. Vaguely I remembered him mentioning a trip to Thailand. I hadn't realized he was leaving so soon. "You said you'll be off the grid?"

"Yup. We'll be living on a dive boat for two weeks." He flashed me an apologetic look as he stuffed another pair of shoes into his suitcase. "Not ideal timing, I know."

Uncertainty hung heavy in the air. We stared at each other for a moment, unspoken questions circling between us. Was this a one-off thing, or was it the start of something real?

What would we tell Leighton? *Would* we tell Leighton?

"Your sister . . ."

Will squeezed his eyes shut. "Right." He looked like he was trying to decide something. Then he shook his head. "I'm still tipsy. I can't think about this right now. Just—don't say anything to her while I'm gone."

"We'll talk when you're back," I said with forced casualness. "Figure everything out then."

Will nodded and then, unexpectedly, grinned. "Technically I only swore never to *date* any of her friends."

"Oh yeah?" I knelt on the bed and wrapped my arms around his neck from behind, resting my chin on his left shoulder. "Wasn't last night a date?"

"Absolutely not," he said into the side of my face. "There were no awkward pauses, no fumbling over the bill, and no weird icebreaker questions. Couldn't have been a date."

"So what was it?"

"Something much better," he murmured, and gave my cheek a quick kiss. "But I really need to get out of here. Tyler'll kill me if I miss this flight."

I watched him scramble around the room. "JFK or LaGuardia?"

"Newark."

"Ew."

"Ah, the New Jersey bias already." Will grinned at me over his shoulder while he finished stuffing clothes into his suitcase. "Look at you, Miss New Yorker." He grabbed a jacket, jammed a Nashville Predators hat onto his golden waves, and crossed the room in two strides. "Check out whenever you want."

"Okay." I swallowed, suddenly despondent that the night

was well and truly over. Will was flying to the other side of the world. Then he'd start his new job at Duke, in North Carolina. I had no idea when I'd see him again. There were so many things I wanted to straighten out. I hated uncertainty. But there was no time. "I—do we—so, I just don't tell Leighton?"

He kissed me gently. "Nothing to tell. We're not dating."

"Right," I said, confusion melting into panic as he disappeared out the door. "Safe flight."

The lawyer in me wanted to sprint down the hall, drag Will back, and conduct a full deposition to clarify what, exactly, he'd meant by "We're not dating." At first it'd sounded like a sweet joke, a reference to our night being too smooth to be a first date. But as the afterglow slowly faded—replaced, cruelly, by a raging hangover—my certainty dissolved. After all, he'd also referenced his promise to never date Leighton's friends. So was our night a one-off? It couldn't have been. That magnetic force—he must've felt it, too. Right? Then I pulled myself together and refused to overanalyze for the next two weeks. When Will was back in the country, we'd figure things out.

The next day, a conveniently imploding merger kept me distracted during my last days in Manhattan. And shortly after my return to Nashville, I ran into Emma at the gas station. Suddenly things seemed like they'd work themselves out. After I nabbed this amazing opportunity for Leighton, she'd forget that Olivia plus Will equaled treachery to the highest degree. Then maybe Will and I could have a conversation about giving things a real shot.

Seeing him now, a tsunami of emotion crashed over me. He was *here*. Not just in the country, but in Nashville and standing right in front of me. Leighton's face popped into my mind: *My brother just landed.* "Hi," I squeaked out. "If you wanted our table that bad, you could've just asked," I added, my brain kicking into gear at last.

"Ha, ha." Will rolled his eyes and turned to Charlotte. "Hi. I'm Will Sawyer. Lived down the street from Olivia growing up." *Slept with her two weeks ago. Current status, undefined.*

Charlotte's eyes widened. "Sawyer, as in *Leighton* Sawyer?"

"Actually, Will, I've got to talk to you about something!" I jumped to my feet and snatched up my bag. "Aunt Lotte, if you don't mind, I'll walk Will back to the range!"

Before Charlotte could protest, I placed two hands on Will's absurdly defined midsection and pushed him away from the table. "Let's go," I hissed.

We beelined across the patio, my heart thrumming faster than hummingbird wings. A million questions buzzed in my head as the shock of seeing him slowly faded. When we reached the path back to the driving range, I tugged at his sleeve. "Is she following?"

"Who? Your aunt?" Will glanced back over his shoulder, amused. "No, she's still at the table. Looks annoyed."

"Good." I picked up my pace. "Quick, let's get farther away."

Will barely had to lengthen his stride to match my near-jog. "Am I allowed to ask why we're fleeing the scene? Was that a drug deal?"

I snorted. "Did Charlotte *look* like a drug dealer?"

"Do Botox vials count?"

We'd reached the edge of the driving range. Ahead of us, thirty or so golfers were clustered in small groups, taking wide practice swings before sending balls sailing upward against the brilliant azure sky. Will tugged me down to sit on a shaded bench. The stone felt pleasantly cool against my legs.

"Leighton's a sore subject with her," I explained. Stalling, I filled him in on the *Southern Charm* magazine competition. Babbling about *SC* took only half of my brainpower. The other half was analyzing Will's every word and gesture. Were we really pretending this was a casual run-in? Like we hadn't hooked up two weeks ago before Will dropped off the face of the Earth? Or like Will had actually told me he was coming back to Nashville, instead of back to North Carolina? "That was my aunt Charlotte. She wants me to be my cousin Kali's maid of honor."

"Aren't you my sister's maid of honor?"

"Yup."

"I don't know much about the sanctity of wedding planning," Will said easily, "but isn't that a conflict of interest? You helping both sides?"

That's *what you want to talk about*? Annoyance flared inside me. Of course it was, but I didn't have time to get into the whole twisted web. "It's not exactly a request you turn down. She's my cousin."

A cousin I barely spoke to anymore, but he didn't need to know that.

"But Leighton said you got her the cover. Nothing about a competition." Will's green eyes crinkled around the edges in confusion. They were the same color as Leighton's, which didn't help. "My mom was talking my ear off about it this morning."

"Yes." I shifted my weight, aware that my story didn't make sense without him knowing about Charlotte's blackmail. "The competition was an unexpected wrinkle. But it'll work out. I'll get Leighton on the cover. I'm not worried."

He threw me a look, catching the half-truth at the end. After Leighton, Will could read me better than anyone else in the world. A familiarity from years of sharing orange-flavored Popsicles and afternoons playing pickup basketball in the Sawyers' driveway. Childhood friends knew you before you knew yourself. Knew you before you'd decided what version of you to present to the world.

"You didn't tell me you were coming back to Nashville," I added, not being able to help myself. It was taking a Herculean effort to hold back the deluge of follow-up questions.

"Didn't I?" Will looked surprised. "Oh, I thought I'd mentioned it. My grandma's ninetieth birthday party is tonight. And my car's here. I'm driving to Durham tomorrow."

"Gotcha." I tucked both hands under my thighs and rocked back and forth uncomfortably.

"Planned on sleeping all day, but Tyler snagged a morning tee time, so I rallied." A knowing expression flickered across his eyes. "I was planning on texting you after I woke up. I didn't forget, Liv. I wanted to see you before I left."

I blushed. "Aren't you awake now?"

"Nope. Half asleep at least." He faked a yawn that turned into a real one halfway through. "Jet lag's no joke. Neither is a sixteen-hour flight."

"But the trip was worth it?"

"Incredible. We spent a week diving off the coast of Thailand and another week lazing on the beach. You wouldn't believe how crystal-clear the water was." He grinned at the memory. "I had a blast. Just lucky to be able to fit the trip in before the new job."

That had always been one of my favorite things about Will: his unconscious habit of gratitude. Like Leighton, Will was easygoing and laid-back. But where his sister was shy and slow to open up, Will brimmed with goodwill among friends and strangers alike. Around him, I found myself complaining less, and letting go and *living* a bit more.

Although that's what had landed us here.

"And there was this one reef—I can't describe it. Most beautiful thing I've ever seen. Let me find some photos."

I leaned a little closer as Will pulled out his phone and scrolled through images of shockingly blue water. His black golf polo smelled like cologne, sweat, and sunscreen. It was intoxicating. I coughed and looked for a new topic, to distract myself.

"Are you looking forward to starting work?"

"Right now, thinking about that ocean?" Will chuckled, eyes on his screen. "Not overwhelmingly. I don't know if it was the right decision. And I won't know until I start. It's an entirely different patient population."

Will was a physical therapist and had worked for years at a fancy private school in Nashville, assisting the sports trainer. From what he'd told me in New York, the hours were good and the pay decent, but he'd felt unfulfilled. So he'd taken a job at Duke in their acute rehab hospital, working with elderly patients post–cardiac surgery. I was supposed to be happy for him. He was pushing himself to take a more challenging position and have a larger impact on patient lives. But, selfishly, I couldn't believe he was moving away right when I'd finally acted on my long-simmering crush. Although maybe that was the universe telling me what I feared, deep down: Pursuing Will would never work. Not if I cared about Leighton.

"Here." He handed over his phone. "The first couple are the Hardeep wreck. That was my favorite."

I took the phone and absentmindedly flipped through photos while Will chattered about various shipwrecks, his face bright with excitement. Then came chagrin as he seemed to remember where he was. "Sorry, Liv. Got carried away. Anyway. I really did want to talk to you today. I had a lot of time to think in Thailand. I don't want to lie to Leighton about us."

"Me neither." I hesitated. "But this is a huge deal to her. When you and Lila broke up—"

His face clouded over. "That was six years ago, Liv. Leighton may be mad at first, but she'll get over it—"

I shook my head. "When you two broke up, Leighton lost one of her best friends. She doesn't want to be put in that position again."

I might've been three states away, but the Lila/Will implosion during our junior year of college was burned into my brain forever. Will and Lila, Leighton's freshman-year roommate and (previous) college bestie, had dated for almost two years before Leighton caught Lila in bed with another guy. Even worse, Will had just given up an acceptance to Washington University's elite physical therapy program to stay close to Lila for her senior year at LSU. Will was devastated and Leighton was furious. Scorched earth was all that remained. With tears dripping from her eyes, Leighton had made me swear never to date her brother; she couldn't lose me, too.

And I'd promised. A promise that'd now been haunting me for weeks.

"What position?" Will's eyes held mine. "What, exactly, are we telling her?"

The air sparkled between us. Once, when I was fourteen and Will was fifteen, we'd sat elbow-to-elbow at a backyard firepit party of Leighton's. The evening was excruciating bliss. It was the most pleasurable torture imaginable: brushing up against him, my entire body charged with possibility.

The same electricity hummed through me now. Our Manhattan night had been incredible. I refused to believe it was one-sided, that it'd been just a hookup for Will. Could it be the beginning of something between us? But Will would be in North Carolina, and I was moving to New York next summer. What could our future be, long-term? And Leighton would be furious. I couldn't lose her. I couldn't jeopardize my as-good-as-sister for the mere *chance* at something with Will.

Not to mention, I had no idea what Will wanted. Or what to say to Leighton.

"I . . . I don't . . . I'm not . . ."

To buy time, I glanced back down at Will's phone and flicked through a few more images. And then my blood froze. I'd reached the end of the underwater photos. Will was standing on a boat deck, wet suit half unzipped and tied at his waist. Next to him stood a beautiful blonde, her right arm around Will's back and her left hand resting possessively on his bare chest. In real life, Will was gazing over the driving range. I flipped through more photos: Will holding the girl in a fireman's carry, both grinning at the camera. Will and the girl sitting on the edge of the boat, hugging. Will and the girl standing wrapped in the same towel. A screenshot of Tyler's Instagram Story from two days ago, a picture of Will and the girl with the caption *Honeymooners <3.*

What the actual—?

"I don't know," I said slowly. My entire body felt like it'd been encased in marble: cold, emotionless, unforgiving. So Will'd had a fling in Thailand. Days after we'd slept together.

A sharp breeze whipped up from over the green, and my dirty-blond hair flew across my face. The color suddenly looked drab and dull compared to Dive Girl's shimmering curls.

Will reached out a hand to tuck a strand behind my ear and then stopped, reading my rigid posture. "I don't want to screw up your friendship with my sister." His hand fell back to his side. "I can talk to her if you want—"

I shook my head. There was no point in telling Leighton about a one-off drunken mistake. Clearly it hadn't meant much to Will. But what had I expected to happen? My best friend would be furious, and even if she didn't care, Will and I lived thousands of miles apart. Already my mind was replaying every moment of our night with this harsher lens, stripping away the magic. Will hadn't wanted to see me to start a relationship. He'd just wanted to get our stories straight. "No. I don't think we should tell her, actually. If it was just a onetime—"

Will didn't appear to be listening. "It's a lot to be keeping from her. Planning your cousin's wedding, what happened with us—"

"I'll tell her about my cousin. Who, by the way, is probably gonna drop out." I jerked my thumb over my shoulder, somehow finding a false cheeriness to stuff into my tone. "The Evil Empress back there? She's the one who cares about the magazine, not Kali. But Leighton's stressed enough right now. She doesn't need to know about us. It's better that way."

"Okay." Will pulled me in for a tight hug. "I trust you. If that's what you think is best—"

"It is," I assured him, grateful my face was hidden in his golf polo. Will had always been able to see through my poker face. But I was a master at hiding the pain in my voice. "Trust me."

4

Being maid of honor for one wedding was stressful. Being maid of honor for two one-week-apart weddings was challenging. Throw in the fact that said brides were in direct competition for a high-stakes magazine profile? That was approaching downright impossible.

Aditya threw a piece of popcorn at me. "No, it *is* impossible. This'll blow up in your face."

I threw a handful right back. Aditya's black Lab, Circe, scampered around my couch in glee, gobbling up the remnants of our fundamental difference in pessimism levels. "No, it's not. Can we please change the subject? Leighton's gonna be here any minute."

Aditya raised his hands. "Let the record show I warned you."

"Hostile witness," I grumbled. The doorbell rang. Uncurling myself from the couch, I padded through my living room and paused in front of the door. "Positive attitude!" I hissed at Aditya.

"Voice of reason!" he hissed right back.

I swung open the door to reveal a determined-looking Leighton, armed with her laptop, a stack of notebooks, and her sketchbook. Her hair was twisted into a messy topknot and she wore head-to-toe Lululemon: she'd come to work.

"Hi!" she said, wasting no time in pushing past me. "Is your radiator broken again? I heard all these weird hissing noises."

Aditya and I made brief eye contact. "Nope, it's fine, no idea what that was," I assured her.

The three of us settled into my cozy living room. In one of his rare outpourings of generosity (always tied to academic achievement), my father had purchased my living room furniture when I'd crushed the LSAT. Leighton, whose creative eye stretched beyond clothing, had designed the layout of the L-shaped sectional, rugged wooden coffee table, and iron-rimmed mirrors flanking the flat-screen TV. Circe bounded into my lap and licked my hand affectionately. At least someone was on my side.

"Okay, Operation Win Magazine Cover starts now," Leighton announced. "Liv, did you send Emma the list of events? Do we know which issues they're running in?"

Flipping open my laptop, I ignored the twinge of academic guilt as I minimized my unread family law case briefing. I pulled up the schedule I'd worked on all week. "Yes. It's now mid-September, and your weddings are both in mid-May, giving six months of content. Emma wants to alternate profiling each bride's wedding events in the preceding issues. November will be Kali's engagement party—"

Leighton's head shot up. "Why is hers first?"

"Because you already had an engagement party."

71

Leighton's parents had thrown Leighton and Matt's engagement party in May. It'd been the last time I'd seen Leighton before leaving for New York for the summer. A four-hour sangria-soaked extravaganza. I'd spent half the time sneaking covetous looks at Will and the other half debating if I could talk Aditya into a platonic marriage pact. Sure, I was only twenty-seven (approaching twenty-eight!), but in the South, that was having one foot in the marriage-able grave.

"She could have another one," Aditya suggested.

I sent him a quelling look. The last thing I needed was another event to plan. "*No*, she can't. Can y'all let me finish?"

"Go on," Leighton grumbled.

"Emma doesn't want to repeat events, so we'll alternate. I've worked it all out. Remember, each issue features an event that happened the month before. And that's super-fast in magazine timing. They're rush-producing the paper issues to stay synced with the social media content."

"Okay."

"The December issue will cover your bridal shower. January will be Kali's cake-tasting. February will be your floral arrangements. March will be Kali's bachelorette, and April will be yours." I paused to let the implications register. "So you'll have the final word, Leighton. Your killer bachelorette will be the last thing on Emma's mind when she makes her decision."

"I thought you said no repeats?" Aditya interrupted. We'd done our Circe walk/cold brew routine at my place this afternoon, and I'd expected him to flee well before Leighton arrived for wedding prep. But he'd been weirdly into it. I suspected he was mining this conversation for a week's worth of sarcastic remarks about bridal minutiae.

"Bachelorette's too big to miss. And the parties will have totally different vibes." I shot a look at Leighton. "Kali'll probably have dropped out by then, anyway."

Leighton nodded, chewing on her bottom lip. "What about October? You said Kali's engagement party will run in November—"

"The October issue's about to go to press." I pulled up the timeline Emma had sent me, laying out the deadline for each of the events. "Each magazine issue goes to press two weeks before the end of the previous month. We're cutting it close with your wedding—Emma warned me the staff'll be working through the weekend if you end up winning."

"But how would we have time to do a cover shoot? My wedding's on May fourteenth—"

"Leighton." I channeled the reassuring tone my father reserved for talking panicked clients out of short-term gains and long-term disasters. "Can you give me a little trust here? I've thought this through a thousand times already."

"Okay. Okay," Leighton repeated, scanning the list of events. "And you're sure this schedule is correct for Kaleidoscope?" This was a fun new habit she'd developed: inventing random full names for Kali, even though I'd told her it wasn't a nickname. Even Leighton trying to be petty was still cute; she didn't have a mean bone in her body.

Aditya snorted, and I sliced my eyes at him again. "*Kali's* events are correct, yes."

"But how do you—"

"Because Charlotte asked me to be her maid of honor," I said fast, like it would be less unpleasant for her to hear this quickly.

Leighton's head whipped up. A few tendrils had escaped her messy bun. Even stressed and about to rip out my throat, she looked like she was modeling for an LSAT prep company. "Excuse me, *what*?"

"It's actually better this way." I started pouring Leighton a generous glass of merlot and didn't stop. "I'll know everything about her wedding! We'll have all the inside intel—"

"How did this even happen?" Leighton shrieked. "Her maid of honor?" She snatched the wineglass and took a long, shuddering gulp. "You don't even talk to Kali! And you hate Charlotte."

"Yes, yes, all true." I nodded hastily, to show my distressed bride-to-be that some facts of the Earth remained intact: I was not actually friends with Kali. Charlotte was evil. Gravity was still a thing.

"Then explain!"

"She showed me an offer letter. From Holmes & Reese."

The creases in Leighton's brows lessened, but she looked even more unhappy. "She's blackmailing you? Help Kali win, or she'll mess with your job offer?"

"Pretty much."

"That's, like . . ." Words momentarily failed her. "Next-level evil, even for her!"

"Right?"

Aditya picked up the wine bottle and silently refilled Leighton's glass. She grabbed it as soon as he was done, her eyes wild. "Couldn't you record Charlotte blackmailing you? Show it to your uncle? Or someone in HR?"

I had a brief and deeply unpleasant vision of filing a maid-of-honor-blackmail-by-evil-aunt complaint to a Holmes & Reese HR rep. "That's not really what they handle."

"Or the police?" Aditya offered. "Kidding. Kind of."

Leighton put her hands to her temples and squeezed her eyes shut. "I'm getting whiplash. You promised the cover was a sure thing. Then I find out I'm competing against your cousin. Now you're also Kali's maid of honor! What's next—are *you* getting married in May, too?"

I pushed Will's face out of my mind's eye. At Leighton's current stress level, hearing about even a one-night stand risked spontaneous combustion. Maybe us fizzling out was for the best. Will had texted me twice this week, asking for Durham recommendations. I was trying not to read too much into it; he'd just moved to a city where I'd lived in college. That was all.

I flopped onto the couch and started kneading the iron-like knots in Leighton's upper shoulders. "There aren't gonna be any more surprises, okay? We have a game plan. I'm on your side."

"And Kalifornia's!"

I grabbed her shoulders. "Leighton. Holmes & Reese always finalizes its new hires by the end of April. Which, let me remind you, is right *before* your wedding."

The back of her head went very still. "Meaning . . . ?"

"By the time Emma makes her decision, the ink will be dry on my contract."

Leighton turned and studied me, anxiety radiating from her invisible pores. "You're sure? You get the job and I still win the cover?"

"Yes." I made the strategic decision not to mention

Charlotte had implied interfering with Leighton's wedding. She was frazzled enough. And I'd be standing guard, anyway. "Let me get some snacks. We've got a lot of planning to do."

Aditya followed me into the kitchen and watched me paw through the pantry. "You seem off, Liv. You're not still upset about the Will hookup, are you?"

I nudged the door shut with my foot. "Watch it. Or are you trying to make Leighton's head explode?"

Traitorously, my phone chose that moment to light up with a text from Will, responding to my coffee shop recommendation. Aditya glanced at the screen and back at me, his eyes narrowing.

"You're still talking to him."

"Just as friends! About Durham. That's it."

"Did you guys text like this before you hooked up?"

"No."

"Okay, shady." Aditya crossed his arms and dropped his voice. "It looks bad. If she finds out y'all slept together and now you're texting all the time, it'll seem like you're dating behind her back—"

"That's not what's happening," I said firmly. *As much as I wanted it to.* Grabbing bags of chips at random, I started assembling a snack platter. "He moved to Durham. I lived there for four years. We're friends and he's asking for recs, that's all. He made it clear we're not dating."

"And you wish you were," Aditya whispered urgently. "You need a clean break. Like me and Boomerang, remember? Don't waste your time on him."

"I know." I opened the fridge and pretended like I was scanning my wine options, mostly to avoid his gaze.

Aditya glanced toward the closed kitchen door. "Liv, I get

that childhood crushes can linger. Nostalgia's a hell of a drug. But you're smarter than this—what the hell is so special about this dude?"

"It's more than a childhood crush." I searched for the words to make Aditya understand. But he'd moved around a lot in childhood; he didn't have any decades-long friendships. I'd grown up alongside Leighton, but I'd grown up alongside Will, too. I'd spent many summer weekends at the Sawyers' lake house, and cheery, shining Will was a cherished part of those memories. As preteens, Leighton and I used to slather ourselves in tanning oil and lie out on the driveway to watch Will's hot friends play pickup basketball. (Well, Leighton watched the hot friends. I was watching Will.)

There were deeper memories, too. When my uncle Mark died, the entire Sawyer family flew to Atlanta for the funeral to support us. Ten-year-old me had broken down unexpectedly at the wake. After Leighton fainted at the sight of the casket, it was eleven-year-old Will who'd hugged me and stayed with me for two silent hours, understanding that some pain couldn't be lessened with words. Eight years later, when my mom passed, the entire Sawyer family came to her funeral, too. By then Will was at college in Texas, and I hadn't seen him for over a year. But when Will had found me sobbing outside the church, his cheeks were almost as damp as mine.

And then there was the raw attraction: his striking height, his radiant blond hair. His easy smile and endless flow of positivity. His remarkable self-discipline, which had nearly propelled him to college basketball stardom. When you combined all that with the power of a shared childhood, how could I resist?

"This dude who hooked up with a surfer chick a week after

you?" Aditya hissed, his voice slicing through the fantasy.

"I don't know that for sure," I muttered.

When we were texting, I'd come *this* close to typing it out: *Who was that girl in your photos?* But I couldn't find a way to ask. On some level, it was probably cowardice. If I didn't ask, there was still hope. Even if nothing ever happened between us again, I found comfort in the idea that we'd shared something special. But if I were honest with myself, there was a shred of relief, too. I'd been so open with Will. Sometimes the memory of the vulnerabilities I'd shared made me feel itchy all over. Starting a relationship with someone who already knew me so well was terrifying—almost as terrifying as the thought of never kissing him again. And then there was the distance, and Leighton's reaction, and . . . somehow, I could never bring myself to send the text. Instead, my brain indulged in my favorite fantasy: Dancing with Will at Leighton's cover-winning wedding. Unrealistic? Definitely. But the allure of daydreams didn't arise from their chance of success.

"Move on, Liv. He's not worth it."

Armed with a bottle of sauvignon blanc, I turned and held it like a shield in front of me. "I don't know why you're being so negative. Just trust me, okay? I'm handling it," I whispered back. Aditya nodded reluctantly.

Back in the living room, we found Leighton examining the radiator with great concern. "I'm telling you, the hissing is unreal," she announced. "Y'all *need* to get that looked at."

As soon as the plane touched down in Atlanta, I could feel it: I was in enemy territory. Even our descent, plagued by stomach-dropping turbulence, had felt unfriendly. Outside, wind gales swept the sodden trees back and forth. I was torn between relief that we'd landed safely and frustration that I'd have to go through with this scheme. If I'd gone out in a fiery combustion, Will would remember me fondly and Emma would feel guilted into choosing Leighton. There were worse outcomes.

Enough of that, I scolded myself. If I'd learned one thing from my hard-ass, I-eat-five-million-dollar-mergers-for-breakfast father, it was that once you made a decision, you had to commit to it. No wondering *What if* or *Was this the right choice?*

"Those are distractions, Olivia," he'd lectured one night at dinner to thirteen-year-old me, too busy scrolling on his phone to notice that I was texting Leighton dog photos. "Indulgences. Commit and move on."

At the time the advice had seemed abstract, so I applied it in the most obvious way: by committing to not eating my Brussels sprouts. But over the years I'd tried to take it to heart. In middle school I committed to debate class over volleyball, even though making the team was a shortcut to guaranteed middle school popularity. I'd committed to Duke for college by applying through the early-decision deadline. I'd committed to a future in law on day one of freshman year, immediately seeking out the prelaw student group and signing up for a law student mentor.

But in many ways, making a choice was the easy part of Dad's philosophy. The hard part was convincing yourself that the not-chosen options then ceased to exist.

Which was what I needed to do now. My original plan—lock in the cover for Leighton so she'd bless my relationship with her brother—was off the table. As was Plan B, the Hail Mary cover competition where Leighton won by a landslide. I hadn't planned on Charlotte's scheming, which in retrospect was a major oversight. Or a freakily bronzed scuba goddess knocking me and Will back into friends-without-benefits territory.

Instead, the choice had been made for me: Plan C. Also known as Plan Help-Leighton-Win-But-Make-It-Look-Close-Until-The-End, which didn't exactly roll off the tongue.

The plan unfolded in my head: *Olivia agrees to act as Leighton Sawyer's maid of honor. Shortly afterward, Olivia enters a verbal contract for a full-time employment opportunity at Holmes & Reese, conditional on her (1) acting as Kali Harlow's maid of honor and (2) making a good-faith effort to help Kali win a magazine competition by planning her pre-wedding events. Which of the following actions will not violate the terms of Olivia's contract?*

A. Persuading Kali to drop out of the competition of her own volition

B. Convincing the magazine editor to choose Leighton for non-event reasons

C. Allotting more effort to planning Leighton's wedding events while still delivering on Kali's events

D. All of the above

I could do this, and I would do this. Come hell or high water.

Although I might've just landed in both. Torrents of water slammed against the plane, and the sky was an ominous shade of purple-grey. A fitting welcome onto Charlotte's home territory.

And Kali's. Thankfully, the Empress was out of town this weekend, so this trip was all about Kali. Hurrying through the airport, I tried to focus on the positives, Will-style. We'd been besties once! (Twelve years ago, but who was counting?) She'd agreed to have me as her maid of honor—that had to count for something. (Had Charlotte blackmailed her, too?) And acting as her MOH would let me be bossy and plan fun parties—two of my favorite things. (Although I'd be much happier planning *one* set of these events, not two.)

Following the signs for passenger pickup, I wandered outside, hugging the overhang to avoid the downpour. I scanned the row of idling cars, trying to remember what Kali drove. It'd been nice of Kali to offer to pick me up. An airport pickup was a big deal—at best, it was inconvenient and boring; at worst, being on call for a delayed flight could eat up an entire day. Leighton or Aditya would do it for me in a heartbeat. But I didn't think Kali and I were on that level. Not anymore.

"Olivia!"

A window rolled down on a black VW Jetta twenty yards away. The trunk popped open. I hurried over, my clothes immediately soaked, and swung my carry-on into the trunk. Blinking away the rain, I slid into the front seat with all the grace of an oiled-up salmon.

"Nice weather," Kali said in lieu of a greeting.

"For fish, maybe," I grumbled, peeling off my drenched jacket. "Thanks for picking me up."

"No problem."

My cousin slid the car into drive, and we rolled away from the curb. While she navigated the maze of airport exit ramps, I snuck a few sideways glances. Kali was as lithe and toned as ever, dressed in leggings, beat-up Nike running shoes, and a quarter-zip rain jacket. Her glossy black hair was pulled into a simple high pony, and she wore minimal makeup. A solitaire diamond glittered on her left hand.

We drove in an awkward but not hostile silence. There was a lot we needed to cover this weekend, and there was also a giant elephant in the room (car?): Why had Kali agreed to this competition? Or to have me as her maid of honor?

I decided to ease into it. "Congrats on the engagement. Your ring is beautiful."

"Thanks. It's lab-grown." She paused and then seemed to decide she had to say something else. "It's been a whirlwind. I'm sorry you had to hear indirectly."

"No worries. You guys probably had a lot of people to tell."

"Mom certainly did," Kali muttered.

"Weddings are right up her alley."

"Event planning, you mean." She shook her head. "I swear she's gotten worse. It's like the same gala obsession she'd always had, amplified times a hundred."

"Amplified, like, she wants you to be on a magazine cover?"

Kali snorted. "All right, we're jumping right in. I respect that." She flicked on her blinker and glanced over at me. "You're wondering why you're my maid of honor?"

"Yup."

"This wedding's for Mom, not me. She's been planning it since I was four." Kali clicked her a tongue a few times. "To a Prince Charming, of course. It took her a while to accept that I was serious when I came out as bi."

"How long's a while?" I'd heard the family gossip, of course, but Kali and I had never discussed this directly. She hadn't come out until college, long after we'd drifted apart.

"Let's just say Greta's the first girlfriend she's acknowledged."

"Oof." From social media, I knew Kali'd dated several women before Greta. I tried to imagine waiting fifteen years for your mother to take your relationships seriously. The thought made me deeply sad for my cousin. "How's Hank? Is he any better?"

Kali waved a hand dismissively. "Hank's interest in my love life is limited. As is his interest in anything not directly billable to a client."

"Oof," I said again, and made a silent promise that my loved ones would never say that about me, no matter how intense the Big Law hours were.

"Mom was hoping I'd end up with a guy. For a while she was really concerned about losing the chance for grandchildren. Had to educate her on that, too." She hesitated again. "I know I don't *owe* her anything. But she's been making a real effort with Greta. Her trying to throw a big wedding— that's her love language. She's trying to show her support. Publicly, I guess."

"And you don't care about the wedding that much," I guessed.

"Bingo. A big win for Mom and a little hassle for me." Kali shrugged. "And I guess a major hassle for you. Sorry about that. I needed someone trustworthy, someone who'd handle things without much input from me."

I ignored the twinge of guilt at the word "trustworthy." "What about your friends in Atlanta?"

She snorted again. "My friends wouldn't be caught dead doing something like this. And they'd do a shit job. You were Mom's first choice." She waved a hand at my glossy rain boots, high-waisted black jeans, and new Theory sweater. "Seems like the sort of thing you'd be good at."

"Gotcha." I waited for her to ask *why* I'd agreed to do this, but she left it at that. Maybe she'd assumed it was cousinly love. Or that the third year of law school was a breeze. "And the *Southern Charm* cover?"

"Oh yeah. Something else I didn't want to deal with." Kali drummed her fingers along the steering wheel. "But important to Mom. And Greta was weirdly into it. She wants to learn more about commercial photography and get some exposure for the foundation."

I filed away this piece of information. The little I knew about Kali's fiancée was all thirdhand through social media and our mutual family members. Born in the States, Greta had spent most of her childhood in South Africa, the daughter of two safari guides. She'd returned to the U.S. for college before landing a job working remotely as a fundraiser for a South African nature conservancy, although she spent a few weeks a year in East Africa freelancing as a wildlife photographer. A way cooler bio than mine. "I'm looking forward to meeting Greta."

Kali winced. "About that . . . I should warn you. Greta can take some time to warm up to people."

I'd interviewed enough clients to know when someone wasn't being entirely forthcoming. "To all people, or to me specifically?"

She slid a sideways look at me. "Both."

"Why's that?"

"She's not a big fan of the bougie Old South, old-money lawyer type."

"What is this, *The Great Gatsby*? I'm not 'old-money'—"

"I know, I know. I told her. But you go to Vanderbilt, and you're almost a lawyer, and you're tight with that influencer."

"Meaning?"

"Y'all probably won't be best friends," she said, dodging the question. "Which is fine. Just don't take it personally."

I stared at the violent storm clouds swirling above us and shivered slightly; my soaked shirt was raising goose bumps on my arms in the car's chilly AC. "Consider me warned."

5

After stopping by Kali's apartment to drop off my luggage and change into dry clothes, we headed to a local coffee shop and snagged a cozy corner table. The aesthetic was old farmhouse: exposed wooden beams, a stone floor, and colorful cloth blankets stacked at each bench-like table. Secretly I hoped that the homey vibe would help Greta warm up to me—I'd chosen it, via Instagram, for this exact purpose.

As soon as we'd gotten settled, Kali glanced up toward the entrance and her face brightened. "There she is!" She lifted a hand.

A clump of people had walked through the door, so it took me a moment to locate Greta. Then two soccer-mom types drifted closer to the bakery counter, and a tall, pale girl with a platinum-blond pixie cut stepped forward. Something about her drew my eye at once. She wore a cropped maroon leather jacket and loose nineties-style jeans, and carried a Trader Joe's cloth bag in lieu of a purse. She moved with the grace of a principal ballerina and the precision of an experienced Marine. But even from across the room, it was obvious this girl belied all the normal labels.

"Can you get our drinks?" Kali shout-called.

Greta nodded and her gaze briefly traveled to me, her face unreadable. Then she turned to the counter to order.

"She's gorgeous," I said to Kali honestly. Greta's features were striking and, alone, might've overwhelmed any other face: a strong Roman nose, closely hooded dark eyes, and wide, full lips. But together, they worked.

Kali sighed happily. "I know, right? I'm a lucky girl."

We watched Greta carry the tray of three drinks over to the table. She sat down opposite us and nodded in my direction. "Hi. I'm Greta. You must be Olivia."

"Nice to meet you," I said brightly. Was that a tremble in my voice? What was wrong with me?

Greta slid a drink toward each of us. "Flat white for you," she said, tapping the rim of Kali's. Then, to me: "Had to guess your order. Got the seasonal pumpkin thing." Her faint South African accent only added to the intimidation factor: she even *sounded* cooler than me.

Color rose into my cheeks: I'd been stereotyped, accurately. "Thanks."

"So." Greta laced her hands under her chin and stared at me. "You're the wedding whiz, huh? The one who's gonna win us a magazine cover?"

"Greta," Kali said quickly, "it's not about winning, it's to keep my mom—"

"If we're gonna do the big white wedding, we should get something out of it!" Greta said sharply. "You know I'd rather be doing this in Cape Town—"

Kali's eyes flashed. "You can't keep holding that over my head. You agreed to do it in Atlanta—"

"If your family's going to blow a crapload of money on this, there's nothing wrong with making sure some good comes of it," Greta said evenly.

The conversation was careening out of control. "I'll help you guys plan some killer pre-wedding events," I interjected. "It'll keep Charlotte happy and get some nice publicity. Kali mentioned you work for a nature conservancy, Greta?"

"Yeah." She hesitated, suddenly reserved. "Laraghai. A privately owned conservancy in South Africa. I plan community outreach to help align local citizens against the poachers."

"The poachers?"

"Rhino poachers," she said, and her lip curled.

"That's amazing!" I didn't have to fake my enthusiasm. "How'd you get into conservancy work?"

"My parents are safari guides, so I grew up spending a lot of time outdoors and up close with the animals. Guiding was never my thing, but I got into photography early. I came to the U.S. for college and spent most of my breaks traveling." Her voice had a slightly robotic tone, like this was a spiel she'd given many times before. "When I was backpacking through Ireland, I met this guy who worked in conservation. We kept in contact afterward and he offered me a job after graduation."

"Backpacking through Ireland? That must've been awesome. I've never been."

Greta didn't take the bait, instead reaching to take a long sip of her drink. A tough cookie.

I switched gears. "Anyway, let's talk scheduling." I handed both women a copy of the pre-wedding event lineup.

Experiencing some serious déjà vu, I explained again how magazine coverage would alternate from November through April.

"We're gonna have to move this one," Greta interrupted, tapping at the cake-tasting date. "I'll be in Ecuador for my scuba re-cert."

"Scuba diving?" I said. My mind jumped to Will. Last night I'd dreamed that we'd gone diving together, but when we'd resurfaced, he'd pushed me off the boat in favor of a faceless blond girl. Didn't need a therapist to decode that one. "I've always wanted to learn!"

"Yeah. Diving."

I opened my mouth to ask a polite follow-up question, like I would anytime someone mentioned a cool hobby. But I saw the challenge in Greta's eyes and decided against it.

"No problem," I said instead. "Let's talk big picture. What's your wedding aesthetic?"

Greta shot Kali an is-she-serious look, while Kali bit back a smile. "Bridal?" Kali suggested.

I kept my smile plastered on, even though my blood had started to bubble. Not quite boiling, but on the way. "What about wedding colors?"

"White," Greta deadpanned.

"Look, Olivia, this really isn't our thing," Kali cut in, apologetic. "Neither of us grew up wanting a big wedding, so we don't have a lot of plans."

"Does everyone do all this shit beforehand, or are we doing it for *Southern Charm*?" Greta interjected.

"A mix," I admitted. "Most people do something for a bachelorette. But can we at least talk engagement party? That's in October, so we've really got to get on it."

Kali shrugged and reached for her drink. "We can get you a guest list. What else do you want to talk about?"

I took a deep, steadying breath, and tried to imagine a universe in which Leighton hadn't put together color-coded inspiration boards for every wedding event. It was almost impossible to compute. Kali and Greta were much more laid-back. I'd have to find a way to work with that.

And then inspiration struck. I could *really* work with that. If they had no vision for their engagement party—well, I could *give* them a vision. My vision. One that didn't match *Southern Charm*'s aesthetic at all.

"You know what?" I slammed my laptop closed and pulled out my phone. "I have a better idea. Let's go figure out what you like. Where's the nearest party store?"

As I hustled my two brides-to-be through the doors of Viva La Party!, my thoughts churned through a smorgasbord of party ideas. I didn't have a clear vision, but I knew the result couldn't be cohesive. There had to be some element of chaos.

"Take these and grab whatever jumps out at you," I instructed, handing them each a shopping basket. Kali took hers with reluctance, Greta with disdain. When they started wandering toward the same aisle, I grabbed Kali's arm and spun her around. "No, you gotta split up! That way we'll, uh, make sure both of your personalities are represented."

"My personality will be represented if we elope," Greta muttered, but she turned and headed in a different direction.

I breathed a sigh of relief. If they'd browsed together, they might've chosen a unified theme. And I couldn't allow that to happen.

A twinge of guilt tugged at me, but I pushed my misgivings aside. After all, neither of them cared about this! Kali wanted to appease Charlotte; Greta wanted publicity for her conservancy. A party disaster wouldn't hurt anyone. And maybe— my spirits lifted at the idea—if the event was a total miss, I'd be relieved of my maid of honor duties. Honorable or dishonorable discharge, I didn't care. I'd take it.

The key, of course, was to execute an awful theme *well.* Charlotte knew I was competent; logistical errors like canceled catering or forgotten vendors wouldn't fly.

But if I just had bad taste . . .

"There's no accounting for taste," I whispered happily, grabbing my own basket and looping down the nearest aisle. This was it. This was my way out. I'd plan the most repulsive engagement party the South had ever seen.

I passed over a display of rustic crates and benches; we had to avoid anything that could be interpreted as "farmhouse chic," which was *Southern Charm*'s preferred aesthetic. My hand trailed along an all-white table display, accented with pops of coral and blush flowers. Way too chic.

My phone buzzed with a text from Will:

So . . . don't keep me hanging. What's Greta like? NY style.

I wrote: *The brilliance of her platinum hair is overshadowed only by the fire blazing behind her eyes, an animalistic fierceness learned on the Serengeti.*

Incredible, Will wrote back. *Although I'm sure she's no match for you.*

I smiled at the message. We'd been texting occasionally since Will had left Nashville two weeks ago. It was a step forward; we'd never talked so much before Manhattan. Aditya disapproved, insisting there was no possible happy ending. He'd even called Will my own boomerang. But I didn't care. My confidence was slowly growing. Maybe the scuba chick had been the drunken one-night stand, not me. Maybe he really was interested.

I added: *And your new boss?*

Like a dragonfly in amber, his patient care methods are studiously preserved and impenetrable to the effects of new and updated research, Will responded.

Oof. Be the change you wish to see?

Something like that.

I tucked my phone away and pressed on. The next aisle was more promising: inflatable rubber decorations. I ducked under two giant palm trees and studied the selection of blow-up flamingos. These would tank the party for sure, but it'd be challenging to pretend I'd chosen them in earnest.

"Birds-of-paradise?" said a sarcastic voice behind me.

I jumped to see Greta standing a few feet away. The shopping basket slung over her arm was empty.

"I was guarding this aisle from you two," I joked. "Can't have you picking a flamingo theme."

"M-hmm," Greta said, and turned to drift away.

I followed her past a display of artificial flowers. "Maybe we

could work something in about the environment?" I suggested, grabbing an armful of blooms at random. "Something flower-heavy?"

"Hmph."

It wasn't a no, so I ran with it. "And lots of greenery!" I
sidestepped in front of her and thrust a spool of fake ivy into
her basket. "Whaddaya think?"

"If I say yes, does that get us out of here faster?"

"Exponentially."

Greta reached for an armful of fake sunflowers. "Why
didn't you lead with that?"

By the time we ran into Kali browsing the balloon arches,
I was tingly with anticipation. If I could steer Kali toward
something that clashed—

But when she turned to greet us, my heart sank into my
knees: her basket held a powder-blue gingham blanket and a
collection of cream-colored teacups.

"I had an idea!" she announced triumphantly, holding up
one of the little saucers. "A picnic tea party!"

Greta almost smiled as she held up a fistful of fake sunflowers. "And I was going for a nature theme. That's perfect."

"Mom'll kill me if we use fake flowers," Kali observed, her
lips pursing in a way that was uncannily reminiscent of her
mother. "We're not actually shopping here, right, Olivia?"

My mouth went dry. I forced myself to think. "I love that
you guys are on the same page," I said slowly, my brain doing
that fun thing where I started sentences without knowing
how they'd end. "But we need to level up. Flowers, at a picnic?" I channeled my best Meryl Streep impression.
"Groundbreaking."

Kali's face fell. "You think it's too boring?"

"Too . . ." I searched for the right word. "Predictable. 'Picnic' is a theme for a twelve-year-old's birthday party. Some magazine writer's going to pen an entire article about this event! You need to give them buzzwords to play with. You need to inject some *interest*."

Greta looked bored, but Kali was nodding along, her eyes wide. "Okay. How do we do that?" For someone who'd been as hands-off as a football dad at a toddler pageant, she was showing a surprising amount of interest.

"Step one is upgrading 'picnic,'" I declared. "Let's brand it 'cottagecore.'"

"Bless you," Greta muttered.

I ignored her. "Step two is to add an element of the unexpected," I went on, pulling bullshit out of thin air. I cast my eyes around the store for ideas.

"Fairy tale," Kali suggested.

"Too similar." *Too cohesive.*

"Casino night." Greta smirked.

"Too different." *Too obvious I'm tanking this.*

I turned in a half-circle, aware that I was running out of time. Kali and Greta were thirty seconds from finalizing their flower-picnic idea. Then my gaze fell on the back corner of the store. *Perfect.*

"Neon!" I announced. "That'll be the unexpected. It'll be *neon* cottagecore."

"Neon," Kali repeated slowly. "You mean, the colors?"

I pointed at the customizable neon sign station in the corner, with examples like *Happy Birthday!* and *Congrats, Grads!* "I mean everything. A neon sign, neon glow-stick bracelets, neon accent pieces—and neon prairie dresses for you two."

My voice almost broke with laughter on the last suggestion. *Pull it together, Liv!*

Kali looked at Greta, her expression doubtful. "What do you think?"

Greta shrugged. "I think I've spent way too much time on this already. If Olivia thinks it's a good idea, it's fine with me."

Kali turned back to me. "Neon cottagecore it is. What else do you need from us?"

And just like that, I got the green light to create an LSD-inspired dreamscape that would send Emma DeVant running for cover.

6

October

Cracking the last of the neon glow sticks across my knee, I scattered them on the final table and stepped back to admire my handiwork. Electric pink and purple rods lay strewn across a mauve flower-print tablecloth trimmed with lace. The overall effect was off-putting and slightly nauseating: excellent.

"It looks like Circe's puke after she ate that box of Nerds," Aditya observed.

"And that's just one table!" I gestured at the hotel ballroom we'd rented for Kali and Greta's engagement party. At my request, they'd dimmed all overhead lights so that the neon *Was it all a dream?* sign would draw guests' eyes as soon as they entered. Other illumination was supplied by neon rod lights strategically placed around the dog-puke-inspired tables. Several large barrels with piles of peonies and baby's breath added a touch of Kali's picnic idea, while a large stack of floral aprons waited as a party favor for the guests. A giant projector screen cycled through photos of Kali and Greta's relationship, all edited to Andy-Warhol-esque levels.

"I *cannot* believe you got Charlotte to sign off on this." Aditya shook his head in disbelief. "Did you run *any* of this by her?"

"Charlotte's blind spot is her age. She might know how to throw a swanky high-society Southern wedding, but she doesn't know the first thing about impressing young magazine editors."

"So she had to trust you on this."

"Exactly."

"And you think she'll buy that this wasn't intentional?" Aditya picked up a flickering glow stick and whacked it against the table until it glowed obediently. "That this was your genuine attempt at a good party theme?"

"The *execution* was flawless," I reminded him. Because it had been; I'd made sure of it. The catering was from the best team in town, the DJ was superb, and the individual cupcakes were frosted with almost-too-pretty-to-eat sugared lilies. Even the bartender had whipped up a killer neon cocktail. To be honest, it'd all taken much more time than I'd expected, even after roping in Aditya to help track down rogue vendor agreements. I'd been letting my schoolwork slide, and I was looking forward to getting back on track. "The premise, on the other hand—"

"Flawed."

"Deeply." With the preparations finally complete, I let out a breath I hadn't realized I was holding. "Thank you again for all your help. And for flying out to help me set up! I owe you." Now that I was thinking about it, I really did owe him. He'd gone above and beyond the call of friendship duty. And I hadn't even asked—although I'd done a lot of moaning about overwhelming party prep. Before I knew it, Aditya had booked flights and was telling me that he'd solved my problems and to stop complaining. In a loving way, of course.

Aditya brushed a lock of dark hair out of his eyes and shrugged. "My Delta miles were expiring. And if you exploded from stress, who'd walk Circe when I'm hungover? Or get rid of boomerangs?"

"Glad I'm worth something to you," I teased. Dressed in a black turtleneck and tailored maroon sport coat, Aditya looked especially sharp tonight. He lifted weights regularly and had the Superman shoulder-to-waist ratio to show for it. Half the women in our law school were in love with him; I knew, because I'd let most of them down gently on his behalf.

"Don't let it go to your head."

My eyes landed on two figures over Aditya's shoulder: Charlotte and her husband, Hank, the first guests to arrive. A few others were visible down the hallway behind them. "Showtime. Ready to sell the dream?"

"Dream or nightmare?"

I elbowed him and hurried forward to greet my aunt and step-uncle. "Aunt Lotte! Uncle Hank! Welcome!" I twirled like I was proud to show off my hard work. "What do you think? Isn't it amazing?" Happily, Charlotte's black sheath dress and Hank's grey suit looked distinctly out of place.

Charlotte was too refined to allow her jaw to gape, but her mouth dropped open all the same. "It's . . . something."

Hank laughed easily, confident that no one expected him

to possess an informed opinion on party decorations. "That's for damn sure! Good to see you, Olivia. I heard great things about you this summer."

"And I had a great experience," I returned. "Did I tell you I got to work with Dave Chadwick?"

"Chadwick?" Hank's eyes crinkled in delight. "Ah, so that's why his golf game got so good—he'd gotten some quality help on his cases! I'll get you assigned elsewhere; he's gotten damn insufferable out on the green."

I laughed, shoving aside the memory of Chadwick screaming at his first-year associates while us summer interns looked on in terror. Not that I could say that to Hank; I couldn't risk appearing ungrateful. "It could be nice to work under a different partner—diversify my cases."

Charlotte was watching our back-and-forth with a sour expression. "Darling, could you get us some drinks?" she said to her husband, who nodded and departed.

"I hope you know what you're doing." My aunt glanced around the room, her lip hinting at a curl. "This all seems rather . . . garish."

Squashing the swoop of triumph in my chest, I rolled my eyes like a teenager dealing with an overbearing mother. "Engagement parties are supposed to be *fun*, not formal. Emma's gonna love it, you'll see." I picked up a neon glow necklace and handed it to her. "In the meantime, why don't you try and fit in?"

Laughing at the expression on her face, I retook my position with Aditya at the gift station. He handed me a violently purple drink and held up his own in a toast. "Liv, you've outdone yourself."

I accepted his toast with mock gravitas. "You flatter me." After taking a healthy gulp, I leaned in close. "Wait until you see what Kali and Greta are wearing."

"Beautiful white dresses?"

"No, yellow-and-orange jumpsuits." I took another sip and suppressed a smile. "With neon-pink flower crowns. I found them online and shipped them right to Kali."

Aditya's eyebrows knit together. "Are they wearing said jumpsuits *under* their clothes? Or is this a costume change sort of thing?"

I whirled and followed his gaze to where Kali and Greta were making their triumphant entrance into the party, surrounded by a gaggle of envious onlookers. Kali's glossy hair cascaded down her back in perfect ringlets, and she literally glowed with excitement. Greta wore a dash of neon-purple lipstick and was, incredibly, smiling. They were both radiant.

And neither was wearing an ugly neon outfit.

"What the hell?" My mouth felt like it was full of cotton balls. Greta was rocking a white crop top with matching wide-legged pants with a neon-blue stripe down the side, and Kali wore a gorgeous ethereal white dress. They looked beautiful and bridal and, *somehow*, like neon cottagecore was actually a thing. "Why aren't they wearing what I sent over?"

"Probably because those outfits are fire?" Aditya suggested. He pulled my phone out of his jacket; I'd asked him to hold it, since my dress lacked pockets. "Leighton keeps texting you, by the way."

"Ugh, I can't deal with that right now." Leighton would want a play-by-play that I didn't have the bandwidth to deliver. I turned to monitor the party instead.

"Saw a text from Will, too." Aditya's tone had shifted.

I glanced at him; there was something I couldn't read behind his gaze.

Feeling suddenly awkward, I avoided his eyes and took the phone. Since Will had started his new job, we'd been talking less and less. I knew he was busy, but it'd also been six weeks since we'd seen each other. Our spark, or whatever it was, was fizzling out. I told myself it was for the best, and yet I couldn't stop answering his texts. But I didn't dare ask if we were friends (with long-distance benefits?) or something more. For now, he was like Schrödinger's boyfriend. If I forced that conversation, there was a chance he'd confirm my scuba-chick fears: sure, we could hook up when convenient, but life (distance, jobs, Leighton) made anything more impossible.

I switched my phone to silent and handed it back to him. "I already know what you're gonna say."

"What if I wrote the text for you?" Aditya suggested, with an attempt at levity. "Let me return the favor. You've done it for me enough."

"Done what?" I asked sharply.

He didn't back down. His thick, shapely brows and upturned nose typically gave him a mischievous look, but there was an uncommon shadow on his face. "Ended something that was never going to work."

A steady stream of partygoers flowed in around the brides-to-be, and the DJ slowly turned up the bass. A thrumming electricity filled the air, breaking the tension. "Thanks for the offer. But I'll handle it."

"Okay." Aditya licked some bright frosting off his fingers and set a half-eaten cupcake down on the bar. A few moments passed. "Is it me, or is this party . . . working?"

I groaned. "Oh God, please don't say that. This is the

opposite of *Southern Charm*! Neon cottagecore is a stupid theme! Everything clashes, I made sure of it!"

Aditya pushed the remaining cupcake toward me. "Yes to all of the above, but . . . it's working."

While I stress-ate the other half of his cupcake, we watched the room fill up with excited guests. I surveyed the scene—thrumming with electricity, this party was in imminent danger of becoming a smashing success.

"Maybe I'm wrong," Aditya offered, handing me a napkin and pointing to the icing smeared on my chin. "Go do your rounds. I'll handle the gifts."

"Thanks." I said a silent prayer of thanks for Aditya. I was leaning on him more and more, recently. Of everyone in my life, he was the only one I wasn't hiding anything from. I didn't second-guess myself around him. I didn't have to watch what I said, like I did around Leighton lately. I didn't overthink things, like I did with Will. And I didn't have to spend all of my energy persuading, like I did with Kali and Greta. I didn't want to argue with him—I needed *something* to stay comfortable and familiar.

As I approached the radiant brides-to-be, I slowed and forced my features into my Happy, Bubbly Olivia mask. A mask I was hiding behind a lot lately, as carefree happiness became harder and harder to find.

"Olivia!" Kali's eyes lit up, and she reached out to squeeze my hand. Up close, she looked downright stunning. I hadn't realized my freckly cousin had grown up into someone so glamorous. "This place looks incredible!"

Greta nodded. "You came through," she added, her tone almost friendly. "Thanks for putting this together."

"You guys look amazing, but what happened to the outfits

I sent over?" I asked, using every ounce of my energy to keep my voice chipper.

Kali's eyes drifted to someone over my shoulder. "Oh, we liked these better. But thanks for sending an option!"

The $300 sales receipt and $80 FedEx fee I'd paid flashed before my eyes. "No worries."

Greta nudged Kali. "Isn't that the editor?"

We all glanced toward the door, where Emma had walked in wearing a tight neon dress. A photographer stood at her side, fiddling with the giant Canon around his neck.

"Should we go say hi?" Kali suggested.

"No!" I flung out an arm to stop them, coming dangerously close to spilling Greta's drink on her bright white crop top. They both looked at me strangely. "I mean, you guys should play it cool. At least right now. I'll go talk to her."

I beelined toward the front of the room, pulse accelerating like a BMW on the Autobahn. Emma was probably only dropping in—editors were busy, right? I'd encourage her to head out before she started enjoying the party I'd planned too well. Maybe I could even slip in a few of the drawbacks.

"Emma!" I beamed at her, hoping my intensity came off as winning. "Welcome! So glad you could make it!"

"Thanks!" Emma smiled at me and turned to continue scanning the room. "This place looks . . ."

"I know, it's a lot, right?"

". . . incredible." Emma motioned to her photographer, who raised his camera and began clicking away. "Like, completely unexpected. But somehow it *works*, you know?"

"Um, sure?"

"This is *exactly* what I'd hoped we'd get from this competition," Emma breathed, her eyes on the Andy-Warhol-inspired slideshow. "Fresh new takes. This sort of engagement party would never run in *Bridal Today*."

"It wouldn't?"

"Absolutely not. But we're not trying to be them. We're trying to be *new*. Cheeky, fun." Emma waved a hand at the dizzying scene before us. "Like this."

A feeling of leaden dread pooled in my stomach, so heavy it could've pulled me down to the basement room where Aditya and I had spent all afternoon cracking glow sticks. "That's great. Well, watch out for the cupcakes," I added hastily. "They look cute, but they taste like sandpaper."

Emma nodded absently. "But they'll photograph great. Frederic, why don't you go shoot the dessert table?"

"And the drinks have a weird aftertaste."

Emma's eyes landed on the violet martini in my hand. "But that *color*. Frederic, get the bar next!" She started drifting away, her eyes on the brides-to-be.

"Someone had a stroke from the flashing lights," I tried.

"Like all the best parties!" Emma laughed over her shoulder and then disappeared into the crowd.

The music swelled. "Let's hear it for our future brides!" the DJ yelled. The crowd cheered and waved their drinks in the air. The bass thudded in my ears, making me regret the two and a half purple drinks I'd downed in my pre-party jitters. The me of an hour ago felt like a totally different person— had I really been worried that the party would bomb?

Tonight was, at least from Leighton's perspective, a total failure. There was only one thing left to try. Maybe I could still salvage things. If I could lay the groundwork for something else, maybe it hadn't all been for nothing.

Ten minutes later, I noticed Kali break off from a crowd of well-wishers to head to the bathroom. Power-walking as fast as I could in party heels, I moved to intercept her.

"Congrats on a great party!" I shouted in her ear.

She grinned, her cheeks flushed with excitement. She'd been dancing hard. "Congrats to *you*! This is so much better than I expected."

You and me both. I forced myself to match her enthusiasm. "Right? Hey, want to grab some fresh air?"

She nodded, and we headed out toward the hotel lobby. After the darkness and pounding bass, the bland lobby was a much-needed palate cleanser, like a swig of cold beer after a plate of Nashville hot chicken. My stomach rumbled and I realized I'd forgotten to eat dinner.

"I forget how to get outside," Kali admitted, squinting down three identical archways. "They all look the same . . ."

"Here's fine." I towed her to an empty couch and half shoved her down. I didn't have much time, and I was desperate not to leave Atlanta an abject failure. "Look, I wanted to apologize if I went overboard in there."

Kali's eyes looked glassy. With some effort, she focused on me. I wondered how many of the neon cocktails she'd had tonight. "Overboard?"

"I know you're doing this for your mom." I lowered my voice like we were confiding in each other. "You don't care about winning! I shouldn't have made this so over-the-top."

A look of faint surprise crossed my cousin's face. "No, I . . . I liked it. You did a great job. The planning wasn't even bad—you made it so easy."

My smile tightened. "And I'm happy to do that—as long as

it's what *you* want." I let that hang for a moment before pressing on. "Greta mentioned an underwater wedding off the Great Barrier Reef—that seems way more y'all's speed. You only get one wedding. Isn't there another way you could show your appreciation to your mom?"

My conscience tugged at me, reminding me of Charlotte's hesitant admission about celebrating her daughter. I slapped it away irritably. Charlotte could show her support in other ways. The wedding was more for Charlotte's society friends than Kali anyway. I was sure of it.

Kali hesitated. "I never thought about it like that."

I could almost see the cloud of uncertainty thickening around her. "I'm here for you either way," I assured her. Best not to push too much. "But just so you know, I'm a damn good travel agent, too."

A sickly-sweet stench distracted me, my nose putting two and two together before my brain had the chance. "Travel agent?" came a familiar drawl. "Are you helping with the honeymoon, too, Olivia?" Charlotte was suddenly towering over us, her eyes narrowed. "Is there anything you *can't* do?"

Escape you. I jumped to my feet, trying for nonchalance. "Something like that! But we should get Kali back inside— she's the one everyone came to see!"

I tried to follow my cousin back toward the party, but a cold hand closed around my upper arm. Charlotte leaned in close. "You did well tonight. You're a smart girl. I know you don't want to risk jeopardizing your future."

Wondering how much she'd overheard, I played dumb. "I don't know what you're talking about. I'm here to help Kali in whatever way she needs."

Charlotte's grip tightened. "She *needs* to win the cover. Nothing else. Got it?"

What was her deal? I knew she was status-obsessed, but this intensity was borderline terrifying. I pulled my arm away. "Yes, Aunt Lotte. Now, if you'll excuse me, I have a party to attend to."

As I hurried back across the lobby, my heels clicking on the glossy marble floor, I could feel Charlotte's gaze burning twin holes in my back. Elation and fear churned through me. I'd found an opening with Kali tonight—she *was* persuadable, I was sure of it. But I had to be more careful. If Kali decided to pull out of the competition, Charlotte couldn't suspect my involvement.

As I neared the ballroom, Aditya strode out, an odd strut in his step. Several of Kali's giggling friends eyed him appreciatively as he walked by, but he didn't seem to notice. His eyes landed on me, and his expression changed. Uncertainty flickered inside me. Something had happened. "Hey, Liv. Gotta show you something."

"What's up?" I allowed him to tow me to another of the featureless lobby couches. We sat. "Everything okay in there?"

"What?" Aditya looked distracted. "Oh yeah. Everything's fine. Anyway. Don't be mad. I did it for you. You needed some tough love." He held out my phone.

"Did what?" With my pulse thudding in my ears, I slowly took the phone. Somehow, I already knew what I was going to find. Opening iMessage, I ignored the unread Leighton thread and tapped on my text chain with Will. And there it was. A text sent from my phone seven minutes ago.

Hey, I want to be up-front—I'm looking for something serious, and I'm just not feeling that with you. Wish you all the best.

As I stared at the screen, my heart still midway through its downward plummet, three dots appeared. Will was typing.

"What the hell?" I hissed. "I told you I'd handle it! Why would you do this?"

"He was turning into *your* boomerang," Aditya said defensively. "I did it for you."

"That's not—it's not the same—" I spluttered. The comparison was insulting. How could Aditya think his two- or three-date clingy ex-flings were anything compared to what Will and I had shared? What we could've been?

You mean your one night? said a nasty voice in my head. *And what you could've built from thousands of miles apart? Behind Leighton's back? He's right. It was never going to work.*

And then Will's response popped up.

No worries, Liv. Thanks for letting me know.

Schrödinger's boyfriend was officially dead.

⟶

October continued in a blur. After exhausting myself pulling together an (unintentionally) killer engagement party, I spent weeks playing catch-up on other areas of my life. Third year of law school might be easier than 1L or 2L, but it was still law school. There was a limit to how chill classes could be. Sometimes I suspected that Vanderbilt Law collected tuition based on pages of reading assigned per week. School-wise, I was hoping to coast this fall, and to use my last semester to get a head start for the New York bar examination. Reese & Holmes required its first-year associates to pass the bar the July after graduation, and a first-attempt failure could tank your career at the company.

I didn't talk to Aditya for almost a week after we returned from Atlanta, which was a lifetime by our standards. My previous appreciation for him was replaced by blinding anger. He maintained he'd intervened for my own good, even lifting the exact wording I'd sent to his boomerang. Eventually I agreed to talk it out on a Circe walk; it was hard to stay angry when receiving happy licks and tail wags. Aditya seemed surprised by the intensity of my reaction. On one level, I sort of understood. From his perspective, I was hung up on a one-night stand. But when I tried to explain that our night had been so much more, I could tell it wasn't getting through.

"It wasn't just sex," I said for the eleventh time. "We talked about my mom's funeral. And about him resenting the athletes he'd worked with, because of his ACL injury—"

Aditya wrinkled his nose. "Sounds more like therapy. And somehow you still hooked up?"

"Exactly! And he's coming to Nashville at the end of October anyway—"

"The facts of the case stand," he said. "He probably hooked up with that scuba girl. You'd be long-distance. And it'd really hurt Leighton. Shall I go on?"

"Court adjourned," I muttered. But after that, I let it go. Underneath my fury was disappointment at how quickly Will had agreed. And I was disappointed at my own cowardly relief. I'd no longer need to wrestle with my fears at becoming totally vulnerable with Will. Aditya had made things simple. Painful, but simple. And I could learn to live with that.

Although Leighton and I texted daily about wedding-related things, I spent most of my time at home or cooped up in the law school library. Either way, Aditya was by my side. He was doing a two-day-a-week remote internship for a Boston malpractice firm on top of all our 3L work.

"I swear, half these cases make me scared to ever set foot in a hospital," he grumbled one evening, after recounting the grisly details of a healthy twentysomething who'd gone into cardiac arrest during a routine appendix surgery. "Definitely never getting my appendix out."

I frowned at him as I held open the door to the law library, gesturing him through. We'd agreed to grind out several post-dinner study hours together tonight. "Is that really optional?"

"What, stepping foot in a hospital or getting my appendix taken out?"

"Both?"

"They should make an appendix-ejecting pill," Aditya declared. "It's pretty small—I've seen CAT scans. I bet you could poop it out."

"Oh yeah. That'll fit nice with all the other organ-ejecting pills on the market."

"It could be the first. Proof of concept!"

"M-hmm. Take that one to *Shark Tank*." We settled at an empty table. I clicked into my Gmail account, procrastinating writing my case brief. "Oh shit!"

"What?"

"Emma sent me an advance of the November issue." With

my heart thumping in my ears, I clicked on the attached PDF. "They're making me sign an NDA first."

"Hurry, hurry!" Aditya scooted his chair around the table, ignoring both the wretched scraping sounds and the looks of ire this drew from nearby students. Vanderbilt's law library had an oppressive silence policy, but this was an emergency. A magazine cover was on the line.

I speed-scrolled through the initial sections of the contract, with Aditya urging me on. The lawyer in me winced at us mutually ignoring every aspect of the due diligence we'd learned in Contracts Law, but the best friend in me was too frantic to delay.

"There!" I pressed submit and opened the article. The screen filled with a two-page spread with a neon-purple title: "Electrifying the Engagement Party." A giant photo of Kali and Greta dancing together filled the left page, while close-up shots of party details like the flower-topped cupcakes, violet cocktails, and floral apron party gifts bordered a five-hundred-word write-up of the party.

ATLANTA, GA—The secret to getting your wedding guests excited about forking over for another present, hopping on another flight, and attending yet another event celebrating your love? Throw a kick-ass engagement party, emphasis on the party. That's exactly what Kali Harlow and Greta Wolfe did in October, hosting a "neon cottagecore"–themed party in a ballroom of the downtown Continental Hotel.

"You have the wedding for formality and romance," said Kali in between long stretches on the dance floor. "The engagement party should be fun! A chance to show off your personality."

"'Show off your personality'? That's how *I* pitched it to her!" I said, glaring at my own laptop in outrage.

> Their "neon cottagecore" event space, which immediately invokes the sensation of an electrified Alice-in-Wonderland experience, was both refreshing and unique—an unexpected combination of overdone party themes that dazzled for two expectation-flouting brides.

"She called the themes 'overdone'!" Aditya highlighted the word on the screen but fell silent at the look on my face.

The article continued gushing over decorative touches, including a special callout of the Andy-Warhol-inspired slideshow and the giant neon dream sign. I picked up speed as I read, my chest growing tighter and the pit in my stomach swelling in size.

> Overall, the engagement party was an impressive showing from Kali Harlow, one of two Southern brides that *Southern Charm* will be following over the next six months. Check in next month for our coverage of Leighton Sawyer's bridal shower. Let's hope that Sawyer brings the same electrifying touch.

I stared at the last few sentences in silence for a moment. "Leighton is *not* gonna be happy about this."

"No," Aditya agreed. "But Charlotte will be. And you were never gonna pull this off without upsetting Leighton. You know that, right?"

I knew he meant well, but one of my biggest pet peeves was being told I couldn't do something. Even if it were true. Not to mention, I wasn't big on Aditya's "tough love" approach after recent events. I took a deep breath and, with great effort, managed not to snap at him. "I've got to do something else for her. Before the bridal shower. Something to take the sting out of this."

"You should show her this." Aditya pointed at the screen. "Before she sees it in the magazine."

"Look, do you *want* me to fail?" I shot at him, finally losing my patience. "You've been a giant buzzkill every time we talk about the competition."

"What're you talking about?" Aditya raised his voice slightly, earning us a fresh round of vicious glances. "I flew to Atlanta with you! Spent my whole weekend prepping for Kali's party!"

This was true, and I'd always believed that actions spoke louder than words. He'd supported me when I needed it. But the constant negativity from the one person I could talk to openly was . . . a lot.

"I know. I'm sorry." I sighed and started packing up my things; I was not in the right headspace to read any more case briefs tonight. "I just wish you believed in me a little more."

"If you want someone to nod and smile and tell you that this competition was a good idea, that's not me," Aditya said flatly. "Friends tell you when you're full of shit, and I'm telling you this wasn't a good idea. You've pitted your own career against your best friend's happiness, and now your cousin's getting dragged in as collateral damage."

"This whole room is collateral damage to your conversation!" hissed a nearby 2L, and a few others sniggered. I hadn't realized our audience was following along.

Silently fuming, we both hurried from the library. I followed Aditya outside to the courtyard and grabbed his arm. "Wait."

He paused and looked at me expectantly, as if daring me to contradict what he'd said. "You're right. I'm sorry. I'm just stressed. *I* barely think I can pull this off, and you're the only one I can talk to about it. *Really* talk to about it—you know I don't talk to Leighton about Kali's stuff the same way."

"You mean honestly."

I accepted the rebuke. "Even if this wasn't the best idea—"

"It wasn't."

"—it's the situation I'm in and I'm trying to make the most of it, okay? I agree it's screwed up, but I think it's doable."

"'Doable' meaning that Leighton wins the magazine cover, but Charlotte doesn't realize until the last minute and you still get your H&R job?"

I flinched. It sounded a little pie-in-the-sky phrased like that. Luckily, he didn't know about my secret bargain with the universe that Will and I would somehow work out if I pulled everything else off. Or that last night I'd spent twenty minutes staring at me and Will's now-dormant text thread, trying to figure out how to undo Aditya's message. "Um. Yes. Exactly."

Aditya gave me a long, searching look, like he was trying to decide how much further to take this. "I already thought this plan was crazy," he said at last. "And then—this sounds dumb, but I'm being honest—after we went to Atlanta, Kali and Greta became real people to me. This is their wedding, Liv! You can't mess with that!"

"I'm not *messing* with it! First, I'm only dealing with pre-wedding stuff. Second—"

114

He gave me a look that could slice through a whole plate of brisket. "Neon cottagecore isn't messing with them?"

"Didn't turn out like that, did it?" I waved aside his eye roll. "And, again, I have nothing to do with the wedding itself. Not that *any* of this matters to Kali—"

"She looked like she was coming around to the wedding thing."

I jumped in front of him and placed two hands on his shoulders. "Aditya. Come on. You know I'm not evil. It'll take some hard work, but everyone *is* going to be happy in the end. Except Charlotte."

Aditya's dark eyes dimmed, his gaze flitting across my face. "As long as I've known you, Liv, you've been a good friend. Loyal. But with this competition . . . it's like you're losing track of what really matters."

He turned and started walking toward the parking garage. I remained rooted in place, turning Aditya's words over in my mind. The twilight deepened around me. What *did* he mean by "what really matters"?

A. Leighton winning the cover and launching a DTC collaboration
B. Me successfully becoming a Reese & Holmes associate
C. Kali and Greta having the wedding they wanted (did they want one?)
D. Will and I living happily ever after with Leighton's full approval (a girl could dream)

All of the above? That was the problem. It *all* mattered. And that wasn't even counting the deliciousness of Charlotte losing. I valued Aditya's opinion, but he was off target on this one. I had my eye on the prize—no, *all* the prizes. I was trying to make everyone's dreams come true.

And right now I was thinking hard about Leighton. I needed to cushion the blow of the glowing engagement party write-up. A killer bridal shower wasn't enough, although I needed to get cracking on that, too. My eyes drifted out of focus as I flipped through possibilities. What could make this better? What was *good* enough to outweigh the *bad* of this article?

Then it came to me. "The dress," I whispered aloud. Leighton was going dress shopping in a few weeks, and there was one bridal shop, Delacour, where she couldn't get an appointment. They wouldn't even take her calls; normally, they served only Predators' wives or country music stars. But I would get her in. I had to.

Failure wasn't an option.

umber of phone calls I made to Delacour: 17.

Number of *answered* phone calls to Delacour: 8.

Average time before the snotty Delacour girl told me they were absolutely booked up: 27.3 seconds.

Number of times I "stopped by" to bribe them with homemade pie: 3.

Number of times the pie was thrown into the garbage in front of me: 3.

My feeling of stupidity when Aditya pointed out that fashion girls don't eat carbs: immeasurable.

Personal cost for a three-month unlimited Pure Barre membership: $249.

The look on Leighton's face when I told her I'd gotten her in at Delacour with two weeks' notice: *priceless.*

The combination of the Delacour victory and my strategic timing (immediately after Leighton's balayage hair appointment, when her self-confidence was at an all-time high) meant that the "Electrifying the Engagement Party" article went over surprisingly well. It helped that I'd promised to pick Emma's brain about bridal shower venues, so that Leighton's first event could be sure to one-up Kali's.

In the days leading up to Leighton's bridal appointments, I had a light week in law school and a temporary respite from urgent MOH tasks. Leighton and I hung out for three straight nights, hitting our favorite margarita spot, borrowing Circe for a walk around Centennial Park, and struggling through a hot yoga class together. Despite Friday's upcoming dress appointments, Leighton didn't bring up the wedding once, and I followed her lead. The wedding respite was, in a word, blissful. Maybe Greta was onto something with this elopement shit.

On Friday morning, I picked up Leighton and her mom, Patricia, from Leighton's apartment, a tray of lattes waiting for them on the passenger seat of my car. "Good morning!" I sang. "Who's excited?"

Even though my role as maid of honor demanded boundless enthusiasm for today, the most holy of wedding-prep days, I wasn't pretending anything. As Leighton climbed into the backseat, I almost reached for some SPF—her smile beamed that brightly. It was the genuine grin she never showed online, the one that she worried made her under-eye wrinkles too visible and made her left eye squintier than the right. It was the grin of our childhood, and it thrilled me to see it. I couldn't help smiling myself.

"Morning, Liv! Oooh, did you bring us coffees?"

"Of course. I'm pretty sure it's in the maid of honor contract."

"Do I want to know what else is in this contract?" Patricia Sawyer opened the front door and smiled at me. "Good morning, Olivia."

As far as today went, the most relevant part of my maid of honor contract was defusing tension between the bride and the mother of the bride, but I'd keep that to myself. Today was all about Leighton: helping her feel beautiful in her future wedding dress.

And maybe making up for the smashing success of Kali's engagement party.

The problem was, once I started thinking down these side paths, more and more started popping up. I'd always thought of conversation as a beautiful, multifaceted tool—like a Swiss Army knife, but for your voice. You could accomplish so many things at once! Like today: in addition to the goals of make-Leighton-happy and make-up-for-Electrogate, I could convince Patricia that Leighton's career really was legit.

Which would maybe soften the blow if Leighton *didn't* end up winning.

"Liv? You ready?" Leighton chirped. I snapped back into reality.

"Yup! Let's go."

As I drove toward the first boutique, I felt a twinge of guilt. Aditya's words echoed in my ears: *It's like you're losing track of what really matters.* In the time it'd taken Leighton to buckle her seat belt, my mind had conjured not one, but two ulterior motives for today. By the time we arrived at Dress to Impress, my cheeks were red-hot with shame.

Luckily, neither Patricia nor Leighton was paying me any attention. A black-attired attendant was waiting for us at the front door. After we checked in, Leighton practically salivating with anticipation, the salesperson released us to browse. I grabbed Leighton's arm as she did her best Usain Bolt impression.

"Hold up." I grabbed the latte from her hand and unsnapped the trendy fanny pack from around her waist. "There. Now you're ready."

As she hurried off to the dazzlingly white racks, Patricia laid a hand on my arm. "You're a great friend to her, you know that, Olivia?"

Another twinge of guilt. Could you strain a conscience, the way you could tear a back muscle from lifting something too heavy? If so, mine was at definite risk, with all this weight I was lugging around.

"She's like my sister," I said truthfully.

Patricia gazed around the store, her eyes lingering on a mannequin in a trendy crop-top-and-full-skirt combo. "Do you really think she'll find a dress, er, here?"

"Oh no. This is a warm-up appointment."

"'Warm-up'?"

"So Leighton can figure out what silhouettes and necklines she wants," I explained. "That's the first step. I didn't want to waste one of our appointments at a top boutique figuring out the vision. That'll be for honing the details."

"Speaking of top boutiques, I heard you got us into

Delacour." Patricia tucked a strand of her glossy brown hair behind her ear, briefly exposing a faint face-lift scar. "*Very* impressive."

"Thanks," I squeaked, and hurried off before she could pay me more compliments I didn't deserve.

At the first shop, Leighton declared she wanted a ball gown with a sweetheart neckline. At the second salon, she was tempted by an intricately beaded mermaid gown. While she deliberated between the two silhouettes, Patricia and I perched on two cream-colored stools with room-temperature champagne (but free, so I was not above drinking it).

"I almost tried to convince her to design her own dress," I mused, watching my best friend twirl in front of a three-way mirror.

Patricia set her untouched glass down on the table. "Leighton doesn't design wedding dresses."

"She's doing the bridesmaids' dresses."

"There's a big difference." Patricia tutted softly. "And she shouldn't even be designing those."

"What? Why not?"

"Don't you think it's prolonging the fantasy?"

The pretzel in my stomach cinched tighter. "'Prolonging the fantasy'?"

"Olivia, I know you're trying to be a good friend. But you should both face the facts. Leighton's been doing this Peach Sugar thing for *years*. What does she have to show for it? Instagram followers and the occasional free purse?"

"She's working on a direct-to-consumer collaboration right now!"

"I'll believe it when her first check clears," Patricia said evenly. "It's a capricious industry. Lord knows I want my daughter to be happy, but she needs a career, not a hobby. It's no way to live."

"If you're worried about money, Matt does pretty well," I tried. "He's graduating from business school this year, and then—"

Patricia didn't appear to be listening. "I'm not asking her to get an assembly-line job, for God's sake. She can still do something she likes. Just something that *pays*. Look at you! You're pursuing your passion *and* a paycheck. They're not mutually exclusive."

A confusing jumble of images appeared in my mind's eye: my triumph at the H&R offer letter, the pride when I'd nailed a deposition prep this summer, Chadwick's beet-red face as he screamed at an associate about his single-digit IQ.

"I know you girls think I'm old-fashioned, but I did not raise my daughter to waste her time on artistic hobbies and then be dependent on her husband for money," Patricia went on crisply. "It's one thing to make the conscious decision to stay home and choose household management as your primary vocation in life. I did that myself. But it needs to be a *choice*, not something Leighton's backed into because she hasn't set herself up for anything else."

A beaming Leighton was heading toward us. I rushed to intercept her. Patricia's prickly barbs would puncture Leighton's floaty happiness faster than a pickpocket nabs your phone at a tourist-trap honky-tonk.

"Here, why don't you try this on?" I grabbed three headpieces at random and shooed her back up to the mirror. "See which accents the dress best!"

With Leighton thus distracted, I retreated to my seat and

said out of the corner of my mouth, "Maybe today we can focus on helping Leighton pick a dress?"

"What happens in three years when this Instagram thing dries up?" Patricia went on, as if I hadn't spoken. "Or when she gets pregnant and can't post pictures in tiny dresses?"

Briefly I deliberated introducing Patricia Sawyer to the gigantic mommy blogger industry. But that was out of the scope of this conversation.

"Leighton's built an impressive following. She's monetizing three different platforms—"

"She needs something more predictable. Sustainable. This magazine cover's the first legitimate business opportunity she's had! When you think about what she spends on hair and makeup—"

Coming from weekly-salon-visit Patricia, this was richer than a country singer's first ex-wife. I opened my mouth to defend my best friend, but then checked myself. Arguing with your best friend's mother wasn't a good look, and it wouldn't win me any points today, which was supposed to be Happy and Stress-Free and Definitely Not Career-Focused.

So instead of fighting, I fled. I grabbed Leighton and barreled into the dressing room.

"Liv, I can't decide!" she wailed, and it took me a second to register what she meant. Right. The ball gown or the mermaid.

"Take off the dress," I ordered, shutting the door behind us. "Let's figure out which one's really your favorite."

After she'd shimmied out of the mermaid gown, I slipped it back into one of the hanging garment bags. Then I turned and stuffed the giant ball gown train into the other bag, zipping both up.

"But I liked those dresses," Leighton protested, her eyes wide. "Both of them!"

"Yes, I know," I said patiently. "Close your eyes."

"What?"

"Trust me."

She closed her eyes. I grabbed both garment bags and swished them around.

"What are you doing?"

"Shhh." I finished my little act and rehung the dresses on adjacent hooks. "Keep your eyes closed," I warned her. Taking both of her hands, I brought them up, palms facing outward. "Now, I want you to really concentrate. There's a dress on the left and a dress on the right. Which one is *calling* you more?"

"Liv! This is ridiculous!" Leighton shook her head, a smile spreading over her face.

"Focus," I intoned.

She quieted and stretched her hands out a little farther. "Left," she declared.

"Open your eyes."

I reached forward and unzipped the left garment bag, which held the mermaid gown. Her face fell ever so slightly.

"So . . . mermaid?" she said doubtfully.

"Wrong!" I reached for the ball gown and presented it to her, triumphant. "You picked mermaid—and you were disappointed, right?"

She thought about it for a second. "Right," she said, her voice rising in excitement. "God, Liv, what a weird way to make me pick!"

"But did it work?"

"It worked. Ball gown it is." Leighton gave me a quick, affectionate hug before turning to gather up the rest of her clothes and belongings. As we picked up a tight-lipped Patricia on our way out of the store, I mused over how little of the wedding stress was actually related to the wedding itself.

After parking two blocks from Delacour, Leighton and I waited on the sidewalk while Patricia hurried inside a bakery for an iced tea. I checked my watch: fifteen minutes until our appointment. I'd timed this perfectly.

"Thank you so much for getting me a Delacour appointment," Leighton said for the fiftieth time. She rocked back and forth on her heels in manic excitement.

"That's what your maid of honor is for, right? Making all your wedding dreams come true?"

"Isn't that Matt's job?"

"Nah, he's in charge of the honeymoon."

"Seriously, though, everyone's been *so* jealous when I told them I was going to Delacour." Leighton twirled down the street in front of me, her flowy skirt catching the breeze. Ball gown had definitely been the right call. "I can't believe you got us in!"

Spirits high, we reclaimed Patricia and sauntered down the street to Delacour. Like all the best bridal salons, it was tiny, fussy, and had no showroom windows—God forbid the street-walking peasants glimpse a Delacour bride in The Dress. Instead, the street window displayed a single, heart-wrenchingly beautiful ballgown. Leighton pressed a covetous palm against the window and then turned to mouth back at me, *Oh my God!*

Grinning, I led the way into the small foyer, which was all-too-familiar after my many persuasion missions. While

Leighton and Patricia oohed and ahhed over the table of tiny bridal figurines—which I'd perused on *several* instances when dropping off my soon-to-be-trashed pies—I headed straight to the pink frosted glass desk and the equally frosty, pink-attired attendant.

"Hi, I'm checking in for Leighton Sawyer, two-o'clock bridal appointment."

The salon attendant was the same one I'd bribed with the Pure Barre subscription, which boded well. I remembered her because of her impossibly perfect topknot that would've looked greasy on me but looked runway-ready on her.

Topknot glanced down at her computer screen, clicked a few times, and frowned. "I don't see your appointment."

I forced myself not to panic. "Can you check again? I got an email confirmation two days ago."

Topknot clicked twice. "I don't have an appointment for you today."

I pulled out my phone and showed her the email. "You guys sent me this on Wednesday."

She glanced at the screen for five seconds before raising her shoulders in a minimal-effort shrug. "I'm not sure what happened. It could've been a systems error, or maybe you canceled your appointment and forgot—"

"I canceled my appointment and forgot?" I spluttered. And then it hit me. "One sec." I hurried over to Leighton and pulled her aside. "Hey—when you said that everyone was jealous about your Delacour appointment, who did you tell?"

"What? Oh, um . . ." Leighton thought for a second. "Some girls from Orange Theory, my hairdresser, my mom . . ."

"Your mom—did she go to any events this week?"

"Um, I think she was in Atlanta last weekend?"

Dammit. "Any chance she ran into Charlotte there?"

"We could ask her." Leighton turned toward Patricia. "Mom, did you see Charlotte Harlow last weekend?"

"Oh yes, we ran into each other at the Red Cross luncheon. Why?"

"Did you talk about Leighton's bridal appointments?" I asked, with a sinking feeling.

"Hmm . . . it might have come up . . ."

Leighton grabbed my hand. "Liv, is something wrong?"

"No, no, they're just running a few minutes late!" I squeezed her hand. "Let me sort out the logistics, 'kay?"

Back at the desk, I leaned over the counter and lowered my voice. "There's been a misunderstanding. Leighton's appointment was accidentally canceled."

Topknot's eyes drifted back to the screen. "Ah. Yes. Your appointment *was* canceled yesterday."

Fighting the urge to ask why she'd neglected to mention that earlier, I paused and considered my options. I had probably ninety seconds, two minutes tops, before Leighton and Patricia picked up on the bad vibes or wandered over out of boredom. Anger welled up inside me and I sent a mental curse southward toward Charlotte, the obvious culprit. That was quickly replaced by frustration at Leighton and Patricia for flaunting my hard-won Delacour appointment—really, what did they think was going to happen?

That's ridiculous, said my soft-spoken and often overlooked voice of reason. *How could they know Charlotte would actively sabotage them?*

FOCUS! screamed a much louder voice of panic. I wrenched

127

my concentration back to the pink-suited problem in front of me.

"So here's the thing. I *know* you remember me. How could you not, right? The relentless girl who wanted an appointment with two weeks' notice, who's not famous or rich or connected, but kept showing up with pies that none of y'all were *ever* going to eat. You cater to a certain clientele, and you want to keep your exclusive reputation. There's probably a company policy against letting people in without an appointment, is that right?"

Topknot studied me. "Yes."

"Right. Well, we're not some randos off the street. Number one, we had an appointment for today, which was canceled due to a misunderstanding. Yesterday. I'm pretty sure y'all didn't change your staffing that quickly. Number two, you know who that girl is?"

She glanced over at Leighton with something like interest. "No . . ."

"That's Leighton Sawyer." I let the name hang in the air for a moment. "Sounds famous already, doesn't she?"

"Um, maybe?"

"That's *Southern Charm*'s next June cover star. You know the June issue, right? The magazine that charges ten thousand dollars for a two-page ad spread. If Leighton chooses one of your gowns, you'll be on the cover for free."

Topknot's mouth twisted like she'd smelled my grandfather's horse stalls after a rainstorm. "What makes you think we care about publicity? You saw for yourself how booked up we are."

"Liv, is there a problem?" Leighton appeared at my side, her brow creased with worry. "Don't we have an appointment?"

"There's no problem," I said confidently, my eyes fixed on the attendant. I directed my next flood of words at her, intending to overwhelm her in a torrent of crescendoing persuasion. At least, that was the plan.

"Half of your appeal is your reputation—you need everyone to *want* an appointment, even though you'll only let in top clients. *That's* what keeps top families coming back and planners referring more brides. *That's* what they're paying for: wearing a dress that precious few are even allowed the opportunity to buy." My eyes dropped to the distinctive bag on the counter. "Delacour's the salon equivalent of a Birkin. The real thing. Is that a knockoff?"

It wasn't, of course, but Topknot's indignation took her off guard for a split second. The Hermès Birkin handbag was the ultimate status symbol for women of a certain social class, as recognizable as a Patek Philippe watch or a checkered Burberry trench. The simplest Birkins started at about ten thousand dollars, but the real thrill was the hunt. You couldn't simply walk into a Hermès store and buy a Birkin, no matter how rich you were. (If you tried, the salespeople would add you to an imaginary waiting list, sell you a scarf, and shoo you out.) Birkins were purchased through carefully cultivated relationships with senior salespeople, a willingness and ability to fly to stores all over the world, and a heaping dollop of good old-fashioned luck.

I knew this not because I pined for a Birkin—their design was kinda boring—but because when my dad had finally secured one for my mom twelve years ago, it'd become a momentous occasion that my parents had celebrated annually. I still thought about my mom and her dumb purse obsession every July 20.

"Do you know how the Birkin got so famous?"

"It was made for the British actress Jane Birkin in the eighties," Topknot said and sniffed. "And I don't see what this has to do with—"

"The Birkin was invented in 1984, but it didn't take off until the late nineties. And you know what brought that bag to prominence? Was it the sheer size of the Hermès marketing department? Jane Birkin signing on as spokesperson? Celebrity endorsements?"

"I don't—"

"Wrong. Hermès doesn't even have a formal marketing department. They never pay for celebrity endorsements. Their entire brand is built on quality and scarcity. That's how the Birkin became legend—they refused to ever make enough. Do you want to be like every other gauche brand, *buying* magazine advertising, or do you want to be so top-tier that your gown's on the cover for free? Honestly, Leighton even paying market price is more than generous."

I clasped my hands together and smiled sweetly at the salesperson. "I know you're smart enough to see the benefits. But if not, I'll stand right here until you close. And for the next month, I'll send one of my old sorority sisters here to do the exact same thing. Stand right here for hours, reminding you what a giant mistake you made when you let Leighton freakin' Sawyer and the cover of *Southern Charm* walk out of here unattended."

Topknot's jaw quite literally dropped. She glanced from me to Leighton to Patricia and then back to me again. "Right this way."

As we followed her down a cramped hallway, Leighton

tugged on my sleeve. "Did something happen to our appointment? Didn't she say it was canceled?"

"There was a mix-up. But it's handled."

"Why were you asking who I told?" she asked suspiciously. "Or about my mom going to—" She stopped dead. Patricia stumbled into her from behind. *Oh my God, did Charlotte cancel my Delacour appointment?*"

"Excuse me?" Patricia snapped. "Charlotte Harlow canceled this appointment? Why would she do a thing like that?"

The assistant coughed pointedly and we all trampled out into a cozy dressing area, where a three-way mirror, a pedestal, and two velvet chairs awaited.

"Because her daughter's also competing for the *Southern Charm* cover," I said wearily.

Leighton's face turned the color of the bridal samples pinned to the wall. Instantly I knew I'd made a huge mistake.

"Competition?" Patricia repeated. "What competition? Leighton, I thought you'd already signed a contract for the June cover."

"I'll pull samples," I muttered, shamefaced, and followed the shop attendant into the next room to sift through racks of snowy decadence. I rustled and shook the plastic-encased samples as much as I could, earning some pointed glares from Topknot, but it wasn't enough to shut out the sound of Patricia's cold fury. Apparently Leighton hadn't told Patricia about the latest twist in the *Southern Charm* saga. Whoops.

"What do you mean, it's a competition?"

I turned to Topknot. "That dress in the front window. She needs to try that one. Now."

"The Sophia Ricardia?" Topknot raised an eyebrow. "It's the most expensive gown we carry."

"How much?"

She named an exorbitant price and smirked, as if daring me to back down. But luck was on my side: Leighton's childless and über-rich godmother had insisted on buying her goddaughter's dress, telling us both several times that there was no budget. I thanked the Wedding Dress Gods for Aunt Kerrin's early Bitcoin investment.

"Great. Bring that one. And some champagne—actually, the whole bottle. I have a feeling we're going to need it."

Steeling myself, I returned to the mirrored room.

". . . completely different from what you told me," Patricia was saying. She turned to me. "Is it true you're the maid of honor for my daughter *and* Charlotte's? Even though they're competing?"

This again. I shoved Aditya's knowing gaze out of my mind's eye. Briefly, I explained that, while this was strictly true, my loyalty was to Leighton. I was helping Kali out of family obligation.

"I'm the one who *got* this Delacour appointment. I had no idea Charlotte would go behind my back and cancel it. Straight sabotage is low, even for her." Now I was shoving my own guilt at the neon cottagecore idea aside. That had been different. Indirect sabotage, not direct. Like manslaughter instead of murder. I was pretty sure that'd hold up in court.

Shaking off the fact that I'd just compared my own actions to manslaughter, I turned to the returning saleswoman. "Can we focus on the dresses? I think Leighton's going to find something beautiful."

Leighton, who'd been chewing on her lip unhappily, lit up

at once. "Oh my gosh—is that the one from the front? The Sophia Ricardia?"

"The best gown in the house," I promised. "And it has all the things you're looking for! Strapless, the beading detail, the satin buttons down the back—"

"—and very heavy." Leighton grunted, accepting the giant garment bag from Topknot.

"The train alone is seven pounds," Topknot offered.

I closed the dressing room door behind us, grateful to escape Patricia's death stare. "I had no idea Charlotte would try something like this," I told her. "I swear."

"I know you didn't." Leighton's face darkened. "But it freaks me out. Was this a one-off thing because my mom was bragging? Or will she really mess with my wedding?"

"Charlotte thinks weddings are the most sacred day of a young lady's life," I reminded her. "There's no way she'd mess with your big day."

"But everything before that?" Leighton pulled her shirt over her head. "My shower? Bachelorette?"

When we were teenagers, Charlotte had once tried to bully Leighton and me into canceling a weekend Smokies getaway to fill two last-minute spots in her charity catwalk show. Leighton had almost agreed—even though the weekend was her birthday present—until I'd physically stepped between them and told Charlotte exactly where she could shove her fake guilt trip. Leighton was the kind one. I was the protector. That's how it'd always been.

"She caught me off guard on this one," I admitted. "But now I'll be on the lookout. I won't let her screw with anything else."

"You promise?"

"Promise." I unzipped the transparent plastic encasing the ball gown, which immediately sprang out and attacked my face. "Wow, this really is heavy," I croaked, tilting my neck back to secure a supply of oxygen.

"Don't worry, I'm working out!"

I helped Leighton into the dress, zipping up the back, fluffing out the several underlayers of the full skirt, and placing a short veil on her head to complete the look.

"Well? What do you think?" Leighton turned toward me, forcing me to flatten against the wall to avoid death by taffeta. There was no mirror in the dressing room, so her green eyes were fixed on me, reading my reaction for a hint at how she looked.

"You look . . . gorgeous," I croaked, astonished to find my own eyes a bit watery. "Oh my God, Leighton. That is *breathtaking*."

"Aww, Liv!" Leighton's expression cleared. "Okay, let's get out there. I need that mirror!"

I darted ahead of her, wanting to catch Patricia's reaction. Leighton was momentarily slowed by her enormous skirt, needing to turn sideways to edge through the dressing room's narrow doorway. Once through, she danced up to the pedestal, and I fluffed her skirts out behind her.

"Well?" I crouch-hopped to Leighton's side and straightened one final fold. "What do you think?"

I glanced up. Both Leighton and Patricia had their hands clasped over their mouths, teary-eyed. Goose bumps ran up my arms as a frisson spread through the room.

"You look perfect," Patricia whispered, placing a tender hand on Leighton's shoulder. "Leighton—I'm so . . ." She choked back a sob.

"Mom," Leighton cry-laughed, her own voice heavy with emotion. "Don't cry. It's so silly. But you're right. I think this is The Dress."

"I agree!" I side-hugged Leighton from the left. "Leighton, it's perfect. *You're* perfect. You're gonna be the most beautiful bride."

"Did I hear that right?" Topknot poked her head in from the hallway, suddenly all smiles and quality customer service. "Is this The One?"

"Yes!"

After Topknot poured the champagne into three slim flutes, Patricia, Leighton, and I raised our glasses in a toast.

"To finding The Dress," Leighton beamed.

"To my daughter's wedding," Patricia added. She was watching Leighton with an expression so tender that I felt I was intruding on a private conversation. But then Leighton turned to me expectantly, her eyes magnified with tears, and a swell of affection rose inside me at my best friend including me in this special moment.

"To Leighton," I said simply. It wasn't my most eloquent work. But from the smiles on Leighton and Patricia's faces, it was exactly the right thing to say.

On Monday, I embarked on a fishing expedition. Obviously, not the type that required rubber boots or wriggling worms. Instead, I swung by the *Southern Charm* offices under the premise of "checking in" with Emma. My bait? Juicy wedding dress details. And Emma bit. Intoxicated by the unexpected success of Kali's party, she spilled everything. Magazine sales were up ten percent, engagement on social media channels was up thirty-eight percent, and the *Bridal Today* editor was furious. "But she can eat glass," Emma added happily.

Most important, she'd referenced an impossible-to-reserve new restaurant, Nature House. Their farm-to-table brunch was legendary, as was their giant greenhouse event space and signature design-your-own-succulent-garden activity. Despite weeks of effort, Emma and her husband had yet to secure a reservation.

"Maybe we'll have the shower there!"

Emma had frowned. "I've heard their event reservations are completely booked, too. I called last week and played the *SC* card. No dice."

"You never know!" I'd said brightly, even as my stomach sank.

"But if you could get in . . ." Emma brought her fingers to her lips in a chef's-kiss gesture. "The shower would be a guaranteed success."

Challenge delivered.

Eleven phone calls and a few drop-in visits later, I'd realized the Delacour brute-force approach wouldn't work at Nature House. The snotty maître d' wouldn't even let me past the hostess stand without a reservation, much less accept a Pure Barre bribe. Dejected, I began browsing alternative venues, but I couldn't forget the thrill in Emma's eyes when I'd mentioned Nature House.

But then I realized I might have another method of nabbing a reservation. One that'd require a different type of groveling. And a whole lot of emotional anguish.

Really, I sent the text for a noble reason. It was all for Leighton. There was no other way I could get us into Nature House.

Will's best friend Tyler was in the Nashville hospitality industry. After a brief stint on a reality TV show post-college, he'd leveraged his fifteen minutes of fame into a steady gig as a local influencer and promoter. Before he'd moved to North Carolina, Will had often accompanied Tyler to various restaurant and bar openings. If anyone could get us into the to-die-for greenhouse event space, it'd be Tyler.

The trouble? A tie-dye dispute during Leighton's eleventh

birthday party had established Tyler and Leighton as mortal enemies. In the intervening sixteen years, their feud had hardened into impenetrable concrete. A certain level of professional jealousy didn't help. Leighton privately moaned about how Tyler's following had fallen into his lap. From Will, I'd gleaned that Tyler considered Leighton to be an online wannabe, not well known enough to bother inviting to events or tagging in posts.

Although Tyler and I had always gotten along, an intermediary was needed. If I DMed him myself, he'd know the ask was for Leighton and refuse on principle. But if one of his bros needed a favor . . . I doubted Tyler would ask questions, and by the time he realized who'd he'd helped, it'd be too late. The trick was persuading Will.

When we'd been texting last month, Will had mentioned a trip to Nashville at the end of October. Tyler was helping promote a glitzy new restaurant opening, and Will was flying back to support him for the weekend. A weekend which was now just a few days away. If the universe *didn't* want me and Will together, the timing wouldn't have worked out so well. I'd texted him asking to meet up, and he'd agreed readily.

So we'd arranged to meet that Saturday afternoon at a local dog park. I hadn't told Aditya why, exactly, I was borrowing Circe. I'd had more than enough of his input on my love life.

"Down, Circe!" I tried for a serious tone, but it was hard to be mad at the adorable Lab. Circe was standing on her hind legs, pawing at my stomach. Lost in thought, I'd committed the grave sin of ceasing to pet her.

"Down, girl! Down!"

This was also happily ignored. I rubbed her velvet-soft ears and looked into her chocolate eyes. "You're lucky you're cute, you know that? Way too poorly behaved."

"I could say the same about you," called a teasing voice.

I glanced up. Will was jogging toward us from across the parking lot. He looked distractingly hot in olive-green pants and a navy bomber jacket. A pair of round mirrored shades flashed in the afternoon light. Part of me couldn't believe he was here. Butterflies soared out of my stomach and into my chest.

"Hey!" I accepted his hug but stepped away quickly, even though no one in the bustling dog park was paying us any attention. Since Leighton randomly dropped by my apartment with wedding tasks, I couldn't risk inviting him to my place. Asking him to coffee or for a drink felt too date-like. An outing to the dog park had felt like a safely platonic activity.

"Relax, Liv." Will crouched down to scratch Circe under the chin. She licked his other hand in appreciation. "We're not doing anything wrong."

"Except for keeping poor Circe away from all her friends!" I hoisted my tote higher on my shoulder. "Let's take her in."

As we strolled into the turf-covered park, I spotted some of the regulars. "That's Sherlock." I pointed out a sleek brindled dog who paced in a terrified circle. "He hates dogs. Also humans. Despises the dog park."

"Why does he come?"

"Not sure. Exposure therapy? Oh, and there's Beasley." A blur of excited fur tore past us, skidding across half of the turf in pursuit of a tennis ball. "She's big on fetch." Rambling about the dogs helped distract me from a sudden avalanche of vivid memories. The gentle tug of his hands running through my hair. The wide shoulders I'd stood on tiptoes to throw my arms around. The sensation of flying, as Will wrapped one muscular arm around my waist and tossed me across the sheets—

"I can see that."

"Here's my favorite!" Blushing, I dropped to my knees as a plump yellow Lab wandered over to me, tail swinging in excitement. "This is Bo. She's an old lady, so she doesn't run much, but she wanders around getting pets from everyone. Such a good girl."

"Hello, Bo." Will grinned as Bo rolled over in anticipation of belly rubs. Circe sniffed Bo's butt contentedly. "I think she's doing it right. Tell your owner you're going to the park for exercise, but walk around getting affection instead?"

"Like when I tell Aditya I'll go to the gym with him, but really I sit in the sauna on Instagram."

Will fake-groaned. "I used to get that from my teenage patients. They'd use their phones to 'check in' at the gym but go to the on-site sauna or juice bar instead."

"Hard to resist the siren call of a Pomegranate Power-Up." I reached into the bag and pulled out a tennis ball. "Ready, Circe?"

Circe leapt to attention. I threw the ball and watched Circe streak across the field, arousing the interest of several other dog regulars. Soon she was being chased by three and loving every minute of it.

"Won't she come back?"

"Nah, she's got friends to play with now." I nodded at the

pack of gamboling dogs. "I usually only throw the ball once. Want to sit?"

We wandered over to one of the open park benches, this one nestled in the shade of the giant oak tree at the center of the circular field. A few other benches circled the tree, but the oak's large branches swept down between each bench, affording us the illusion of privacy.

Not that we were doing anything wrong, I reminded myself. This was a simple pet-sitting and venue-securing excursion.

"It's good to see you," Will said at last. He'd left a full foot between us on the bench.

"You, too."

I re-crossed my legs and pulled my jacket tighter. Now that he was here, twelve inches away, the reality of the situation sliced across my face as cold as a Manhattan winter. Deep down, under that harshness, lay something more powerful. Familiarity. Comfort. Home. Childhood friends were a rarer gem the older you got. I'd managed to hang on to a diamond of a best friend. No wonder I felt so drawn to Will. But there was so much layered above. Aditya's voice echoed in my ears, repeating the facts of the case: the girl from Thailand; Leighton's disapproval; the hundreds of miles between us.

"How's Leighton's stress level been?"

His tone was casual, but the reference to his sister made my skin prickle. "She's booked most of her vendors, so that's been a relief."

"And yours?"

I smiled weakly. "Fluctuating wildly."

"Wedding stuff?"

"Among other things." I sighed before I could stop myself. I'd wanted to be my winning, charming self with Will, but the situation was so complicated. "I don't want to bore you."

"You, bore me?" Will chuckled and flipped his sunglasses to the top of his head. "I'm not worried. Go ahead, let it out."

Something brittle snapped inside me, and I stopped thinking about how to say things right, or what Will would think, or how to manage his impression of me. The words just flowed out.

"After New York . . . we'd had that amazing night, and then you went to the other side of the world while I had no idea where we stood. Then I ran into Emma and the *SC* cover felt like the perfect way to smooth things over with Leighton. Except my evil aunt found out, and it became a competition, and then I got roped into helping both sides, and 3L year of law school is *not* as chill as everyone made it out to be. At least not when I've got all this on my plate." I took a deep breath, wishing I could inhale confidence along with oxygen. "I have a preliminary offer from Holmes & Reese, but my aunt's holding it hostage until I help my cousin. My step-uncle works at H&R and could tank my job, so nothing's official until I sign in the spring."

"Your aunt's doing *what*?" Will blinked.

"Holding my job offer hostage, yup."

"There's no way she'd actually—"

"You don't know Charlotte like I do," I said grimly. "She totally would."

"It's like something out of—I don't know, a reality TV show. Or a fairy tale."

I chuckled weakly. "Nah, that's evil stepmother, not evil aunt."

Will propped his fist on his knee and appeared to be thinking deeply. "Well, has she banned you from attending any balls lately? Given you any poisonous apples? Pricked your finger with a spinning wheel and sent you into an endless sleep?"

"I think I'd have noticed. Although endless sleep sounds amazing right now." I glanced at him. "Impressive fairy-tale knowledge, by the way."

Will grinned. "I did a lot of babysitting." Then he cleared his throat. "But back to what you said—I didn't mean to leave you hanging. We just ran out of time that morning. My return flight was to Nashville, so I figured we'd talk then. Which we did, right? Said we didn't need to tell Leighton."

Technically. "Yeah. I guess. But then you kept texting me afterward . . ."

Will leaned back. "Because I like talking to you, Liv. Remember that speakeasy? And those espresso martinis?"

I smiled despite myself. "Twenty-seven-dollar espresso-and-honey martinis. How could I forget?"

The bar, hidden behind a barbershop front, had been our second stop of the endless night. Over overpriced and indulgent cocktails, the conversation had turned to the unexpected twists Will's life had taken.

As a high school basketball star, Will had been courted by top college programs. He'd had his heart set on playing Duke basketball, a dream almost within his grasp. And then an ACL tear had stolen most of his junior season, and a secondary meniscus tear during rehab had taken professional sports off the table forever. He'd landed on his feet, so to speak. Strong STEM grades won him acceptances to multiple physical therapy programs, and he'd been hired right out of

PT school. His primary interest was sports medicine, and he'd started off as an assistant PT for the Tennessee Titans' practice squad.

"I chose PT to help athletes recover from injuries like mine," he'd told me. "It made sense, right? Sounded great in my interviews. At first, at school, in clinicals, it felt good to be working in sports. To still be involved. I was so motivated to help players return to the games they loved. But then, with the Titans . . . something flipped. I started resenting the players I was working with."

"Resenting them?" I'd stirred my martini. Will's eyes followed the honeyed swirl. "Did they take it for granted, being in the NFL?"

"No. And that's the thing," Will said unhappily. There was a darker undertone to his voice, one I'd never heard before. "They were great guys. Most of them were grateful to even be on the practice squad. And I *still* resented them. This thing that had happened to me when I was sixteen—it'd taken away a future I thought I deserved." He barked a laugh. "No one *deserves* to play pro sports. I knew I was being petty and immature. But the jealousy made it impossible to work there. That's why I moved to the private school. Dealing with high school girls was easier. They didn't remind me of what I didn't have."

"I hadn't told anyone that," Will said now, his voice low. "About—why I left the Titans. So . . . yeah. Talking to you was so easy. But when you texted and said you were looking for something else . . . I didn't mean to give you the wrong impression."

When Aditya texted you, I corrected mentally. The neurotic dog Sherlock trotted up to us, seeking a respite from forced canine socialization. I petted his head.

"It's not that I was looking for something else—" I began.

Will shook his head. "Don't worry about it, Liv. We're on the same page now. I'm happy to have you in my life as a friend."

An ax chopped my heart in two. *Friends.* Slobbery wetness on my knee offered a distraction. I glanced down to see drool smeared all over my leg and a happy Circe panting at my feet. "Circe! Did you get tired, you good girl?"

Will rubbed Circe behind the ears. The black-haired Lab stared up at him with pure adoration. I replayed the conversation in my head. *We're on the same page now.* Had we *not* been on the same page earlier, when Will thought I was blowing him off?

"Ah shit." Will was staring at his phone. "Tyler's freaking out about the kegs not arriving in time. I might have to dash to help him deal with this." He grinned up at me, his green eyes crinkling around the corners just like Leighton's did. "Guess we both have a stressed event-planning friend to talk off the ledge."

Concentrate, Liv! My own feelings aside, I reminded myself I had an actual mission. Back on familiar ground, I felt my anxieties subside. Planning and convincing and persuading. This was my forte. Big, existential swings in my love life? Not so much. "Actually, before you go, there *is* something you can do to help me talk your sister off the ledge."

Will chuckled and shook his head in amusement. "Walked right into that one, didn't I?"

"You know your friend Tyler?"

"I thought we wanted to chill Leighton out, not rile her up."

"And you *can*, once Tyler gets us a reservation at Nature House." I explained about Leighton's bridal shower and how everything needed to be two hundred percent perfect to make up for the one hundred percent perfect neon cottagecore party. "He doesn't need to know it's for Leighton."

"Won't it be in a magazine? He's going to find out."

"Yeah, but not for weeks." I adopted my best puppy-eyes expression, although it was hard to compete with Circe's adorable gaze. "And by then it won't matter. Also, I doubt Tyler reads *Southern Charm*. He might not even find out."

"It's still dishonest."

I bit my lip. "I know, but I'm in a tough place here. Emma specifically recommended Nature House, and I *need* Leighton's bridal shower to be a success. If I had another way to get a reservation, believe me, I would." I paused, watching the hesitation play out on his face in real time. "I'm not asking for me, Will. I'm asking for Leighton."

A few seconds passed. Will's eyes narrowed as he studied me. "Fine," he said at last. "I'll talk to Tyler. But just this once, Liv. We're already keeping something from Leighton. I don't like all this sneakiness."

"Sneaky" was a nice euphemism for *blatantly lying*, but, hey, I'd take it. Besides, Tyler and Leighton's beef was petty nonsense, not a real injustice. I gave him a big hug and snuck a whiff of his cologne. "Awesome! Thanks so much, Will! I promise to make the shower a huge hit. It'll totally be worth it, and your sister will love it."

"She better." Will pointed a warning finger at me, and Circe barked in excitement. "When Tyler finds out he accidentally helped Leighton Sawyer, I'll be paying his bar tab for *weeks*."

9

November

Your network, my dad used to say, was your net worth. As a kid, I'd never been clear on how acquaintances translated into dollars, but I'd had some childish idea about people buying tickets to visit my father in his office. Growing up, it was one of my favorite things to do on his firm's annual Take Your Kid to Work Day. I'd dress up in my flounciest party dress, sip my morning milk from a coffee mug like Dad, and ride with him to work. There, us kids would spend a half-hour touring the office, with its breathtaking views and quiet thrum of possibility, before we were rounded up for a series of PR-friendly photo ops. Then we'd be herded off to a conference room and placated with movies and donuts until our moms arrived to pick us up for lunch. I always left on a sugar high and dreaming of the day that I, too, could have the Knowing Important People job. To seven-year-old me, that was the coolest thing in the world.

And to twenty-seven-year-old me, dressed in a similarly flouncy party dress and staring around at the reward of my (extended) network, it was hard to feel any differently. Nature House's event space was more gorgeous than I'd dared to hope: a giant dome-shaped greenhouse, like a snow globe that had melted into a moss-carpeted wonderland. Green garlands snaked up artfully arranged wooden trellises, and pockets of greenery bloomed amid gurgling fountains. Small mirrors hung from the trees like wind chimes. Three long farmhouse-style oak tables had been decorated with colorful pink potted succulents, adding a pop of color to the sea of greens and neutrals. A DIY flower-crown station had been positioned off to the side. Even nature itself had cooperated, gifting us with a gorgeously sunny day and the most coveted accessory of all: flattering lighting.

I flipped my phone around and pulled up the *Southern Charm* Instagram account. Emma had asked me to film some behind-the-scenes content before the party started.

"Hey, guys!" I chirped, immediately hating the sound of my voice. I wasn't good at the social media stuff; this was Leighton's domain. "Olivia here, checking in to show y'all what an amazing setup we have for Leighton's bridal shower." I prattled on about the venue and panned over the setup for a few minutes.

"Damn, dude!" I turned to see Aditya standing slack-jawed in the doorframe. "*How* did you get this place?"

"Ask me no questions, and I'll tell you no lies!" I stopped the video and gave him a quick hug. I'd been crazy busy over the last few weeks pulling everything together for the bridal shower, and Aditya was in the thick of recruitment season.

The little free time I had was spent on the phone with Kali or FaceTiming with Leighton, with a seemingly endless list of wedding questions to run by the brides. I'd barely seen Aditya lately, so when he'd offered to help set up for the bridal shower, I'd gladly accepted. But not for the free labor. Although an extra set of hands would've been nice, I'd been determined not to exploit Aditya's generosity like I had in Atlanta. I didn't want him to think I took him for granted.

"But—it looks like everything's done." Aditya frowned and plopped down on a nearby stone bench. "What do you need me for? Liv, I'm risking my Y chromosome by even being here."

"I wanted to clear the air. Things have felt a little weird between us since Kali's article came out, and I wanted to show you I'm not using you for party prep."

Aditya looked half exasperated, half pleased. "Liv. You didn't need to do all this on your own to prove a point. But I appreciate the effort."

"It was a *lot* of effort," I informed him.

"And I didn't mean to come on too strong. I only meant . . . you've always been a good friend. You don't want to mess that up. For you and Kali, or you and Leighton. I get you're in a weird position, but don't you feel like you're lying to everyone, just a little?"

I tried to ignore the heat in my cheeks. "Lying how? Everyone knows I'm in both weddings, it's not a secret—"

His skeptical eyebrow raise said it all. "Lying in that you're not genuinely doing your best for both weddings, lying to Leighton about how much Kali cares—"

"Kali doesn't care," I insisted. On our calls, she sounded completely disinterested, perking up only when I asked about

Greta. Two days ago, we'd spent thirty minutes planning a surprise trip to Chile for Greta's birthday. The time before that, I'd lent a sympathetic ear while she vented about Charlotte's latest wedding demands (something about calligraphy quality for the invitations). I'd started to look forward to the calls, even though jotting down soft-sabotage ideas during them made me feel a little icky. I'd enjoyed having a pretense for reigniting my relationship with my cousin.

Aditya held up both hands. "Okay, okay. I'll leave it at that. Anything I can help with?"

I cast an eye around the room. The honest answer was no, but admitting that felt like tempting fate. "Will you do a trial run for the flower-crown station? I haven't had the chance."

"Liv, I need to leave with *some* of my testosterone intact—"

"You don't have to wear it!" I cajoled. "Just make one. It's not hard. Press the leaves in a circle. It doesn't even have to be pretty."

He rolled his eyes so far into his head he briefly looked possessed. "Fine. But after that, I'm crushing half your mimosas."

"Deal. Oh, and one other thing." I handed Aditya my phone. "Emma wants us to do regular Instagram Lives from the *Southern Charm* account. I've done a bunch this morning, but could you take over during the party?"

Aditya looked horrified and tossed the phone right back to me. "No way! I'll do background prep, but I'm not starring in a women's magazine Instagram account."

Now it was my turn to roll my eyes. "Funny thing about women's magazines. A ton of beautiful young women watch their content. Didn't you say you needed a date to Law Prom?"

"Olivia, you've outdone yourself!"

I whirled to see a delighted Patricia and a beaming Leighton making their way through the greenery. I shoved the phone back to a grumbling Aditya and went to greet them. Leighton wore an adorable white minidress with satin bows on the shoulders, looking like a glammed-up Taylor Swift as she wandered among the greenery. Her golden hair was pinned with small pearls to cascade prettily down her back.

"This is gorgeous, Liv," Leighton breathed, hugging me delicately to avoid crushing her hair. "Like a real-life fairy tale."

Pride swelled through me, blooming ever higher as each new guest walked in and paused, dumbfounded by the unexpected beauty around them. It was one thing to book out a trendy club or reserve a skyline view of Nashville. But to create a magical forest *within* city limits? Now, that was something to write about.

The first hour of the event passed pleasantly. As an official cohost—and the one footing the bill—Patricia stood at the door to welcome guests and accept gifts on Leighton's behalf. Stationed at her side, I helped guide guests to the mimosa bar and the flower arrangement setup. The mirrors hanging from the trees, compact mirror party favors, were also a smashing hit.

"This really is impressive," Patricia whispered to me after everyone had arrived. She gazed triumphantly at the mingling guests, who surrounded her radiant daughter like planets circling the sun. "How much is this costing me?"

"Under budget, which is all that matters!" I named the figure. "Will's friend helped get us a good deal."

"Did he?" Patricia smiled wider. "Well, I guess it takes a village."

"That it does."

The event continued smoothly into the brunch portion. Attendees exclaimed in delight over the photo-worthy avocado toast, maple spice pancakes, and low-carb, low-fat vegan donuts. I sat with Leighton and the other three bridesmaids. Shane and Samantha were twins and two of Leighton's sorority sisters from LSU; I'd met them before at birthday dinners and Nashville hangouts during our college years.

"Olivia! Great to see you again! How fun is this?" Shane squealed, giving me a tight hug, while Samantha cheered in delight. The twins were dressed identically, as always, in burgundy sweater dresses and high-heeled leather booties. Only their hairstyles separated them: Shane rocked a tight ballerina bun, while Samantha's hair was braided down her back.

The third bridesmaid, Nikki, was an aspiring YouTuber Leighton had met at a networking event. Her platinum-blond hair was slicked back like she'd just gotten out of the shower, and she barely glanced up as I waved awkwardly. "Hi, I'm Olivia!"

"Nikki," she drawled, and my stomach jolted. The voice coming out of Nikki's artificially enhanced lips was nearly identical to Charlotte's Southern drawl.

Leighton leaned across the table and dropped her voice. "Have you seen Emma?"

"No, but she told me she'd be late—some breakfast meeting."

Leighton's green eyes were wide with worry. "What if she doesn't come? Or doesn't like it?"

"It's *exactly* what she asked for," I reassured her. "She's gonna love it, I promise. And she'll be here any second now." Did most maids of honor spend so much time reassuring their brides?

Just then, my prayers were answered: Emma appeared in the doorway, flanked by two cameramen. Leighton looked at me with wonder as I rose to greet the editor.

"Emma! So glad you made it!"

"Olivia, this is *absurd*." Emma removed her cat-eye sunglasses with exaggerated slowness as she gazed around the greenhouse. "I'd seen photos, but the *atmosphere . . .*" She looked over her shoulder and her tone sharpened. "Did you bring your wide-angle lens? We've *got* to get this skyline."

She gave me an approving nod and strolled off to the mimosa bar.

After brunch, Patricia and I led the guests through a few guessing games before the obligatory appearance by the groom-to-be. As Matt and Leighton posed for photos and chatted with friends, I sipped my mimosa in satisfaction. Behind me, staff cleared the tables for the final group activity, flower-crown crafting. As we herded the guests back to the tables to begin assembling their crowns, the Nature House manager appeared at my elbow.

"How is everything going, Miss Fitzgerald?"

"Amazingly! The venue is breathtaking," I gushed. "I'm so glad you suggested the flower crowns—I know the succulent garden is your normal activity, but this is even better." In front of us, Leighton was meticulously crafting a crown of ivy and white-dyed roses. A few spots away, Shane and Samantha were comparing designs, while Nikki wandered off alone in search of optimal lighting. Fueled by a generous number of mimosas, Aditya had abandoned his reservations about disintegrating Y chromosomes and was bonding with my best friend's mother.

The manager looked confused. "I appreciate the compliment, but it was your party planner's idea."

I blinked back at him. "Party planner?" We hadn't hired a party planner; Patricia and I had worked together on the event. By which I mean I dealt with all the logistics and Patricia micromanaged but supplied her credit card.

"Yes—the one who handled all the flower supplies."

We were standing in a pool of golden sunlight, but that didn't stop a chill from slowly seeping over me. I'd arrived two hours early to arrange the table settings, set up the mimosa bar, and hang the mirror decorations. The flower-crown supplies had been waiting on a side table when I'd arrived, and I'd assumed the Nature House staff had prepped them for us. But if not . . .

"So Nature House didn't put together the flower-crown kits?" I asked urgently.

The manager looked startled by my tone. "I suppose it's possible one of the assistant managers did—but that greenery doesn't look like anything we grow here." He drifted closer to the nearest table, where a few of Leighton's cousins were adjusting their leaves-to-flowers ratio. Then he stopped dead. His face whitened. "Good Lord."

I grabbed his arm. My eyes scanned the table for killer hornets, hidden ink capsules, or anything else Charlotte could've snuck in with the crowns, but all I saw was an idyllic bridal shower activity. "Good Lord *what*?"

"Hey, Liv, can you take a look at this?" Aditya tapped me on the shoulder and held out his hands. A spotty, angry red rash had erupted across both of his palms. "Isn't that weird? I don't know what—"

The manager pointed at Aditya's hands as the realization crashed over me. "Poison ivy!"

"Whoa, whoa, whoa." Aditya glanced from me to the manager and then at his half-finished flower crown, which was made of shiny green leaves. "Please tell me you're kidding. That was a joke, right? I didn't spend twenty minutes playing with poison leaves, *right*?"

I grabbed Aditya and the manager, whose name I really needed to find out in case he sued us, and towed both behind a large shrub. Arousing panic was the last thing I wanted to do. "Are you sure it's poison ivy? Why doesn't everyone have a rash?"

"It takes time to develop," the manager said hoarsely. "Hours to days."

Aditya and I locked eyes. "I tested out the crowns a few hours ago . . ." he mumbled.

We both peered through a gap in the shrubbery at the happy scene in front of us. Thirty-seven fabulously attired women, unknowingly rubbing poison oil all over their faces, arms, and heads. It was almost too much to process. My hairline felt distinctly wet, and panic puddles bloomed under my arms. But I had to keep it together.

"We've got to stop the flower-crown making." I thought fast. "And everyone'll have to wash off. Maybe we can say there's pesticides on the leaves?"

"Good idea. You don't want people to freak out," Aditya said nervously, looking like he was barely keeping it together himself. "If they hear the crowns are made of poison ivy—"

"They're made of *what?*" Five feet away, Leighton's bridesmaid Nikki froze and slowly lowered her phone mid-selfie. I hadn't noticed her drifting closer to us. "*Poison ivy?* You gave us *poison ivy crowns?*"

Heads whipped around. The babble of chattering women faltered and was replaced by anxious whispers. Leighton looked confused, while Shane and Samantha yelped and tore their crowns off their heads. An old aunt scowled in our direction and repeated, "Poison *what?*"

"So much for avoiding panic," Aditya muttered.

"I think this really is poison ivy," one of Leighton's high school friends declared, dropping her crown and examining it from an exaggerated distance. "I thought the leaves looked extra-shiny, but maybe they were saving money with fake flowers—"

Patricia's offended huff blended in with the commotion as thirty-plus women collectively lost their heads. In under ten seconds the elegant fairy-tale bridal shower devolved into panicked chaos. Guests frantically pawed at their heads, trying to extract leaves from intricate hairstyles. A mad dash for the restrooms resulted in a near-mob of sorority sisters clawing their way in. Others rushed over to the fountains and plunged their forearms into the water, attempting to rub the oil off with abandoned napkins. Somehow the Taylor Swift music was cut off, leaving a frantic yelling the only soundtrack available.

"I'm, like, *so* allergic, do you think it's too late to wash off?"

"It got in my *hair!*"

I hopped onto one of the chairs and cupped my hands around my mouth like I'd seen in movies. "Everyone, please relax," I called, to absolutely no effect. "There's plenty of time to wash off—"

"I'm gonna sue!" someone shrieked.

"We are *not* liable for this!" the manager shouted, standing on a chair himself. "These were not Nature House affiliate crowns—"

Aditya rammed the manager's chair with his hip, wobbling him enough to shut him up.

"Olivia, what's going on?" Leighton appeared at my side, her eyes red and swollen. "It's not actually poison ivy, right? Right? No one has a rash—"

"I think it is," I said grimly. "Everyone'll need to wash off and change their clothes. Hopefully we can get most of it off—" I glanced down and registered her swollen face. "Leighton, it's okay, we'll fix this, there's no need to cry—"

"I'm not crying! This was Charlotte, it had to be! What kind of monster—"

"It's okay, you don't need to be embarrassed, don't cry—"

"I'm not crying," Leighton snapped, and I took a closer look. Her eyes were red and swollen, but there weren't any tears, and her cheeks looked puffier then normal. Then she sneezed.

"Leighton . . ." I kept my voice calm. "Where's your crown?"

Back at our table, we peered down at the white-dyed crown, the special one that'd been reserved for the bride-to-be. It was hard to judge the sheen of the leaves through the white glaze, but there was another, smaller plant tucked between the leaves—

"Ragweed." I fought to keep my anger under control. The one thing that Leighton was allergic to. "Holy crap. Is there anything Charlotte won't do?"

By now at least half the guests had grabbed their coats and fled, likely in search of somewhere else to wash off. The remaining guests were packing up their things. Leighton appeared to be twenty seconds from spontaneous combustion.

"At least the shower was almost over?" I tried. "Everyone had a great time, and I'm sure Emma got loads of good pictures—"

For the last three months, the *Southern Charm* cover had occupied a large percentage of my waking thoughts. Even when I wasn't consciously thinking about it, some part of my mind was reviewing a mental to-do list of chores for Kali's wedding, tasks for Leighton's, or sabotage-prevention techniques for Charlotte. But standing in the eye of a hurricane of poison-ivy panic, the magazine had slipped my mind. In the chaos, I'd completely forgotten about *Southern Charm* and the all-too-powerful editor twenty feet away from me.

The editor who was halfway to the exit, shouting at her cameramen to capture every second of the disaster unfolding around us.

"Hold that thought," I said to Leighton. I hurried over to Emma, ignoring the half-circles of sweat inching down both sides of my dress. "Hey, Emma, I'm so sorry about all this—"

"Olivia, I really need to get home and shower this off." Emma pushed past me. "We'll chat later! Don't worry, this'll make for a hilarious article!" she called over her shoulder.

"Hilarious," I repeated to myself. "Great. Because that's *totally* what we were going for."

One of the two *SC* photographers paused to give me a reassuring pat on the shoulder. "Seriously, don't beat yourself up. Emma loves a good disaster story."

And then the three *Southern Charm* staff members exited the greenhouse, taking with them my last chance of salvaging this poisonous day.

I'd had setbacks before. As much as I'd fought for what I wanted in life, I learned that you couldn't always win. When I was in fifth grade, I cried for a week after losing the class president election to Tom Brady, who won the entire male vote by sharing a name with a football star. During my first semester of law school, I'd come close to failing my Contracts Negotiation class, and had been convinced my dreams of Big Law would be lost forever.

But this was harder to swallow. Because it was Leighton I'd failed, not myself. I'd always tried to shield her from Charlotte's bitchiness, and I thought I'd done a good job. But now I knew I'd been kidding myself. I hadn't protected Leighton, not really. The only reason she hadn't been hurt in the past was because Charlotte's barbs had been aimed at me. But now that Charlotte was targeting Leighton directly? I was as effective as a Broadway bouncer trying to keep out underage college kids—that is to say, not at all.

I woke up the next morning feeling determined. There were three things I needed to do:

A. Apologize to Leighton
B. Damage control with Emma
C. Call Charlotte out on her bullshit

I just couldn't figure out which order was best. Will had texted me yesterday afternoon with his condolences:

Heard what happened. Here if you want to talk about it. L's pretty upset.

Thinking about my best friend's public humiliation made me feel physically ill. Leighton had rushed out in tears, with Patricia throwing me a filthy I'll-deal-with-you-later look over her shoulder. I'd gotten stuck with the manager, who made me sign paperwork stating we wouldn't sue before I'd finally escaped. I'd tried calling and texting Leighton with my apologies, but it was no use; she was ignoring me completely. Patricia had texted me once:

Leighton's recovering. Please let her rest.

Like she had the plague, not that she'd been poisoned by the Evil Empress of Atlanta.

I'd almost called Charlotte about seventeen times last night. This was a new low—almost unthinkable, really. But I needed to handle things delicately. Fighting fire with fire didn't work with Charlotte. I needed something subtle. I didn't need to beat her; I needed to outsmart her.

I glanced at my class schedule for the week and did some quick mental math. If I met with Emma on Monday morning, made it to my midday M&A seminar, and then left directly afterward . . . I could get to Atlanta a few days before Thanksgiving. I'd have time to set Charlotte straight. And approach Hank directly. And maybe even start working some magic on Kali. If I had to spend the holiday with the Empress, at least I could get something out of it.

For now, it was time for some damage control.

10

I n the end, I didn't even need the $40 box of fancy Five Daughters donuts. I was pleading my case to the snobby *SC* receptionist when one of the photographers from the Nature House event strolled into the lobby. He laughed out loud when he saw me.

"You! Poison ivy girl!" The photographer, a man with impossibly glossy dark hair, grinned in recognition. "That story *kills* at happy hour. Literally, cannot make this shit up."

"Thanks," I mumbled. Maybe Leighton would think it was funny if I dressed up as the villainess Poison Ivy for Halloween in ten years. Or twenty. "Can you help me get in to see Emma? I wanted to apologize—"

"Sure," the photographer said carelessly, flapping a hand at the receptionist to cut off her arguments. "But do yourself a favor and hide those donuts, mmkay? Emma hates the sight of non-vegan carbs before ten a.m."

As we rode up in the elevator, I stuck the baker's box behind my back, attempting to defy the laws of physics. Outside Emma's office, the photographer paused and raised an eyebrow. He glanced pointedly at the four inches of cardboard visible on either side of me. In my defense, it was an extra-large box.

"Okay, okay!" I sighed and stuffed the box into my shoulder bag, crumpling it to get it to fit. I'd either squished all the donuts or released their contents into my purse, but this was crisis management and tough choices had to be made.

"Good. I'm Frederic, by the way." He extended a trim hand. "You're the maid of honor for both weddings, right? Emma told me all about it. Crazy . . ."

He said "crazy" like it was an adjective, like there was another word to follow. Crazy cool? Crazy stupid? Crazy crazy, like straight-up insane?

". . . impressive." His voice was monotone but somehow still conveyed his genuineness. "I helped my sister plan *one* wedding last year, and I barely kept my head above water."

I sighed. I didn't feel very impressive. "I'm already drowning, and we've still got six months to go."

"Hang in there." Frederic patted my shoulder supportively. "I had a blast shooting the shower, even before the ivy stuff. If it were up to me, I'd do a profile on *you*. Maid of honor for two warring weddings? Now, that's a cover story."

He wandered off, leaving me feeling slightly less miserable. Frederic's words had been kind, even if a third June cover contender was the last thing I needed. I glanced at Emma's door and was relieved to see it pulled tight. Putting me on the cover was a surefire way to anger everyone and create maximum chaos. Like when a rogue jury tried to convict someone for a crime they hadn't been charged with. (It's happened.)

I reached into my purse to reapply my lip stain and touched something gelatinous. "Ugh!" I half whispered, half shrieked. The donuts had escaped their box; I'd need this purse dry-cleaned for sure. Did the universe really have to kick me when I was down?

The office door swung open, revealing Emma wearing a tweed jumpsuit and a surprised expression. "Olivia! How do you keep getting in here?"

Not the greeting I was hoping for, but I stuck my jelly-covered left hand behind my back and laughed it off. "What can I say, I'm persistent."

But she didn't look annoyed; if anything, her birdlike features beamed with excitement. "You saved me a call! I've had the best idea for our wedding coverage. Come in, come in."

She ushered me into the office and sat down. Her desk was covered with images from Leighton's bridal shower, which had at least photographed gorgeously. The white linens glowed in the sunlight, and Frederic had captured the greenery's lushness surprisingly well.

Emma followed my gaze. "Perfection, right? We'll barely have to retouch. Exactly like I wanted."

My eyes landed on another photo, this one less idyllic. Four guests were crouched at a fountain, frantically scrubbing their forearms. Sheer panic was etched on their faces, and their hair hung in tangles from hastily discarded crowns.

"And the drama!" Emma said happily. "You've given my writer the easiest job in the world."

"I have?" I blinked. "So you're not mad about it . . ." I glanced down at her bare arms and hands, which were rash-free. One stroke of good luck, at least.

"Honestly, not at all. The engagement on Aditya's Instagram Live, when he was showing his rash?" Emma raised her hand above her head for emphasis. "Through the roof. Our audience is dying to find out how the rest of the party went down."

"The ultimate cliffhanger," I said weakly.

"And great eye candy." Emma smiled devilishly at me. "Well done, you. Let's have your boyfriend host the next Live, too."

"Oh no, he's not—"

"And it gives us an easy angle for the story—how do you recover from something going wrong?" Emma picked up the gift bag I'd had messengered to all the guests yesterday, containing aloe vera, anti-itch cream, a mirror party favor, and a vegan cupcake. "Such a great idea. Love, love, love. But you need to tell me what vendor you used for flower crowns, so I never book them! Name and shame."

Unfortunately, "My Evil Aunt" didn't sound like a believable florist. "I'll look and get back to you," I lied, and then tried to recalibrate. "So, Leighton's given Kali some stiff competition, right?"

"Absolutely." Emma nodded several times. "But the comments on the Live got me thinking—our audience has loved following along. It's so interactive. We've gotten thirty DMs asking when the next event will be! So we're taking this one step further."

"'One step further'?"

"We'll let the *readers* decide who wins!" Emma leaned back in her chair and spread her arms wide. "After the final event coverage is published in April, we'll have a one-week voting window online. And until then, we'll keep some live coverage on the website." She spun her computer around to show me the screen. "My digital team was working all weekend!"

Previously, the online version of the article announcing the Leighton-versus-Kali competition and the "Electrifying the Engagement Party" write-up had been lumped in with general lifestyle pieces. But now a new tab had been added to the *Southern Charm* home page with the title "Charming Bride."

"Brilliant, right?" Emma beamed. She clicked on the tab, which led to a subsection of the website dedicated to the Charming Bride competition. In addition to the two previous articles, dozens of photos from both events had been uploaded, along with a link to the bridal shower Instagram video. A poll in the right-hand column asked visitors to vote for their favorite event: Electrifying Engagement or Greenhouse Shower. Underneath, another poll asked for their vote on who should be the Charming Bride. Leighton was winning, but the two little bars looked very close in height.

The hope in my chest transformed into real excitement. I'd never expected *SC* to invest so much effort into the competition. An advertisement on the left-hand side for the bridesmaid company Azazie caught my eye. I pointed to the ad. "You're drawing in new advertisers?"

"Like you wouldn't believe," Emma confided. "The eyeballs speak for themselves. Of course, *Bridal Today* is about to pop an aneurysm, but I specifically re-reviewed our contract, and they have an exclusive claim on wedding dresses and engagement rings only. Everything else, fair game! We're leaning into it." She glanced up at me with a wry smile. "So you can stop sneaking into our offices. You don't have to impress me anymore. Your job is to impress the people!"

I smiled back. This was good news, indeed. I might not be the best at social media, but I knew someone who was. My best friend, who'd built an entire career on impressing people. On influencing them.

I'd never been so thankful for poison ivy.

I'd planned on heading right to the law library, but then my phone lit up: Leighton wanted to meet for an early lunch near her apartment. And after Ivygate, I wasn't exactly in a place to say no. On the way over, I rehearsed my talking points for why the newly fleshed-out Charming Bride competition was a win for us, including:

A. More event coverage in the magazine
B. More social media posts on Instagram, TikTok, and the *Southern Charm* website
C. Leighton was an influencer! This was right up her alley.

I'd planned to open with small talk, but as soon as I slid into the juice shop's booth, Leighton flipped her phone around. "What is this?" She had the Charming Bride web page pulled up; maybe Emma had sent it to her.

Okay, so we were dispensing with greetings. And small

talk. And ordering food. My stomach rumbled, and I glanced covetously at the acai bowls a few feet away. Leighton cleared her throat.

"The bridal shower livestream got a ton of engagement on Instagram, so Emma wants to make the competition more interactive," I explained. "They built out a whole website section and are planning on expanding their pre-wedding coverage. This is a good thing!"

Leighton's hair was arranged in a fishtail side braid, and her mock-neck black turtleneck and layered gold necklaces were right on trend. She must've been filming content this morning; Leighton was never this put-together before noon. But her hands and arms were covered with a splotchy red rash that was still developing. I looked away, pushing past the guilt.

She played with the braid, reluctant to admit this was a positive development, given her annoyance at me. "Engagement how? Everyone laughing at how the shower ended in disaster? Or wondering *how the hell poison ivy got in the crowns?*"

"To answer your first question, no," I said calmly. I pulled up the saved Instagram Live from the *Southern Charm* account and showed her the comments. The vast majority were fans praising the venue, the décor, or Leighton's outfit. A good minority speculated on Aditya's identity and relationship status; his ego would appreciate that. Near the end, when Aditya showed the camera his hands, the comments turned surprised, and then helpful, with many suggesting remedies. Plenty of people commented that they wished Leighton and her guests a speedy recovery. And there were dozens of comments on *SC*'s latest Instagram post, asking for an update on the poison-ivy situation. "See? It made the party way more interesting to follow online."

"Don't act like you planned this," Leighton snapped. Her tone was harsher than normal, but I tried to cut her some slack. She was under a lot of pressure, her publicly streamed bridal shower had gone up in flames, and she was probably very itchy.

"I didn't. We both know what happened—"

"Your psycho aunt!" Leighton looked like she could breathe fire. "She crossed a line. *Multiple* lines. It was bad enough that she turned this into a competition. Then she canceled my Delacour appointment and snuck poison ivy into my bridal shower! Who does that?"

"I know, Leighton. It's messed up. I'm really sorry. I'm heading to Atlanta this week to talk to her—"

Leighton took a deep, shuddering breath. "To be honest, I wish I'd never said yes to the competition! I should've let Kali have the cover." She looked close to tears. Another rumble, and I realized it wasn't just my stomach that was talkative today.

I held up a quick finger. "I hear you, and we're gonna talk about this. Can I grab us some acai bowls first? Things look better when you're not starving."

"This isn't a Snickers commercial," Leighton mumbled, but she nodded.

Five minutes later, I was back at our table with two heaping bowls of frozen acai, topped with bright berries and coconut shavings. I placed Leighton's photogenic lunch in front of her, careful not to mess with the mountain of toppings, and watched her reluctantly take out her phone and post a photo.

As annoyed as she might be, she also knew her brand, and she wasn't about to miss an opportunity to stir up some follower interaction with a pink-and-purple breakfast bowl.

As I watched Leighton rearrange the berries for a close-up, a pang of sadness accompanied the thought of how little most people thought of her career choice. People like Patricia, who thought influencing was a joke or a phase. People like Tyler, who'd had their followings dumped in their lap by being in the right place at the right time. Even her other friends, like Samantha and Shane, thought of it as a fun hobby, not anything with real potential. When Leighton had joined me at a law school event, my school friends had been shocked—although they tried to be polite—that Leighton would disclose such an embarrassing career choice. It made me bristle, even though Leighton brushed it off.

To be fair, I always tried to consider what opposing counsel might argue—if you'd happened across Leighton's Instagram feed, it'd be easy to write her off as another shallow twentysomething coasting by on her looks, sacrificing at the altar of consumerism. But I had the inside story. I'd known Leighton since Peach Sugar had originated as a fashion-driven Tumblr blog. Back then it really had been a hobby, but then Leighton started designing clothes. By the time we were in high school, she was sewing some of her own things. She started a YouTube channel on how to DIY your own prom dress and slowly started accumulating followers.

Junior year of high school had been stressful. Leighton had dreamed of attending the Parsons School of Design in New York, but her parents had forbidden it, telling her she could attend a "real school" and get a marketable degree or pay for school herself. I remembered several stressful sleepovers counseling Leighton on the pros and cons of committing to fashion design so early in her life. And several screaming matches between a normally mild-tempered Leighton and a frustrated Patricia, where I'd slumped into the backseat of Patricia's SUV and tried to pretend I didn't exist.

In the end, Leighton had decided to play it safe, although it wasn't the student loan debt that scared her off. No, it was because she wasn't set on fashion design. By then she'd started an Instagram account and was posting outfit inspirations, mostly sewing to re-create high-fashion pieces she couldn't afford to buy.

"I don't know if I want to be a fashion designer," she'd told me, the night she'd agreed to attend LSU to study communication. "I like styling clothes. I want to be a stylist. And I don't think I need formal training for that."

To me, this sounded like incredible insight at the age of seventeen. My approach to the college search had been decidedly formulaic: I listed off universities until I hit a name impressive enough for Dad to look up from his laptop. But Patricia had interpreted Leighton's college decision as reassurance that her daughter was finally acknowledging her mother's wisdom.

A third of the way through her breakfast, Leighton laid down her spoon and addressed me again. "As you know, I'm moving in with Matt after the wedding. We're looking at apartments now."

"That's great," I said cautiously.

"But with him joining a start-up, we need more income. I'm making good money from YouTube ads and sponsored posts, but it's not going to be enough." She glanced down at her lap. "Influencing was supposed to be a stepping stone. To get me a clothing collaboration, or land me a styling job. It was my way of being in fashion without, you know, *being in fashion*."

She waved her hand vaguely and I understood this to mean a whole host of things: without obtaining a hyper-specific fashion degree; without living in an NYC shoebox while working for peanuts; without enduring the abuse of the hierarchical fashion industry. "I'm thinking about taking a break from Peach Sugar. Maybe getting a full-time communications job."

"*What?*" I put down my own spoon for emphasis. "But you love Peach Sugar!"

"I love the styling," she corrected. "But you know how much goes into it. I can't take photos on a mannequin and sell that to followers. Instead, I have to make this whole persona. Dress up. Watch my appearance. Create new content. *Always* create new content. It's too much, Liv. I've been doing this for five years. Maybe it's time to accept that this isn't gonna work."

"Leighton, I really think—"

"When the *SC* opportunity came around, I thought maybe I'd have a real path to expand. But now that it's a competition, and a *public* one—I don't know if I can go through with it, Liv. I've already got wedding planning on my plate, and my normal Peach Sugar content. I'm working my butt off on prelims for Kenne's. Then I've got these really adventurous designs for the bridesmaid dresses, and . . . it's too much. I'm barely sleeping."

I had not been expecting this. In all my weeks of scheming, I'd never expected *Leighton* to consider dropping out of the competition. After all, she was the one who really wanted it. Who had a career path dependent on leveraging additional exposure. Who had something to prove to her mother.

But was this what she really wanted? Or was it the overwhelm and calamine lotion talking? This was my best friend in the world, my best friend of twenty years. I knew her better than anybody, and I knew when to push her. Just like she knew when to push me. Three times during my LSAT study period—when my practice scores weren't anywhere near where they needed to be—Leighton had dropped what she was doing to pump me up. Including, if I remembered correctly, a time in which she walked away mid-photo-shoot because I'd called her crying. She'd always been there for me. I needed to give that same tough love back to her.

"You are *not* giving up this close to the finish line," I said, my voice ringing with conviction. "You've worked your butt off for years to get an opportunity like this for Peach Sugar! I know it's a stressful time. Wedding planning usually is. From what I hear," I amended. "But if you walk away, I know you'll regret it. You'll regret not putting five more months into this, to see where Peach Sugar really could go." I lowered my voice. "I think part of this is embarrassment from the bridal shower. You don't want something like that to happen again. I get that. But it won't. I swear."

Leighton looked conflicted. "But Charlotte—"

"Forget about Charlotte!" I waved my spoon hand dramatically, and a bit of purple acai flew off and landed on the wall next to me. Whoops. Leighton cracked a smile. "I'm going to Atlanta this week to set her straight."

"But your job—"

"And I'm going to confront Hank," I said confidently. "I'm done letting Charlotte hold this job over my head. It's ridiculous. I've done the internships, I've demonstrated my worth, and I'll talk to Hank directly. Enough of this behind-the-scenes bullshit."

Leighton nodded slowly. "I guess—even if I lose, the competition will be over by the wedding. So she won't have any reason to mess with that."

Charlotte doesn't need a reason to mess with me. I pushed that nasty thought aside and nodded back. "Exactly. And you've already gained, what, nineteen thousand followers?"

Leighton nodded. "And another five thousand YouTube subscribers. My sponsorship posts are bringing in even more. I guess I can talk to Matt about seeing it through the summer."

"Exactly." I latched on to a happier topic. "How're the bridesmaid dresses going, by the way?"

This was the right thing to ask. Leighton's eyes brightened like they always did when clothing design came up. "I wanted them to be unique, you know? So I've spent a while reviewing the current market. And there's a ton of room for novelty. Because all the big bridesmaid dress companies . . . well, they make dresses that scream 'bridesmaid dress.'"

I nodded like I knew what that meant, even though Leighton/Kali was my first time being in a wedding, and I'd never worn a bridesmaid dress myself. But Leighton could read my face like the back of her eye shadow palette. "There's this

tradition of a bridesmaid dress 'not showing up the bride,'"
she explained. "So they're never low-cut, never form-fitting.
Most of them are A-line or sheath. And chiffon. So much
chiffon because it's cheap."

I loved hearing Leighton talk about her thought process.
If only Patricia could hear all of this. "Okay, gotcha. So most
of the market is purposefully unflattering?"

"Yup. And that's why bridesmaid dresses are notoriously
not re-wearable."

"Is this all a lead-in to you telling me our dresses are intentionally ugly?" I joked. "Because if you're worried about us
showing you up, Leighton, let me tell you—that ain't gonna
happen."

Leighton smiled, accepting the compliment. In our teenage years, I'd often struggled to overcome the shadow cast by
my best friend shining so brightly. I didn't consider myself
*un*attractive, but it was hard having a genetic-lottery-winning
bestie when you were struggling through acne-prone skin
and hair that self-greased overnight. Maybe that's why I'd
developed such a "loud" personality, as my mother had called
it. At parties, people were drawn to us for Leighton's looks;
they stayed for my conversational talent.

"No, but it gave me an idea. What if, when I designed the
bridesmaid dress, I sewed in a pattern for getting it tailored
after the wedding? To transform it into something you'd
actually want to wear again." Leighton grabbed a napkin and
rummaged in her purse for a pen. She sketched a simple
V-neck, floor-length gown. "If I added a lace piece around
the V here, and then sewed in a fold or two across the
thighs—"

"You're designing a dress that's *meant* to be tailored." Echoes of our earlier conversations danced in my ears. She'd mentioned this before, but I'd never asked for an explanation. Or to see a design.

"Exactly. It's intentional. Predictable. Instead of the result depending on which tailor you go to." Leighton sketched another dress next to the first, presumably the result of post-wedding tailoring: a slightly deeper V-neck, and a higher asymmetrical hemline that skimmed the mid-thigh.

"Leighton, that's brilliant!"

"You think?" She studied me anxiously. She'd been working on this for months, but it wasn't like Leighton to brag about her ideas. That was one of the things holding her back. She didn't self-advocate enough. I realized that if I'd ever asked her about the bridesmaid designs, she would've been delighted to show me. But I'd never asked. I'd been too focused on everything on *my* plate to support my best friend's best idea yet.

"Absolutely! Leighton, I can't believe you were thinking of withdrawing. Not with an idea like this up your sleeve." Another stab of guilt. Leighton did get overwhelmed easily; she'd never handled stress well. But this was a great idea, and *SC* could provide the perfect launching point to help her find a business partnership. I would *not* let Charlotte's antics rob her of her best chance at making this dream a reality. "Are you hoping to turn Peach Sugar into a real start-up?"

Leighton shuddered. "No. I don't have the business background. Pitching investors, designing a business plan—that's not my thing. And it's too unpredictable."

I couldn't argue with that. It wasn't my thing, either. All I could do was draw up contracts. "What about Matt?"

"He wants to get into health care, not commercial fashion. He offered to put me in touch with some other MBA classmates, but I want to have a deal under my belt before I ask someone to take a chance on Peach Sugar."

"So, maybe a collaboration with an existing brand?"

"Yeah. Someone like David's Bridal or Azazie. If I can partner with them and design my own line, I can stick to what I do best. I don't want to be a CEO." Her face took on a dreamy quality as she sketched more draping into the shorter version of the dress. Her now-melted acai bowl sat forgotten. "Just a stylist."

"A visionary," I corrected.

She rolled her eyes. "Creative director."

I ate the rest of my bowl while Leighton walked me through her preliminary ideas for the bridesmaid dresses. A sense of purpose washed over me. It was time to stop being reactive to Charlotte's unpredictable schemes. I'd drive to Atlanta and sort things out. With Charlotte, Hank, *and* Kali. Charlotte needed to back off. Hank needed to know about his wife's blackmail. And Kali—Kali needed another conversation about this competition. Because if Leighton had been considering dropping out, maybe Kali had been, too. Maybe I could help her see the light. I might've accosted Emma DeVant in a Mobil station out of girl-code guilt, but the cover had grown to mean so much more. I wanted this so badly for Leighton.

I had a lot of work to do in Atlanta.

11

The door to the Evil Empress's lair swung open.

A sad combination of circumstances had landed me in this predicament. First, Thanksgiving-week hotel rates were sky-high, and my bank account was still recovering from the Delacour Pure Barre bribe. Kali had already promised her couch to another out-of-towner, so I'd had no choice but to shack up with the Empress. Then two separate car crashes on I-75 had added ninety minutes of traffic to the already five-hour drive from Nashville to Atlanta. Leaving me cranky, disheveled, and now staring directly at Charlotte Harlow. Life was not, shall we say, perfect.

"Olivia," Charlotte said. "Lovely to see you. Come in."

"Hi, Aunt Lotte. Thanks."

"Although you're not exactly punctual," my aunt added, her mouth curling wickedly.

I feigned deafness and stepped inside, happy to escape the

gleaming ruby-eyed stone lions that flanked her doorway. Flying monkeys would've been less intimidating.

Charlotte wore a cashmere sweater and pencil-cut black trousers, dressed for a corporate takeover even at eleven p.m. A stark contrast to my jeans and Vanderbilt Law pullover. *Underdressing can be a power move,* I told myself. Like I didn't care what she thought of me. I pulled my suitcase behind me, feeling like the world's most unwanted guest.

She led me through the marble-paneled atrium, which I'd always secretly admired but could never admit. Two arching staircases swung around from a balcony high above us. When we were little, Kali and I used to wrap our sheets around ourselves like ball gowns and practice descending the twin staircases in perfect synchrony. It'd been the only time my cousin ever agreed to put on a dress, pretend or otherwise, and only because of our shared love of all things Happily Ever After. Nostalgia tugged at my heartstrings. Things had been simpler then. Much simpler.

I followed Charlotte into her kitchen, which she'd redone when I was at college. The walls were whitewashed limestone, disappearing behind shiny white granite with van Gogh swirls of grey. The only color came from the overhead exposed wooden beams, which had been painted a brilliant blue that reminded me of Greece. Everything gleamed. Impractical, but Charlotte and Hank seemed the eat-out type, anyway. I was surprised to see an open bottle of merlot and two waiting glasses. Sharing a glass of wine at the kitchen counter felt strangely intimate. Like something I'd do with Leighton. Maybe even Kali.

"Would you like a drink?"

"Yes, please."

As she poured us each an even portion, my feeling of weirdness intensified. It felt odd to be sitting in Charlotte's kitchen, sharing wine like old friends.

"The kitchen looks nice," I offered.

"Thank you." Charlotte handed me a glass. "Your mother helped me with the design. We were working on it together that summer. I haven't changed a thing. I only repaint the white every year." Her voice was quiet. "So it's as bright as she wanted. She loved Santorini. That was our inspiration."

My throat tightened, and I took a sip of my wine for something to do. "She always loved Greece," I said after a moment. "Your trips together—she'd talk about them for months." For as long as I could remember, Charlotte and Mom had taken annual June trips to a Greek island of their choosing. I used to resent them. It was another instance of Charlotte stealing Mom away. Hearing Charlotte talk about them was . . . nice. I liked thinking about the memories my mom must've made on Mykonos, Paxos, Crete, and the rest. I was probably romanticizing things, but I liked to imagine her and Charlotte relaxing on a sandy beach, recounting childhood memories, watching the sapphire waves, and giving zero thought to philanthropy work.

"I enjoyed them as well. I haven't been able to face going back since."

We drank in silence for a moment. There had been a time, five years ago, when I'd thought Charlotte and I might build a real relationship. During my senior year of college, I'd passed out in front of my roommate. She'd called 911 and then Leighton and my dad, the two emergency contacts in my phone. Leighton picked up; Dad, on a business trip in Singapore, did not. I'd been rushed to the hospital and taken into emergency surgery. So Leighton had called the only other family member she knew. When I woke up in recovery, it was Charlotte dozing in the pleather recliner next to my bed. I'd had a ruptured ectopic pregnancy. As the OB-GYN explained to us both the next morning, I'd been pregnant, but the pregnancy had been inside my abdomen, not in my womb. Its rupture had caused a life-threatening amount of internal bleeding.

I hadn't been dating anyone seriously at the time. I hadn't known I was pregnant at all. But none of that mattered to Charlotte. She held my hand when the surgeons did their daily dressing changes, and she helped me to the bathroom when I was too weak to get out of bed alone. We passed the time watching *Seinfeld* reruns and systematically rating the entire cafeteria menu. She'd stayed for three days, until I was discharged. I sent her a thank-you card the next week. She sent a generic get-well-soon bouquet, and we never spoke of it again. When I next saw her at a cousin's wedding, there was no warmth in her greeting. It was like those three days had never happened. Except I had the scar on my abdomen to prove it.

Charlotte's phone buzzed against the granite countertop, startling us both. She picked it up, poorly concealing her thrill of excitement. "Please excuse me."

"Sure."

Alone in the kitchen, I sipped my wine and amused myself by imaging what late-night call would make Charlotte Harlow so excited. An illicit affair? Doubtful; she'd married Hank only three years ago, and she didn't seem the type.

More likely it was a benefit coordinator calling to discuss some new gala. Thrilling stuff.

A sudden crack of thunder made me jump, and my hand knocked over my glass of red wine. Rain pounded the bay window as the skies opened in an instant. A blood-like pool spread over the counter and began to drip onto the floor.

"Shit, shit, shit," I muttered. Red wine stained like crazy; Mom had drilled this into me, even as a child. Charlotte would probably think I'd done it on purpose. I glanced around for a paper towel, but only pristine snowy hand towels hung from the stove. Beautiful, but impractical. She had to have paper towels *somewhere*. I darted down the hall to the pantry and located a roll of Bounty. *Perfect.*

". . . even better than I'd hoped." Charlotte's voice floated down the hall from a half-closed door. I rolled my eyes; probably some fundraiser goal, but her next words stopped me dead. "And Olivia's playing her part brilliantly."

Playing what? I grabbed the paper towels and inched closer to the open door.

". . . especially dramatic," Charlotte was saying. "It's a great B plot. Yes, for the younger audience. We want this to be widely accessible."

I frowned at the door. "Widely accessible" was the polar opposite of the $500-a-head fundraisers Charlotte normally organized. And I doubted there were plots involved, except about separating donors from more of their money.

". . . but tasteful," she was saying. "Tasteful drama." She laughed. "You know I've done my market research. I've got to go—Olivia's here now. Talk soon."

I hurried back to the kitchen and dropped the

wine-soaked paper towels into the trash as Charlotte reappeared. Her cheeks were flushed with pleasure. I eyed her suspiciously; what had that been about? What part was I playing? And could drama ever be tasteful?

But my aunt had already retaken her seat. "What brings you to Atlanta so early in the week? It's unlike you to prioritize your family around the holidays." She sipped her glass. "Learned that from your father, I suppose."

Maybe because this is the welcome I get? I ignored the insult to both me and my father. Sometimes I thought Charlotte showed a sliver of heart just to throw me off balance, and then she'd snap right back to her typical icy ways. It never failed to unnerve me. "Leighton's bridal shower, actually."

"Oh?" My aunt raised an eyebrow innocently. "Is she holding it in Atlanta?"

"Aunt Lotte, please." I set my glass down for emphasis. "Can we cut the crap? I'm here to tell you to back off. Since apparently you didn't get the message the first time."

"As I told you before, Olivia—"

"None of this is Leighton's fault," I snapped. "This cover was supposed to be hers. I agreed to help Kali anyway. And I threw Kali an amazing party. You sabotaging Leighton was never part of the deal!"

"Sabotage?" Charlotte sniffed. "Hardly. If Leighton can't handle a few road bumps, marriage will be—"

"Road bumps? That's what you call canceling her Delacour appointment? Sneaking poison ivy and ragweed into her bridal shower?"

"That's what mothers do," Charlotte said primly.

"What, poison their competition?"

"Fight for their daughters." Her eyes nearly glowed. "If your little friend wants this profile so badly, she should fight harder. Instead of expecting everything to fall into her lap."

This was beyond rich, coming from a woman born into family money and an even more valuable network of powerful connections. But there it was again: the insinuation that Leighton didn't work for anything, that she didn't deserve any success of her own. It made my blood boil.

"Leighton *has* been working hard," I growled. "She works her ass off on Peach Sugar. Leave her alone, Charlotte. I mean it."

"Olivia, I thought I'd made myself clear. I am the one giving instructions. You are the one carrying them out. You plan perfect events for my daughter, and I don't interfere with your job." Charlotte looked almost bored. "I'm not unreasonable. I'm not asking *you* to sabotage your best friend. I could ask you to do that, but . . ."

The threat hovered. I clenched my fist around the barstool seat, trying to channel my fury into something other than slapping Charlotte across the face. Or throwing my red wine across her white kitchen. Or on Charlotte herself. "Whether you do it or I do it, Leighton is still hurt," I said coldly. Charlotte had clearly used up her daily allotment of humanity on reminiscing about Mom, so I pulled out my backup card. Grabbing my phone, I brought up the comment section of the Instagram Live from Leighton's shower. "Read that."

Charlotte took the phone and frowned at the screen. "'There's no way this was an accident, right? What if it was the other *SC* wedding?'" The comment had attracted half a dozen replies and forty-six likes.

184

"Imagine if they knew about the Delacour cancellation. That would really grease the conspiracy wheels."

Charlotte's eyes narrowed. "What are you saying?"

"The Charming Bride competition means that a hell of a lot more people are following along. A lot of eyes on *everything* to do with Kali and Leighton's events. If you do anything else like this, Kali will get blamed. And she'll never win the competition if *SC* readers think she's a tasteless cheater." I folded my arms. Was it my imagination, or had she flinched at the word "tasteless"? "The poison ivy was a mistake. If you'd chosen something less obvious, you'd have some plausible deniability . . ."

My aunt was too refined to sweat under pressure, but a trace of anxiety flitted across her face. Bad publicity was to Charlotte what humidity was to Dolly Parton's wig stylist: the ultimate enemy.

"If you so much as hint that I was involved with *any* of the mishaps caused by your poor planning," she said coldly, "I will make sure you never work at Holmes & Reese. Or at any law firm worth knowing. We are family, Olivia. There are some lines we do not cross." An icy force radiated from her, and I could practically see the tendrils of power rippling around her. How did an Atlanta housewife exert so much influence over my future career in New York? But that question was easily answered: a well-timed marriage to a Manhattan law partner.

If only I could work at another firm. There were hundreds of law firms in the city. And at least a dozen as prestigious as Holmes & Reese. But that wasn't how the world worked. The top Big Law players, the ones with the five-figure signing bonuses and the most prestigious clients, hired exclusively through summer internship pathways. This allowed firms to lock down talent early and evaluate them over the course of two three-month summer stints. I'd chosen Holmes & Reese two years ago, halfway through my first year of law school. If it hadn't worked out—and not every summer associate made it to an offer letter like I had—I'd be left scrambling and re-recruiting into a new industry, like Aditya.

But things had worked out for me. *Had been* working out, until Charlotte's new husband had suddenly transferred firms. If I walked away from my Holmes & Reese offer, it would take years to scrabble into the top echelon of Big Law. If I made it at all.

"So we're family when publicity is involved, but enemies otherwise?"

"Don't be dramatic," Charlotte sniffed. "We're simply working at cross-purposes."

"Is that what we're calling it?" I swung my legs off the bar-stool. I needed to exit this conversation before I completely lost my cool. "You're right, Aunt Lotte. We *are* family. That's why I agreed to help Kali in the first place. So focus on the ceremony, and let me get back to what I agreed to do: helping your daughter get exactly what she wants."

Unfortunately, I was Charlotte's houseguest, which really limited my dramatic exit options. All I could do was turn and whirl out of the kitchen, hoping desperately that I hadn't just made a huge mistake.

Some would say that I'd lost my cool with Charlotte. That I'd let my anger get the best of me, and lost control of the conversation in a way that was very unlike Olivia Fitzgerald. It'd been a humbling experience, and one I wasn't keen to repeat. Keeping my cool under pressure was one of my strengths. Or at least it was supposed to be.

"You're being too hard on yourself," said Aditya when I'd finished word-vomiting all that over the phone. "She's family. She gets under your skin like nothing else."

I nodded to myself, pacing back and forth outside of the shiny red diner where I'd scheduled my next confrontation.

"She's like poison ivy," I muttered. "Vicious. Sneaky. Rash-inducing."

"Rash-inducing?"

I stopped pacing and eyed my reflection in the diner window. A splotchy stress rash had broken out across my neck. Or was that late-onset poison ivy? "Yes! From stress!" Stress. It had to be stress. I refused to consider the alternative.

Aditya chuckled. "So you told her to back off? How did that go over?"

"Not too well," I admitted. "She doesn't like being told what to do."

"Sounds like someone else I know."

"Ha, ha." I paused uncomfortably. The depths of Charlotte's evilness were sort of . . . embarrassing. Why was my aunt so hell-bent on getting her disinterested daughter onto the cover of *Southern Charm*? Why did she act like she'd just stepped off a reality TV show? Why had my mom been so drawn to Charlotte, and why was my dad's definition of success so narrow that it was Holmes & Reese or bust? How had I let myself get into this mess in the first place? "Maybe I can get through to my uncle instead."

"Isn't that risky? If he's the one with the real power at your firm?"

"Yes, but he may be easier to reason with."

"What's he like? *NY* style?" After two years of friendship, Aditya had picked up on the *New Yorker* gag. Again, I had the answer ready because I'd drafted one for Will. "Generic affability conceals a steely-hearted ruthlessness and a devotion to client needs bordering on worshipful."

"Worshipful. Nice one."

I lifted a hand to wave to Hank, who was exiting his car nearby. "Got to go, he's here." I ended the call. "Good morning, Hank. How'd you play?"

"Morning." Hank wiped the sweat off his brow and zipped up the Stanford sweatshirt he'd thrown on over his golf gear. As far as I could tell, Hank never worked when he was in Atlanta—at least not in the office. Most of his time was spent schmoozing on golf courses or tennis courts. Charlotte and Hank "kept residences" in both Manhattan and Atlanta, and Hank flitted between the cities at his leisure. "Not well enough to talk about. But coffee'll help. Shall we?"

We settled ourselves inside a dusty booth. The place hummed with conversation, punctuated by the clang of silverware against plates. After the waitress had taken our orders, Hank leaned back. "So, to what do I owe the pleasure?" He smiled easily, deepening the wrinkles that swung down either side of his face. Their symmetry was oddly satisfying.

"Actually, I—"

Hank's phone chimed, and he held up a finger. "Hold that thought."

"Of course."

I stared around the diner absentmindedly while Hank typed away on his iPhone, muttering half-formed comments under his breath. A few booths down, a blonde and a brunette around my age were huddled over the blonde's phone. The brunette threw her head back and cackled with glee. The blonde swatted her playfully, hiccupping with laughter. Both were dressed in leggings and old college sweatshirts, their hair pulled back as an afterthought. I watched them wistfully. They looked like the me and Leighton of six months ago, before I'd run into Emma. Before Patricia had given Leighton the ultimatum about figuring out her career. Before every hangout was consumed with strategy sessions and obsessions over *Southern Charm*'s social media platforms. I missed that. I missed us.

Hank set his phone down with a clatter. "Sometimes I'd like to pour coffee on top of that thing," he said ruefully.

"Everything okay?"

"No rest for the wicked." At my confused look, he tapped the phone. "You remember how tethered you were to your email this summer? That's corporate law. Constant accessibility to your clients. I hope you're ready for that."

"I think I am," I said honestly.

He nodded. "It's easy to be ready when you're in your twenties and have no real responsibilities. Spouses, kids, things like that. At your age, it's hard to think long-term. If you're willing to sacrifice future you's priorities along with today's."

I'd seen my father's commitment to his work. He'd fought hard and provided for his family, but it'd come with a non-monetary cost to his family life. A not-insignificant one. In the last few years, I'd realized that Dad's inaccessibility had probably played a big part in Mom drifting so close to Charlotte. This had somewhat cooled my idolization of his high-powered career. "Definitely important to think about. But I—"

"Have you talked to any of the junior associates?"

"I've worked with a bunch of them—"

He waved this aside. "I don't mean when you're staffed on cases. Or at H&R-sponsored happy hours. I mean *really* talk to them. Preferably one-on-one."

"About . . . ?"

"The realities of being a junior associate," he said grimly. "Take it from me, Olivia. There's more to life than working at a firm that everyone's heard of. Go in with your eyes open. Got it?"

I swallowed and nodded. "Got it." Part of me wanted to ask more, to figure out what was driving this line of conversation. But I had to switch topics. When I'd asked Hank for a private chat this morning, he'd slotted me in after his morning golf but was due back at the house soon to assist with Thanksgiving preparations. Time was limited.

"Hank, I wanted to talk to you about something delicate. In confidence."

The phone beeped again, but Hank's gaze stayed on me. "Okay. Go ahead."

"I really enjoyed my time at Holmes & Reese, and I'm excited to have received a preliminary offer," I began.

"But . . . ?"

"I almost feel silly bringing this up," I confessed, allowing a hint of embarrassment into my voice. It was crucial to nail this delivery; that's why I'd rehearsed a dozen times to the bathroom mirror. "But your wife asked me to plan Kali's pre-wedding events for this *Southern Charm* competition. Which I was—am—happy to do."

"Olivia, pretend I'm the senior partner and you need to distill our case down to one sentence. What's going on?"

If he wanted facts, I'd give them to him straight-up. "Charlotte has implied that if I don't help Kali win the competition, she'd get my Holmes & Reese offer rescinded." I let that hang there in the silence. The sentence burned like vodka without a chaser.

Hank's grey eyes darted back and forth between mine. "Implied?"

"Made it very, very clear. A competition that was never supposed to exist. Against my best friend in the world," I added.

I watched his face closely, trying to read the subtleties. I didn't know Hank very well; he'd married into the family three years ago. For obvious reasons, I didn't seek out their combined presence, and most of our interactions had been at family holidays. I'd found him pleasantly witty, tolerant of his wife, and more glued to his phone than a teenager. I'd seen him around the office a few times this summer, but we'd never exchanged more than brief pleasantries. I'd gotten the impression that he was keeping his distance to avoid accusations of nepotism. I appreciated that, especially since I'd gotten my first Holmes & Reese summer position long before Hank had joined the company. But the timeline wouldn't matter to snarky office gossips; if word spread that Hank was my step-uncle, my own merits would be dismissed in an instant.

It'd been a risk, approaching him like this. I didn't like to gamble in high-stakes conversations; I liked to go in knowing everything possible about the outcome. But you couldn't know everything about your opponent. From what I knew about Hank, there was a reasonable chance he'd see the ridiculousness of Charlotte's actions. And as a fellow highly motivated professional, he wouldn't want my blossoming career stifled by a trivial wedding dispute. Plus, significant others could sometimes rein in their partner's worst impulses; they could get through where no one else could. And I certainly wasn't getting through to Charlotte on my own.

And then Hank broke into a grin. "Olivia, Olivia," he said easily. "I like you. I like you a lot."

Uh-oh. In my experience, never had the phrase "I like you" ever been followed by anything good, unless you counted the time Scott Waterhouse had asked me out in third grade. But he was only acting on a dare from his buddies, so that barely counted.

"I'm going to give you two pieces of advice." Hank paused as the waitress returned with our food orders: pumpkin pancakes for me, an egg-white omelet for him. He was disciplined even in his food habits. (This I found supremely unrelatable.) "At the highest level, a lawyer's job is to shape the facts to the best interest of the client. Whether that's setting up a merger, defending an antitrust claim, or shielding internal operations in compliant language. That's Big Law. That's high-level corporate law. We're not talking traffic court."

"I understand."

"So think of this situation as an opportunity to flex those muscles. On a smaller scale," Hank added. "I understand there are personal stakes for you. That makes it even better. Being able to secure, navigate, and deploy social capital is crucial to making partner."

"That's sort of my specialty," I said without thinking. "But it's not as simple as that." If it had been, I'd have figured out the solution a long time ago. "The personal relationships involved complicate things. With Leighton, with Kali, *and* with Charlotte—"

"Everything is personal," Hank countered. "You're never working alone. As a junior associate you'll work with peers, senior associates, and your partner. Then there's the relationships with opposing counsel. And with judges. And, of course, with the clients. These are the people you'll build relationships with over the next few decades. Once you get a few years out of law school—and shed the people who don't have what it takes to climb the ladder—you'll see how small a world it is. Navigating conflicting priorities is essential. And finding a compromise out of thin air, in a situation where it feels impossible?" He grinned and took a sip of his coffee. "That's lawyer 101."

I could sort of see his point, but another part of me bristled with indignation. This was all well and good. But I hadn't come here for a lecture about compromises and relationship management.

"I understand," I said again, the more professional version of *I know all this already!* "And part of all that is using every connection you have. And thinking outside the box for alternate approaches. Which is what I'm doing now, by coming to you."

"Ah, very nice," he said appreciatively. "Shaping the facts differently. There you go."

I waited, but he was busy with his omelet. "So will you talk to Charlotte?" I asked at last.

"That brings me to my other point. Excelling in Big Law means making a lot of personal trade-offs. The ones I was alluding to earlier. Some call it sacrifices, but I don't like that word; it has a negative connotation. 'Trade-off' implies an active choice, which is more accurate." Hank set his utensils down. "My first marriage ended because I traded quality time at home for quality time in the office. That's a statement of fact. Now, at this stage in my career? I have other priorities. One of which is my marriage to your aunt."

I didn't like where this was going. "Yes, but—"

"The competition is important to her, end of story," he said. "I don't pretend to understand what my stepdaughter wants. But supporting my wife is a priority to me. I'll always back her."

"Meaning you'd interfere with my job offer?"

Hank smiled again. For a corporate lawyer, the guy sure did a lot of smiling. "I don't think it'll come to that, Olivia. From everything my wife tells me, you have a habit of getting your way." He stood and dropped four twenties on the table. Either he was overpaying for dramatic effect or was so wealthy that he had no concept of diner pricing. "And remember— nothing's sealed until it's in writing."

And with that, my uncle smiled that goddamn Cheshire Cat grin of his and sauntered back out to his car.

My audience was over.

12

There are two types of people in this world: people who run Turkey Trots on Thanksgiving, and people who have not gone insane. Unfortunately, Kali was one of the former. As we drove to the start of the torture I'd paid $40 to experience, I reflected on the multiple things wrong with this scenario:

A. The temperature was thirty-nine degrees
B. It was not even eight in the morning
C. I would shortly be expected to run more than three miles (only a tenth of a mile more, *but still*)

The singular bright spot, and the reason I'd dragged myself out of bed to accompany Kali, was that Greta had retained her sanity and declined to join the race. Yesterday, Kali and Greta had driven over to Charlotte and Hank's house, and we'd all had a superficially pleasant dinner. After-ward, I'd tried to pull Kali aside for a glass of wine, but Greta had followed us into the den. With Leighton's wedding plan-ning, Matt took the uninvolved-groom stereotype to the next level; I doubted he knew anything about his upcoming nup-tials besides the date. But Kali and Greta were inseparable. So the three of us had chatted about ideas for their joint bachelorette and then watched a climbing documentary on Netflix (Greta's choice). Minus the Charlotte interaction, it'd been a surprisingly fun evening.

But I'd had no chance to talk to Kali alone, and Thanks-giving itself would be flooded with relatives, my own father included. So when Kali had started to (lovingly) whine about Greta's refusal to run with her, I'd volunteered with-out thinking it through. After a quick five-minute online registration, I'd officially become Sucker #4392 for the Atlanta Turkey Trot.

Kali parked and glanced over at me, her eyes bright with anticipation of early-morning exercise. In that moment I severely doubted we shared an iota of DNA. "Ready?"

"As I'll ever be."

She'd parked on a side street a few blocks over from the start line, and we joined a crowd of brightly attired runners bundled up against the unseasonable chill. For many people this seemed to be an annual tradition. Flocks of families chatted in matching T-shirts, while race veterans compared turkey costumes.

"People really do this every year?" I asked doubtfully.

"Religiously."

"And you run it alone?"

"Not this year." She elbowed me playfully, but then her

face tightened. "Growing up, I used to run this race with my dad. It was sort of our thing. After he died . . . it didn't feel right not to be here on Thanksgiving." She paused. "Plus, my mom always meets me at the finish line with apple-cider donuts."

Damn it. I had less time than I'd expected with Kali. I'd planned on walk/running the 5K, emphasis on the walk, but now I'd have to keep up with my fleet-footed cousin.

"Do you mind if we run together?" I asked. "Warning: I'm pretty slow."

"Of course we'll run together!"

A warm feeling welled up inside me, and somehow the crisp morning air didn't have such a strong bite. I felt silly for even asking, but her surprise sweetened the moment. To distract myself, I knelt and fiddled with my shoelaces. By the time I stood up, an enthusiastic MC was hyping the crowd up with a one-minute countdown.

"Damn, they really pack us in here," I muttered. We were shoulder to shoulder with hundreds of other runners, all enthusiastically stretching or bobbing in place. The constant motion meant that everyone repeatedly bumped into one another, but no one seemed to mind. A far cry from my summer in Manhattan, where an accidental brush with someone's elbow could earn you a hairy eyeball and a ten-second cuss-out.

Kali shrugged. "It's for charity. So the more the better, I guess?"

"Which charity?"

Kali looked sheepish. "I'm not sure, exactly. I'm set up to auto-enroll every year. But it must be a good cause, right?"

"Imagine if Charlotte found out!" I teased. "Her own

daughter, not even knowing the name of the charity she's running for. What kind of philanthropist *are* you?"

Kali elbowed me, but she was grinning. "Don't tell my mom."

A bullhorn sounded, announcing the start of the race. The crowd surged forward as one, with participants power-walking until they passed the red start line, and then starting their run.

"Here we go!" Kali said cheerily, breaking into a light jog as we crossed the start line. Matching her stride for stride, I was relieved that my lungs weren't immediately on fire. We trotted down a cordoned-off street, the crowd slowly thinning over the first few blocks.

Briefly I wondered how long it took endorphins to kick in. Probably more than three city blocks, but how long would my legs last? "I'm glad we're getting to spend more time together," I said between breaths.

Kali smiled. "Me, too." We followed the trail of runners around a fountain. "That was part of my ulterior motive. I told Mom I'd only do the magazine if you were the maid of honor."

"On a scale of one to ten, how bad has all the wedding planning been?"

Somehow, my cousin slipped a fluid shrug into her running stride. "Maybe a seven? Not as bad as I expected. You're handling most pre-wedding things, and my mom's running the actual day-of. But it's still a lot of time, and money, and stress, over just one day."

Bingo. I accidentally sped up in my excitement, which was a mistake. Kali matched my increased pace easily. "Crazy, right? Imagine if y'all had eloped. Or done the destination-wedding thing. The only thing you'd decide is which reefs to dive. Or which mountains to hike!"

That was the first of the two tricks I'd stuffed up my sweatshirt sleeve this morning: if you're trying to talk someone into something, get them to imagine it vividly. "Pretend the magazine thing doesn't exist," I went on. "Where would you want to go?"

Kali's face took on a dreamy quality, which I resented, since I'd already started sweating. We coasted for a few minutes as she thought about her answer. "I'd love to do it in Southeast Asia. Maybe Taiwan? Supposed to be insane scuba diving."

"Beach wedding?"

"Yes! The dream. And we could pop down to Australia for the honeymoon."

"I've heard," I puffed, "that destination weddings are usually cheaper, can you believe?"

"Really?"

"Because the guest list is so much smaller," I invented. Luckily, it was hard for her to fact-check me halfway through a 5K. "And I've got a ton of Delta miles saved up with no plans to use them. Maybe I'll upgrade you to first-class as a wedding present." This was true; my dad had promised to take me to Europe last June but canceled when a court date was moved. I still had the unused credits sitting in my account.

"No way, first class is a scam! Save them for yourself—you'll need a vacation from lawyering."

"They'll expire!" I insisted. Ever since Aditya'd mentioned using expiring Delta miles for our Atlanta trip, it'd been on my mind to use mine before the one-year mark. I hadn't bothered looking at flights for Thanksgiving, since they were always so expensive. "You'd be doing me a favor." Were we halfway yet? My legs were fading fast.

"I don't think Delta miles expire. Aren't they known for that?"

Up ahead, I spotted a large marker with the number 1. "Oh, look! A mile down!" *Okay, a third done.* I could work with that.

Kali laughed. "That's the kilometer marker."

"Is a kilometer more or less than a mile?"

She grinned. "You don't want me to answer that."

We ran in silence while I reflected on the poor life choices that had led me to this race. The things I did for . . . I realized I didn't have a clear end to that sentence. For Leighton? For my job? For Kali? For Will? Not the last. He'd made it clear he only wanted to be friends.

"At least my mom's not involved with the honeymoon," Kali said after a bit. The crowd had dispersed even more. There were only a dozen runners in eyesight as we ran through a small park. "Greta's handling that. So that part'll definitely be fun."

I chose my words carefully, using precious energy that should probably have been diverted to my thighs. "I know you're doing this for your mom. But why does Charlotte care so much about this magazine cover? You shouldn't be talking about your honeymoon as 'the only fun part' of your whole wedding. That's not fair to you. Or to Greta."

Kali kept her gaze on the road. "You know how she is. Big into the social scene, always looking for flattering publicity.

Ways to raise her profile. It'd be a . . . What's the expression? Feather in her crap."

I snorted. "Feather in her cap."

"You wouldn't believe what she'll do for a spot on a museum board. One time, she slipped ipecac into some lady's cocktail at an important benefit. Sent the rival off puking while she worked the crowds."

"I— What?"

"Ipecac. She makes it from some plant in our greenhouse."

I had a flashback to my sudden-onset nausea at MM Baxter. How Charlotte had gotten me out of the way for the pitch meeting with Emma. How she'd spilled my margarita and given me a replacement, *just like that.*

"Your mom is unbelievable," I said, when I found the words to speak.

Kali laughed again. "Agreed. Although . . . don't hate me, but I see some similarities between you two."

I stopped dead. Kali ran several yards ahead of me before noticing. "Come on!" she called.

"Not until you take that back!" Other runners had started to stare, but I didn't care. Every fiber of my being had been insulted. Sometimes you had to take a stand.

My cousin jogged over. "I take it back," she said, rolling her eyes. We resumed running, although I set a much slower pace. Mentally I was turning over her words in my head. If there was one thing I knew about Charlotte, it was that we valued wildly different things in life. She cared about press coverage and gala invites and rubbing elbows with millionaire donors; family was an afterthought. Sure, I wanted that shiny Big Law career and the associated professional success, but I also cared about my loved ones. Aditya's words echoed in my ears: *You've pitted your own career against your best friend's happiness, and now your cousin's getting dragged in as collateral damage.*

No, I argued back. *It's not the same thing at all.*

"I only meant that you're both ferocious about going for what you want. Cutthroat."

"I don't poison people," I muttered.

Kali winced. "Okay, so the timing of the comparison was bad." She looked even more flustered as she added, "Speaking of . . . I saw the Instagram about Leighton's shower. You think that was my mom?"

I tilted my head and gave her a what-do-you-think? look.

"That's screwed up," she declared. "I'll talk to her."

Maybe I could use this turn in the conversation to my advantage. "Do you really want to reward this kind of Charlotte bullshit?"

"What do you mean?"

"You and Greta are making this huge, generous gesture by letting your mom throw the big society wedding of her dreams. Of *her* dreams, not yours."

"Yes, but—"

"And even that's not enough. She forced y'all into a magazine competition, and then poisoned my best friend—"

We jogged in silence past the halfway point, where enthusiastic volunteers were handing out mini-cups of water. I would've loved to detour over, but Kali was staring ahead, and I couldn't risk ruining the moment. I was making some real progress.

"That's all true," she said at last. "But we've already planned so much—"

"That doesn't matter. It's *your* day, Kali. Yours and Greta's."

"Greta was open to it," Kali said doubtfully. "Emma promised her a write-up for Laraghai—"

Inspiration struck. "True, but that was before the Charming Bride thing blew up," I pointed out. "Has Greta seen the new content schedule? I don't want to stress you out, but it's . . . a lot. Emma wants content from y'all every week, minimum."

Kali winced.

"You don't owe your mom your wedding day." Time to pull back; I couldn't push too hard. "Talk to Greta. See what she wants to do. I'm sure I can get Emma to write about the conservancy either way. Your wedding should be about you two. Not your mom's power addiction."

I pulled my sweatshirt over my right hand and crossed my fingers. If I was reading Greta right, she'd opt for an elopement in a heartbeat.

Kali nodded. "It could be a good twist," she said, almost to herself. And then, to me: "I'll talk to Greta. Because you're right. This *should* be about us."

Newly energized, she started to accelerate, and I wasn't even mad about matching her speed.

By the time my father arrived at Charlotte and Hank's house, a hot shower, a pumpkin latte, and an apple-cider donut had more than made up for the chilly Turkey Trot. I wasn't sure how many calories running burned, but when you factored in the mid-race scheming, I'd definitely earned a donut. Or three.

"On a sugar bender?" My father swept into the kitchen, catching me mid-bite. He was dressed informally in a crisp button-down and tailored slacks. He must've left his suit jacket in the car; my father never stepped outside of the house without one.

"Hi, Dad." I hugged my father, reveling in the softness of his non-suited chest. "I ran a race this morning."

"Intentionally?" Dad turned and lugged my mom's old Lilly Pulitzer suitcase into the kitchen. He'd always hated the neon-pink-and-green flamingo-patterned atrocity, which Mom had loved and vehemently defended. After she died, he'd started using it when we visited Charlotte for Thanksgiving. The sight of it still made my throat feel tight.

"Yes, intentionally." I rolled my eyes. "I ran the Turkey Trot with Kali. How're you? How's work?"

Dad took a long slug from his Starbucks cup and picked up his phone. He drank black iced coffee year-round, sometimes with an added espresso shot when a deadline was approaching. When I was in high school, Mom and I always hid our pumpkin spice lattes from him to avoid a lecture on the insult PSLs ("commercial coffee parodies") represented to the unadulterated bean-derived elixir.

"Good. Busy." To him, these were synonyms.

"Any interesting cases?"

He finally put the phone down. "Are you a basketball fan?"

"Um, not really."

"Well, I've just been called in at the eleventh hour to resolve the NBA Players' Association strike," Dad said, unable to fully hide the pride in his voice. "Good chance I'll be able to get courtside tickets for the next five years. If you and Leighton wanted to go."

My mind conjured up an image of Will and me courtside at an NBA game. He'd love that. I could get into basketball, for Will.

Stop it, Liv!

"Maybe we could go to a game," I said instead. "You and me."

Dad looked surprised, as if this hadn't occurred to him. "We could do that," he said after a beat. "Maybe a Knicks game. Madison Square Garden isn't too far from the Holmes & Reese offices."

"Yeah, that'd be great. I promise I'll learn at least one player's name first."

"I used to take your mom all the time." Although Dad barely talked about Mom, he remembered her in other ways. Like how Dad had continued the Thanksgiving-in-Atlanta tradition even after Mom died. We'd never discussed it outright; that wasn't Dad's way. The first November after her death, I'd received an email with a plane ticket to Atlanta, and that was that. "She didn't know anything about basketball. But she loved the energy in the arena."

"I'm my mother's daughter, then," I said awkwardly.

Dad picked up his phone again while I sipped my coffee and gazed around Charlotte's kitchen. My eyes landed on a framed black-and-white print of Libreria Acqua Alta, a beautiful Venetian bookstore known for displaying books in overflowing gondolas. Mom had given the print to Charlotte for Christmas the year before she died.

Mom had always loved books. She'd been a high school English teacher, and she'd always wanted to write a book. She'd written all the stories she read to me at bedtime, but she wanted a real, hardcover-in-bookstores sort of book. Dad made plenty of money, so she quit her job to pursue writing full-time once I was in school.

And she had, until my uncle Mark had died. She'd spent several months splitting her time between Nashville and Atlanta, trying to support Charlotte. After Charlotte had gotten "back on her feet" (Mom's words), my aunt had started coming to visit. She filled more and more of my mother's time with things that only glancingly resembled volunteer work. I watched my caring, bookish mother transform into a Junior League and Pure Barre groupie, always seeking her elder sister's approval. She'd won it, but it wasn't worth the price. At least not in my book. Or in my mom's, the book that she'd now never write.

Although, if I were honest with myself, the sisterly support may have gone both ways. Both Mom and Charlotte had been dealing with absent husbands. Both needed a way to temper the loneliness. It was a weird feeling to reexamine the assumptions you'd held as a teenager about your parents and the adult lives they led. Life was more complicated than it looked when you were fifteen and thought you knew everything.

My father put the phone down again, and I suddenly felt the full weight of his attention. "Have you gotten your finalized Holmes & Reese contract yet?" he asked.

"Not yet. It's contingent on our 3L fall grades." A half-truth.

Dad frowned. "No one gives a shit about your 3L grades. They only say that to give themselves an out if something major happens."

"I know—"

My father was too experienced a litigator to miss the tone of my voice. "*Did* something major happen?"

I thought of Charlotte's increasingly less-veiled threats, of Hank's refusal to get involved in anything that threatened his happy-wife, happy-life priorities. Nothing had happened, and if I handled things right, nothing would happen. "Nothing major's happened," I said forcefully, focusing on the true part of my half-truth. That was another trick Dad had taught me. If you had to twist facts, focus on the truth of what you were saying; it came off more genuine.

Dad eyed me for a long while. "Well, get that contract signed," he said at last. "If you want Big Law, Olivia, this is your ticket—"

"I know," I said irritably. For once, I was grateful when his phone chirped.

He raised the phone at me. "I have to take this." His eyes landed on my pumpkin latte. "And you shouldn't drink that sugary shit. Full of carcinogens."

"Yeah, you've mentioned."

Left alone, I munched my donut and reflected on my father's ability to reduce me to a petulant teenager in under five minutes.

I spent the rest of Thanksgiving weekend avoiding my relatives, a challenge on a holiday that was ostensibly all about family time. I settled for avoiding one-on-one time with most of them. I evaded Charlotte for obvious reasons, but I didn't want to hear Dad's too-smart questions about my Holmes & Reese offer. And I had no idea how to handle myself around Hank.

The result was a lot of time sneaking off with Kali and Greta. Sometimes it was hard to third-wheel such a happy couple; it made me regret the loss of a future with Will more deeply than I had in weeks. But by now I felt at ease around my cousin, and I was somewhat comfortable with her fiancée. I seemed to be making real progress with Greta.

"I think she's really warming up to you," Kali whispered to me on Saturday night. She unfolded herself from the couch next to me. "Going to get some more wine," she announced.

After she padded out of the basement, Greta glanced over from the recliner she was sprawled across. "How much do you think we've gone through?"

"Not enough."

She snorted and raised her glass to toast. "Cheers to that."

I mirrored her and took another sip of wine. One of Charlotte's few redeeming qualities was her impressively curated wine cellar. That'd been our secret act of rebellion all weekend: drinking the best vintages we could find.

"This is all new for me," Greta said, swirling her cabernet meditatively.

"What is?"

"Thanksgiving." She looked at me like I was an idiot. "It's not exactly a big holiday in South Africa. My parents were expats, but we never celebrated."

"Right. Of course." I drank some more wine for something to do. "Do you want to go back?"

"Go back? Sure. Live there?" She shrugged and twisted a lock of her platinum hair. "I used to think I would. My parents wanted me to. And it was on the table, until I met Kali." There was no regret in her voice. "I think she'd be happier living in the States. And I like it here, too, as long as we travel."

"Was that weird?" I asked tentatively. This was way more information than Greta normally shared with me. "How things changed after meeting Kali?"

She nodded. "Sure. I was used to doing my own thing, making my own plans. Then I meet this woman, and suddenly it's two sets of plans and careers and opinions to manage." She chuckled. "I didn't see it coming."

Hank's words echoed in my ears. Did I want to sacrifice future me's priorities? "In a good way or a bad way?"

Now she was looking at me like I had three heads. "A good way. A complicated way, but I wouldn't trade meeting Kali for anything. We're partners. Some things are more important to me now."

I nodded. "Makes sense."

"It wasn't easy at first," Greta went on. "We met while hiking around Mount Rainier. Dated for six months before I moved to Atlanta. I was in SF at the time."

I hadn't known this; I'd assumed they'd both lived and met in Atlanta. Moving cross-country had been a leap of faith on Greta's part. I thought of the hundreds of miles separating Nashville and Durham, and the hundreds more between Durham and New York. "How'd you know she was the one? When you moved to Georgia?"

"I didn't. I hoped she was. But I didn't know for sure. Not then."

"But you still moved for her?"

Greta shrugged. "I could work remotely full-time; she couldn't. What I did know was that I could see a future with her like I hadn't with any other girl. I didn't know if that future would happen, but I couldn't have lived with not trying."

Maybe it was the cabernet clouding my head, but I couldn't shake the image of Will's face. Aditya and his list of factual barriers had never seemed farther away. Will *was* the kind of guy I could see myself ending up with. Despite our conversation at the dog park, was it possible we could still give things a shot?

We sipped in a comfortable silence for a moment. And then I made my decision.

I couldn't have lived without trying.

I pulled my phone out and typed without thinking.

> *Hey, Happy Thanksgiving. I've been thinking about you a lot recently. I know things are complicated, but would you want to meet up next time you're in Nashville? I'd like to give us a shot. If you're interested.*

My entire body tingled with anticipation, adrenaline pumping through my veins like I was awaiting a jury's final decision. Certainty rolled over me; at least I'd acted. Whatever Will's answer, it would bring clarity.

"How's your guy?"

I froze. How the hell had she known I was texting Will? Maybe she was psychic. "What?" I coughed. "I don't—I don't have a guy. Right now."

Greta frowned. "Who was that dude you brought to our engagement party? Indian, I think? Pretty hot?"

"Oh, him." I relaxed back into the couch. "That's Aditya.

A friend from law school. He was helping me set up for the party."

"Came all the way to Atlanta? Damn. I need more friends like that." Greta snorted. "He's cool. I chatted with him for a bit. You should bring him to the wedding."

"Yeah, maybe." Normally I'd love to invite Aditya—he was a blast at parties, he held his alcohol impressively well, and he was a dance-battle master. But deep down I really wanted Will as my plus-one. I glanced at my phone: no response yet.

"Kali told me about your conversation at the race."

I forced my face to stay relaxed. "Oh yeah?"

"Yeah." Greta stared at the TV screen, where we'd pulled up a looped video of a crackling fireplace. It'd seemed silly at first, but it gave the dark basement a distinctly cozy feel. "That new content schedule? *Not* about it. And this whole competition . . . it's made Kali so stressed. I keep catching her checking the standings on the *Southern Bride* website."

Charming Bride, I corrected her mentally, but held my tongue.

"And you know what pisses me off the most?" Greta didn't wait for an answer. Her skin seemed to glow in the candle-light, her platinum hair shimmering in the darkness. "Kali's not stressed because *she* cares. She's stressed because her mom does. And she doesn't want to disappoint me. I told her Laraghai could use the publicity, and now she thinks it's all I care about."

I thought about Leighton's constant need to prove herself to Patricia. How her stresses about the competition were tinged with anxiety about my job offer. Kali wasn't wired like that. She wasn't as cutthroat as me or as softhearted as Leighton. "She's not usually such a people-pleaser."

"Exactly." Greta gazed moodily at the fire. "I don't know why she has such a blind spot here. I wish I hadn't said anything about publicity for the conservancy. If I hadn't, I still think I could get her to walk away—"

"Tell me more about Laraghai," I interrupted, seeing an opening. "Because I have a few ins at *SC*. Maybe we can get an article in without the competition."

Something ignited in Greta's eyes as she saw what I did: a way out. "All right. What if I told you the secret to getting American millennials to give a crap about wildlife conservation in East Africa?"

"Which is?"

"Social media. Which means a new kind of wildlife photography."

My phone vibrated. Will had sent only three words back:

I'd love that.

With triumph coursing through me, I leaned forward. "Tell me more."

13

December

Christmas was a magical time. It was when long-lost twins reunited, almost-divorced couples reconciled, and miserly old men discovered the true spirit of Christmas. There were Mariah Carey marathons, artfully wrapped presents, and delicious gingerbread treats. Anything could happen at Christmas.

Or at least that's what I was telling myself as I paced back and forth at the entrance to Cheekwood, a sprawling botanical garden twenty minutes outside of downtown Nashville. As I waited for my first official date with my longest-standing crush, anticipation filled my chest like helium, threatening to send me spiraling up toward the velvety night sky. Will and I had been texting nonstop since Thanksgiving, and I'd been looking forward to tonight so intensely it almost hurt. My friends had noticed, asking me (Leighton innocently, Aditya suspiciously) why I seemed so happy. "Holiday spirit," I'd explained.

I sensed his presence a split second before the tap on my shoulder. I turned.

"Hey, there." Grinning, Will pulled me in for a hug. "Aren't you a sight for sore eyes."

Melting into his chest, I let myself get lost in him for a few seconds. "I've missed you." I took a step backward for the sole purpose of drinking him in with a slow, exaggerated once-over. Will looked every inch the Christmas prince in dark jeans, a grey peacoat, and a red scarf that Leighton had given him last year for Christmas. "The scarf's a nice touch."

He grinned. "I figured since she gave it to me, she'd think twice about strangling me with it."

"Did you invite her along?" Alarm bells rang in my ears. "I didn't think we'd tell Leighton tonight—"

"Relax." Will squeezed my shoulder, which immediately glowed at the tactile memory. "I didn't invite her. But this place looks like peak influencer bait. Wanted to be prepared in case we ran into her."

He wasn't wrong. Cheekwood was a rolling flowered estate, usually featuring a local artist's sculpture installation tucked among the blooms. Every December, thousands of hanging lights were draped across the foliage to create a magical holiday experience. Along the main walkway, twelve-foot candy canes glowing with red and white lights towered over us. Leighton *did* shoot holiday content here every year. But she'd done it last weekend; I'd made sure of that.

"Ah, thinking two steps ahead. Makes me proud."

Will chuckled. "You must be rubbing off on me."

We wandered down the main walkway, hands dangling by our sides. I'd been here many times during the day: it was gorgeous then, but truly enchanted at night.

"I'm really glad you reached out, Liv."

My cheeks reddened, and not from the cold. "Me, too." I coughed. "I—I had to be honest with you. How I was feeling. I couldn't not give this a chance."

"So you felt it, too?" Will said earnestly. "Didn't that night in New York feel different to you? I still can't think of it as a first date. It was too—too natural."

My many awkward Tinder-derived first dates bore no resemblance to our Manhattan night. With Will, there was the familiarity of a shared childhood with the excitement of a first date: an intoxicating combination. "I agree. But if first-date vibes are what you want, I can do that," I teased. "Should I overshare about my exes? Ask awkward icebreaker questions?"

"Only if I can unload personal baggage and invite you to meet my parents way too fast."

"Deal." I laughed. "Although unloading personal baggage is basically all I did in New York."

Will grinned. "It was a joint effort. And I liked it, Liv. We already know each other. We can skip past all the superficial crap."

The path curved around a large glassy lake. Glowing red and green orbs drifted silently back and forth. "I always had a thing for you," I admitted. "Pretty much since I met you."

"Really? You were, like, seven."

"Well, back then liking you meant I wanted you to play the Prince Charming doll instead of Leighton."

"Hey, don't pigeonhole me. I play a great Ken doll, too."

"Of course. Wait." I nudged his shoulder. "Does this mean you didn't like me when we were kids?" The thought was strangely off-putting. Was I over-romanticizing our shared history?

He glanced down at me and grinned. "Liv, I was eight. All I cared about was Xbox and basketball. Girls had cooties back then, remember?" His gaze traveled to the glittering spheres on the lake. "Of course, once I started noticing girls, I noticed you. But you were Leighton's friend."

"So was Lila," I countered.

He shrugged. "She made a move on me. The hormones made me think I was in love. I made a stupid grad school decision, but things worked out in the end."

He framed his past like the plot of a Lifetime movie, with a predictable storyline and the unspoken assurance that everything would be wrapped up in a neat, shiny bow.

"And after that," Will added, "Leighton made me promise to stay away from her friends. Seemed like an easy one to keep, after what happened the first time."

I bumped him playfully. "St. Louis isn't all that great, anyway. Wash U wasn't for you."

"Did you know, when they built the Arch, they predicted thirteen people would die?"

"Who predicted?"

"The insurance people. It was included in their project analysis. Construction is dangerous."

"And they still went ahead with it?"

"Had to put St. Louis on the tourism map somehow, didn't they?" Will grinned at me. "Ask me how many people actually died."

I deliberated. Mom and Charlotte had undertaken an impressive number of home renovation projects over the years, and a constant theme seemed to be contractors underestimating project cost and duration. "Twenty-seven."

"Zero."

"Wow. They really got lucky, didn't they?"

"Mhmm. Learned that when I visited for my PT school interview."

"Must be a hit at cocktail parties."

"Mostly I save it for first dates."

"How's that been working for you?"

He held my gaze, his eyes playful. "You tell me."

The backs of our hands brushed. My insides ached with longing; I wanted to grab his hand so badly. I wanted to *kiss* him so badly. But as well as (I thought) this was going, I'd made the first move by asking him here. There was so much at stake. I needed him to reciprocate.

We were nearly halfway around the lake. The path was quieter now, our way lit by a tunnel of bistro lights that stretched a hundred yards ahead of us.

"How's work?"

"Going well," Will said, as I'd known he would. Will could never be trusted to give a fully negative review about anything. I'd learned that lesson the hard way, when he'd warned me a terrifying horror movie "wasn't really that bad," and that the Tough Mudder race he'd convinced Leighton and me to run in high school "wasn't that intense, actually."

"I'm finally out of the probationary period, which makes things less stressful. The patients are really sick, unlike the ones I worked with in Nashville. Or the ones I saw in school."

"Sick how?"

"At my last job, I helped schoolgirls recover from sprained ankles." Will rolled his eyes in a self-deprecating way. "My Titans job had been better—players were generally recovering from major injuries. But at Duke, I'm working with rehab patients who've spent time in the ICU. So they're really deconditioned, and it's a much longer road to recovery."

"Do you like it?"

He considered. "More than the prep school. And I'm learning a lot, instead of coasting. But it's not what I envisioned when I signed up for PT school. I chose PT because I liked working with injured athletes. I could relate. That had been me. And that's an easy patient population."

"Easy?"

"Young, healthy. They bounce back fast. And they're highly motivated—they'll do whatever you tell them, if it'll help them get back on the field."

"And that's not the case for the post-ICU patients?"

Will tilted his head from side to side like he was trying to be fair. "There's a different type of motivation. They want their lives back. Their independence. Their dignity. It's less flashy, but it's . . . deeper. I never would've chosen this sort of work, but . . ." He shrugged. "It's very meaningful. At the same time, I can already tell I don't want to do it long-term. But it's a good change for now."

"Sounds like you're already thinking about what's next."

Will shoved both hands deep into his coat pockets. "I'll probably need to stay there for a year. Durham is cool, don't get me wrong. But it's a sleepy college town. I think a year is enough. I might have a lead on getting back into pro sports."

"Yeah?" There was a hint of suppressed excitement in his voice, so I phrased my question delicately. "Do you think you'll have any of the same . . . issues . . . you had working with the Titans players?"

"You mean the immature jealousy and resentment?"

I matched his light tone. "In your own words, yes."

We were drifting toward the end of the glowing tunnel. Ahead of us, the path meandered through glistening fir trees dripping with lighted icicles.

"Seeing the aftermath of *true* misfortune—strokes, open-heart surgery, sepsis—helped me keep things more in perspective." Will tapped his left knee, where I knew his old ACL surgical scar stretched nearly three inches long. The injury that had ended his basketball dreams and changed the course of his life. "My favorite part about PT was working with top athletes, being on the cutting edge of sports rehabilitation. Throwing that away because I felt the universe had stolen something I was owed as a kid? That's dumb, even for me." He chuckled self-consciously. "Wow, I sound like a real asshole, don't I? Took working with post-ICU patients for me to stop being petty about a decade-old injury."

"I think it sounds like growth," I said honestly. "Perspective takes time to develop. And I think it's awesome you've been trying different PT specialties and being honest with yourself about what brings you fulfillment."

"Thanks, Liv." Will reached for my right hand and squeezed it softly. And then kept holding it.

As my heart accelerated to dangerous speeds, I tilted my head up to gaze at the stars. We walked in silence for a few minutes before Will spoke again.

"What about you, Liv? Is Big Law really going to bring you fulfillment?"

"Hey, now." I nudged him with my shoulder, able to reach only as high as his mid-chest. "Why'd you slip that 'really' in there?"

"Because you've never given serious thought to anything except Big Law," he said easily. "You said so yourself in New York."

He'd caught me off guard. I was still figuring out how to answer when he went on. "From what you've told me, it sounds like you've never *let* yourself consider anything else. Not after your mom died. I know it's what your dad wants, but there are other paths. Even within law."

"There's a lot I like about Big Law," I said slowly, considering each word. "I like working on the biggest cases, for the highest-profile clients. I like the fast-paced environment. And yeah, I do like the idea of following in my dad's footsteps."

"And you like all that enough to outweigh the downsides?" Halfway through a lighted grotto, the shadows concealed Will's face. "The hierarchy, the insane hours, the administrative bullshit?"

A tiny part of me regretted being so honest with him in the third Manhattan bar. When I'd confessed the flaws in the aspirational career I'd built up in my head for years—flaws I could no longer ignore. That was how Will got through to me. His gentle, consistent questioning had cracked the lock on a vault of doubts I'd kept hidden from everyone. Including myself.

I must've been scowling, because he glanced at me and quickly backpedaled. "Take it from me. Sometimes you can be happy doing something totally unexpected. Or at least learn from it. There's nothing wrong with a few detours. Or seeing where life takes you."

"Seeing where life takes you is not exactly my speed," I muttered.

Will studied me, a half-smile playing on his lips. "I know. It's one of the things I like about you." He tugged me toward a refreshments hut decorated like a giant present. "Should we get some spiked hot cocoa?"

"Obviously."

After we'd acquired two cocoas and a s'mores-making kit, we settled at a firepit nestled in a large clearing. Plaid blankets were spread across the ground, and toasting sticks had been left next to the cheerful flames. We settled into our task. As much as my mouth watered in anticipation of gooey s'mores, my mind was already mourning the loss of Will's hand in mine. So far, the vibe between us tonight felt just like Manhattan—familiar yet thrilling, comfortable yet unpredictable. The hand-holding had been a good sign. But I needed certainty. I needed to know where we stood.

"I'm really glad you agreed to meet up with me again," I began, tucking my free hand underneath my thigh. My marshmallow was browning nicely on one side but was pasty white on the other. "I still feel weird with Leighton not knowing, though."

Will kept his eyes on the flames. "Agreed on both counts."

"I don't think we should tell her about a one-night stand. That's the sort of thing we could bury and never speak of again. The only reason to have that conversation with Leighton"—I summoned all my courage—"is if we actually want to pursue something serious."

"Do you want to pursue something?" Will asked. There was a smile in his voice. I glanced up to see his eyes crinkled in amusement, the corners of his mouth pulling upward.

"You are not making this easy for me."

"You're the smoothest talker I know. I like seeing you off balance once in a while." Will laughed at the expression on my face. "Of course I want to pursue this, Liv. Why do you think I reached out so much this fall? And was so eager to see you again tonight?"

The air between us crackled with promise. "To have this conversation?" I said hopefully.

"No. To do this."

His hand found the back of my neck and pulled my face toward his. I'd replayed our Manhattan kisses over and over in my head, but today his lips were both softer and stronger, his mouth moving with mine in a way that felt oh-so-right. Vaguely I was aware of both our toasting sticks clattering to the ground, forgotten. His other hand ran through my hair. My legs swung over his lap, and I curled into his chest. I was in heaven. I was kissing my childhood crush in front of a roaring fire. It was practically the same thing.

After several blissful moments, I pulled away. There was still so much we needed to discuss. I forced myself to think rationally, to voice the concerns that had been worrying me for weeks. "You really think this could work? Even with Leighton? Even long-distance?"

He considered. "I've never done long-distance, but I feel strongly about you, Liv. And I've really liked having you more in my life these last few months. If that's what a long-distance relationship feels like, I'm a happy guy."

A warm, tingly feeling spread over me, totally distinct from the fire's heat. Will wanted a relationship. With me. The elation made me feel light as air, like a balloon that would soar up to the heavens if released. Scuba girl must've been a vacation fling, but now he was ready to commit, even long-distance. I already felt high, high on life and love and Will. And definitely not thinking straight. I dug my heels into the ground, like I could tether myself to prevent gliding upward by mistake.

"That doesn't bother you?" I pressed. I envied his simple confidence, his ability to leap into the unknown without a second thought. "Never having done it before? Not knowing how—"

"How it'll work out?" Will picked up his stick and attached a fresh marshmallow. I waited anxiously for him to finish. "You can't control everything in life, Liv. Doesn't mean you shouldn't take some risks."

"But this means . . . we need to tell Leighton." The happy fireworks exploding inside me dampened immediately, like an unexpected downpour had opened in the skies. But then I remembered my original plan. How I could take the wind out of Leighton's fury and betrayal. "Luckily, I do have some good news to tell her."

"I'm all ears."

As we gathered fresh toasting sticks and popped new marshmallows over the flames, I caught him up on how everything had snowballed into the Charming Bride social media phenomenon. "I just got back from Atlanta, and I made some real progress. On all fronts."

"On all fronts?" Will raised an eyebrow. "What is this, a war?"

"Sort of!" I extracted my perfectly browned marshmallow and plopped it onto a graham cracker. "I yelled at Charlotte and warned her to back off. And then I spent the drive home brainstorming ways to keep Leighton in the lead."

"Such as?"

Excitement swelled over me. I'd been working so hard, and I relished the chance to finally tell someone about it. Like how cartoon villains indulged in self-promotional monologuing after capturing the pesky hero. Except I wasn't the villain here. Charlotte was. "I got so creative," I gushed. "First, I spent forever tracking down Kali's day-of wedding coordinator. Because those coordinators are crucial. And if I got rid of her, Charlotte would have to spend ages finding a new one."

"Got rid of . . . ? What'd you do, take out a hit?"

"Would've been simpler," I admitted, sliding a fresh marshmallow onto my toasting stick. "I wanted to outbid Charlotte, but that was way out of my price range. So I went down an Instagram rabbit hole, figured out the planner's anniversary with her boyfriend, and got an old sorority sister to reach out with an insane deal for an elopement wedding—"

Will blinked. "You did *what?*"

"So now Kali's coordinator has canceled, since she's eloping on May twenty-first!" I explained. I'd spent so many hours concocting the scheme that I'd forgotten how insane it must seem. But it'd been a series of tiny decisions—if I scroll through her Insta I might find something; maybe I can convince her boyfriend to plan a conflicting event; isn't Tori from Tri-Delt now a luxury travel agent? And so on. Really, the plan had assembled itself. All from the comfort of my snuggly bed. The Internet was amazing.

Will nodded once. "So when you said 'keep Leighton in the lead' . . . you meant sabotaging your own cousin?"

My armpits prickled. "'Sabotage' is a little dramatic. It's not like I'm burning down her venue."

"*That's* where you draw the line?" There was a pang of something new in Will's voice. Something I didn't like.

"No, no. You don't understand," I said quickly. "I talked to Kali in Atlanta. And Greta. They're considering dropping out anyway, maybe eloping—"

"Dropping out because they want to? Or because you talked them into it?"

The honest answer was a bit of both. I really did think that they'd be happier without the society wedding, but they needed a few nudges to get there. "You don't understand," I said again. "It's complicated—"

Will set down his toasting stick. He'd been neglecting his latest marshmallow, a charred blob that now oozed black goo onto the ground between us. "I was gonna let this go, but now I think you should know. You know how Leighton's shower blew up on social media?"

Sour regret filled my mouth, erasing every trace of delicious s'more. "Let me guess—Tyler saw?"

"Yeah." A muscle jumped in Will's jaw. "He put two and two together and realized that 'favor' had been for Leighton. He was pissed."

"It was a *restaurant reservation*," I said, trying to inject some perspective. It wasn't like I'd sabotaged Tyler's wedding. Or given him poison ivy. Or slipped a vomit-inducing elixir into his drink. Those were things to get upset about. "It wasn't that big a deal—"

"It was the *lying*, Liv. The fact that you thought it was okay to ask me to do that. To put me in that position." There was real anger in his voice.

"So why'd you do it, then?" I challenged. "It's not like I forced you into anything."

His features crumpled in frustration. "I did it because I *liked you*, Olivia." I felt the sting even before I registered the past tense. "We had that amazing night together, and I hoped we'd maybe give things a shot. I didn't want to mess that up. I thought the lying was a one-off thing. But now? Hearing everything you're plotting? It's not a one-off. It's a pattern."

Heat rose in my cheeks. "That's not fair," I said, stung. "I made sure Charlotte would have time to find a replacement! I needed her distracted. So she couldn't mess with Leighton's events. You know what they say," I added desperately. "Offense is the best defense."

He stared at me for a long moment. Had I gotten the saying wrong? Sports had never been my thing. But his eyes hardened, and I could tell that wasn't the problem. Frustration welled inside me. How had things turned so wrong, so quickly?

"Have you ever thought," Will said at last, "that what you think is persuasive is really just manipulative?"

The word sliced through me like ice. *Manipulative.* Had he really called me that? Me, who'd been running myself ragged for months trying to keep everyone happy? Who'd let my schoolwork slip and kept my career in limbo to help my friends? "You don't know the whole story. I'm only—"

"I know enough," he said quietly. He stood and shoved both hands deep into his coat pockets, like he was trying to keep them as far away from me as possible. "Maybe this is for the best. Long-distance would've been hard. And now we don't have to tell Leighton anything." His hair shone brighter than ever in the firelight. "What's one more lie, right, Liv?"

And with that awful parting shot, Will Sawyer turned and strode off into the darkness, leaving me alone with a pile of burnt marshmallows, two half-drunk cocoas, and the gnawing uncertainty that there might've been a kernel of truth hidden inside all of that hurt.

⟶

In the wake of Will dumping me before we ever officially dated, I:

A. Consumed three pints of mint chocolate chip ice cream
B. Spent a whole day watching straight-to-Netflix rom-coms
C. Repeatedly googled "Why are physical therapists so judgmental?"

In said wake, I definitely did not:

A. Tell Leighton about sleeping with her brother
B. Cease-and-desist my interference with Kali's wedding events

To be fair, I also agonized over everything Will had said, second-guessing myself in a way I hardly ever did. Was he right? Was I manipulative, or was I getting everyone what they wanted?

Or was Will lashing out for other reasons? Maybe the indecision had been eating away at him, ever since the me/Aditya let's-not-do-this text. Add in the Tyler argument, coupled with the potential stress of telling Leighton, and it'd been the perfect storm. A perfect, horrible, fairy-tale-ruining storm. It'd been radio silence from him since Cheekwood, for two whole weeks.

Aditya considered all this. "Sounds like it got pretty ugly. Sorry you had to go through that, Liv."

We were lounging together on his couch, surrounded by the remnants of the Chinese takeout we'd already polished off. After spending the whole day in the library prepping for finals—where I should've been—Aditya had swung by, taken one look at me, and ordered an emergency pick-me-up on Grubhub. With the promise of such fortification, I had found the strength to leave my bed, walk thirty feet to Aditya's apartment, and collapse onto his couch instead.

"I put him in a bad position with Tyler," I admitted. "And I sort of expected Tyler to find out, since the shower would be all over social media."

"But you didn't warn Will?"

"No," I muttered. "I probably should've. But it's not like Leighton ever did anything to Tyler. If they had some real history, it'd be different. But it's a small, petty thing—"

Aditya rolled his head around and gave me his patented cut-the-crap look. "Liv. Stop trying to justify everything. It was shady of you to ask Will to do that, regardless of how dumb Tyler and Leighton's beef is. It was also pretty judgy of Will to blow up at you like that."

"So I'm not allowed to defend my position?" I demanded. Circe licked my ankle supportively, responding to the anger in my voice. "Because, if so, let me know now. I'm in the wrong career."

"That's not what I said." Aditya looked annoyed. "I told you before, the Will thing was never going to work out. I don't get why you even reached out to him."

"The Nature House shower was a mistake," I conceded, following my own train of thought. "And not because of the poison ivy. You're right. I shouldn't have asked Will to lie to Tyler. But maybe it's for the best." I plopped a half-eaten fortune cookie into my mouth and chewed morosely. "Leighton doesn't need any more stress right now."

"Exactly. And you don't need to let this Will thing drag on any longer," Aditya said. There was a strange ring to his voice. "You can move on, too."

"I think I'll swear off romance for a while." I stroked Circe's head. "I've got enough on my plate. And I'm moving to New York in a few months, anyway."

"You were ready to try long-distance with Will," Aditya countered. Whose side was he on? What were we even arguing over?

"Yeah, and you kept telling me how it'd never work."

"Maybe Will wasn't the right guy."

I glanced over at him, but he was staring into his wineglass. "What're you talking about? I've got no time for dating apps. And I doubt I'd meet anyone who'd be cool with an LDR in a brand-new relationship."

A beat of silence, and suddenly a sourness spread throughout me. *No,* I insisted, like I could force it not to be true. Emma's voice echoed in my ears: *Great eye candy . . . Let's have your boyfriend host the next Live, too.* Greta's surprise that a friend had flown out to help with party prep. *He had miles,* I argued back, but then Kali's voice came next: *I don't think Delta miles expire . . . Aren't they known for that? . . .* Aditya sending that text to Will, always arguing against pursuing him . . .

"You never know," Aditya said quietly. He met my gaze, and there was the chance of something different behind his eyes. A complication I couldn't deal with right now.

So I didn't. "Too late, I've already sworn off men," I said in a jokey tone. "Anyway. It's for the best. Leighton's my priority."

"That's the spirit," Aditya said, forcing lightness into his own voice. "Keep that in mind when you're dreaming up new schemes."

"You make me sound like a villain," I grumbled. "Who says 'schemes,' anyway?" I set down my wine and stretched. "I've got some more wedding planning to do. Thanks for the vent."

"Off to your lair?" Aditya called after me as I padded back toward my apartment. To my relief, his voice sounded normal again. Maybe I'd imagined the subtext. "Shall I alert your henchmen? New plots in progress?"

"I'm one of the good guys," I threw back.

"Yeah, yeah. That's what they all say."

December and January passed in a blur—a coffee-infused, sleep-deprived, existential-crisis-driven hurricane of action. I divided my time among assisting Leighton with wedding tasks, pretending to law professors that I still cared about my grades, sending Kali possible elopement packages, and implementing benign acts of sabotage for Kali and Greta's wedding.

Frederic the *Southern Charm* photographer and a new writer were deployed to cover Kali and Greta's December cake-tasting, where I'd arranged for the worst possible pairings: orange-flavored cake with peanut-butter icing, and rosemary-infused cake topped with marshmallow ganache. Frederic had raised an eyebrow but snapped photos obediently, while the *SC* writer valiantly attempted to write halfway flattering descriptions.

A few weeks after the New Year, Frederic and Emma accompanied Leighton and me to design Leighton's floral bouquets. Determined to avoid any disruptions, I'd called the very confused florist daily for weeks to ensure that nothing was canceled. I'd also made backup appointments with two other florists *and* arrived early to personally inspect every single bloom. The afternoon went off flawlessly.

Although that might've had something to do with the offensive strategy I'd developed. I'd realized that to keep Charlotte away from Leighton, I needed to:

A. Create minor chaos that sucked up as much of my aunt's time as possible
B. Ensure that nothing Kali or Greta cared about was disrupted
C. Maintain plausible deniability so that Charlotte couldn't pin anything on me

A tall order, to be sure. But after Will had closed the door on us for good (*Stop that, Olivia, put it out of your head*), I devoted most of my free time to this noble pursuit. After the cake-tasting, I called Kali's wedding venue and explained that the stressed mother of the bride wanted to begin weekly meetings to review logistics. I reached out to the stationery store that'd done Kali and Greta's save-the-dates and requested a specific indigo ink for the wedding invitations. Then I tracked down their invitation calligrapher and hired her to do the signage for our upcoming Law Ball, delaying her delivery times by several weeks.

But I got the most mileage out of a lucky instinct back in November. When raiding Charlotte's kitchen for a late-night snack, I'd noticed a Post-it stuck to the side of the fridge with a Santorini magnet. Quick snooping revealed a list of Charlotte's passwords, including her Gmail. Half asleep, I'd snapped a photo on my phone and promptly forgot about it until a boring seminar in late January. Within ten minutes I'd logged in to Charlotte's Gmail. Within twenty, I'd emailed thirteen wedding vendors to request real-time updates. "No question too small," I typed cheerfully. "Happy to give feedback on every detail."

When I checked later after my Torts seminar, Charlotte had already received five responses. The florist recommended expanding the bridesmaid bouquet radius from twelve to fourteen inches and had attached an updated proposal. The band had requested her input on the included song list and the proper set order. Even the linens rental had reached out to invite Charlotte to their storeroom to feel the softness of her selection in person.

"Bingo," I whispered happily. Then I wiped the sent emails from her account. I knew my aunt; she was a control freak, and she wouldn't be able to resist following up on all these new minutiae. Offense really *was* the best defense.

Despite my increasingly puffy eyes, my confidence rose as January melted into February. Emma was pleased with the coverage of the cake-tasting and flower-arranging events, and *Southern Charm*'s social media engagement continued to climb. I'd used this goodwill to strategically float the idea of featuring Greta in *SC*'s July philanthropy issue, which Emma had agreed to consider. Multiple party-planning services had contacted me offering to coordinate the upcoming bachelorette parties, enticed by the promise of free publicity on *SC*'s social media accounts. I was happy for the help; I was being stretched tighter than ever in the lead-up to the bachelorettes.

Even Holmes & Reese had given me reason to feel cautiously optimistic. My fall grades, while not spectacular, had met their minimum. With every pre-employment hurdle I cleared, it'd be harder for Hank to raise any red flags. Holmes & Reese needed to fill their first-year associate class; as the academic year wore on, it'd be increasingly challenging to find a talented replacement. And Kali had already received a considerable amount of media coverage. Which would hopefully temper Charlotte's wrath if Leighton won the cover.

When Valentine's Day rolled around, I spent the evening drinking rosé and rewatching Katherine Heigl classics. Aditya had offered to keep me company—a big favor, since he hated rom-coms—but a V-Day hangout felt like unstable territory for us. He'd been acting normal since that one weird conversation, and I'd matched his approach, doing my best not to think about the awkward uncertainty of his exact feelings for me.

So instead I watched *27 Dresses* and *The Ugly Truth*, ignoring the ugly truths in my own life. The echo of what Will and I could've been hung over me, but I fended off the regret with a third glass of wine. When I'd texted him to apologize again for the Tyler thing, he'd responded with a terse *Thanks*.

But maybe it had been too good to be true for everything to work out. Maybe losing Will was the price for keeping the rest of the balls I was jugging aloft. "Breakup" seemed a strong word for two people who'd never officially dated—and had spent only one night together—but my childhood history with Will made the loss much more painful. Maybe I would've felt differently if I'd made a noble choice to let Will go, to put aside my feelings for the sake of my friendships and my career. But I hadn't. I hadn't walked away from him; he'd walked away from me.

And I still didn't like being told I couldn't do something. Couldn't pull something off. But Will had made his viewpoint clear. I'd texted him once more, to ask to meet up and talk. Just to torture myself, I pulled out my phone and read his response again: *Are you still manipulating your friends?* I hadn't known how to answer.

Olivia Fitzgerald, at a loss for words? That was a new feeling. But Will wasn't interested in hearing my point of view. As much as I enjoyed the thrill of debate, I also knew a lost cause when I saw one. My target needed a sliver of an open mind for my persuasive tricks to work. And Will? Will wasn't interested.

And that, I told myself, was that.

14

February

When Kali and Greta had first decided on a "mountain retreat" for their bachelorette, I'd have been lying if I said I was thrilled. As I stepped out of my car and watched my breath puff out into a cold cloud, I shook a metaphorical fist at the sky. The various freebies we'd been offered flashed through my head, all from companies eager to be featured in a weekend of live *Southern Charm* content. We could've been in Miami! New Orleans! Vegas! Puerto Vallarta!

"Mexico," I mumbled covetously.

"What was that?" Kali appeared around the side of the car, cheeks pink from the cold.

"Nothing." I glanced up at the wooden cabin we'd booked deep in the Smoky Mountains and tried to convince myself this would be fun. Okay, so I was bundled up in leggings, boots, and a parka, and there was an unfortunate amount of hiking in my near future. But from the photos online, the two-story cabin had a fantastic view of rolling Tennessee mountains and an in-deck hot tub big enough for all six of us. Emma had warned me to keep the vibes of the bachelorette parties as distinct as possible. Until now, *SC* had made a conscious choice to cover different events for each wedding—engagement party, bridal shower, cake tasting, and floral arrangements. Some lower-key events had also been posted to *SC*'s Instagram—Leighton giving a sneak peak of her bridesmaid designs, Kali hinting about her honeymoon destination—and there had been absolutely no repeats. But soon readers would be directly comparing the two brides' bachelorettes.

"Not to put any pressure on you," Emma had said to me yesterday, "but everyone is psyched for the bach weekends. You know *Bridal Today* hasn't even started live coverage like this?" Then she'd lowered her voice. "And if there were to be any drama, no one would be too mad, hmm?"

I tugged my woolen hat down around my ears like I was adjusting my helmet before battle. Emma had issued my marching orders: deliver a weekend full of interesting, engaging content for *SC*'s online audience. But this was also my last Kali event. My last chance to ensure her wedding wasn't chosen for the cover. For once, my job seemed simple. *SC* readers had been sending in suggestions for months: New Orleans! Vegas! Scottsdale! Readers wanted trendy restaurants, glamorous pool parties, and exclusive nightclubs. Preferably with lots of penis decorations.

But my cousin and her fiancée? That wasn't their style. And there wouldn't be a penis in sight. Their bachelorette weekend was in serious danger of being *b-o-r-i-n-g*. But boring was what Kali wanted. And as maid of honor, I served at the pleasure of the bride-to-be.

"This place is epic!" Greta popped out of the backseat and grinned at Kali. "Nice find, Liv."

She patted me on the shoulder as she followed Kali inside. I blinked in surprise: My first compliment from Greta. It'd taken only six months. Baby steps.

Another car rolled up, and three of Greta and Kali's mutual friends piled out: Mila, Bella, and Polly. I'd met them briefly on a previous Atlanta trip and had retained one fact about each of them: Mila worked at a dog shelter; Bella was huge into vegan cooking; and Polly had a streak of purple hair.

"The brides are inside!" I announced. I reached into the trunk and pulled out a giant bag of decorations, which I handed to Mila and Bella. Polly received the cooler of spiked seltzers. "Polly, you distract them. Mila and Bella, get decorating!"

"Aye, aye, Cap'n," said Bella, saluting. She and Mila hurried inside.

Briefly I reviewed the weekend's itinerary in my head. Tonight we'd hang out at the cabin, soak in the hot tub, and play icebreaker games. Tomorrow we'd tour the Smoky Mountains' best waterfalls. We'd have dinner at a local restaurant before hitting a few low-key neighborhood bars. On Sunday we'd planned one more hike, followed by lunch at a brewery before driving back to Nashville. Overall, it was low-key, low-stress, and exactly what Kali and Greta had asked for.

It was true that I could've planned more, especially with

the added publicity of *SC*. Emma must've passed along my info to local companies, because I'd received offers for a free helicopter ride of the Smokies, a heavily discounted brewery tour, and a private tasting menu at the local steakhouse. A posh spa retreat had even offered to comp us a full day of treatments (in exchange for live coverage on *SC*'s Instagram). All of which had the potential to greatly improve *SC* readers' assessment of the bachelorette party.

And maybe how much Kali and Greta enjoy it, said a tiny voice in my head. *You didn't even ask.*

The bachelorette was supposed to be a surprise for the bride(s), I argued back. They'd asked for hiking, breweries, and nothing over-the-top. I had delivered. End of story.

"Hey, Olivia." Polly shifted the cooler onto her other hip and tucked a lock of lavender hair behind her ear. "Quick question. Did you get this message, too?"

She held out her phone, and I saw an Instagram DM from Mountainside, the spa retreat, again offering complimentary treatments.

"How'd they know you were coming to the bachelorette?" I said without thinking.

Polly gave me a strange look. *Whoops.* That's definitely not the first thing a totally innocent, non-scheming person would've said. "I think Kali did an Instagram Live this week? And someone asked who was coming? I got a bunch of new follower requests right after."

"Gotcha." I put on my best relaxed smile. "Thanks for showing me—yeah, they reached out to me, too! But it wasn't really the vibe that Kali and Greta wanted."

Polly looked doubtful. She swiped to a photo gallery of Mountainside's gorgeous infinity pool, which swung out in a graceful arc over miles of forested mountain. "Are you sure? Because this would be epic for a post-hike soak, and they said they can work us in—"

"I'm sure," I said firmly. "But thanks for showing me! I'll let them know we're not interested."

As Polly walked into the house, laden with seltzers and a distinct air of disappointment, I pulled out my phone and paused before sending a firm decline to Mountainside's Instagram account. A post-hike soak did sound nice, but Kali and Greta wanted the weekend to stay low-key. And if it kept their bachelorette from being must-watch content for *Southern Charm* followers, that was an added bonus.

Speaking of, I'd been neglecting my duties. I started a new Instagram Live on the *SC* account. "Hey, guys!" I said brightly. "Olivia here, checking in to kick off Kali and Greta's joint bachelorette. We've just arrived at our awesome Airbnb." I turned and panned the camera over the cabin behind me. "Hope you guys are excited to follow along!"

A few comments popped up on the bottom of the video:

Damn was hoping they'd go to Vegas

Cabin bachelorette? Really?

Hope Leighton does something better . . .

Things were going according to plan. If law school had taught me anything, it was that it was way harder to identify sins of *omission*—something you should've done but didn't—versus sins of *commission*—bad things you actually did. I could've pushed the envelope on this weekend a little more. But instead I'd done exactly what Kali and Greta requested: lots of wilderness, no flashy clubs, and no fancy restaurants. And no one could get mad at me for that.

—

"And that was our fourth and final waterfall," I panted, tucking a sweaty lock of hair behind my ear. "Vote for your favorite in the comments! Who's planning a visit to the Smokies?"

Greta plucked the phone out of my hand. "Okay, I'm cutting you off. You've almost tripped five times filming this thing."

"I have not!" Traitorously, my ankle immediately caught on a tree root, causing me to half stumble into Greta.

She grabbed my shoulders and righted me with a raised eyebrow. "Make that six."

"Not everyone has been blessed by the hiking gods," I muttered, as she leapt over a fallen log and rejoined Kali at the head of our little line. Dressed in matching camouflage leggings and black down jackets, Kali and Greta looked like twin huntresses, totally at ease on the terrain of the Smokies. They moved effortlessly up the steep trail, whereas I kept my gaze trained firmly on the path to avoid constant stumbles. Even more annoyingly, they looked happy to be out here in the wilderness. I thought back to Kali's unbridled joy during the Turkey Trot. Maybe we really weren't related.

"Don't feel too bad," Mila said from behind me. "They're total pros. You know Greta almost did the Appalachian Trail this year?"

"Doesn't that take months?"

"Three to four, usually," Greta called back from up the trail. "I was aiming for fourteen weeks. But then Kali proposed, so I pushed the trail back a year. I'll head out around this time next February."

I spent the next ten minutes brainstorming the many ways I'd rather spend fourteen weeks of my life. It was a long list, so I switched to things I *wouldn't* choose over the Appalachian Trail. Maybe hiking Mount Everest? Or trekking across Antarctica?

After breaking through the tree line, we were rewarded with a glorious view of the snowcapped trees around us. It was gorgeous, but the novelty wore off fast. How did someone choose to do this for months? To wake up every morning and walk in the woods? Lost in thought, I stepped awkwardly onto a misshapen rock and lost my balance.

"Ahhh!" As I toppled over a small ridge, my throat emitted an embarrassing sound between a shriek and a yelp. I landed hard on the ground with the wind knocked out of me. "Oof."

"Olivia! *Liv!*"

The other girls scrambled down to me, where I'd landed halfway into a large, prickly bush. Greta reached me first, her eyes scanning me for damage. "Anything hurt?"

Kali was right on Greta's heels. I was touched to see no laughter in her eyes, only concern. I'd fallen all of seven feet, but they were taking me seriously. "You okay?"

"Only thing bruised is my ego," I said suavely, grabbing Kali's outstretched hand to swing myself up. That was the intention. In reality, I crumpled the second I put weight on my left ankle.

"Woah," I said intelligently.

"Maybe not the only thing." Greta crouched down and rotated my left foot.

"Ow!"

"Greta's trained in wilderness first aid," Kali explained. *Of course she is.*

"You probably strained a tendon." Greta glanced up at me. "Do you think you can bear any weight at all?"

She and Kali helped me up onto my right leg. Tentatively I lowered my left foot. My ankle throbbed angrily upon contact with the ground. "Umm, not much?" From the trail above, the other girls peered down nervously. I was relieved no one had thought to film this for *Southern Charm*. One of Leighton's bridesmaids definitely would've. Maybe there was something to this escape-from-the-world thing, after all.

Greta produced an ACE bandage from thin air and gently removed my sneaker. While she wrapped my ankle, Kali pulled out her phone and made a face. "No service." Maybe I'd spoken too soon on the being-out-in-the-middle-of-nowhere-was-a-positive thing.

"How're we gonna get help?" I asked, fighting to keep the panic out of my voice. I stared wildly around, searching for a clearing. We'd hiked for nearly an hour to get to this ridge, and we still hadn't reached the summit. "Can a helicopter even land out here?"

Greta and Kali exchanged an amused look. "Liv, you were tripped by a tree root, not mauled by a bear," Kali said kindly. "We don't need a helicopter."

"The ACE wrap will help," Greta promised. "I'll stay with you, and we'll start the walk out, with me supporting some of your weight."

Kali nodded. "We'll all go slow, no worries."

"No, no," Greta and I said together. My motivations were selfish (it'd be embarrassing for the whole group to witness me hobbling), but Greta's were purer. "I've hiked this peak before; you guys haven't seen it yet. You should finish. Catch up with me and Olivia on your way out."

Kali hesitated. "You sure?" She turned to me. "Liv, is that okay with you?"

"Absolutely." I turned my left ankle back and forth experimentally. The tightness of the bandage was reassuring. "You'll catch us on the way out. But promise me you'll take some pictures at the summit for *SC*!"

My cousin rolled her eyes but nodded in agreement. After Kali and Greta helped me clamber back to the trail, Kali disappeared up the ridge with her friends in tow. Greta found me a large stick to use for balance as I adjusted to my unsteady left ankle, and soon I was able to walk slowly without leaning on her too much. We began the long, plodding downhill.

"You really are single-minded, aren't you?"

"What?" I glanced up and she had to throw out an arm to steady me.

"Eyes on the ground," she ordered. Then, softer: "You've just had a nasty sprain, and the first thing you're thinking about is photos for the magazine."

"My first thought was cursing you two for wanting to hike on your bachelorette party," I admitted.

She snorted. "I bet."

We walked in silence for a few more minutes before she spoke again. "I'm glad Kali has you to make the big wedding less . . . shitty. To make sure some of it is what she wants. Like this weekend."

I snuck a peek sideways. "Have y'all given eloping any more consideration since Thanksgiving?"

"I know you guys have been discussing it." Greta sounded thoughtful. I wondered if she knew what an understatement that was; I'd been walking a fine line between encouraging and hounding Kali to consider a last-minute elopement. "And we talked about your idea to get Laraghai in the philanthropy issue."

My heart rate sped up even faster than when I'd tumbled through the Smoky Mountains underbrush (priorities). "Yeah?"

"But then I saw some of the DMs she's been getting. And Emma forwarded us a few reader emails."

"DMs?" I frowned; this was the first I was hearing of any of this.

Greta paused to help me over a large log. "It's been different for me," she said, almost to herself. "I grew up in Cape Town, one of the most LGTBQ-friendly places in all of Africa. My family was progressive. Being gay wasn't a big deal at all, not to them. I don't even remember 'coming out' to my parents. We all just knew. Isn't that crazy?" She whistled once. "Every coming-of-age story about an LGBTQ kid has some big dramatic scene when they come out to their parents. Either it goes amazing or it goes horrible, no in-between. For me, it was way easier. For Kali, not so much. For a lot of girls in the South, not so much. Even now. Kali being the first queer bride covered by *Southern Charm*?"

"It must mean a lot to them."

"She's been getting messages every week. From girls as young as ten or eleven. Saying they're rooting for her, how cool it'd be for a girl who *likes girls* to be chosen as the ultimate Southern bride. And you know what?" A genuine smile broke across Greta's usually composed features. She looked younger than I'd ever seen her. Less guarded. "She's replied to every single one. It's awesome to think that our wedding being picked for some stupid magazine cover could mean so much."

"It is," I agreed, trying to digest my own reactions. A sense of pride in my cousin. Empathy for all the Southern women who didn't fit the traditional young Christian mold that was so prized, especially once you'd gotten a few whiskeys into the older generations. And something else—consternation. Rationalizing my approach to the Charming Bride competition was easier when there weren't any upsides to Kali winning. Except there were. "But also—even more pressure?"

"Exactly." Greta sighed. "This pressure to be a role model— it's awesome, and it means a lot to me and Kali. But it's also not something we signed up for, you know? First Kali was doing this for her mom, and then she said it was for me and Laraghai, and now she doesn't think she can walk away from the chance at real LGBTQ representation in Southern media. Sometimes I want to shake her and say: *But it's our wedding!* It's okay to not want so much extra external pressure on the event. It's okay to focus on what we want. Not everyone else."

"That's a lot of other people to keep in mind." I felt a pang of empathy for Kali. In some ways, we were facing similarly difficult decisions: a lot of competing priorities, and a dwindling amount of time to figure out the best way forward. "I didn't realize—"

Greta flashed me a wry smile. "She keeps it locked away. You gotta know what you're looking for. Probably like you, hmm?"

That took me off guard. I peeked up at her, even though another tree root would probably take this chance to finish me off. "What do you mean?"

"You like to be in control. You don't like showing weakness. I'm the same way. But I've started to understand how special weddings are. They have a way of opening up even the most locked-down people."

I waited a beat. "Where do you think Kali's head's at? On the magazine versus the elopement?"

The answer came faster than I was expecting. So fast that I wondered if Greta had been leading up to this all along. Had she orchestrated this intimate but seemingly spontaneous conversation? Did she suspect the motives driving my near-weekly calls with Kali, during which we looked over elopement vision boards and last-minute vacation packages "just in case"?

"She needs more time," Greta said firmly. "She wants her options open as long as possible. The more you can help with that, the better." She gestured vaguely at the woods around us. "Like getting us the best write-up possible for this weekend. And positioning Kali so that if she decides she wants the cover . . . it's there. And for all the girls looking up to her."

Recognizing the expertly laid guilt trip didn't stop it from working. Greta was tugging on my heartstrings as effectively as Taylor Swift's latest rereleased album. Because she wasn't bullshitting me. Kali on the *SC* cover meant her love story being highlighted by a cultural icon, one which had so far neglected anything outside of "traditional" heterosexual relationships. I'd known that in the abstract, but hearing the heartfelt messages from fans? That hit differently.

Very differently.

Later that night, I stood on the balcony of a local brewery doing three out-of-character things all at once: drinking beer, ignoring social media notifications, and second-guessing my decisions. After my conversation with Greta, I'd found myself looking at Kali differently all afternoon. Had she really written back to every girl who'd reached out to her? I knew my cousin; she didn't seek out the spotlight. Had she taken on this trailblazing role because she wanted it or because it was expected of her? How many expectations had this competition forced upon her?

More than anything, I wished that I could talk to Will. During those few months when we'd been texting regularly, I'd grown used to confiding in him. That had been one of the hardest parts of losing him. And things were off with Aditya—I wasn't as comfortable around him, not anymore.

"Penny for your thoughts?"

I turned. Kali was shrugging on one sleeve of her jacket, holding her other hand straight up to keep her beer steady. I rescued the jeopardized drink and set it on the balcony railing. "I've got a lot of thoughts. How many pennies you thinking?"

She dug in her pocket and pulled out a nickel. "What's this get me?"

"Not much. Inflation's a bitch."

She snorted and raised her glass in acknowledgment. I picked up my phone and snapped a quick photo of her in her white ski parka, polka-dot hat, and knee-high velvet boots. Under the soft fairy lights strung across the balcony, she looked like a wintertime angel.

"I'm so glad Emma didn't send any *SC* crew to the bachelorette," Kali said. "Would've totally killed the vibe. Which has been awesome, by the way. You did an amazing job."

That had been my idea. Emma had planned to dispatch a writer and photographer to join both Kali's and Leighton's bachelorette parties. But I'd pushed back. Everyone would want to unwind, not worry about performing for the cameras or being photographed from an unflattering angle. So I'd convinced Emma to allow DIY media coverage: self-recorded videos, amateur photos, and post-weekend interviews between the bridesmaids and the *SC* writer. It'd been a fight, but Emma had come around. And it'd been a nice change, using some of my old charm to help *both* Leighton and Kali. Instead of always being forced to choose.

"If only my ankle can pull it together," I joked, displaying the makeshift splint that Greta had whipped up back at the cabin. "For safety, my exercise should be limited to ellipticals. With no tree roots around."

"I'll keep that in mind when we're planning your bachelorette," Kali said, grinning. Warmth spread across my chest. A year ago, I never would've considered including Kali as one of my bridesmaids. Now I couldn't imagine going through a major life event without her.

"It's a deal."

We sipped our beers in silence.

"Fifty-fifty," Kali said.

"What?"

"Fifty-fifty. That's how I feel about going through with this whole thing."

"The wedding?"

"The big society wedding. The magazine." She kept her gaze on the moonlit hills in front of us. "I know we're coming down to the wire. But every day I wake up and have a different opinion."

Her wedding was three months away. If it were anyone else, I'd have long given up any chance of an elopement. But

Kali had always done what she wanted to do. She flouted expectations with the carefree nature of someone who barely registered their existence. A week ago, I'd have been thrilled that Kali was contemplating walking away. But things were more complicated now. Sensing her need to vent, I kept quiet as she went on.

"If we didn't go through with it . . . I don't even want to think about all the money we'd lose. Mom would be furious. But she's already gotten more than she thought—the Charming Bride thing blew up more than any of us expected. She can't deny that," Kali added, almost to herself. "When I agreed to let her pitch me . . . I didn't think I'd mind not having control over my own wedding. But I resent it more than I thought I would."

Her voice held the same frustration that I felt deep in my soul: frustration from talking in circles, not knowing the right thing to do. I knew the feeling. Abstract decisions needed concrete tools; otherwise you'd spin your wheels for hours. I held up a finger. "One sec."

Five minutes later, I returned to the balcony with a fresh glass of beer and two empty glasses. "Okay. You've got way too much swirling around in your head. Let's settle this." I put the two empty glasses on the balcony. "Start talking about the pros and cons: elopement versus wedding."

"How is this going to—"

"Just trust me," I said patiently. A flash of déjà vu distracted me: Leighton, doubtfully closing her eyes when choosing a wedding dress. "Start with the pros."

"Okay." She was humoring me. "Elopement: it's what we'd always planned to do."

I poured half a shot's worth of beer into one of the glasses, the one with a sketch of the Smoky Mountains engraved on the side. "Keep going."

"No regrets about letting other people dictate our wedding." Another pour. "Truer to what me and Greta want." A third. "The chance to have a badass scuba wedding."

I finished the fourth and waited. "Okay, now the pros for the wedding."

"It'd make my mom happy."

I poured a smaller pour into the second glass, the one with a black bear emblazoned on the side. "That one gets half points."

"We've already put so much time and effort into planning." Another half-pour. Kali sighed. "Me being the *SC* bride would mean a lot to a lot of people in the South."

I gave that one a generous pour, which brought the level in the wedding glass within striking distance of the elopement glass. "Greta mentioned that. Said you've been getting a lot of DMs from readers?"

"Thirty-two," Kali admitted. "One high-schooler messaged that she used my *Southern Charm* article to convince her old-school parents to let her ask her girlfriend to prom. A woman ten years older than me told me she'd been nervous to hold a big wedding in her small Georgia town, but the coverage gave her the confidence to go ahead. It's crazy. I never expected any of this. It's the twenty-first century, for God's sake. But just because homophobia's now socially uncool doesn't mean it's not still rampant behind closed doors. Especially Southern ones."

"A place where cultural influences like *Southern Charm* still carry a lot of weight," I said quietly.

"Doesn't it sound silly? That a magazine cover—which really means social media content—matters this much?"

"Media is part of culture change," I countered. "All forms. You've got to reach people in multiple ways. And meet them where they're at. We need more than just *New York Times* write-ups of Supreme Court cases."

Kali raised an eyebrow. "You mean sandwiched between mascara ads and sex tips?"

I shrugged. "Hey, whatever works. Now, what about the cons?"

"Wedding: always wondering 'what if' about not doing what Greta and I wanted."

I tipped the black bear glass, emptying a few swallows of beer over the railing.

"And even if I see it through, there's no guarantee that I end up on the cover." Kali propped her chin in her hand. "That'd be the worst-case outcome: that I do all this, give up what *I'd* wanted for my wedding, and don't even get the media representation to make the sacrifice worth it."

"A definite risk," I agreed, spilling out an even more gen-erous amount. About a shot's worth of beer remained in the wedding glass. "Okay, now the elopement."

"My mom's pissed."

"I said con. Besides, you already used keeping Charlotte happy in the pros column for the wedding. No double-counting."

She snorted. "You have a lot of rules."

"It's a scientific process."

My cousin thought for a moment. Finally, she said, "The regret of walking away from the chance to make life better for some LGBTQ folks in the next generation. I didn't ask for this. But the chance still landed in my lap. I might regret walking away."

"You could make history," I teased.

She rolled her eyes. "It's a magazine cover. Let's not get carried away."

"But a meaningful one." I tipped the elopement glass and watched all the liquid pour downward into the darkness. Belatedly, I wondered if watering the bushes of eastern Tennessee with beer was an environmental harm. Beer was mostly water, right?

Kali's dark eyes stayed on the empty glass. "That's it? We've decided?" There was a palpable sense of relief in her voice.

"*You've* decided," I corrected. "I only poured beer out dramatically." I pushed the one-third-full black bear glass toward her. The one that represented her going ahead with the wedding. The one that meant me giving up control. I'd tried to be the mastermind for too long. As one of my law professors liked to say, *At the end of the day, you can prime the jury however you want. But you can't control what goes on in that room.*

Kali smiled. Relief hovered in the air between us—whether hers or mine, I couldn't tell. Some things *were* out of my control. I didn't know if Kali would win, or if Leighton would be upset that the competition went ahead as scheduled, or how Charlotte would react to the outcome. I'd spent six months balancing on a tightrope, and maybe it was time to let go. I lifted my beer and clinked it against hers. "Now, that's a decision to toast to."

My cousin smiled, drained the black bear glass, and gave me a quick hug. "Thanks, Liv. I'm really glad you're here."

"Me, too." I hugged her back and allowed myself a moment of peace before whipping out my phone. If I wanted to give Kali a real chance at the cover, I had one more day to turn her snooze-fest bachelorette into an envy-inducing, magazine-worthy celebration. All while staying true to Kali and Greta's very specific tastes . . . *and* without letting them know that I'd had a change of heart.

A renewed sense of purpose settled over me as I turned over the challenge in my mind. "We are people of action," my dad liked to say. I always felt better when I had a plan. Quickly I opened Mountainside's Instagram account and began crafting a new response. The DM really was mightier than the sword.

15

The only bad part about the last day of Kali and Greta's bachelorette was that I didn't get any credit for pulling it off. As maid of honor, I'd taken charge of the planning; no one else knew the itinerary. So it was easy to announce our newly spectacular plan (morning helicopter tour, afternoon at the spa, and a picnic in a glamped-out tree house) as if it'd been scheduled for months. My success had some alarming implications for the work-life balance of Smoky Mountains tourism employees, since so many responded to my desperate messages at nine p.m. on a Saturday. But then again, the promise of flattering *Southern Charm* coverage ensured access to luxury concierge brands, ones that prided themselves on 24/7 accessibility. Even then, concocting these eleventh-hour plans required several last-minute surcharges to Charlotte's credit card (another perk).

The day kicked off with coffee and pastries to stave off the morning's hangovers. Then we took an hour-long helicopter tour of the Smoky Mountains, which garnered nearly two thousand live followers on the *SC* Instagram Live. Next was a series of relaxation treatments at Mountainside. Even skeptical Greta warmed up to the idea after the manager prattled on about their sustainable sourcing. After exfoliating facials and full-body seaweed wraps, we relaxed in the sauna and played a cheesy bachelorette Guess-the-Bride game. (Who takes longer to get ready? Who initiated the first kiss?) I spent most of the time wiping sweat off my phone screen to add real-time poll questions to the *SC* Instagram story account, but everyone else seemed to be having a blast.

Our last stop before piling in the car to drive to Nashville was a tucked-away tree house Airbnb. As a top-rated stay, it hadn't been available when I'd first planned this weekend, but they'd had a last-minute cancellation. We stopped at a grocery store on the way to the tree house, picked up charcuterie and wine, and had ourselves a cozy picnic on the floor of the tree house. It was the opposite of the flashy, glamorous activities Emma had requested.

"We want them to be *aspirational*," she'd drilled into me. "Take advantage of all the freebies *SC* can get for you!"

"I will," I'd promised, thinking instead of the damage to Charlotte's black AmEx. My aunt never needed to know she could've gotten this stuff for free.

And yet—Kali's bachelorette was blowing up across social media. A silly TikTok of us in cucumber face masks lip-syncing to Carrie Underwood had racked up ten thousand views, and the Instagram videos of the tree-house picnic were garnering hundreds of comments. Viewers loved the low-key nature of the Kali/Greta weekend. Nothing that we'd done was that thrilling—explored the Smokies, gone to a spa, picnicked in a tree house. But a touch of Olivia magic had transformed the weekend into something worth reading about in a magazine.

Not that I had much time to rest on my laurels. The week after Kali and Greta's bachelorette, I helped coordinate phone interviews with the bachelorette attendees, so the writer could draft the March issue's official write-up. Next came weeks of photo emails with Frederic, going back and forth on exciting issues such as file sizes and exposure levels.

Aditya's knock provided welcome relief. I'd been in the middle of crafting another group-text plea for a specific uncropped image of the Smokies helicopter that Frederic swore would make or break the entire feature. I opened the door to reveal Aditya with a leashed Circe at his side.

"How slammed are you?" Aditya asked. "Want to go for a walk?"

I groaned. "Pro-wrestler-level slammed."

"Want some licks to make it better?"

"Obviously." I knelt and hugged Circe, wishing I could absorb her unworried, happy attitude.

"How's all the bachelorette planning going?"

"Fine. It'd been going fine."

"Until . . . ?"

"Until I realized I couldn't go through with talking Kali out of it." I stroked Circe's velvety fur. "I changed plans mid-weekend to give her a chance at winning."

"Yeah, I saw all the posts. It looked awesome."

"I know," I groaned.

"Which is . . . bad? Good?"

Sure, I was proud of the last-minute sorcery I'd worked, creating a smorgasbord of Insta-friendly glamping content. But the March issue hadn't even landed yet, and Kali had already edged Leighton out in the Charming Bride online poll. Leighton's bachelorette needed to kick some serious ass. I contemplated screaming into my pillow, but that felt melodramatic, even for me. "I don't even know anymore! And I have an interview at *SC*'s office today. Emma has a new idea she wants to discuss. Some fresh torture, I'm sure."

"You're almost done," Aditya said in a calming voice, like he was talking to a furious toddler. He paused, and I readied myself for the told-you-so part of the conversation. "And you created some special memories for your cousin. Be proud of that."

My conscience twinged uncomfortably as I thought about how last-minute that change of heart had been.

"Thanks," I said weakly. I wasn't due in the *SC* office for another few hours, but I grabbed my stuff and pulled on a jacket. I needed to escape Aditya's supportive gaze. As I hurried out the door, I tried to channel the down-on-her-luck heroine of a cozy mystery TV show. The one who tied everything together in a shiny bow in under sixty minutes, including commercials. Instead, I felt like the cautionary tale in some made-for-Hallmark special: this is what happens when you wait too long to make a decision.

"You can do this, and you *will* do this," I muttered to myself. But the words had never sounded more hollow.

"I thought Emma told you to come freshly showered." The petite hairdresser sighed, exasperated.

"I did!"

"Freshly showered, like *today*."

"I showered this morning!"

The hairdresser peered down at my greasy roots. "And you're sure you, um, washed everything? Because this looks like three days' worth of grease, and I only have twenty minutes to prep you."

"I'm sure!" I spluttered, torn between embarrassment at the state of my roots and indignance at being cross-examined on my cleanliness. Yes, my personal hygiene had been slipping lately, but I could be counted on to know when I'd last showered (today). "Besides, I'm not one of the brides. No one's gonna watch this interview."

The hairdresser clucked her tongue. "I wouldn't be so sure. That Charming Bride thing is a smash hit. We can't have you looking like a pig that got into the compost heap."

I glared at her in the mirror. "Thanks for that mental image."

"You're welcome," she said, deadpan, and gave my hair an extra-sharp tug.

Thirty minutes later, after a makeup artist had beautified me (thankfully without comment on the state of my neglected eyebrows), Frederic arrived to escort me to the interview. Although he was a photographer, not a cameraman—he'd been insulted when I'd asked if he did both—he'd volunteered to help with the lighting so that he could sit in.

"After the stories you gave me last time, I've signed myself up to work any event where you'll be there," he informed me.

"Thanks," I grumbled. "Glad I'm such a selling point."

The interview setup was simple: an ivory stool in front of a brilliantly pink wall. It was the same setup they'd used in interviews with other bridesmaids, with the mothers of the bride, and what they'd use for the brides themselves. Emma was standing next to the cameraman, texting furiously, when I arrived.

"Olivia! Ready to bang this out?" she said without looking up. "I know you're rooting for Leighton, but I need you to act neutral, okay? Sell them both. We want a nail-biter." She waved impressively long fake nails and added, "Figuratively, of course."

Once I was mic'd up and more powder had been dusted onto my already-oily forehead—"How does she grease up so fast?" the hairdresser sniffed to the makeup artist—Emma wasted no time. She started off with a few softballs, asking about how Leighton and I had met, and then about my favorite childhood memory with Kali. Finally starting to relax under the heavy, blinding lights, I missed her next question.

"Sorry, what was that?"

"Give me your best pitch for each bride," Emma repeated. She was shrouded in darkness, an invisible voice floating up from behind a wall of blinding lights. "Why they should be on the cover."

I uncrossed and re-crossed my legs. Drops of sweat had started to appear on my forehead. *She asked you to be neutral,* I reminded myself. Even if I did want Leighton to win. But did I? The more time I spent with Kali and Greta, the more my surety faded. Maybe that was the problem. I'd spent so much time with them lately and not enough with Leighton. Maybe I was being affected by a recency bias. That had to be it, I decided. That had to be why I was feeling so conflicted.

"The June cover has always featured an aspirational Southern bride," I began, forcing some razzle-dazzle into my voice. "Aspirational but accessible. The big Southern wedding that feels like it could almost be yours. The South is an area with strong regional culture—and they're proud of that. That special flavor in Southern weddings takes je ne sais quoi, and that's Leighton Sawyer.

"She's a true Southerner, born and raised in Tennessee, with family roots stretching back nine generations. And she's a creative visionary." My voice strengthened as I imagined persuading an invisible audience about my amazing best friend. "She's built an online following for her incredible style and her ability to stay relatable and down-to-earth. And when I say 'built,' I mean with blood, sweat, and tears. She's worked her ass off on Peach Sugar, and she's hoping to take the next step in her career by launching a dress collaboration. Leighton on the cover means celebrating everything special about Southern weddings *and* helping a self-made star launch her style career."

"Showing that you really can have it all," Emma said.

"Exactly. What's more impressive than a picture-perfect wedding that also unveils your custom line of bridesmaids' dresses?" I turned my palms up and shrugged. "Now, that's a strong Southern woman."

"Amazing. Great tagline." Emma clapped her hands together. "Now pitch me on Kali."

The Leighton pitch had been easy. I'd rehearsed a dozen variations before meetings with Emma. But Kali? I didn't have anything prepared. Nothing polished. By the camera was rolling, and Emma's expectant gaze rested heavy on my shoulders.

"Kali . . . is not your traditional Southerner. She's from Atlanta, went north for college, and only recently returned to Georgia. But she's a total badass who's never worried about what anyone else thought. She made her own way, and she defied expectations. She's traveled widely and lived elsewhere in the U.S., so she's got a more varied style. The South has a strong historical culture, but it's not as progressive as other regions. Kali on the cover means celebrating the modern South and how its traditional culture can mix with new and fresh ideas. *SC* has never featured a queer wedding."

"It would absolutely be a first," Emma agreed.

"Kali's the perfect choice to bring a modern twist to the *SC* June cover," I went on. "The face of an eclectic new South. One which draws from a wider array of influences."

Emma's face popped out from behind the camera. Her smile outshone the wall of lights behind her. "That was *excellent*, Olivia! Have you had media training?"

I smiled weakly and slid off the stool. "Nope. Beginner's luck?"

"Even *I* couldn't tell who you wanted to win," Emma added cheerily. "Well done."

I nodded and wiped my glistening forehead. Her approval felt hollow, because I hadn't done anything fancy: I didn't know who I wanted to win, either.

Two days later, when my phone lit up with a text from Will, I almost dropped it into the toilet in surprise. After months of silence, I'd nearly succeeded in putting him out of my head. I'd chalked our failed almost-relationship up to collateral damage, regrettable but unavoidable in the grand scheme of the bridal wars I was waging.

Can we talk? I want to clear the air.

My fingers felt like they were twice their normal size. I fumbled at the keyboard.

Sure.

"What happened?" Aditya said as soon as I walked out of the bathroom, reading my shocked expression. He and Circe were sprawled on my couch watching some game; Aditya often came over to mooch my cable subscription for live sports.

I didn't want to mention Will to Aditya. I already knew he'd tell me not to reopen that can of worms. "Just—wedding drama. Won't bore you with it."

Aditya shook his head and returned his gaze to the TV. "Never ends."

My phone vibrated with an incoming call, startling me again. Since Will no longer lived in Nashville, I'd expected him to vanish into the North Carolina distance. I felt that way about all my exes; they should cease to exist as soon as

our relationship did. The few times I'd run into one in public, it'd been as jarring as seeing Elvis walking around in the
flesh. But Will was different.

I ducked into the bathroom and closed the door behind
me; I didn't need Aditya overhearing this. Thanking my
lucky stars Will hadn't FaceTimed me, I answered the call. My
avocado face mask and three-day-old hair were not meant for
anyone's eyes. (I'd made a point of dressing extra-casually
around Aditya lately, so he didn't count.) "Hey, Will. What's
up?"

"Hey, Liv." Will's voice was polite but distant, like he was
phoning a relative for an obligatory birthday call. "How've
you been?"

A dozen responses flashed through my head, but I settled
for the simplest. "Good. Busy. Both with law school and bachelorette planning. You?"

"Not too bad. Work's going well. Can't complain." Will
paused. "I wanted to clear the air before Leighton's wedding.
So there's no weirdness."

My heart fell one rib space lower in my chest. A small part
of me had clung to the hope that this call could've gone
another way. "There won't be. That day's about her. We both
want her to be happy."

"Yeah. Exactly."

A silence. I rushed to fill the void. "I really am sorry about
the Tyler thing. I hope you guys worked things out."

"We're dudes. I brought over a few six-packs of craft beer
and we called it even, so long as I promised not to pull anything like that again. So, yeah, we're good."

God, it was hard to read people over the phone. I wished

I could see Will's face, to search his eyes for a hint of his true feelings. Would they show any leftover affection for me? Or a resigned obligation to a girl he could no longer stand?

"Good. I'm . . . I'm glad to hear that."

"I have a question for you."

I locked eyes with my green-skinned reflection. "Yeah?"

"I've been following all the *Southern Charm* wedding stuff," Will said. I knew him well enough to notice the care he was taking to keep his voice neutral. "And I don't know anything about wedding planning . . . but from what I saw online, it looks like you've been planning awesome stuff for both my sister and your cousin. Is that true, or is your sabotage too sneaky for me to pick up on?"

My heart lifted. I forced myself not to get too excited, not to read too much into what he was asking. "No. I gave up on all that. Just tried to plan great events for them both. And let the competition turn out how it would."

"Olivia Fitzgerald, letting go of control?"

Was that a teasing note in his voice? I tilted my chin up. My reflection copied me. "Are you impressed?"

"Yeah," he said. "I am. I'm glad you came around, Liv. Really."

"Me, too."

Uncertainty simmered through the phone. It felt like there was more that he wanted to say. There was definitely more I wanted to say. More I wanted to *know*: Was I forgiven in a let's-put-this-behind-us-and-get-back-on-track sort of way? Or in a no-hard-feelings-I'll-see-you-at-the-wedding-buddy sort of way? I closed my eyes and concentrated on picturing Will's face. I knew him so well; surely my subconscious could read his tone, could intuit the feelings underneath. But try as I might, I couldn't conjure up whatever he was holding back.

Will cleared his throat. "Anyway. Good luck with the rest of the planning. I'll see you at the wedding?"

"Yeah. Sure. See you then."

I put the phone down on the sink and glanced back up into the mirror. A glob of avocado mush dripped from my reflection's cheek onto her Vandy Law T-shirt.

"It's for the best," I told her firmly.

She raised a skeptical eyebrow, and another green glob splashed onto the sink.

16

March

Over our two-decade friendship, Leighton had never wavered in her desire for a "hometown" Nashville bachelorette. We'd been planning it together in bits and pieces over the years—a night out on Broadway, a pedal tavern through Midtown, photo ops at all the brightly colored murals. Not only was Nashville the top of any bachelorette destination list, it was also *Southern Charm*'s HQ city and an ideal fit for the brand.

Emma had signed off with a grin—and a request. She wanted a "fresh, unique twist" on "Nashvegas" for Leighton's bachelorette. But fresh and unique were a mighty tall order. Most *SC* subscribers had either attended, knew someone who'd attended, or dreamed of attending a Nashville bachelorette. So they already knew the staples, like coordinated cowboy hats and boots for the whole bridal party.

"It's like trying to reinvent the wheel," I'd moaned to

Aditya. "Except a triangle or square wheel literally wouldn't roll. It's a circle for a reason!"

But despite my panic, I'd come up with an impressive itinerary. The girls were coming in on Friday for brunch at MM Baxter, the rooftop spot where I'd barfed on Emma's shoes. The lighting was incredible and the mimosas even better, so it'd be the perfect place to kick off the weekend. Then I'd used my *SC* publicity clout to secure private shopping sessions at three of Nashville's chicest boutiques. Hot chicken and line dancing would round off our Friday night. On Saturday, we'd lounge at the rooftop hotel pool in our matching bikinis before getting glammed up for a dinner out at a trendy new restaurant and a table at a local club.

Before things officially kicked off, Leighton insisted on a top-secret bridesmaid dress fitting at our hotel. Absolutely no photos would be taken or shared with *SC*. She wanted the reveal of the dresses to happen at her wedding, on her terms.

"This suite is *the most*," drawled Nikki. She lowered her sunglasses for emphasis. *"Ever."*

I waited expectantly for an adjective, but Nikki seemed to think she'd made her point. "Thanks! Leighton's got the dresses in the bedroom if you want to head on back."

I eyed the back of Nikki's blush-colored jumpsuit as she sashayed by me, tossing her Prada moto jacket onto me like I was a human clothes rack. Blush was a little too close to white for my liking: who wore white to a bachelorette party?

"Ho-ly shit," Shane shouted from the doorway. "This—place—is—amazing!"

"Although please tell me you got it comped," Samantha

added, her mouth agape. "Because I definitely couldn't afford my portion."

"It's comped," I assured her. Satisfied that both twins were wearing brightly colored sundresses, I surveyed the luxurious penthouse. Every inch of the suite was covered in buttery soft leather, impossibly polished mirrors, or fluffy shag carpets. Floor-to-ceiling windows afforded an impressive view of downtown Nashville, with the neon-lit honky-tonks of Broadway visible a few streets away. Thank God for *SC* publicity connections. "Let's go try on the dresses!"

The twins followed me into the master suite, where Leighton had already dressed Nikki in her champagne-colored bridesmaid dress. The dress had a mermaid-inspired silhouette, with ruffles starting at the knee and flowing out around Nikki's ankles. The figure-hugging shape was more flattering than the average bridesmaid dress, but the high neckline deflected any threat of stealing attention from an actual wedding gown. Inwardly I marveled at Leighton's deft touch: it was a delicate balance to strike.

"That's gorgeous, Leighton!" Samantha gushed. "I love it!"

"Honestly the best-looking bridesmaid dress I've ever seen," Shane commented.

Leighton's eyes brightened. "Wait till you see yours!"

Nikki turned from side to side, studying herself in the mirror. She ran her hands down her tiny waist and over her hips. "I do like it . . . but isn't the neckline a little high?" She tugged at the collar with an expression like she'd stepped in one of Circe's legendary poops.

"Isn't that part of the tailoring?" I said quickly, before Leighton's face could fall too far. "The neckline, right?"

Leighton nodded and stepped next to Nikki. "After the

wedding, the mermaid ruffles can be detached, converting it to a bodycon cocktail dress," she said, pointing out the hidden seam at Nikki's knees. "And the neckline will drop down into a cowl."

Nikki looked unconvinced. "What if we made those alterations now? I think it'd look so much better—"

"Shane, Samantha, let's get you two into your dresses," I said loudly. "Nikki, it looks amazing, and you want to highlight how it's two different dresses in one, right?" Tugging Leighton away to help the others, I didn't wait for an answer.

Ten minutes later, all four of us were wearing our custom Leighton Sawyer convertible dresses. Samantha's was a wrap gown with detachable sheer sleeves and a hidden mid-thigh hemline, while Shane wore a strapless trumpet-style dress that could be tailored into a high-low. My own dress—my personal favorite—was a one-shoulder Grecian-inspired column dress that tailored into a romper. I mean, how ingenious was that?

Leighton bustled around with an alarming number of pins in her mouth, making tiny adjustments as she turned us this way and that. She looked so completely and utterly in her element, like how I felt when I crushed closing arguments during mock jury cases. It helped that Shane, Samantha, and I were blown away by the amazing dresses. Even Nikki had come around; I caught her checking out her own ass in the mirror more than once.

Finally, and with only thirty minutes until our MM Baxter brunch reservation, Leighton declared us ready and authorized a change back into street clothes.

"Ten minutes until departure!" I bellowed at the scattering girls. "No stragglers! No excuses!"

Nikki traced the high collar of her dress one more time. "Are you sure we can't—"

With one fluid motion, I knocked a huge glass of water off the dresser and onto Nikki's blush-colored jumpsuit. Not the nicest thing to do, but it distracted Nikki from commenting on her dress *and* prevented her from wearing an almost-white outfit to my best friend's bachelorette.

"Oh my God!" Nikki shrieked.

"I'm so sorry! It was a total accident!" I lied. "Don't worry, I have some extra dresses you can borrow."

Over her shoulder, Shane winked at me and mouthed, *Good one.* Samantha had her hand over her mouth and was desperately trying to stifle her laughter. Even Leighton was fighting a grin when I added, "And the neckline can be as low as you want."

Thirty hours and at least that many collective drinks later, I was thanking my lucky stars and the bachelorette-planning gods for catapulting me into the Maid of Honor Hall of Fame. (Did such a Hall of Fame exist? I made a mental note to pitch Emma on creating one after the Charming Bride competition ended.)

Yesterday had been an amazing whirlwind of shopping, photo shoots, and a surprisingly fun line-dancing lesson. Even Nikki, who'd tried to bow out of the line dancing, had relaxed and let loose. And all of Saturday's daytime activities had gone as planned, with impressive engagement numbers across *SC*'s social media channels. Emma had texted me a simple: *Keep up the good work!*

Most important, my best friend was having the time of her life. I smiled in satisfaction as she threw back her head in laughter, glossy tresses cascading over her shoulders as she cackled at Samantha's joke. Next to her, Shane was pouring another round from the dangerously tasty sangria pitcher, while Nikki snapped a few group photos. After nearly two days together, we'd all loosened up and bonded. Instead of "the twins," I now thought of Samantha as the wisecracking jokester to Shane's bubbly party-girl persona. Even Nikki had acquired a redeeming quality; after Leighton mentioned her difficulties with Patricia, she'd opened up about her own struggles for legitimacy in her parents' eyes. I found myself looking forward to hanging out with all three women during Leighton and Matt's wedding weekend.

Best of all, I could taste the freedom stretching ahead of me as soon as Leighton's bachelorette wrapped up. I'd received two emails from the Holmes & Reese onboarding office, with plans to start my initial employee paperwork next week. Charlotte was pleased with all of Kali's events, and even more pleased about the neck-and-neck Charming Bride voting. I'd convinced Leighton that her bachelorette would be enough to clinch her victory, although in truth I had no idea where the dust would settle. But as I'd thought about where things stood, I was convinced:

A. Even if Leighton lost, she'd gotten a lot of publicity. And she'd signed a pilot collaboration agreement with Kenne's.
B. Even if Kali lost, it was too late for Charlotte (and Hank) to do much about it. Plus, Kali was already

becoming a role model to so many women and I'd planned Kali some kick-ass events. So:

C. I would be one of Holmes & Reese's first-year associates this summer.

A tiny part of me wondered if, (D) Will and I could rekindle things at Leighton's wedding. We seemed to have buried any ill will during our phone call. But maybe that was asking too much. That was another one of my dad's rules for effective deal-making: Don't get greedy. Your goal outcome should be achievable; otherwise, you'll always be disappointed.

And if I had pulled this off while maintaining my friendship with Leighton, rebuilding a relationship with Kali, and keeping my hard-won job offer?

See? It's all about framing, I told myself. When I thought about things like that, it was easy to feel grateful for how everything had worked out. Will notwithstanding.

Samantha reached over and tapped my wrist, eyes dancing. "*Please* tell me we're going to Broadway after this," she said playfully. "Let's get Leighton onstage with a band."

Leighton laughed. "What if we just go someplace fun and dance?"

"It's your bachelorette! We all flew into town for the privilege of embarrassing you," Shane countered. "Honestly, you sort of owe us."

"I know the guy headlining at Dierks Bentley's bar tonight," Nikki announced. She pulled out her phone and began typing. "I'm sure he'd do me a solid. Or we could do karaoke!"

"What song should we make Leighton sing onstage?" I asked, grinning at my half-laughing, half-terrified bestie. "Wrong answers only."

"'Livin' on a Prayer'!"

"'Despacito'!"

"Anything Britney, obviously."

Fishing out an old eyeliner from my purse, I sacrificed it for the good of the cause by jotting down their answers on a napkin. "Awesome. We're gonna have a whole set list." I twisted the napkin around so that Nikki could snap a photo. I'd leaned into Nikki's YouTuber background and asked her to take over as the official bachelorette documenter. She'd accepted with only one snide comment about how we'd finally get some flattering angles.

"How do you know the guy playing Dierks Bentley's?" Shane was asking with interest.

"I dogsat his evil puppy last year."

I laughed. "And you kept in touch?"

"He's actually an instructor at Barry's Bootcamp in Atlanta," Nikki said. "I started taking the Tuesday-evening classes, kept running into him, and we started hooking up."

"Ah, the modern love story," Samantha joked. "Dogsitting leads to fitness classes leads to . . . friends with benefits?"

"There's got to be a dating app to qualify as a modern love story," I countered.

"I matched with him on Rover for the dogsitting. Does that count?"

Our sangria-fueled laughter was so loud that heads at nearby tables turned. I'd considered asking for a private room at the upscale Mexican restaurant. Instead, I'd chosen one of the three raised tables surrounding the pink-and-orange-tinted fountain in the middle of the room. The elevation helped add to our allure. The faces turned toward us looked on with envious interest.

Leighton reached over and squeezed my hand. She wore an off-the-shoulder white crop top with dramatic sheer sleeves overlaid with polka dots, exposing two inches of tanned, toned midsection. "I'm so glad I didn't pull out of the competition," she said. "The publicity's been amazing. Totally worth the stress. Even if I don't win."

I grinned back at her. Relief filled my lungs like super-charged helium, threatening to lift me right out of my seat in happiness. I'd hoped Leighton felt that way, but I hadn't known for sure. "I'm so glad. You deserve this, Leighton!"

"You were gonna pull out?" Samantha asked, overhearing. "Why? It's an online contest and you're an influencer! It's a perfect fit." Shane and Nikki both looked up, their attention piqued. I'd managed to avoid the Charming Bride topic all weekend, but it was bound to come up eventually.

"It's also been a ton of stress," Leighton admitted. "It's a big transition year. And Matt's decided to join a start-up after graduation, so his salary's not as high as we'd expected. Not to mention unreliable. I've spent a lot of time figuring out if I can earn enough from Peach Sugar. Or maybe it was time to stop influencing. I mean, I'm not twenty-one anymore," she added with a small smile. She was putting on a brave face, but the vulnerability was there.

"But you're so talented," Nikki said, with unexpected warmth in her voice. "And you love doing it."

"I love conceptualizing content," Leighton corrected. "Or, at least, that's how I've felt recently. I still get excited dreaming up new post ideas and fresh takes on old outfits. The actual getting-glammed-up-and-scheduling-my-life-around-photos? Not so much."

The other girls nodded in understanding, but I doubted

any of them—except maybe Nikki—had a shred of insight into the effort Leighton put into Peach Sugar. Or how much more the Charming Bride competition had demanded. "Well, we're only two months from your bridesmaid dress unveiling," I said brightly, maneuvering the conversation into safer waters. "Then all the brands will come knocking."

"Cheers to that!" Shane said, raising her glass of sangria. "Let's all manifest it. This time next year, Leighton's bridesmaid dresses will be the talk of every wedding planner in the South!"

"In America!" Samantha insisted, and we all clinked glasses.

I drank my sangria, relishing the light burn of the alcohol as it coated my throat. As I chewed on a wine-soaked raspberry, my thoughts returned to the cover competition. Back in September, I'd been convinced that the players in this negotiation wanted incompatible outcomes: Leighton needed the cover to impress Patricia and to snag a clothing collaboration; Charlotte demanded the cover-or-bust for Kali; Kali wanted to plan as little as possible and to please her mother; and I needed to keep everyone happy so I could keep my future at Holmes & Reese *and* my lifetime friendship with Leighton. But now there was more uncertainty about who'd grace the June cover—more uncertainty than I usually allowed!—but everyone seemed okay with that. Maybe life wasn't as black-and-white as I'd always thought. Maybe it didn't have to be such a winner-take-all, zero-sum, talk-your-opponent-in-circles free-for-all.

Olivia Fitzgerald, are you going . . . soft?

"Leighton, is that your brother?" Nikki's voice sharpened with interest. We all turned to the front of the restaurant, where Will and Tyler were walking in alongside a few brawny men I recognized from the Nashville Predators, the city's NHL team. *I might have a lead on getting back into pro sports . . .*

"I see Tyler, so it must be a Preds event he's helping with." Leighton rolled her eyes. "Everyone, please ignore that my brother's crashing my bachelorette!"

My eyes followed Will as he crossed the restaurant with the others, clearly headed for an event space in the back. My mind insisted that I should *stop looking now*, but my heart wanted to drink in the sight of him. He looked good. Just as tall as the professional hockey players, Will cut an impressive figure in a sharp blue suit jacket and crisp white button-up.

"Has he always been that good-looking?" Samantha sighed dreamily.

And then it happened: Will looked up and our eyes met. My insides ignited with the thrill. The millisecond before his face changed was excruciating. But when his face did shift, there was something there. Something that made my heart skip even faster, and heat rise in my cheeks. He looked . . . *happy* to see me.

Almost automatically, I grabbed my purse and rose from the table. "Restroom," I announced, and headed toward the back of the restaurant.

Luckily, the restrooms were in the hallway leading to the private event space. I turned the corner, preparing to negotiate my way inside, but found Will standing in the hallway alone.

"Hi," I said breathlessly. My four-inch going-out heels closed some of the seven-inch height gap, but I still had to tilt my neck back.

"Hi," he said back, and that familiar half-smile softened his face. The smell of his birch cologne wafted toward me and threatened to weaken my knees. "Would you believe me if I told you this was a complete coincidence?"

"Maybe," I teased. "Are you that overprotective? Can't let your little sis have one last wild night of freedom?"

"I'm actually on Matt's payroll," he joked. "Here under strict orders to keep all men away from y'all."

"Ah, that's too bad. I already put a deposit down with the strippers."

One of the Predators players exited the men's room and we both flattened ourselves against the wall to let him pass. There was a beat of silence. "Tyler's done a lot of work with the Preds PR office," Will said at last. "They had an opening for a team PT. I'm here tonight on sort of a social interview. See if I get along with the guys."

"Oh, that's awesome. Congrats." I felt a flash of awkwardness at Tyler's name. If this was a sort-of interview, shouldn't he be in there schmoozing? Not out in the hallway with me?

Will stuck his hands in his pockets, looking as uncomfortable as I felt. "But while I've got you . . . I've been thinking a lot since our call, and I owe you an apology."

"You do?"

"I might have overreacted at Cheekwood. I didn't agree with what you were doing to your cousin, but it was more than that. All fall, I'd wanted to see where things could go with us, but then you told me you didn't want anything serious. I finally started moving on, and then you wanted to give things a try. But you didn't want to tell Leighton anything, so I couldn't tell if you were serious. Or if you were still stringing me along."

"I'd always liked you. I'd always wanted to give things a try—"

"Then why'd you tell me you didn't want anything serious?"

I sucked a breath back through my teeth; he wasn't going to like this, but he deserved the truth. "I didn't. My friend did, without me knowing."

This took him off guard. "What? Why?"

"He thought *you* were stringing me along. Because of that girl from all your scuba pictures. And that it'd never work long-distance, anyway." *And maybe Aditya had an ulterior motive.*

Will ran a hand through his hair, his surprise intensified. "McKayla? What does she have to do with anything?"

"Will, you showed me a dozen photos of you two all over each other," I said impatiently. "Right after we'd hooked up. Of course I thought you didn't want anything serious. And Tyler posted that photo of you two captioned, *Honeymooners—*"

"McKayla was my *diving* partner," Will said, his expression befuddled, like he still couldn't process why we were talking about her. "That's it. The first day, the captain thought we were on our honeymoon, and it became a running joke. She's in a relationship. With a woman," he added. "Not me."

"Oh." I felt relieved, stupid, and furious, all at once. I looked down at my feet, suddenly unsure of where this left us. "I wish we'd had this conversation a long time ago."

Will shrugged. "Me, too. But I didn't want to put too much pressure on us and freak you out."

"Freak me out?" I frowned. "By coming on too strong? That was never going to happen, believe me."

"No, not that." Will rubbed the back of his neck with one

hand. "Freak you out by forcing you into a situation you couldn't control. Like with my sister. You don't like that. You run away from that."

"I don't run away," I said, stung. Even though he was right. "And it's different for me," I argued. "You're her brother. If she found out about us in the wrong way . . . well, she can't disown you. But she could pull a Lila with me."

"You really think that?" he asked. "She and Lila were close for a few years. Leighton thinks of you like a *sister*, Liv. She couldn't disown you any more than she could disown me."

It was a good point. Sure, Leighton had already lost one best friend over a failed relationship with Will. But that had been years ago. We were adults now, with fully developed frontal cortexes and our own health insurance plans. Had I been using the Lila thing as an excuse? Maybe Will was right. Maybe I feared that conversation with Leighton for other reasons. Because I didn't know if I could persuade my best friend like I did everyone else. I didn't like situations I couldn't control. And maybe because telling Leighton would make this thing with Will real. Realer than any other relationship I'd had. It was a weird thing to realize, given that Will and I had been on all of two dates. But I knew what life with him could be like. The potential was endless.

"Maybe not," I admitted. "Maybe I was making excuses. Telling Leighton, and the long-distance, and the scuba girl . . . All those reasons it could never work between us. Because the alternative was scary."

Will's eyes held mine. "Scary because of Leighton's reaction . . . or scary because of what it would mean?"

Two giggling teenagers emerged from the women's room

and struck up a loud, gossipy conversation. We edged down the hallway, away from the Predators room. The delay gave me time to land on an answer.

"Because of what it would mean," I said, with more bravery than I felt. And then I swallowed hard. "What it *could* mean."

His green eyes softened at the corners, and one half of his smile tilted upward. A tremble of excitement swept through me as we stared into each other's eyes. Even though we were surrounded by gossiping Preds groupies, the clanging sounds of the kitchen, and a distinct bleach odor, it was possibly the most romantic moment of my life. We'd said so little and yet so much. Maybe there was still a chance for us.

He reached for my hand and pulled me a step closer to him. "Liv, I really—"

But then a loud, thumping bass started blaring from the dining area. Shrieks and whoops filled the air. I glanced at Will and saw my confusion mirrored on his face. Together we headed toward the commotion. As we turned the corner, my jaw dropped in horror.

Five scantily clad men were writhing and gyrating around a mortified Leighton. One of them carried an old-school boom box over his shoulder, the source of the earsplitting club music. Another jumped onto the table and pulled a confused Samantha up with him, dancing suggestively. Two others were taking turns twerking in Shane's face. The last was straddling Leighton and performing a lap dance, which Nikki was filming with one hand clapped over her mouth.

"I thought you were kidding about the strippers," Will said, baffled.

"I was!"

Most of the patrons were cheering and whooping, enjoying the show, but an angry-looking manager was storming toward Leighton's table. I hurried across the restaurant to intercept him, dragging Will along behind me.

"I'm so sorry about this," I shouted into the manager's ear. "A prank from the groomsmen. I'll get rid of them!"

"You have sixty seconds!" the manager snapped. "Or I'm throwing your group out!"

I nodded and nearly sprinted to the table. I grabbed the stripper with the boom box and pushed him toward Will, hoping he'd get the hint and turn the music off. "Show's over!" I announced to the other strippers. "Thanks for coming! Get the hell out of here, now!"

"What about our tip?" shouted the one on the table.

"Fifty bucks each if you're gone in thirty seconds!" I yelled back. That did the trick; all five of them began scrambling for scraps of discarded clothing.

I turned to Leighton, who was scarlet-faced and shaking with rage. "How could you let this happen?" she screamed over the still-blaring music from the stupid boom box. "You promised you wouldn't let Charlotte screw anything else up! You freaking promised, Liv!"

"I'm sorry!" I shouted back. "I've been trying, Leighton, I swear—"

Her normally beautiful face twisted in anger. "Really? Or did you let this happen because you wanted Kali to win all along?"

My intuition told me there was something I was missing, that this was about more than just the strippers. Leighton grabbed her phone and shoved a glowing web page at me: an article from the *Southern Charm* home page. The headline blared out at me: "Maid of Honor Says Kali Is 'Perfect Choice' for *SC* Cover."

My heart sank. "When did you see this?" I said blankly. The strippers gawked at us, arms full of clothes, blatantly rubbernecking. Were people really that voyeuristic? And for the love of God, could someone please turn the music off?

"Just now," she snapped. "We were checking the online votes. When were you gonna tell me about this, Liv? That you've been sneaking off to give interviews supporting Kali?"

The injustice cut too deep. Months of frustrations welled up inside me. In one instant, my internal barriers crumbled to dust, and the truth poured out.

"Do you have *any* idea how hard I've been working to help you win?" I screamed back at her. The music cut off halfway through my sentence. "I chose a stupid theme for Kali's engagement party! I planned the most boring bachelorette possible! I picked a disgusting cake flavor and forced Kali's coordinator to cancel!" My words echoed around the entire restaurant, but I was too angry to lower my voice. "And I've spent six months trying to talk Kali into eloping! So don't you tell me that I haven't been helping you."

A stunned silence followed my words. The entire restaurant looked from me to Leighton in anticipation. Nikki still had her phone up and was turning it from me to Leighton, her expression gleeful.

"So that's why you wanted me to drop out," said a tight voice behind me.

If my heart had already plummeted underground, now my stomach did, too. I turned slowly to see a shell-shocked Kali.

My mind crashed, like a laptop trying to process too many commands at once. It didn't compute. What was Kali doing in Nashville, at Leighton's bachelorette? It couldn't be a coincidence. There was no way.

"Kali, that's not what I meant—" I tried.

"Isn't it?" Leighton threw back, her voice like ice. "You can't have it both ways, Liv. You're gonna change your story now that Kali's standing there?" She waved the phone in the air. "You already told the whole world who you wanted to win. Just admit it."

"I think Olivia's made it real clear who she's helping," Kali said, her voice equally venomous. "Herself." She turned and stormed out of the restaurant.

"Kali, wait—" I called desperately, but broke off as Leighton grabbed her purse. "Leighton, come on, let me explain—"

"There's nothing to explain," she said coldly. "I thought I could trust you." Her voice wobbled slightly. "And I saw you. Holding hands with Will. One more thing you were lying about."

For someone who prided herself on conversation skills, my brain had completely shut down. There was too much happening, all at once. My composure had evaporated, along with my dreams of this whole situation working out okay. "Leighton, it's not what it looks like, I swear—"

"Save it," she snapped. "Come on, girls. Let's get out of here." She swept by me, taking care to ram my shoulder as she passed. Shane, Samantha, and Nikki scurried after her, all avoiding my eyes.

I suddenly felt totally naked, standing alone on the raised platform. Hundreds of eyes watched me as whispers started to fill the empty air. Half a dozen phones were pointed at me, having recorded the entire conversation. I'd never felt more alone in my life.

"I thought you said you gave up on all the sabotage," said Will quietly.

In the whirlwind of confrontations, I'd almost forgotten he was there. His face was steely. "I did, I swear. Everything I said was stuff I did before—"

His face twisted in a mirror expression of his sister's. I'd never thought Will and Leighton looked much alike, but their identical distaste for me was uncanny. "Stop lying, Liv. You can't talk your way out of everything. And you can't talk your way out of this."

And then he left, too, and I hit a new lifetime low, thirty seconds after the first. *This* was now the most alone I'd ever felt. And worst of all, I knew the truth: I deserved every bit of it.

17

April

Failure was not something I handled well. I hated feeling inadequate, feeling that I wasn't good enough. Powered by a pure, unadulterated fear of insufficiency, I'd learned to morph every situation to my advantage, to stack every deck, to exert every possible shred of control. Consciously or not, I'd always chosen situations I could bend to my desired outcome, through sheer force of will and an uncompromising desire not to lose. I'd built my entire identity around overachieving and winning others over.

So in the aftermath of Leighton's bachelorette, having failed in every possible way, I'd never felt more wretched. Both brides refused to talk to me. Will wasn't returning my texts, either. The only message I received was from Charlotte, a simple gloat: *Well done.* Like I'd blown everything up on purpose. Like I'd wanted to ruin my best friend's bachelorette.

To add insult to injury, if none of the three people I cared about wanted to talk to me, it felt like everyone else in the world did. Nikki had been shooting an *SC* Instagram Live when the strippers first appeared, and she'd captured the entire showdown. One clip of me screaming about my sabotage efforts had briefly trended on Twitter with the hashtag #MaidofDishonor. My social media accounts were flooded with criticisms and followers announcing their devotion to Team Kali or Team Leighton. After changing my accounts to private, I'd stayed off the Internet as much as possible.

I moved through life like I was in a trance. I went to class, did my work, and kept my head down. I filled out onboarding paperwork for Holmes & Reese and scheduled phone calls with the second-year associate assigned as my work mentor. But even those calls didn't lift my spirits. The Holmes & Reese job felt so far removed from everything I'd been dreaming and scheming about all year. After months of balancing schoolwork with all sorts of life work, the thought of eighty-hour workweeks on corporate mergers didn't thrill me like it once had.

The only person on my side was Aditya, but even our friendship had lost its old comfort. Something subtle had changed between us. My intuition told me that he might want more than friendship, but I couldn't risk alienating the only friend I had left.

Instead, we spent many evenings sharing six-packs and a *Seinfeld* marathon, with Aditya never pushing me to talk about what had happened. That is, until one evening in the beginning of April.

"How're you holding up?" he asked during a commercial break. "Leighton still not talking to you?"

I sighed. "Nope. Not Kali, either." *Or Will*, I added in my head.

Aditya stroked Circe's head and waited a moment. "So, what're you going to do about it?"

"What?"

"What're you going to do to fix things?"

I sighed. "It's not like that. This isn't fixable. I can't make it right with people who won't talk to me."

"Here's the thing." He cracked the top on another beer and took a fortifying sip. "You did some shitty things. But you genuinely feel bad about doing them. Not just that you got caught."

I frowned. "So you're saying my wallowing is . . . good?"

"It proves you have a conscience," he pointed out. "And that you're not ready to give up on any of these people. So you have to figure out how to fix things."

"I don't know if there's a way to make everyone happy."

Aditya shook his head. "Dude. Have you learned nothing?"

"What do you mean?"

"That's what got you into trouble in the first place." His expression softened. "You were so convinced you could talk your way through anything, but it's really because you were scared of making a choice."

I turned his words over in my head. "I guess . . . I didn't want to admit that I couldn't make it all work. I didn't want to give up anything—not Leighton's cover, not my H&R job, and not Will. I thought I could control the situation. Make it work out the way I wanted."

"Except it didn't. It couldn't, Liv. There was no way."

"Yeah." I took a long sip of my beer. "You know what's funny? Right before the strippers showed up and everything went to shit, you know what I was thinking about?"

"Um . . . what a great friend I am?"

I rolled my eyes. "How *lucky* I was that everything had worked out so well. That Emma had launched the Charming Bride thing, and both brides had gotten so much publicity. How both of them were okay with possibly not winning. How I'd navigated the minefield and somehow kept my Holmes & Reese offer."

Aditya winced. "It was terrible luck. Having Kali and Will both show up, ten minutes apart? Neither of them even live in Nashville!"

"Ain't that the truth." I reached for a new beer myself. Something ignited in the back of my mind. "Will . . . that could be a coincidence," I said slowly. "Tyler's done a lot of work for the Predators. But Kali? What the hell was she doing at Leighton's bachelorette?"

It was a question that had been tugging at my subconscious, but I'd been shutting down any train of thought about That Awful Night. But I was now two beers in, and we were getting into it.

"Maybe Charlotte sent her, along with the strippers?" Aditya offered. "Maybe she wanted to orchestrate a fight between Leighton and Kali?"

"Why bother? She had to know the strippers would be disruptive enough."

"Why does the Empress do anything?" Aditya said wisely. "Isn't being evil for the sake of being evil enough?"

I snorted, but part of me took the idea and ran with it. "Now that you mention it . . . I know I joke about Charlotte being evil, but this was next-level. She's usually more subtle."

"Poison ivy crowns? Public stripper attacks? Definitely not subtle," Aditya said. "But effective."

I put down my beer and began pacing around the room.

"When I did something to Charlotte as a kid, she'd always be sneaky about getting back at me. Something that she could feign innocence about. Like 'accidentally' shrinking my favorite jeans in the dryer. Or spilling her cocktail on my finished science project. There'd always be this shred of doubt. Nothing like this."

"Maybe housewives get less subtle with age?" Aditya suggested. "Like wine."

I sped up. "No, there's got to be a reason. I can't believe I didn't see it before. And her being so insistent that Kali get the cover . . . I always thought there was something she wasn't telling me." Then something Aditya had said clicked. "*No*. No way. But maybe . . . Oh my God, if that's why she's doing this—"

"What, what!" Aditya barked impatiently. I pushed past him and grabbed my laptop. "Liv, what're you talking about?"

Nearly vibrating with excitement, I pulled up the Gmail home page. "I was in Charlotte's Gmail account before, but I didn't go snooping. I was only emailing vendors . . ."

"Glad you follow the stalker code of ethics."

I typed in Charlotte's email and the password I'd written down: kali31992. Then I found the search bar and typed one word: *housewives*.

"What're you looking for?" Aditya asked impatiently. "Liv, come on—"

The screen refreshed, and there it was, right in front of me. Like it'd been all year, if I hadn't been so distracted. If I'd put the pieces together.

I twisted the laptop screen to face Aditya and watched his face as he read. His mouth slackened. "Holy shit. Charlotte's being recruited for a reality show?"

"Yes!" I scrolled through the email thread. "Looks like a *Housewives* spinoff . . . but for charity work. Called *The Gala Life*. Described as 'a look behind the curtain into the glamorous, intriguing work of high-impact philanthropy . . . Drama and dollars galore!'"

"Who the hell would watch that?"

"If Andy Cohen hosts, literally millions of women."

"Andy who?"

"So *this* is why she's been pulling all this crap." I pointed at one email from a senior producer describing plotlines for Charlotte's "sizzle reel." The producer was encouraging Charlotte to up the drama around her daughter's wedding competition.

"But it's not like there's been TV crews around," Aditya said, looking confused. "We would've had to sign releases, right?"

I scanned a few more emails. One jumped out at me: *making the final casting decision this spring. Exposure from the* Southern Charm *cover would go a long way . . .*

"I bet Charlotte's trying to prove her life is dramatic enough for the show," I said, thinking out loud. "Plus, there's a ton of social media videos from all the events. They could use those and intercut with confessionals, if they wanted to include it on the show."

"Wow," Aditya breathed, and we both stared at the screen in silence.

"But this doesn't change anything," he added after a moment, his tone dejected. "I mean, now we know Charlotte's motives. But that's not going to change anything else . . ."

"It gives me leverage," I said slowly.

"Liv," Aditya said in a warning tone. "Last time you ran around trying to manipulate everyone, it didn't work out so well—"

I winced; I really didn't like the *m*-word. An idea was crystallizing in my head. Will had said I couldn't talk my way out of this one. And maybe I couldn't talk my way *out* of anything. But I could still use my words. Armed with some intel on Charlotte, maybe I could find a way to save my relationships with two very special people. If I made a choice. And played my cards extremely, extremely well.

"Well, well, well. If it isn't my *favorite* maid of dishonor." Emma grinned widely as she swung open her office door. "Come in."

I tried to return the smile, but my mouth got stuck in a grimace. "Can't say I'm sad for my fifteen minutes of fame to pass."

She chuckled and settled into the chair behind her desk. "I've been eyeballing the spread for Leighton's bachelorette. You planned a stellar weekend."

I glanced politely at the screen, which had retouched images of us posing at brunch, shopping at boutiques, and line-dancing from Friday night. I barely recognized the light-hearted me of three weeks ago. "Looks great."

"So what can I do for you?"

I took a deep breath and began the pitch I'd rehearsed with Aditya. "All this wedding coverage has been great for *SC*. Especially on your digital media channels, which are the largest source of growth for eyeballs and advertising revenue."

Emma nodded slowly. "Yes. This is true."

"And your readership has become invested in *both* Leighton and Kali," I went on. Emma's face shifted like she knew where I was going. "So why limit yourself to one? Feature *both* weddings in the June issue. Give your readers closure on *both* of the brides they've followed so closely."

Emma was already shaking her head. "Out of the question." She held up a finger. "First, I only have space for one wedding. We're just two months out from the June issue going to press, and I've booked every other page of that issue."

"What if you split the space?" I suggested. "Half to each of them?"

Emma flicked up a second finger. "Second, the whole point of this Charming Bride competition was that it's a *competition*! It's been a huge success, yes, but that's because there's a prize on the line. If I feature both brides, we lose the stakes. And the competition's already been greenlit to repeat next year," she added smugly.

Frustration welled up inside me: Didn't Emma feel any gratitude toward me? I'd come up with the competition idea. I'd made her look good to her bosses. But resentment wasn't helpful; I pushed it aside. "That's great. But aren't there extenuating circumstances here? Me being maid of honor in both weddings and all the drama that went along with it?"

Emma's eyes lit up. She leaned forward eagerly. "Now that you mention it, that had crossed my mind. I'd like to make you our June cover star. Our subscribers are so curious about the girl helping both weddings. Your face would garner a lot of clicks. And it'd get the *Bridal Today* editor off my back. Although annoying her has been a plus," she added in a musing tone.

Success lifted my spirits: she'd played right into my hands. "It's an interesting idea," I said, feigning thoughtfulness.

Emma nodded enthusiastically. "And we'd feature photos of you at both weddings, so both brides would still be included."

"But I can't take that offer," I went on. "It wouldn't be fair to Leighton *or* Kali."

She eyed me. "So you've made up with them? That was quite the fight."

"No," I admitted. "But if you won't put both brides on the cover—"

"Impossible. Devalues the whole competition."

"—then I have another way of capitalizing on the maid-of-dishonor thing."

"I'm listening."

I took a deep breath. "You said my face would garner a lot of clicks . . . but what about my voice?"

She frowned. "What do you mean?"

"An interview on the *Southern Charm* podcast." I watched her face carefully. This was what I'd been building up to; it was why I'd come back to her office. "Where I talk about being the maid of honor in dueling weddings, and all the behind-the-scenes drama your subscribers don't know about. Yet."

Emma leaned back and regarded me. "An interesting idea. I like it. It'd be popular."

"Exactly." I waited for the *but* that I could hear in her voice. I was so close. This podcast was the answer. I knew it was. I'd made my choice.

"But, Olivia—I've got to ask, why would you want to do that?" Emma drummed her fingers on the desk. She actually looked torn. "While it'd be great for *SC*, I can't make any promises about how you'd come off. It might make things worse. And if you want your fifteen minutes of fame to be over, this'll do the opposite."

I nodded. I knew all this; I'd lain awake for hours last night thinking it over. "I know. But it's the only way to get Leighton and Kali to listen to me. And to believe what I'm telling them. If I make it this public."

"Okay, well, if you're sure—" Emma jumped to her feet and pressed a button on the phone on her desk. "Candace? Can you book the studio for this afternoon? We've got a podcast to record."

[Transcript of the *Southern Charm* podcast episode #112, released on April 11]

CANDACE: Hi, everyone, and welcome to a *very* special episode of the weekly *Southern Charm* podcast! I'm Candace, your host, and joining me today is Olivia Fitzgerald. Hi, Olivia!

OLIVIA: Hi! Thanks for having me.

CANDACE: If Olivia's name sounds familiar, it's not because she's a Kardashian hanger-on or a rising TikTok star. She's been in a ton of *Southern Charm* coverage over the last six months as the maid of honor for *both* of our Charming Bride weddings!

OLIVIA: [*Laughs.*] Quite the claim to fame, I know.

CANDACE: So, let's go back to the beginning. Tell me about how the competition started. I heard it was your idea?

OLIVIA: Yes. But it wasn't the original plan. I'm a long-time *Southern Charm* reader, so I knew about the June wedding cover. And my best friend, Leighton Sawyer, had just gotten engaged. Leighton runs an online fashion and lifestyle brand, Peach Sugar, and I thought she'd be a perfect cover star. So I set up a meeting with a *Southern Charm* editor to pitch Leighton for the cover.

CANDACE: And how'd that meeting go?

OLIVIA: Not too well. [*Pauses.*] I actually got pretty sick and had to duck out. But my aunt Charlotte—Kali's mom—ended up taking over the meeting and making a pretty good case for Kali as the cover star.

CANDACE: And were you already both brides' maid of honor?

OLIVIA: No, just Leighton's. So I convinced Emma, the editor in charge, to run a competition to give both Leighton and Kali a chance.

CANDACE: Gotcha. So how'd you end up as Kali's maid of honor, too?

OLIVIA: Well, my cousin wasn't originally planning on having a big wedding. And if she was going to go that route, she wanted someone she could trust by her side. It was also really important to my aunt. So, I'd say family reasons.

CANDACE: Did you think it was a conflict of interest, to say yes to weddings in direct competition?

OLIVIA: Deep down, yes, although I didn't want to admit it to myself. I'm usually pretty good at talking people into things, so I thought I could handle the conflicting personalities. I also have trouble accepting when I *can't* pull something off. So I was a little bit in denial. I thought if I worked hard enough, everyone would be happy in the end, no matter how the competition turned out.

CANDACE: All right, let's get into the dirt. Everyone's seen that clip of you fighting with both brides at Leighton's bachelorette last month. For listeners who haven't seen it, we'll include a link in the show notes of this podcast.

OLIVIA: Lovely.

CANDACE: There's a lot to unpack there. Leighton accused you of supporting Kali over her. She also said that you "promised you wouldn't let Charlotte screw anything else up." Is this your aunt Charlotte she's referring to? Kali's mom?

OLIVIA: Yes.

CANDACE: So what else had Charlotte "screwed up" for Leighton?

OLIVIA: [*Pauses. Deep breath.*] My aunt really wanted Kali to win. And to her, it wasn't enough for me to plan great events for Kali and see how readers voted. She was actively trying to interfere with Leighton's chances.

CANDACE: Sabotage.

OLIVIA: Your words, not mine. But she did cancel a dress appointment at Delacour, this impossible-to-get-into boutique that Leighton was so excited to shop at. And I'm convinced she was behind the poison-ivy debacle at Leighton's bridal shower.

CANDACE: You mean when poison ivy found its way into the flower-crown-making kits? That was pretty crazy.

OLIVIA: Yeah. Pretty unbelievable, if you ask me, that a professional florist would accidentally include poison ivy in those kits. Or that they wouldn't recognize it. And you know who has her own private greenhouse?

CANDACE: [*Gasps.*] No.

OLIVIA: Yup. My aunt Charlotte.

CANDACE: And did she send those strippers? Because, by the look on Leighton's face, those men were *not* well received.

OLIVIA: Yes. That was easier to confirm. I called their manager and got him to tell me who booked them.

CANDACE: It's like something out of a TV show.

OLIVIA: [*Snorts.*] Yeah, well, the things mothers'll do for their daughters, right?

CANDACE: Speaking of Charlotte's daughter, let's talk about the rest of the accusations from that clip. When you were defending yourself to Leighton, you rattled off a whole bunch of things *you'd* done to sabotage Kali. Not knowing that Kali was standing right there.

OLIVIA: Yeah. [*Pauses.*] I definitely would've handled it differently if I'd known.

CANDACE: [*Papers rustling.*] But what you said—that you'd picked a bad party theme, planned a boring bachelorette, and canceled Kali's coordinator—that was all true?

OLIVIA: Yeah.

CANDACE: Why agree to be Kali's maid of honor if you were planning on disrupting every event?

OLIVIA: Let me start by saying none of this is me defending what I did. I shouldn't have done any of it. It wasn't fair to Kali, or to Greta, or even to Charlotte.

CANDACE: Noted.

OLIVIA: But I do want to give some context. When I first agreed to be Kali's maid of honor, there was a lot of family pressure involved, especially coming from my aunt. I didn't think the competition was that important to Kali. She and Greta—her fiancée—kept talking about eloping. That always seemed more their speed.

CANDACE: In the clip, you mentioned trying to talk Kali out of the competition. Was that your reasoning?

OLIVIA: Yeah, exactly. I genuinely thought that eloping would make Kali and Greta happier and that doing this whole big society wedding was a major sacrifice. It was supposed to be *their* special day, not Charlotte's.

CANDACE: [*Laughs.*] I'm sure a lot of brides can relate to that.

OLIVIA: So, yes, I did spend a while trying to talk Kali out of the competition. Partly because I wanted Leighton to win. But also because I thought Kali deserved the wedding *she* wanted. [*Pauses.*] And it turns out I'm not that good at sabotage. I tried to pick a bad theme for their engagement party, but it was a huge hit, anyway.

CANDACE: And the bachelorette?

OLIVIA: They'd asked for something low-key, and that's what I'd planned. But halfway through, Kali started sharing with me some of the messages she'd received from the magazine's LGBTQ+ fans. Readers and viewers who were thrilled about queer representation on the June cover. And that's when I realized Kali might actually want to win. So I made a bunch of late-night phone calls, and pulled together an awesome last day for us.

CANDACE: So you haven't been trying to talk Kali out of the competition since then?

OLIVIA: No, definitely not. Once I realized that she wanted to win—not just to please her mom—I focused on planning the best events for both Leighton and Kali. And supporting them in all the other crazy parts of wedding planning.

CANDACE: Where do you stand with the brides now? Are you still the maid of honor for them both?

OLIVIA: [*Forced laugh.*] I don't even know if I'm *invited* to their weddings anymore. They haven't been taking my calls. Which is part of why I wanted to do this interview. There's been so much back-and-forth over the last six months, and I haven't been entirely honest with either of them. That ends now. This is me telling the truth, in as public and permanent a way as I can. I'm trying to own all my mistakes.

CANDACE: If Leighton and Kali end up listening to this podcast—as it sounds like you hope they will—what would you want to say to them?

OLIVIA: [*Takes a deep breath.*] Kali—I'm sorry. I'm sorry for not being up-front about all the pressure your mom was putting on me. And I'm sorry for trying to ruin your events. I kept justifying it to myself and saying that you didn't care about the competition and you'd probably end up eloping. But none of that made it okay. It was an *honor* to be your maid of honor, and I'm glad we got to rebuild our friendship this last year.

CANDACE: You've referenced family pressures a few times when talking about your aunt—care to elaborate?

OLIVIA: Some things have to stay in the family.

CANDACE: Very mysterious. Okay. And Leighton?

OLIVIA: Leighton, I'm sorry. I'm sorry for over-promising on the cover because of my own pride. I'm sorry for letting Charlotte mess up your beautiful events, and for letting this competition come between us. I never should've gambled with your wedding like that. And I'm sorry for not telling you about Will. I never knew the right way to do it, and I don't know what the right way was. But I know the wrong thing was keeping it from you.

CANDACE: Will? Is this a love interest? Do tell!

OLIVIA: [*Another forced laugh.*] Haven't I spilled enough of my guts today?

CANDACE: Touché. One last question before we let you go, Olivia. The Charming Bride voting wraps up in two short weeks. Who do you want to see on the June cover?

OLIVIA: The truth is, both Leighton and Kali are amazing women with incredible reasons to be on that cover. Leighton's a self-made fashion designer who's launching her own line of convertible bridesmaid dresses, and Kali's a total badass who represents a huge step forward in representation for a Southern magazine like *SC*. I know the last six months have been building up to this either-or decision, but why should we need to tear one woman down to lift the other up? I want Leighton *and* Kali on the cover.

CANDACE: Quite the ask! I don't think we've ever had dual cover stars before.

OLIVIA: But you've never had dueling weddings before, either.

CANDACE: [*Laughs.*] Can't argue with that! All right, listeners, that wraps up our special edition of the

Southern Charm podcast. Let us know in the comments and on social media—and on the Charming Bride home page, of course—what you think of Olivia's idea for a shared cover! And remember to pick up the April issue of *Southern Charm* for an inside look at Leighton's bachelorette—the source of all this fun drama.

OLIVIA: Thanks, Candace. Listeners, it's up to you now.

18

If my life were a Hallmark movie, things would've played out like this: When I got home from recording the podcast, emotionally spent and guilt-ridden, both Leighton and Kali would be waiting on my doorstep with flowers to signal complete forgiveness. Then Will would show up, maybe with a boom box on his shoulder, and Leighton would declare she'd always wanted us to end up together so we could be sisters for real. Then Will would kiss me, the girls would cheer, and we'd all live happily ever after.

In reality, things were a lot more anticlimactic. There was a two-day delay before the podcast would air, so after the recording I went home and watched a movie with Aditya, who reassured me that I'd done the right thing, and Circe, who contributed lots of supportive licks.

The day the podcast came out, I did finally get a text back from Leighton.

Heard the podcast. At least you owned up to all your shit. I'll see you at the rehearsal.

I'd texted back offering to help with any last-minute wedding prep, but she responded only:

All set, thanks.

"At least you're still invited to the wedding," Aditya pointed out. Circe wagged her tail in agreement.

Three days later, Kali reached out. I wasn't surprised by the delay; Kali had never followed *SC* social media as closely as Leighton.

Listened to the podcast. Thanks for apologizing. I appreciate all the help. We're okay.

We're "okay." Not "good." Not "forgiven." Just . . . okay. I tried to tell myself that this was natural; both Leighton and Kali needed time to process. Not to mention we were now only a month out from both weddings. From watching other friends get married, I knew how stressful those last few weeks were. It broke my heart to not be there for either of them in the last sprint, especially Leighton.

"She's got so much going on," Patricia said, not unkindly, when I called her to offer help. "She and Matt are moving two weeks before the wedding, which is a whole different hassle."

"I could help with the move."

"Oh no, no," Patricia said hastily. "We're hiring movers. We'll see you at the rehearsal, hon."

Will's text had been the shortest of all:

Heard podcast. It was the right thing to do.

So short that I didn't know how to respond, so I left it there. As much as I wanted to pursue a future with Will, that potential didn't even register next to the relationships I'd damaged with Leighton and Kali. There was no way to reach out to Will that wouldn't go behind Leighton's back, and she was my priority.

My biggest win came the day after Kali texted. I'd known it was coming: Once Kali knew about the podcast, Charlotte would, too. My phone rang one afternoon when I was out with Circe. I'd been walking Circe a lot lately, out of guilt for taking Aditya for granted all year. I glanced at the caller ID and sighed.

"Hi, Aunt Lotte."

"What in God's name were you thinking, airing all our dirty laundry on that podcast?" my aunt shrieked. "Are you out of your *mind*, Olivia? Where are you?"

I surveyed the park to establish that there were sufficient eyewitnesses to prevent Charlotte from murdering me. Well, and get away with it. "Centennial Park. Why, are you in Nashville?"

"I'll be there in ten minutes," my aunt said curtly.

"Looking forward to it," I said sweetly. Circe and I settled on a bench near the lake and watched the ducks while we waited for Charlotte to arrive.

"She probably won't like you," I warned Circe, giving her an extra-long scratch under the chin. "She doesn't like animals. Or anything that brings people joy."

Charlotte found us so quickly that I made a mental note to check my bag for a tracking device. But maybe fury gave her superhuman smell. She stormed up to us, looking over-dressed in an olive peplum dress and red-soled pumps. The smell of Givenchy was overpowering, like she'd bathed in perfume. Maybe that was her stress response, because otherwise my aunt looked as put together as always.

"Olivia," she hissed, in lieu of a greeting.

"Charlotte." I made a show of brushing dog hair off the bench next to me. "Care to join?"

She eyed Circe. I swear her lip would've curled if that hadn't been so gauche. "No. But I *would* like an explanation. What possessed you, making all those accusations against me? Did you really think I wouldn't find out?"

I stood and adjusted my shirt and leggings; it drove her crazy when people did that in public ("inelegant"). "It wasn't a secret. The whole point was for everyone to hear the full story."

"That was *slander*," she snapped. "You have absolutely no proof. You're blaming me for a poorly executed bridal shower—"

"Cut the crap, Aunt Lotte," I said evenly. "I could've said a lot worse. I didn't mention you blackmailing me over the Holmes & Reese job, or you poisoning me to get the pitch meeting—"

Her eyes hardened. "Baseless accusations, Olivia. Completely unfounded—"

"Unfounded?" I took out my phone and pulled up the document I'd prepared in anticipation of this conversation. "It took me a while to figure it out. But then Kali told me about your habit of slipping ipecac into people's drinks. Lucky for me, I went to my doctor the day after my sudden-onset sickness, and she ran a few tests. So I've got lab results documenting ipecac in my blood, *and* Leighton'll corroborate that she saw you put it in my drink."

Charlotte squinted at the phone screen. "Circumstantial," she said at last, but her voice held new uncertainty.

"Maybe." I shrugged and tucked the phone away. "But I think the Bravo producers would be *really* interested in a poisoning plot for your first season on the show, don't you? Should be a perfect reality TV controversy. I have to say, I don't think viewers will approve, but you might get two or three episodes before the Internet cancels you for good."

My aunt glared at me and then at the phone in my pocket, like she was weighing whether to throw it in the lake. "You found out about the show?" She didn't wait for a response. "I suppose that's not surprising. You've always been nosy."

"Yup," I agreed. "I have."

Charlotte's eyes narrowed. "You've made a real enemy now, Olivia. I don't care that we're family. It may be too late to pull your Holmes & Reese offer, but my husband is still a partner. I'll make sure that you're staffed on the toughest deals with the worst workloads. Ninety-hour workweeks will be your new normal. You won't see the light of day for *years*."

I half expected her to jab a finger at Circe and add, "And your little dog, too!" Or maybe pull out a broomstick and zoom away. But instead, she whirled and stalked off, somehow avoiding getting her stilettos stuck in the muddy grass. Now, *that* was an ability I truly envied.

"Looking forward to it!" I called after her. "At least I'll save on sunscreen!"

I texted Aditya a thank-you for mocking up a convincing

fake lab report—having a friend in med mal was proving unexpectedly helpful. Then I went home and continued my newest hobby: engaging with *SC* readers on my reinstated social media accounts. Since the podcast release, the tone of the messages had shifted to generally positive. I deleted the trolls' comments and encouraged everyone else to petition *Southern Charm* for both weddings to be featured. I didn't know if the campaign would work, but the *SC* readers were definitely doing my bidding. Emma had emailed me twice asking me to please stop; she was being inundated with reader outreach.

Otherwise, I filled my weeks with school, onboarding for my new job, and weekly phone calls with my Holmes & Reese mentor. Now that I'd signed all the paperwork, the tone of these calls had shifted. I'd known the real Big Law experience would be worlds apart from the cushy, luxurious lifestyle I'd enjoyed as a summer intern, but I hadn't realized how *wide* those worlds would be. And as someone who'd spent the last year pursuing interests outside of law—even if those interests revolved around wedding sabotage and secret relationships—it was jarring to realize how limiting my new career would be.

"It's all about trade-offs," my mentor said, and I had an unpleasant flashback to my conversation with Hank at the diner. "You trade a few years of your life for the ability to work at any law firm in the city."

"What's a few?"

"Five, if you're lucky."

"What about the partners?" I asked. "What's their work-life balance like?"

My mentor laughed unkindly. "Never let them hear you

asking about work-life balance," she warned. "And if that's on your radar, partner track isn't for you. Focus on the money. Get in, collect a fat paycheck for as long as you can stand it, and get out."

It was humbling to realize how little I'd investigated the realities of Big Law life. My dad had never talked about the downsides, only about the thrill of pulling off a tricky deal. I'd been so focused on breaking into Big Law that I hadn't stopped to examine what life looked like after. I'd spent two whole summers working at Holmes & Reese, and not once had I bothered to buy a junior associate a coffee to ask what their daily life was really like. Instead, I'd hung out with the other pampered summer associates, happily ignoring the dark side of the world I thought I wanted.

Existential dread was a big part of those weeks. It helped to pass the time, even if it kept me up at night and worsened my caffeine addiction. My phone calls with my mentor grew longer and longer, and I reached out to a few other alumni I knew in Big Law for more advice. In the end, their wisdom came down to one thing.

"If you're torn between two paths—or if you can see yourself doing *anything* else—Big Law's not for you," one past Vanderbilt grad advised. "There are easier ways to make good money."

"Are you sure you're not obsessing over this to distract yourself from the wedding mess?" Aditya asked, as I unloaded my day's research onto him over some Chinese takeout.

"No," I admitted.

"You've wanted Big Law since I met you."

"Maybe because it's the obvious path. It was the high-achiever thing. What my dad expected. But spending so much time helping Leighton defy *her* parents' career expectations, or even you, walking away from an offer to re-recruit for a better fit, there are more options than I realized."

"Mhmm." Aditya put down his fork. "Don't use me as an inspiration. I still haven't found anything I'm thrilled about."

"Still set on medical law?"

"Yeah, but I want something that excites me. And I don't know what that is yet. So I'm just working on bar prep for now."

I patted his arm. "You'll find something. Any firm would be lucky to have you."

"Thanks." He grimaced. "Speaking of bars, there's an open bar this weekend, right? I need a distraction from being unemployed."

"Absolutely," I promised. Kali and Greta had specifically invited Aditya to the wedding, citing his help with their engagement party. We were flying out the next day, although this time I'd insisted on buying his flights to Atlanta.

Kali and Greta's rehearsal dinner was held at a beautiful Mediterranean restaurant right outside of Atlanta. As Aditya and I walked in, I waved hello to the other bridesmaids and made a beeline for the bar. I'd made a promise with myself to talk to both Greta and Kali tonight. As guilty as I felt accosting them at their rehearsal dinner:

- A. It was marginally better than accosting them on their wedding day
- B. I needed to clear the air before I spent all morning with Kali tomorrow
- C. Kali hadn't given me much choice

310

"Tequila soda," I said to the bartender. "As strong as you can make it."

The bartender eyed me with something like concern. "This is a beer-and-wine event, ma'am."

"Ah. Shit. Okay, hit me with a sauvignon blanc, please. The healthiest pour possible." I needed to get some alcohol in me, quick. Liquid courage and all that.

"Glad you could make it," said a dry voice behind me. "Sorry we didn't spring for the full bar."

I whirled to see Greta, looking stunning in an ivory jump-suit and with the slicked-back hairstyle that looked good on a select few and made the rest of us (me) look like we had super-greasy roots. Behind her, Aditya mouthed, *Good luck,* and melted into the crowd. "Greta! Hi! You look amazing."

"Thanks." She accepted a second wineglass from the bartender and handed me my own. We turned to survey the party together. Fifty or sixty people milled across the court-yard, bathed in a soft golden light from the fairy lights strung overhead.

"Emma told me they've officially decided to feature Lara-ghai in the philanthropy issue," I babbled, fumbling to fill the silence. "Great news, right?"

Greta gave me a sideways look. "You know conversations don't always have to be tit-for-tat, right?"

I blushed. "Excuse me?"

"You don't have to win me over all the time. With compli-ments and good news and all that. Just . . . say hi. Have a conversation."

"Well, you're hard to impress."

She raised an eyebrow. "I'm more reserved than you, and that makes you uncomfortable. You like being able to read people. You find it harder to predict them if they're not talking as much as you're used to."

I sipped my wine while I thought about how to respond. "You're . . . not wrong. Wow. Read me like a book, didn't you?"

She smiled and inclined her head slightly.

"I really am sorry," I said after a beat. "I don't know if you heard the podcast—"

"I did."

I hesitated, but Greta didn't offer anything else. "Well, I directed most of my apology to Kali, but I owe you one, too. I'm sorry about trying to mess up your events. And trying to talk y'all out of the competition."

"I can't blame you for thinking we weren't into the wedding," she said. "We weren't, not for a long time. And Kali's happy you spent so much time together. She told me how close you two had been growing up. So in my book, the good outweighs the bad."

"Thanks, Greta."

She drained the rest of the wineglass and patted me on the shoulder. "I hope we keep seeing you. If you're not too busy with your fancy New York job."

I returned her smile. "I hope so, too."

The engagement party passed in a pleasant, heartfelt blur. It was a relief to attend an event that I hadn't planned; my only job was to show up, eat a free dinner, and clap after toasts. As fun as it had been to explore life outside of law school, a future in event planning was definitely not for me.

Charlotte, who shot daggers at me all night, had seated me and Aditya at a remote table with random third cousins and twice-removed aunts. It was meant as an insult. But I considered myself lucky that, as far as I could tell, she hadn't brought any actual daggers. Still, I made sure to always keep my drink within reach.

After the formal dinner and toasts concluded, the guests began milling about. I took a deep breath and prepared myself for the second tough conversation of the night. One I'd been putting off for far too long. I turned to Aditya, who looked especially handsome in his tailored navy suit. "Hey. I need to talk to you about something."

He rotated his body to face mine and matched my serious expression. "What's up?"

"I'm . . . so grateful for all the help and support you've given me this year." I waved a hand vaguely around at the festivities. "And for calling me on my shit when I needed it."

He grinned. "You do need that. Often."

"Rarely."

"Sometimes."

"Occasionally," I conceded. "I should've said something earlier, but you're so important to me, and I didn't want to ruin what we have. In all honesty, I really value you"—I paused—"as a friend. And I think we're best as friends."

Aditya's face remained impassive, but the vibe between us shifted. His features hadn't moved, but there was a new sadness there.

"Maybe I was misreading things," I went on, fumbling along uncertainly, "but I respect you too much to lead you on. And if I'm off base, we can forget this conversation ever happened."

He hesitated. "You're not off base, Liv. I don't know when it started—it snuck up on me. Over the last year. The more you talked about Will, the more I hated the idea of you with anyone else. I was just . . . too scared to do anything about it." He paused again, and I could feel him steeling himself. "So . . . you don't have any feelings for me? Romantic feelings?"

The candlelight reflected across his dark hair, which looked almost purplish in the warm glow. His brown eyes held mine. There was at least one universe where Will and I hadn't met up that night in Manhattan. Where Aditya and I spent our 3L year sharing our Big Law disillusionments, and maybe something more. The attraction was there; the friendship was there. But in this universe, reconnecting with Will had changed everything for me. My heart was elsewhere.

"No," I said instead. "I love you, Aditya, but as a friend. A truly valued friend."

He ducked his head, taking a moment to absorb the blow he'd seen coming, the devastation not at all lessened by anticipation. Then he cleared his throat and reached for his wine. "I value our friendship, too. I don't want to lose that."

"Okay. Good. Me, too." I reached for my own glass and we both took a long sip.

Finally, Aditya half smiled and added, "But can we still pretend this conversation never happened?"

I snorted and raised my glass in a mini-toast. "It's a deal."

"I'll draw up the contract." Aditya finished his wine and then jerked his head toward Greta and Kali. "Why don't you let me lick my wounds and go finish your apology tour?"

"Go find the bridesmaid with the purple hair," I suggested. Polly had been eying Aditya all night. "I think you'll forget about our conversation real fast."

Leaving him scanning the room, I headed for the happy couple, seated behind their greenery-draped sweetheart table. Greta glanced up and nudged Kali as I approached.

"Hey, Kali. Can I talk to you for a moment?"

My cousin was already rising from her chair. Either an artful spray tan or the Georgia sun had turned her skin a glowy bronze, which popped against her ivory column dress. "Sure."

A few other guests drifted closer to us, but Greta stood and ran some interference while Kali and I escaped to a far corner of the patio.

"The party's beautiful," I offered.

"Thanks." Kali smiled without malice. She looked like she was floating, unencumbered by all the stress and guilt weighing me down. Was this what it looked like when you were about to marry the love of your life? "That podcast was ballsy."

I cracked a grin. "I needed to get your attention. And Leighton's. And neither of you were talking to me."

"Wonder why," she said, but her tone was light. "I saw you were trending on Twitter. I bet the publicity was great. Was Emma happy?"

"She was." I nodded. "Although less happy when I started encouraging all of Instagram to email her begging for dual cover stars."

"Understandable."

Above us, the open Georgia sky stretched endlessly onward. Against the glow of the fairy lights, it looked inky black, without a star in sight. I knew it was the light pollution masking the stars, but it still made me sad to see them swallowed up.

"I'm sorry," I said after a bit. "For . . . all of it. For not being honest with you."

"It's okay." Kali followed my eyes upward. "I just wish you'd been more up-front. Like, why didn't you tell me my mom was blackmailing you?"

315

I considered. Pride? Fear of Charlotte's retribution? Shame that our shared childhood nemesis had finally gotten some real leverage over me? "I thought I could handle it," I said at last. "I thought—"

"You could get me to drop out," Kali finished.

"Yeah," I said weakly. "And if I delayed long enough, she wouldn't be able to mess up my job offer." The false dichotomy seemed so empty to me now. Was it only eight months ago that I'd seen the world as so black-and-white? Like this whole situation was some problem that I could solve if I schemed hard enough? "And back then . . . I was still getting to know you again. When being your maid of honor came up, part of me was happy we'd be spending time together. Even with all the strings attached. Plus, I didn't know how you'd react. What if you didn't believe me, and it blew up into this huge family drama?"

Kali rolled her eyes. "Give me a little credit, Olivia. I've gotten engaged, not gotten a lobotomy. I know what my mom's like."

I chuckled. "Fair enough."

"And here's another." Kali's gaze drilled into me. "Why didn't you tell me my mom was using this competition as a storyline for her TV pitch?"

I froze. "You know about that?"

"I do now," she said grimly. "Found her highlight reel on her laptop last week. We had a huge fight about it. She knew you were Leighton's maid of honor. She *wanted* this whole situation to be crazy and dramatic. That's why she suggested you as my maid of honor in the first place. And why she lured me to Nashville last month, to try and cause a big scene at Leighton's bachelorette."

"That's next level," I said, impressed in spite of myself. Charlotte really had been a few steps ahead.

"But you knew about the TV show—Mom thought you'd told me, until I showed her the laptop. Why didn't you tell me? It would've explained a lot. Helped me understand the position you were in."

I traced my fingers along the wooden fence bordering the patio. It was true I'd been tempted to text Kali as soon as I'd figured out Charlotte's ulterior motives. Hell, I'd pulled up Google Flights and considered hopping on a plane to tell her in person! (Dramatic, but so was puppeteering your daughter's life for a spot on a TV show.)

But something had stopped me. As much as I liked to paint Charlotte as a one-dimensional Disney-type villain, there had been genuine emotion in her eyes when she spoke of wanting Kali to feel accepted and celebrated. In her own way, she had tried to take care of me after my mom passed. And as I knew myself, it was totally possible to do something for multiple reasons. So Charlotte had wanted to stir up some drama around the competition. It was also possible she'd wanted to celebrate her bisexual daughter publicly. And with all the heavy emotions that weddings swirled up, I'd wanted to give her the benefit of the doubt on that one.

(But only that one.)

"She'd told me she regretted not being more supportive when you came out," I said at last. "That this was her way of publicly celebrating you and Greta. And maybe it was. I didn't want to ruin that for you."

Kali blinked, and even in the dim lighting her eyes looked misty. "Thank you," she said finally. "And . . . for all of it."

She'd hugged me a few times this year, but this embrace

was different. In the tightness of her grip and the powerful emotions surrounding us both, I felt a sense of relief, and love, and restored friendship. And something else: hope. Hope and happiness that we could rebuild the close friendship we'd shared as children. That I hadn't totally screwed things up with my shenanigans.

"Aw, how adorable!" Frederic cried. Bright flashes blinded me as he snapped a few photos for the *Southern Charm* coverage, which we still didn't know the outcome of. But in that moment, I didn't care at all. "Give me another pose, ladies."

I slung my arm around my cousin and grinned for the camera.

19

May

Eight days later, I was smoothing my one-of-a-kind bridesmaid gown and holding back tears. Patricia and I were helping Leighton into her wedding dress, and the enormous skirt was putting up a real fight.

But the giant train was nothing compared to the tension in the tiny hotel bedroom. I still hadn't cleared the air with Leighton. I'd pulled her aside at the rehearsal dinner last night and repeated my podcast apology in person, but it hadn't broken the ice like with Kali. After all, the Charlotte-reality-TV reveal had helped my case with my cousin. But Leighton had known about the Charlotte situation from the start.

I desperately wanted to fix things before she walked down the aisle. I knew we'd get past this eventually—and clearly Leighton did, too, or she would have fired me as maid of honor—but I didn't want things to be rotten between us when my best friend said her wedding vows. Maybe it was superstitious, but I felt an impending sense of pressure. Time was running out.

"Oh my God," Patricia breathed, as the last layer settled into place. "Leighton—you're—" Her voice choked up, and she put her hand to her mouth to stifle a sob.

"Beautiful," I said softly, tears welling up in my own eyes. Leighton turned. For a precious half-second, the sanctity of the moment overpowered everything else. My best friend stood framed in front of the window, rays of light shining around her like an aura from the heavens. Her golden hair was twisted into an elegant updo, with carefully arranged tendrils spilling out to frame her face. A sapphire-studded hair clip held everything in place: her something blue, and something borrowed. I'd lent it to her ages ago, and I was glad to see she'd still chosen to wear it.

Leighton smiled and became, impossibly, even more stunning. But then the tension poured back into the room like an unwelcome, icy draft.

Patricia glanced between us. "Let's get the photographer back in here," she said quickly, and bustled out of the room.

"Leighton, can we—"

"Don't, Liv," she said, her voice sharper than usual. "Please," she added in a softer tone. "There's too many people around—I can't, okay?"

Shrieks of excitement cut out my response; the other three bridesmaids were crowding into the room, excited at their first glimpse of the bride in the dress.

"You look incredible!" Samantha gushed.

"In*sane*," Shane agreed. "Matt's going to lose his mind."

I edged past Nikki into the larger hotel suite and tried to focus. *Think, Liv.* I needed a way to talk to Leighton alone. We had to fix things.

Do we *need to fix this, or do* you *need to fix this?* said a snarky voice inside my head. I almost recoiled. Was I being selfish, forcing this conversation on the morning of Leighton's wedding day? Should I let things go and regroup with her after the honeymoon?

But that felt wrong. I knew I'd regret not addressing this— and that Leighton would, too. This was one of the most important days of her life, and I wanted—*needed*—to stand by her side. To support her without this wall of awkwardness between us. But Leighton's wedding planner ran a tight ship; her itinerary had less wiggle room than the Marines' training schedule. If I wanted a private moment with Leighton, I'd have to earn it. And that meant flexing conversational muscles I was reluctant to use. My quick-thinking skills now felt like a liability; I didn't want to *manipulate* Leighton into forgiving me. And yet . . . a little smooth talking could go a long way. It could create the opportunity for reconciliation. I'd just need to finish the job myself.

I paced in a tight circle. Beauty-prep remnants littered the room: shiny champagne wrappers, abandoned bobby pins, and lipstick bottles that had rolled halfway underneath the couch. In this suite were:

A. Three other bridesmaids
B. The aforementioned wedding planner
C. The photographer
D. Patricia

Sorting my opponents into groups made the problem easier to tackle. I sent two quick texts for help and started with Leighton's first line of defense: the other bridesmaids.

"Shane, Samantha, Nikki!" I called. "Can you come here for a sec?" They trooped out of the bedroom and stared at me expectantly, responding to my intrinsic authority as maid of honor.

I lowered my voice. "Don't freak out, but Leighton's ceremony bouquet is missing."

"Her flowers are right there," Nikki said, pointing. Leighton's bouquet was indeed sitting on the couch behind me.

"That's her prep bouquet, not her ceremony bouquet," I said, forcing exasperation into my voice. "Didn't you guys read Patricia's email? We're supposed to keep track of all the bouquets. Come to think of it, I haven't seen the reception bouquet, either."

Samantha's eyes were wide. "Shit," she whispered. "Patricia's gonna kill us."

"Not if she never finds out," I insisted. "The last time I saw the other bouquets was downstairs near the rotunda. Can you guys track them down? I'll stay here and keep Patricia distracted."

Shane frowned. "Do you think we all need to go?"

"Absolutely." I herded them toward the door as I talked. "The rotunda's huge and you only have fifteen minutes before you need to be back up here. Go, go, go!"

The bridesmaids scurried off as Frederic appeared at the suite door, right on cue. "I got your text," he whispered. "On a scale of one to ten, how dramatic are we talking?"

"Ten."

He nodded. "Aye, aye, Captain." He raised his voice and nearly bellowed, ". . . and the film is *completely* overexposed! It's an absolute nightmare, I don't know *how* we'll shoot anything!"

"I said drama ten, not volume ten!" I hissed.

He shrugged. "Gotta sell it, right?"

The photographer poked his head out of the bedroom. "Couldn't help but overhear—you're having issues with your film?"

"Are you the wedding photographer?" Frederic said in faux-relief. He strode forward and grabbed the man by the arm without waiting for a response. "I'm the lead shooter for *Southern Charm.* I'm so sorry to interrupt, but it's an emergency. The lighting in the rotunda cut out, and I don't know how we're going to shoot the ceremony!"

The photographer's jaw dropped. "*All* of the lights cut out?"

Frederic nodded vehemently. "Disaster, right? Can you help us figure out how to shoot?"

The wedding photographer glanced back into the bedroom, his bald head going shiny with stress sweat. "I wanted to—But if the rotunda's that dark, we may need to rework—"

"Did I hear you right?" the planner squawked, marching out of the bedroom. "Get down there and figure out the lighting! Go, go!" She shooed the photographer and his assistant out the door after Frederic.

"Is there a problem?" Patricia called from the bedroom.

"No, no," the planner said, straightening her black sheath dress. For a tiny, four-foot-eight woman, she radiated authority. "Everything's going perfectly." Her eyes landed on me, now alone in the living area. "Where is everyone? Where are the bridesmaids?"

"Starbucks run," I said innocently.

Her face turned a shade of purple I'd have assumed incompatible with human life. "They went to *Starbucks*?" she hissed. "Get them back here ASAP."

I nodded and pulled out my phone, pretending to text. My mind churned frantically; I had maybe five minutes before the bridesmaids returned. What was taking Aditya so long?

"My friend just texted me," I said, plunging ahead without him. I was running out of time. "The, uh, singer is looking for you. Says she can't start without her fee paid in full?"

The planner eyed me suspiciously. "The singers are in the green room; there shouldn't be any guests in there. Who's your friend?"

I shrugged again. "I'm just the messenger," I said, playing for time. "Maybe you should go and check it out?"

"I don't leave my bride's side until she walks down the aisle," the tiny dictator said coldly. "What're you trying to—"

And then, finally, Aditya burst into the room. "Where—is—the—coordinator?" he panted, bending over and resting one hand on his side. He never did cardio. "Disaster—downstairs—"

The planner glared at her. "What're you talking about? Who are you?"

"I told you there was a problem with the singer!" I said loudly.

"Appendicitis!" Aditya said at the same time, and then looked panicked. "The singer!" he added quickly.

The planner grabbed his arm. "Is this a joke?"

Aditya nodded. "Right-lower-quadrant pain, tender to

palpation, classic case—writhing in pain, they've just called an ambulance—"

The wedding planner's face paled. "Good Lord. We'll need to adjust the ceremony timing, and—" She started toward the door, and then glanced back to the bedroom, clearly torn.

"I'll stay with Leighton," I volunteered. "I got this. Don't worry."

"I'll show you where to go," Aditya offered. "Hurry, the ambulance is on its way—"

"Don't leave her side," the planner shot at me, and then followed Aditya out the door. "Are you a doctor?" I heard her ask, as they disappeared down the hallway.

Thanking the heavens Aditya had gotten into malpractice law, I turned to face my last and greatest obstacle.

"What's going on out there?" Patricia stood in the bedroom doorway, gazing at the empty room in confusion. "Where'd everyone go? What was that shouting about?"

A dozen ploys flashed through my head. I settled on the truth. "Nothing's wrong. I needed the chance to talk to Leighton."

Understanding appeared on her face, shadowed by sadness. "Olivia, I'm not sure now's the best time—"

"It is," I insisted, slamming raw emotion into my voice. I had to make her understand. "Leighton's like a sister to me. I need to make this right for her." Patricia's protective instinct was too strong; I could see in her eyes I wasn't getting through. Desperate, I played my last card: "And I have some good news. I heard from Emma this morning. *Southern Charm* has decided to feature both Leighton and Kali on the cover."

Patricia's eyes widened. "Oh, how wonderful! What a great opportunity for Leighton. I'm so proud of her."

"Make sure you tell her that," I said softly. "Your approval is everything to her. That's why she was so desperate to win the cover."

Patricia looked startled. "I didn't mean to add more pressure."

"She wanted to show you that her designs could be a real career." I spread my arms and twirled back and forth. My dress fluttered helpfully. "She's proved she's got what it takes, don't you think?"

Raised voices from the hallway distracted us both. I could hear the muffled sounds of the wedding planner's shouts. My heart sank: I'd run out of time.

"Go talk to her," Patricia said. "I'll lock the door. Ten minutes."

"Really?" My hand was already on the bedroom knob. "Thank you!"

I tumbled into the bedroom and closed the door behind me. Leighton was standing at the window, staring out at the streets of Nashville.

"I know something's wrong," she said without turning. "It's why everyone's hurrying out and telling me to stay here. What's going on?"

"Nothing's wrong."

She turned, frowning. "But all the yelling—"

"A manufactured crisis," I admitted. "Several, actually. So I could talk to you alone."

Her mouth formed a tiny O of surprise before her beautiful features hardened again. She was protecting herself. Against me. It made my stomach lurch. "So you could convince me to forgive you? Persuade me that everything's okay? Talk me into forgetting how you lied to me?"

Each accusation was like another arrow in my heart. But I deserved every one. "I don't want to talk you into anything," I said quietly. "But I do want to make things right." The fact that Leighton would be on the *SC* cover floated into my head: What better way to defuse the tension? But just as quickly, Greta's words echoed in my ears: *You know conversations don't always have to be tit-for-tat, right?*

So instead I spoke from the heart. I let go of my pride, my guilt, and my shame, and focused on the woman standing across from me. The three-foot distance felt like an endless chasm, one that I'd created along with the entire Charming Bride competition. A canyon that could only be bridged with the truth. So I went back to the very beginning.

"I've always had a thing for Will," I admitted.

Leighton's eyebrows raised. "*That's* how you're starting off?"

I pushed on. "Always. But ever since the Lila fiasco, I never let myself entertain the idea. And then I ran into him in Manhattan. In a different environment, things flowed so easily between us. I wanted to be with him. I was nervous about your reaction."

She didn't say anything, so I kept talking. "When I landed the pitch meeting with Emma, it felt like the perfect solution. I knew you were struggling with monetizing Peach Sugar. I thought if I got you the cover, I could get your approval with Will."

"Glad to know the real reason you helped me."

"It wasn't the only reason," I said honestly. "I've always believed in Peach Sugar. In you. I haven't been supportive enough. It was selfish of me, to not be there for you on that deeper level. When you brought up concerns with your mom, or with figuring out your career, it was easier to deflect and make a joke. But you deserved more than that. *Southern Charm* was my first step toward paying back that debt."

"So if Charlotte hadn't messed things up—you would've told me about Will back then?"

I thought for a second. "Yes," I said at last. "If Will and I were actually— Yes, I would've. But I would've been using the cover as leverage. Which would've been a shitty way to tell you. So I guess maybe it worked out better this way."

Leighton's eyes met mine, and for a second my best friend was back, giving me her cut-the-bullshit look.

"Or maybe not," I amended hastily. "You get my point. Anyway, Will and me . . . it's not like we've been dating all this time. I thought he had a fling in Thailand, and then Aditya cut things off, and there was the distance, and the idea of telling you—"

"So you haven't been together?"

"We met up in December to give things a try, but . . . we got in a fight about the *SC* stuff, and I think I self-sabotaged, anyway." I shrugged. "I was scared about how real things felt between us, and how painful it'd be if things went wrong."

"The *SC* stuff?"

"Me talking Kali into dropping out and wreaking some mild havoc on her wedding plans." I took a deep breath. "Even after Charlotte got involved, I still thought I could handle everything. I thought I could win you the cover without losing my job. You know the rest."

Leighton was gazing out the window, her fingers tracing the fold of the pearl-trimmed veil that lay in her lap.

"That interview I gave—I told Emma why I wanted you on the cover, too. They edited that part out. I swear."

Leighton tucked one tendril of hair behind her ear and sat down on the bed. "Do you still have your job?" she asked after a moment, and I was reminded again of how much she cared for me.

"I think so," I admitted. "Charlotte's promised to make my life a living hell, although that might be status quo for Holmes & Reese junior associates, anyway." I sat down next to her.

"I believe you," she said after a moment, and leaned over to rest her head on my shoulder. "I'm sorry, too, Liv. This has been such a stressful year. I was expecting you to read my mind about how to be there for me. It was easier to lash out at you for the Kali stuff than to admit I needed more support."

I hugged her tightly. "Thanks for not firing me as maid of honor."

"Your dress is the centerpiece of my new line," she said, her voice muffled by my shoulder. "I couldn't not let you wear it."

We both laughed and released the hug to nestle deeper together. "I have some other good news," I added. I told her about Emma's decision to feature both her and Kali.

Leighton sat straight up, her eyes bright. "Are you serious? Oh my God! I can't believe you didn't start with that."

"Yeah, well . . ." I flipped my hair to the other side of my neck and grinned at her. "I'm turning over a new leaf. Trying to just have conversations, instead of planning out every second."

"Olivia, giving up control?" she teased. "What if someone says something unexpected?"

I elbowed her. I had one last conversation pivot to pull off, to bring this moment back to the special day we were here to celebrate. "You ready to go marry Matt, or what?"

And if her eyes had brightened at the news of the cover, they now absolutely shone with joy. "Will you walk downstairs with me?"

"Of course." I squeezed her hand. "I'll be right by your side."

Leighton's wedding planner may have been terrifying, but she was supremely talented. The ceremony flowed perfectly into a cocktail hour overlooking the Nashville skyline, the patio drenched in golden-hour sunset. I'd fancied myself an amateur planner, but professional planners were in a whole different league. The reception was studded with subtle, elegant touches: customized cocktail napkins, orb candles floating in reflection pools, and silk pashminas for the surprisingly crisp spring evening.

"This is the best wedding I've ever been to," Aditya announced, appearing at my side with two glasses of the custom Leighton-and-Matt cocktail. "I bet the food'll be awesome, too."

"Agreed." I accepted my glass. "Glad to see you're still alive—did the planner not rip your head off when she realized you were lying?"

Aditya smiled mischievously. "I played it off. Told her I screwed up the diagnosis—it was a kidney stone, and the singer had passed it while we were in the elevator."

"You're amazing. Thank God you pivoted into medical law," I said fervently. "And that you came to this wedding."

"Yeah, no kidding." Aditya grinned. "The best man over-heard me talking about kidney stones, and we started chatting. Turns out Matt's new start-up is a direct-to-consumer primary-care firm, and they're looking for a general counsel. Lots of red tape in health care. Works to my advantage."

"No way!"

"Yup. We're getting beers on Tuesday to talk it over more."

"That's awesome." I gave him a hug. "We'll see each other all the time if you're in business with Matt."

"Have you told Leighton the good news?"

We both turned to see Emma DeVant grinning wickedly at me, dressed in a high-low floral gown that I'd seen in the pages of *Vogue*.

I returned her smile. "Yes, she's thrilled. You made a great choice."

"I figured you'd told her. You two looked pretty happy in all the photos," she observed. "I'm sure that helped smooth things over."

"Actually, we worked things out beforehand. But the cover was a nice bonus."

Emma arched an eyebrow. "That's the first time I've heard a *Southern Charm* cover described as 'a nice bonus.'"

"First time for everything?"

Emma chuckled. "I'm glad I found you. I've got a proposition for you."

"I'll leave you to it," Aditya said quickly, and drifted away into the crowd.

"I'm not taking the cover away from them," I told her firmly. "I worked so hard to get you to feature them both—"

Emma rolled her eyes. "Believe me, I know. The number of emails I've received? Your campaign worked, although we'll be wriggling through some minuscule legal loopholes. We'd promised *Bridal Today* to feature only *one* bride per calendar year. It'll take some creative negotiations." She shuddered and then straightened up. "But anyway. The podcast was a hit. You spilled most of the tea, but not all. Left some intrigue."

"That was the idea." Some family skeletons—cough, cough, Charlotte's poisonous hobbies—didn't need to be made public.

"We'd love to have you back," Emma said. "Possibly as a regular contributor. We could do a spin-off podcast all about wedding prep events—like a Bridesmaids 101."

She'd taken me by surprise. "Wow. That's quite an idea."

"But . . . ?"

"But I've got a job lined up," I told her. "I'm starting at a Manhattan law firm next month. I don't think podcasting's for me."

Emma eyed me. "What if I had a better idea?"

And then I sensed it: She'd done the old bait-and-switch right back at me. She hadn't expected me to accept the podcasting gig. Whatever was coming next, that was her real pitch.

"There's an opening for junior associate in-house counsel at Marshall Sheldon. I think you'd be perfect. They wanted someone creative, someone who'd work well with magazine staff and understands the industry." Emma's eyes glowed with excitement. "I sent over your LinkedIn profile and put in a good word. They'll be reaching out on Monday."

My jaw dropped. "But I have a job—"

"And now you have options," she corrected. "Take the interview, Olivia. I look forward to hearing how it went."

And with that killer final line, she disappeared back into the crowd, leaving me slightly stunned and staring after her. I'd been hit by a fellow persuasive master. And I was feeling more than a little open to the idea.

As if sensing my dazzled, vulnerable state, the universe chose that moment to inject another blast of chaos into my life. The crowd parted to reveal Will Sawyer, looking unfairly handsome in his groomsman's tux. I'd glimpsed him yesterday at the rehearsal, but we hadn't spoken. It hadn't felt right, not when things had been rocky with Leighton.

But two hours ago, as I'd waited with Leighton at the top of the aisle, counting the beats until my musical cue, she'd whispered, "You should talk to Will at the reception."

I glanced at the bride, startled. "I don't think he wants to talk to me."

"Trust me" was all she'd said in return. And then she'd squeezed my hand.

Now Will was walking toward me. "Hi," I said.

"Hi," Will said back. "You look great."

"You, too." It was almost unfair, how good he looked. Like staring directly into the sun. After lying dormant for months, a flame in my heart flickered to life at the sight of him. What was it about Will Sawyer that short-circuited my brain and melted my insides? Maybe it was the hormones: my body remembering the night we'd shared, the ecstatic pleasure of losing myself in Will. Or maybe it was nostalgia, a stubborn fondness for the boy I'd grown up with, now maturing into admiration for the man he'd become. Or maybe it was the wispy beginnings of a very real adult love.

"The podcast," Will said. "That was brave, putting yourself out there like that. I'm glad you owned up to everything. It took some real courage."

"Thanks," I said awkwardly.

"Especially since you didn't know how people would react," he added. "Quite the gamble."

"Next thing you know, I'll be a card sharp in Vegas," I joked weakly. "Taking chances left and right."

Will laughed. Then his face grew serious. "You did some crazy things, Liv. But I should've given you the benefit of the doubt at Leighton's bachelorette. I should've known there was more to the story."

"So much more," I muttered, thinking of the ipecac. "But I'm turning over a new leaf. I promise."

"Not a poison-ivy leaf, I hope?"

I nudged his shoulder with mine. "Oh my God, don't even joke about that."

"Too soon?"

"Give it ten years." We both sipped our drinks and gazed around at the smiling, chattering crowd.

"I'm taking the job," Will added. "The Predators one. Back into sports rehab for me."

"Hey, that's awesome! Congrats!"

"Thanks." Will grinned down at me. "Best part is, I get another month off between jobs. I've already lined up my next diving trip. Costa Rica."

"That'll be amazing," I said wistfully, thinking of the strict ten-day vacation policy that H&R enforced on its first-year associates. I wouldn't be taking any long trips for years.

"And I'll be based in Nashville," Will added shyly, his gaze heavy with meaning. "So I'd be here if you . . . for when you came back to visit."

Emma's Marshall Sheldon proposal shimmered in my mind's eye. Certainty flashed inside me: I'd take that interview. If I was offered a media law position here in Nashville, and Will was moving back to work for the Preds—

With Herculean effort—maybe it'd get easier over time—I stopped that train of thought in its tracks. *One step at a time, Liv. See how things work out.*

"Leighton and I made up this morning. For real. No more drama. No more lies."

Will nodded. "I know." The late-afternoon sunlight glinted off his golden hair, just as the light had framed his sister this morning. Two annoyingly genetically blessed people. I wanted them both in my life. "She told me to come talk to you."

I blushed again. "She said the same thing to me."

Will grinned. "Is Leighton . . . *matchmaking*?"

I took a half-step closer. "That depends. Do you think we'd make a good match?"

"I think there's only one way to find out." His eyes held my own, and suddenly I felt like we were the only two people on the patio.

He pulled me in to him and kissed me, long and deep and passionate. I kissed him back, reveling in the moment. Despite all my charming and persuading and smooth talking, things had maybe worked out okay. I didn't know how the Marshall Sheldon interview would go, or if Will and I could make long-distance work, or if the *Southern Charm* cover would land Leighton any long-term collaborations. But for once, none of that bothered me. Normally I had to convince myself not to worry about things. But in this moment even I found a way to let go.

The kiss ended, and Will hugged me tight to his chest. Across the patio, Leighton and Matt nuzzled against each other, beaming. Vicarious joy bloomed in my heart at the sight of her, radiant, hand in hand with her husband. The rest of our lives flashed before me: Leighton teary-eyed at my wedding; me cradling Leighton's first child; the two of us lounging on a sunny porch, grey-haired and full of hard-won wisdom. A deep, powerful emotion burned within me. I'd known Leighton for more than two decades, but now I was seeing her with brand-new eyes. With a new appreciation for how deep the waters of our friendship ran. Clarity arrived at last: I'd never felt such raw, unbridled love for someone.

Ten yards away, Aditya chatted with Matt's best man. Behind him, Emma and Frederic were bent over Frederic's Canon, examining the moments he'd immortalized for *Southern Charm*. The emotion of it all tugged at my heartstrings—or maybe it was the champagne—but suddenly I felt almost teary-eyed at the thought of how many beautiful moments had yet to unfold in our lives. Somewhere across the Atlantic, I knew, Kali and Greta were creating a whole constellation of memories on their South African honeymoon. So many moments to cherish. So many people to treasure. My own life glittered like an expanse of Tennessee sky, stretching before me with endless possibilities, shimmering with the starlight of the people I loved.

Leighton inclined her head toward Will and me and smiled, as if to give her blessing. Frederic snapped a photo of us and winked.

"So." I grinned up at Will. My childhood crush, my best friend's brother. My potential future. Will reached out and traced the side of my face. My cheek glowed, and for an instant the world paused as I savored the perfection of this snapshot. "Can I talk you into giving us another chance?"

He grinned back at me. "You don't have to talk me into anything."

And his lips found mine again.

ACKNOWLEDGMENTS

So many people supported and encouraged me on the long journey to publishing this book. Endless gratitude to my amazing agent, Erin Niumata of Folio Literary, who sharpens every manuscript with diamond-edged precision. Maddie Woda, my editor, has a rare talent for enhancing manuscripts while retaining the author's voice; this book is ten times better after her insights. It's been a delight to work with the entire Zibby Books team, and I'm so grateful to have joined such an impressive group of Zibby Books authors.

Steph Hart and Mark Naguib deserve a special shout-out for reading early drafts of this manuscript and insisting this was something special.

Chris and Gail Erath, although related to me, went above and beyond the familial call of duty with their early support.

Teresa Dinter, Sophia Setterberg, and Collette King may as well work in publishing themselves after endless conversations about plot specifics and industry updates.

ACKNOWLEDGMENTS

My parents, Kellianne and Chris, indulged my love for writing from the age of four, and are the reason I've grown into the reader and novelist I am today.

Finally, my husband, Alan, has supported me every step of this publishing journey and has always been my role model for hard work and persistence. Although he loves his surgery textbooks, he'll always choose an Elle Evans novel first.

ABOUT THE AUTHOR

A Boston native, Elle Evans spent five years in Nashville enveloped in sweet Southern hospitality and even sweeter iced tea. She now lives in Philadelphia with her husband and rescue dog, Calypso, the first of many pets named for Greek mythology characters. Evans enjoys hiking, rock climbing, and attempting ambitious cocktail recipes. She writes under a not-so-secret pseudonym to maintain separation from her academic research papers and day job as a doctor.